Skywatch

Skywatch

Steve Davala

For my family, for your support through this all.
And for all the sci-fi out there, thanks for inspiring me to create my own worlds and stories.

CHAPTER 1

Ever look up into the sky and say, "That's where I belong?" I don't mean riding around in a skimmer or on a skyboard, I'm talking about really flying. You know, just you and the sky?

That's me. I've always wanted to be up there as far back as I can remember. No, I take that back. Not wanted. Needed is the right word. I was meant to fly. That's why I'm going out today. Going out to the Edge.

"Hey Daj, what are you doing in there? You almost ready?"

"Yeah, hold on, Kie."

Kie. My best friend. Always here for me. At least when I'm ready to make a new stream, and especially when he can get in on something this big.

"Did you get the notes from Scitech?" Kie says. "They're pinging me to get you out there."

"Sponsors. Don't they know about showmanship?"

With a quick flit of my eyes, the Nanosite fills my vision. Bright lines pulse and respond to every eye twitch, displaying news feeds, weather, maps, friends, vids. Everything I need. I activate the stream and link it to the server.

"Whoa, three hundred thousand Maglans on the 'site already?"

"And growing fast," Kie says.

The stats from the stream scroll across the lower edge of my vision, bigger numbers than I've ever seen this early on. Messages stream faster than I can process as the early log-ons try to get my attention. My display starts to fill up with alerts so I minimize a bunch of them.

"Thanks for watching!" I respond to a few.

The message board erupts and there's no way I can handle it, so I let the AI response software deal with it.

Three-fifty.

A single line of text in the upper right of my vision blinks its question. *"Initiate program?"*

Four hundred thousand.

"Initiate."

A thumping bass line thuds in my head as the opening sequence of my program starts. The lights in the living area slowly come on highlighting my old skyboards right above the couch. I stare into a mirror with my four arms crossed over my purple Scitech jacket. The music lowers as my old Camdrone hovers above my head to give a sweeping view of the room and funnels it right into the stream.

"Do you really need that old thing?" Kie texts on screen.

"Cam? Of course. She can get some angles I miss. Right?"

"There are plenty of other cameras around," Kie says. *"I'm just saying it's clunking up your look."*

"You can barely see her. Now, if you don't mind, I've got a show to do. So get off my feed."

The vid feeds light up as I watch myself on the 'site display in my eyes. I blink and cycle through the possible camera positions until the new focus is on the Sky Deck.

"Look at her. Sick right? You've never seen anything like it."

I rub my hand over the tight mag-fiber design, making sure to show the blocky Scitech symbol, as "per our contract."

"She's lighter and more maneuverable than any other board." That's also a part of the contract. Kind of soul-selling, but what are you gonna do? "And I'm going to test it out in front of all of Magla. Are you with me?"

Seven hundred thousand viewers. And still going up.

Yes, everyone in the city, and yes, they are definitely with me. No pressure.

Blood pumps loudly in my head. My breathing quickens.

"Need a tranquilizer?" a calm voice in my head prompts. I can almost feel the nanomeds just waiting, primed to click out their tiny injectors into my bloodstream.

I click negative on my 'site. I can't tone down my reflexes, not on today's course.

I hold the sled over my head with one hand and let go. The glider freezes in place, locked into the magnetic field. Cam hovers into place right behind me.

Time to cue the voice controls, fade out the music a bit. Take a deep breath.

"Ever look up into the sky and say, 'That's where I belong?'"

Fiftieth floor. Sixtieth. The rocky ground outside the ringed city of Phen spins out of sight. I shake my head and focus on what's in front of me. As I travel up and the lower Rings disappear, my feed streams in the corner of my vision. Chatter from my fans fills most of the screen but I ignore it. They're busy watching a montage of my old stunts on different screens, now scattered all around me, while in the center I head to the jump site.

I blink at the weather icon. Light winds, cold. Not what I expected, but it could be worse. Automatically, my internal nanos adjust and my arms heat up. They say you can't sense the nanos working, but I swear I can feel them crawling around under my skin.

"Thanks, bots." Better not piss them off, I always say.

I prompt the next part of my program and a glowing arises across my boring gray arms developing into lines and complex patterns like fire. They even flicker like real flames. I check the feed for the general reaction.

The first responder includes a symbol with a frown on it.

That's what you get when you upload an untested designer. Well, that Maglan is fired.

"No, not that one. Choose tattoo pattern *Zaylee*."

"Are you certain?" a computerized voice warns. "This is not sponsor approved—"

"I know what I'm doing."

Don't piss off the nanos, but the sponsors? Screw 'em. I'm the best they've ever had.

The glowing flames on my arms disperse into pixels and regroup into thick lines like lightning bolts. Blue energy throbs through them and pulses with my music.

"That's better." I check the feed and smile as the approval ratings light up. Zaylee's sub feed pops in with her signature burst of sparks.

"*Thanks, D,*" it says. "*I owe you.*"

"*Thank me later,*" I reply with a winky response.

The elevator slows as I approach the top of the Ring. The sun sets and the moons, Naglor and Cadea, fill the night sky blanketed by the glow of the auroras. Cadea freaks me out. I wonder if the Cadeans are watching this feed right now. Probably better than anything they can get on their pathetic world. Still, they make a nice backdrop for my show.

The elevator clicks to a halt and the door opens, letting a gust of wind in to blow my hair back. I eye my vid from the feed. Yeah, it caught that. That little Camdrone is the best. She focuses on the Sky Deck and pans around the top of the Ring. From here I'll be able to get out to the Edge and make the dive. First one to ever do it.

"Adjust profile image?" my internal AI prompts.

I look at myself. Stupid blotches on my narrow purple face. My too narrow face. And the stumpy face spikes? These won't do. A quick swipe and the image I now see on the sample feed looks better. Much better. I cycle through the eye colors and settle on a nice shade of green. Face filled out a bit. Spikes sharpened.

"I don't know how you do it," I say. "Every time."

Over a million and a half logged on to my feed and the count keeps ticking up. I'll have all of Magla on here before long.

A strong bass line kicks out of the speakers on my shoulders and I make my way onto the deck with the glider following me. My boots whir and click as the mag grips lock onto the decking.

"Disengage grips," I key into the Nanosite command screen.

A sharp beep and a flash respond. "Negative."

"I said *disengage grips.*"

Again the alarm sounds abruptly and still the mags hold on.

Well, it was worth a try. Probably for the best with the winds and all. It would have boosted my ratings, though.

A large shadow falls over me. It's the first of the Dust Field coming in tonight, a massive rock tumbling slowly amongst rocky debris. High above that I catch a glimpse of one of the silver freighters out on a mining run. They've got one rule up there: dodge rocks or get pulverized. That's where the real flying happens.

Ping.

"*Stay on schedule,*" a text on the side of my 'site reminds me.

Right. I hit the prompt and Scitech's prerecorded spiel starts. "Ever since he was young, he's dreamed of flying in the Dust Field."

True enough, but cheesy.

"I think every kid has. Free of the planet."

Stupid planetary lockdown keeping everyone on Magla unless on Scitech business. Luckily my eighteenth birthday is coming up and I can finally get out of here.

"Thanks to the innovation and support of Scitech lifting him up, he is about to live his dream of leaving the Rings and entering the sky.

Could you be next?"

The silver freighter spins around the tumbling rock, locking into its trajectory, perfectly synched up.

"Magnify."

My 'site focuses on the ship and zooms in until I can almost see into the cockpit. A single pilot flies this thing. That'll be me someday, and soon. I watch for a few more seconds until the rock blocks the ship from sight.

A beep interrupts me and I glance over at the script in the corner of my vision. I'm supposed to be heading over to the Edge now if I want to keep in time with the next song queueing up. So I drink in the sights and cold night air whipping past, and stamp in the direction of my drop off. The whir and clank of the mag boots beat in rhythm with my playlist, while the Sky Deck hovers patiently behind, tethered to my lower right arm.

"Looking good, Daj," Kie whispers in my sub channel. No one can hear that on my feed. "I can't believe how many Maglans are watching. I think Scitech really liked when you panned up to their ship."

"Holy shit." My eyes bulge as I check out my account funds. Scitech's initial amount has doubled. Doubled! "You're not kidding."

"See any more?" Kie says.

"Not yet, but I'll have Cam keep an eye out for anything. Can you do that?"

The drone beeps happily and the blue eye scans back and forth across the horizon while keeping the main camera in front of me.

"You ought to link that thing to your Nanosite display," Kie says. "It'd save time and they'd be able to edit your feed on the fly."

"I'm good," I reply. "I've had her so long I don't want to upgrade and lose whatever she's learned."

"*She?*"

"Yeah she, dumbass. And she takes way better vids than my nanos ever could."

"Don't say that too loud. You know, Scitech's gonna make you do it when you upgrade next month, anyway."

I glance back at the drone, and the little thing winks her blue eye happily at me. "We'll see."

After a minute more, my final song drops and it's time to go. The Edge marks the end of the smooth contours of the city and the beginning of a rocky cliff face. This part cuts straight down to the surface of the planet nearly a mile below through spinning rocks held right in the mag field. I've got to rip that new Sky Deck so hard that I don't end up splattered all over the feed. And right before I get there, I'm going to flip and arc into the city ring, going faster than anyone's gone before. Nothing can do it. Nothing except this new ride. I've practiced so many times on the sim but man my stomach drops a mile as I near the Edge for real. I got one chance to do this. I'm not going to screw it up.

"Hey, Daj?" Kie asks, this time not texting.

"Not so loud," I say. "This is it. Everyone's watching." Two million hits. The counter in my feed doesn't lie.

"Daj?"

"What?" I shout this time.

"Look up."

I slowly turn my head up to the skies, to the sharp and jutting rocks at the Edge. "This better be good." My stomach drops even farther this time when I see what Kie noticed in the live feed.

A Maglan. Some black-haired girl perching right on one of the floating rocks about thirty feet up. And staring at me. My Nanosite zooms in another few times until I can see the delicate spikes on her face.

Oh great. She's waving.

Well, if she thinks she's going to show me up, she obviously doesn't know who I am.

I lift my deck above my head with my top arms. And flip her off with my lower two.

"Watch this." I slam the Sky Deck to the ground and it bobs in the city's magnetic grip.

Before I can do anything, the girl, young like me, steps off one of the spinning cubes of rock. My chest tightens for a moment as she drops, but she smoothly catches onto another rock with her... bare toe claws? Wait, no boots? How is she doing this without any equipment? She's insane. She props her chin up with two hands and blinks at me. For half a second, I almost think she's seriously checking me out, but then she just rolls her eyes.

"Um, you better get moving," Kie says. "And get your cameras off her."

He's right. The music I was supposed to be listening to as I gripped the mags on the Edge is already blasting. And me standing around like an idiot staring at some girl. A warning light on the side of my stream flashes suddenly, insistently.

"We will sever your feed if you do not start moving," it reads.

Scitech. Shit.

"I'm going, I'm going." My boots click and lock into place on the Deck. The interface for the machine lights up and overlays my regular Nanosite giving me access to the controls.

Steering. The Deck spins 360 degrees. Check. I tuck down and then I flip backward in a tight loop. I edge forward slightly so that I can peer over the side of the arcing city wall down to the bottom. Boulders caught in the mag field sway back and forth in my path. I let out a deep breath. I've been training for this. I can do it.

Someone taps me on the side of my head. I spin around but no one's there, but then I look up. It's the Maglan girl hanging upside down from a floating cube. Her toes are clutching the stone as she peers down at me with her crystal blue eyes. And then she shoves me so hard I fall back onto my ass. Meanwhile, she floats gracefully toward the edge of the mile-high chasm I'm about to dive down. She's still sitting on that rock and she stretches her four arms and yawns intentionally at me.

"What do you want?"

Bright static lines shoot across my 'site; must be some sort of interference. Nanos shorting out isn't a common thing. It's got to be the intense mag field out here messing with them. The weather report called for low intensity mags tonight, though. After a few quick taps to the side of my head, the lines disappear and I can see again. Well, almost everything. Things seem a little out of focus. I can't see the girl's face clearly but I can tell she's still smiling. I hit the *request info* tab on my 'site but no stats pop up from her. No name, no age, nothing.

Either the interference is blocking me, or she's got no Nanosite. No Nanosite? Not likely.

"Can't you talk?"

Nothing. Great. A mute whack job hanging around on my vid feed. That's going to go over well.

All right. I've got a dive to take, or I'm going to lose my sponsorship. And that's not going to happen. Not with my training day coming up soon. Kie already rewound my music sequence and I'm ready to drop.

"Cam, make sure you get this."

The little drone zips past me and focuses on the girl. The hanging girl blows a little kiss at the camera. Cam shies away, seemingly embarrassed.

"Not her. Me. Going down there." I point down and Cam beeps an apologetic sound at me. She zips to my side and points down.

A high-pitched sound rises above the music and shreds into my ears. I swear loudly, but my recording software mutes it out. This is a family show, after all.

What's causing this? More interference? The girl drops down another few paces and slickly catches the next floating cube with her feet spinning herself over into a few graceful flips. She's good.

Annoying, but good.

"*Ending vid feed. Return to your domicile.*" Scitech streams this banner over the top of my sight in bright red letters.

"Wait, what? With all these views? I've still got this." I urge the Deck forward and it tilts dangerously close over the ledge. A gust of wind blows past me and my stomach sinks. This is going to be one crazy ass ride.

"Cam, keep up."

The drone beeps affirmatively.

The girl, still spinning on the floating rock, salutes me and swan dives off the edge.

"No way."

I jam forward on the control panel of my 'site, and the Sky Deck speeds down the city wall's grav field. The building whizzes past, wind shoves my eyes back into my head. I don't think I've dropped this fast before. Nanos jack my reaction times, and I juke back and forth between the grav rocks spinning about.

"Vid... closed..." Kie's voice cuts in and out of the comm channel.

I spare a second to check out the vid feed and see what he was talking about. "Cam, I got no video through my 'site. Don't you stop now! Stay on me and right up ahead."

Cam, still next to my side, beeps. Sounds like a terrified beep, but it could be just me.

I try to zoom in up ahead to stay ahead of the debris in my way, and also to look for the girl, but there's something wrong with my Nanosite. A sharp pain tears through my right arms. I don't even see what caused it, but it had to be some rock debris smashing into me.

My video feed, the one thing I needed, is now completely shut down. Viewer count is at zero.

The whine of the Sky Deck as it fights to stay locked to the city wall cuts into my brain. I'm inverted now as the building begins to bend back on itself and I can't see anything ahead of me. Not even the girl.

The Sky Deck comes to a complete stop, and my body crumples within a safety net. The last thing I think as the pain of stopping after traveling faster than I've ever gone fills my entire body is that the girl must be dead.

And how much I frickin' hate inertia.

CHAPTER 2

"You up yet, kid?"

The slurred, gruff voice stabs into my ears and rattles my already jostled brain. I squeeze my eyes shut.

"I said, *you up?*" The Maglan gets so close, the reek of whatever he's been drinking makes the last meal I had creep its way up to the back of my throat.

The harsh glare of flickering light burns through my half-opened eyes, waking me further. Where am I?

The bum is right in front of me now, and I get a close-up look at his elongated face spikes through his patchy gray beard. I reach up to push him away and turn over on the hard cot.

Only to look through a set of solid metal bars.

I'm in a holding cell?

The hell?

I jerk upward and slam my head into the low bunk right above me. Another jolt of pain tears through me and my 'site beeps a warning.

"*Repeated head trauma is not advisable.*"

Yeah, no shit.

"Maybe give me some pain meds, you think?"

"*Negative. Access to your Nanosite is restricted.*"

I must have hit my head harder than I thought to make my nanos tweak out like this. A quick scan over my 'site shows that almost all of the readouts are empty.

"Contact Kie."

"*Access denied.*"

"Play my latest feed."

"*Access denied.*"

"Jeez, is there anything I can access?"

"*Answer to that question denied.*"

"All right, that's it." I carefully sit up this time and brush past the

10

faded blue Maglan bum sitting next to me in this shared cell. "Nice tat, grandpa."

Surprise crosses the old man's face for a second as he pulls his sleeve over his forearm with a stump of a hand. Gross. What happened to it?

"That would've been some jump if you actually did it," he says.

"Oh, you saw that?" I tear my eyes away from his stump. "How much did you see?"

"Before or after you chickened out?"

"I didn't chicken out, you old drunk. Why don't you go back to your bed and sleep it off?" Outside my cell, a screen lights up with today's highlighted vids. Must be for inmates without access. At least my nanos can still reach the wireless port and relay the feeds to my head. I grip the bars with all four hands. My knuckles turn white.

"You ain't on the top of the feed, are you, HotDaj?"

No. I'm not. But for the life of me, I can't figure out why. I had two million plus viewers. Hell, why am I not even in the top five? I need one of those spots if Scitech is going to give me that upgrade. Hell, if this old guy knows my screen name, you'd think I'd be in there somewhere. It takes a bit and then a headline pops up next to my HotDaj username, but it isn't even close to what it should be. It should say something like, *HotDaj makes his most epic drop off the Edge*, but there's something else.

"*Suicide off the Edge by one of the Maglan radical group, Eldane, postpones Scitech's maiden Sky Deck flight. Reschedule TBA.*"

"Well that sucks."

Old drunk guy chuckles behind me, and while he's at it, he coughs up something chunky.

"What, you gonna cry because you didn't get your special spot on the list?"

The blood inside my head begins to boil and I punch the bars. "Some Nonno jumped on my feed."

"*Nonno?*"

"Yeah, you know? A Maglan with no nanos? Nonno. Man, you are old. Anyway, her killing herself in front of my feed kind of took over my show."

Now the old geezer is really laughing. "Dead, huh?"

"Watch the news feed. She jumped off the Edge without a suit or anything. The fall protection wouldn't catch her if it couldn't detect her. Splat. She's dead."

The old guy slaps me on the back. "Son, if she's an *Eldane*, then she flew better than you ever could."

"You're crazy. Too bad my nanos shorted out on the Edge before I could jump, or I would have caught the vid." My chest clenches and I look around me and search all over and under the bed.

"What you looking for?"

"Where is she?"

"Who?"

"Did you see an old drone come in with me?"

The old man shrugs. "Impounded, probably. Why?"

"Because it's mine, that's why."

"What's the model?"

"Why do you care?"

"I like old stuff, that's all."

"Me, too." I sigh and press my head against the bars. "She's a Camdrone Mark I. She can prove I jumped."

"Really? A Mark I." The drunk moves in a little closer and taps something on his wrist. "That's some real old tech."

"Yeah. It is."

"Special to you?"

"What do you think?"

"Step away from the door," a robot says in a cold voice.

It's a security bot. Can't really tell how old, but if the number of scuffs and score marks on its chassis tells me anything, it's pretty old. Barely any chrome left, now. Pity. It could have really been something if the security station kept it in any semblance of shape. A single glowing red eye scans the cell.

"Are you going to let me contact anyone?" I say. "I don't even know why I'm in here."

"It says you were in violation of the city of Phen's safety code 2115. You were also trespassing."

"Huh? See, I was out there on Scitech's time. Why don't you go give them a call and you'll see. They're my sponsor. You might have heard of me. Daj?"

The old bum nods to the bot and then points to me.

"HotDaj?" the bot asks.

"Yeah, that's—"

And the next thing I sense before I pass out is the sizzling smell of my own flesh.

***

Something beeping really loudly wakes me up. I'm still in my cell, but at least stinky old drunk is gone.

"Get up." Rough hands grab me under my arms and drag me into the hall.

"Why did you—?" I start to say, but my lips aren't working right so I stop.

The guard leads me to some sort of interrogation room and sits me down. All four hands suddenly lock down onto the table in front of me. My head still spins from that security bot. How long was I out?

A middle-aged Maglan stands over me. He's wearing a security force standard uniform and it fits snugly over the top of his well-rounded midsection. He's carrying a datapad. A literal datapad.

"What's with the ancient tech? Don't they have you on nanos yet?"

The man grunts and turns around. He's probably running Nanosite version 15, or older. I guess I'd be upset, too, if I had to read the uploads off that thing.

"*Run diagnostics*," I key out with my eye board. The results pop up and tell me my nanos are back online, or at least some of them are. Whatever burned and shocked me into unconsciousness earlier, there's no scar or any pain left, so I know the base healing nanos must be working. I cycle through the systems to see which are online.

In the corner of my 'site there's a readout of my whole body. The epidermal scan shows all cuts and lacerations that were healed up in the past couple of hours. All right, all right. No scars, at least. The next scan, the skeletal scan, shows the nanos working on both top and bottom left arms. A cluster of them at the forearm. There must be a pretty serious break if they're still active, and judging by the amount of warmth in there, the nanos must've injected me with the proper anesthetics. The final scan for soft organs appears to still be in diagnosis.

Something like a concussion would take a lot longer to heal up compared to a regular bone fracture, and with my placement exams coming up for flight training, I can't afford to wait. The scan first goes through my head. It pauses for a moment but then flashes green.

Phew. The scan continues downward.

On to my hearts.

They both check out.

Digestive stuff.

Good.

Balance and mag center.

The scan runs a diagnostic here for a full minute. Back and forth. Scanning the hard bio-metal lump right below my gut. Oh man, if my balance or reaction time is off at all, I'm going to get thrown out. And screw getting into the flight program if that happens.

Finally, the green light kicks out and I'm clear. Even bigger sigh.

Well, one more.

Got to be sure I can make some little Maglans someday.

And… check.

"You almost done here? I want to get home."

The security guy sits down right across from me and places the data pad propped up away from me so I can't see anything on it. "You've been grounded, kid."

"Hah. What do you mean?"

"After that suicide, Scitech is holding off on letting any more of you stunters up to do your tricks. Pity that's what some Maglans want to do. Steal a vid just to say goodbye to the world. You should have gone down before she jumped in front of your camera." He spins the data pad around and there's my feed I shot. "I was rooting for you. My whole family was."

I watch the vid silently.

Vertigo fills me as the camera pans out over the edge. My voice plays on the feed. *"With all these views? I've still got this. Cam, keep up."*

Really good footage, despite not being Cam's, flits over to the girl floating on the rock. She has a sad expression on her face. Huh, I must not have caught that the first time. But man, she's bummed, because in the next second she leaps off the edge. Suicide all right. She didn't have any nanos in her. No wonder she jumped.

A terrified scream trails off as the camera peers down the drop, but there's no sign of the girl. The feed turns to static and cuts out. I rub my eyes and pound the table.

Scitech didn't actually see me drop. They don't think I did it.

"I went over, too. There's got to be more footage. I know there is. Rewind that."

The guard glares at me.

"Rewind that, *please.*"

With a swipe, the video scans back until I'm looking over the edge again. The sad Maglan girl waves farewell to the world and jumps. Bye. But no, I'm not even moving close to the edge. Stupid interference from the mag field. Why didn't they check for that before sending me up there? I hope whatever footage Cam got is better.

The guard's datapad dings. He picks it up and stares at the screen. "Scitech posted your bail just now. Stay off the side of the city walls from now on, kid. Leave that to the window washers." He eases himself out of his chair and limps out of the room.

Too much sitting around will do that to you, buddy.

"It's about time." The magcuffs disengage with a click. "Kie," I begin messaging into my Nanosite. "You're not going to believe where I was last night."

No reply. Probably some interference with my nanos coming back online. Ugh, this sucks.

"Hey, where can I pick up my stuff?"

The guard outside points two arms to the right.

The halls are empty as I quickly walk to the checkout wall up ahead. An eye scan interfaces with my 'site sending my ID to the bored looking Maglan on the other side. While I wait, I type a message to Scitech.

"Sorry the drop didn't work out. I can get back up to the Edge as soon as you need me there. My vid feed cut out before I could jump off."

The Maglan clears her throat. "Here's some clothes, a backpack, and a water tube."

"Umm, what about my Sky Deck?"

The attendant stares at me with her tired gray eyes.

"I came in with a Sky Deck. And an older drone."

"This is all that was in your bin."

"Well, check it again. I think you might have missed the half million cred new tech in another locker." She keeps staring at me. "Go and check again!"

She glowers at me for a bit and then pushes her chair back to get up. Without a word, she heads to the back room.

All my hands are clenched into fists. I'm about to slam something. I scan through the diagnostics in my Nanosite just to focus on something else. I pick out a solemn music track and turn it on. The deep bass resonates in my skull. Thankfully that's running again. Nano-tats are online, too. I scroll through some of Zaylee's designs. Electric growth, digital waves. Maybe I can get her to make the tat that old guy

15

had. It was a pretty sweet design. Simple, but it would really go perfectly with my next jump. Some overlapping diamond shapes on it. What did it look like, exactly?

I rewind through my vid log of the past couple of hours. There's some time of me just lying there passed out. A bit more. And then I'm back in the cell with the drunk prisoner and the security bot. Right there, there's his tat. I take a still snap and upload the image into the tattoo software.

The diamonds appear on my palm as the nanos in my skin light up. With a flick of my hand I swipe the image onto my forearm and expand it a little bit. Add some glowing outline to it. Color it... purple? Perfect.

"No, nothing back here, but there's a message for you."

I stand expectantly and wait. "And?"

"Here." She swipes at the datapad in front of her toward me and I instantly get the message across my 'site.

"Sky Deck appropriated until further notice. Payments withheld."

They're banning me? And they didn't have the nerve to tell me to my face? Is it all because I didn't get vid coverage? I smack my hand against the metal wall and it rattles.

"Where's my drone?"

"There's nothing else, sir. No record." She slams the gate down. "But nice tattoo. I'm seeing that a lot lately."

I clutch the gate and rock it back and forth. "If you lost my bot you're going to pay!"

"Yeah, I bet." She starts to walk away and something hits me.

"Wait, you've seen this symbol before?" I gesture to my glowing tattoo.

She nods. "Some old drunk and his bot checked out of here a couple of hours ago. It had that freaky red eye. Now, will you get out of here and let me get back to work?"

My head spins. "What did the old guy want when he came here? Please."

She sighs and flips through a data pad. "The bot put in a requisition order. Huh. Now that's odd."

"What?"

"There's no record of it happening. I logged it in, picked up the package and gave it to them. I know I did." She stands up and walks back to another Maglan and begins talking.

That old man sure was asking me a lot about my drone. He must have taken her. My blood burns thinking about it.

Maybe I can remote activate her. I run through the Camdrone startup sequence. A message pops up. *"No drone detected."*

Crap. Too far out of range. But not far enough to engage the tracking device. A few more gestures and the signal in my 'site flashes once and then stops.

That tracker has at least a five-mile surface range on it. There's no way he's out of Phen's rings. Maybe he disabled that thing.

But why? Why would he want it?

Then I remember our conversation. I told him I had footage of my jump. Dammit. That video could make him a lot of money if he ever figured out what to do with it. And considering he knows how to disable the tracker, he can probably find the vid. I'm going to have to find that old bastard first.

As I run out of the station, I send a message to Kie and Zaylee. *"Need your help. Meet me at Bruho's."*

My stomach rumbles in response to having spent all night in the hole. It's late in the day already and Cadea and Naglor are setting. I pull up the map of this quadrant of Phen and the outline of the city's interlocking rings fills my 'site. Bruho's is a little greasy, but it's my favorite spot in the upper Ring.

I sit on one of the benches near the street side and a destination request pops up on my 'site.

"Bruho's, up on Phen Prime."

The charge for the ride displays and I type out the payment on the eye board. A bar wraps across my lap and the bench glides to the center of the street where other riders are also going wherever they need to go. In a second I'm whipping past the curved buildings on my way to the top, hundreds of feet up.

Ugh, this is going to take forever. Better check today's feed. Man, I had a record video stream going right before they cut me off. Two million. That was all of Phen, for sure. Definitely other rings around the globe, too. My comment feed is full of followers dropping the usual things.

Hot.

I want your baby.

Sweet Eldane suicide dive.

Daj, you f-ing wuss.

You know, the usual stuff. I don't spend too much time with that though.

The other bench riders are all staring off blankly, probably catching a video, maybe even recaps of mine. A long bench enters the travel zone next to me. It contains four giggling girls all with bright blue hair and the tips of their face spikes glowing different colors. They must recognize me because they all scream and wave. Bright flashes emit from their eyes as their 'sites snap some pictures of me. One of them attempts to pry up the bar keeping them seated, but the thing is locked tight.

I smile at them and shrug, but by now they're not even looking at me. They're all silent and swiping their hands in front of their eyes.

The bench cuts through the midsection of the ring and ascends the vertical section of the city. I get a view of the open sky beyond that. The bright green aurora fills the sky with its pulsing glow. The whole nightscape is alive. I gesture to the girls and point to the sky but they're still locked onto their screens. Oh well, their loss.

The silhouettes of the asteroids in the Dust Field around Magla flit by. My 'site magnification zooms in on the massive debris field scanning for any of the mining ships. That's going to be me once I get off this rock. It's been my dream to be a pilot since way before my parents left. I've been working way too hard on this promotion for Scitech, and nothing is going to stop it.

A message from Kie blips onto my notifications. "We're almost there, m'bacho. Can't wait to hear all about last night."

By the time my bench reaches the top, the sun is down and the aurora is in full green and purple mode. I flip off my nanos, and even without the 'site filters on, it's amazing. The rest of Phen is dead, though, so I turn them back on and the lights and shops and billboards appear in my eyes. Man, I love this city.

The old diner door dings as it opens, welcoming me inside. My two friends are already sitting there waiting for me. I slide into the booth next to Zaylee and reach over for a kiss, but she pulls her spiky cheek away.

"Phew, you're ripe." She wrinkles her nose.

"That's what happens when you spend a night in jail." I get a little closer to make her squirm a bit. She smells nice, though. Looks like she spent a little time primping, too. Each of her tiny face spikes are covered in a lightly glowing shade of blue.

"Jail?" Kie stares at me.

"Yeah, jail. You didn't try to find out what happened to me?"

"Messages all bounced back, said you were offline," Kie says. "But jail, man? That's one way of getting more viewers."

"They said I was trespassing."

"But Scitech cleared it, right?"

"That's what I told them!"

I try to put my arm around Zaylee but she shrugs me off. "Why'd you turn off your 'site? Right at the beginning of your jump. You were right there about to make the biggest dive in Phen history."

I shrug and grab a handful of fried strips off of Kie's plate. "That girl showed up. She was crazy. Didn't have any boots. Or anything."

"No gear?" Zaylee says.

"Yeah, she had *some* things, just not the things needed outside the Rings."

"You mean she could have just floated away?" Kie asks.

I nod. "As soon as she jumped, a bunch of interference cut my camera. I jumped anyway, and Cam got most of it."

Kie coughs on the strips. "You got footage of the jump?"

"Don't worry, I'll let you edit it up for me. I need something to help me get back in with Scitech."

Kie gestures with all his hands in a gimme gimme motion. "So where is it?"

I snag the last strip off his plate. "That's the thing. When I was in the hole, I think some old crazy drunk and his bot stole my stuff."

Zaylee raises her eyebrow at me. "They stole it? How'd they know about it? You and your big mouth?"

"Yeah, me and my big mouth." I open wide and grab some food off of her plate next.

"So, any other footage from this shit show?" Kie says.

"I don't think so. Just Cam's. At least I *hope* Cam's." A waitress walks up to me, but I wave her away. "Scitech cut me off."

"But Daj, you already spent those creds." Zaylee backhands my chest.

"Yeah, I did." On you and your clothes. "Do you mind?" I point to her plate and pick off some of her food.

"Apparently not. Hey, what's that?" She points to my arm.

"Oh yeah," I say through food. "The bum, he had this on his arm. I made a copy. You ever seen anything like it?"

"Let me see." Zaylee gets in close.

I can smell her perfume from behind her neck as she bends over to the glowing mark on my arm. "All right." I gulp and then swipe the design over to her. She holds two hands up in front of her face and begins to make intricate motions with her fingers.

"I'll look into it." She stands up.

"What? Now?" I back out of the booth to let her out and follow her to the door.

"No, next month when you're completely broke and living on the streets." She wrinkles her nose again as she looks out over the patrons of the bar and the open sky outside. "Why do you like coming up here again? Oh right, the *view*."

As if on cue, a mining rig touches down on a landing pad on the other side of the diner.

"Come on, you never get to see a landing or a takeoff to the Dust Field from down below. Or get to see the stars. Thought you'd like to live a little up here."

"Let's stay down in the ring next time you get your raggedy ass thrown in jail." She plants a kiss on my cheek and the heat fills my head. "And take a bath."

She sits on a bench and slides away quietly into the night. The heat flows away from my body; I'm not sure if it's from her leaving or a trick from the nanos.

"You done staring?"

"Jeez, man." My hearts jump nearly out of my chest.

"You didn't tell her the other reason you come up here," Kie says and leads me back into Bruho's.

My 'site scans through the patrons at their tables registering the Scitech logos on their uniforms. "You're right." I settle into the booth next to Kie.

"So what now?"

"That tattoo is the only thing I have to go on. I was thinking maybe I could ask around..."

"Why don't you let Scitech track your drone?"

I laugh.

"Oh, you're serious. I'm pretty sure I've told you before, *no one* gets access to it."

"Why not?"

"Why are we still talking? Now are you going to help me with this, or am I on my own?"

Kie shrugs and then gestures to himself. I take that as a yes and slide him the tat design, too. He nods that he got it. "You want to hang for a bit?"

"I'm going to head home. It's been a long day and I need a real bed." I stand up and take the rest of his strips. "Thanks though. I'm sorry, man. I'm just tired."

Kie says something like wondering if he could crash the night on my couch, but I just answer with a grunt. I'm too busy watching another mining tug land on the pad right outside the diner. I strain to see the pilots climbing out of the rig. Not who I was hoping for so I head for the door with Kie right behind me.

CHAPTER 3

Sunlight. Warming my face. A cool breeze blows across my skin.

If I have to get up, at least my 'site's wake up function makes it less painful. It's still too damn early, but I've got to meet with the Scitech reps to see about extending my contract. And to figure out why the hell they cut my 'site privileges. I bet they're just upset I didn't get any footage off that jump after spending all that time and money on the Deck and boosting my feed. I'd be pissed, too, I suppose.

The usual bits of info populate my feed. Weather. News. But if my vid from the other night is on there somewhere, I can't find it. I mean, not anywhere. Not on any of the highlights. Nothing. Normally, I'm used to days and days of sharing, commenting, remixing, building my network. Now, I'm barely searchable. All that pops up when I do find some about me is the whack job jumper killing herself.

I do spot a remix of my jump, or the "Walk of Shame" as some Maglans are calling it. The sad-eyed girl is just sitting there on the rocks waiting to jump off. Cued with the depressing music, the bootless girl jumps off the edge.

"*Fail,*" the screen says. An advertisement for Scitech's mag-grip boots pops onto the display complete with a hot girl in said boots. And not much else.

"A tragedy that could have been prevented," she says. "Remember, never leave the city without Scitech boots."

Sad.

A chime sounds signaling the top of the hour. Time to make my call. Usually, I take this call with my agent, but Scitech wants to talk to me directly. Whatever they want, man, whatever they want. I'll take this out in the living area, as my room is covered in clothes. Kie is still passed out on the couch, but I can block him. With a few swipes, I switch the display to private and Kie fades out of view, and luckily his snores get muted, too. I open the channel and an image of a woman I've never seen before in a well-cut suit appears in the chair next to me.

She's the image of corporate. Perfect black hair. Face spikes manicured. Outfit expertly pressed with no lines. I know she's not there, but man she looks real.

Real pissed, too. This doesn't look good. Figures they'd send some rep I don't know. If I wanted to let someone go, this is how I'd do it, too. Okay, I've got one chance, so just like I rehearsed.

"Good morning, Ms. Pontane." Luckily, her name is tagged on the display. "First off, I'm sorry about the jumper and the interference in my dive."

"Have a seat, Daj."

She says this with a finality that cuts me off and I sit down. I remind myself not to fidget, but I'm already clutching the arms of the chair with my lower hands. So much for my speech. My heart races and sweat drips down my back.

She sits there staring at me with her disapproving expression for several seconds. Her black hair pulled back tightly matches the glare in her eyes. "We are very disappointed about this whole incident. You have tarnished the good name of Scitech."

"I have the footage of my jump." Got to get right to the big guns, I guess.

My nanos pick up a slight alteration in her expression, but instead of interpreting whatever it was she just did, the body language software goes blank. And before I can think, she's back to her austere expression.

"What do you mean you have it? Your Nanosites shorted out under the interference. There is no record of your so-called jump."

"I have a Camdrone."

She smiles, but if there's anything friendly in it, I don't sense it. "An unregistered video device. Go on."

"Well, I mean, I *had* one. You see, when I was in jail—and thanks for posting my bail, I appreciate it—someone took my drone. Stole it. I'm looking for it, and once I find it, I'll be able to edit up the jump so it's not a total disaster."

Ms. Pontane taps her fingers on her chair arm without expression. My guess is she's off call right now discussing this with someone else. At least they haven't let me go quite yet.

After a moment, her eyes focus back on me. "We can help you find your drone, but we'll need access to your encrypt codes."

"The guy who stole it is out of surface range, and I can't track it."

There's no way he disabled the long range tracker, right? I encrypted it really tight.

"We can help you. Register its codes and we can search as well."

I want to say no. From the look of it, I don't think this lady has been told no her entire life.

"Just give me a day; I know I can find it."

She smiles again and the temperature in the room seems to drop a few degrees. "It is imperative we get this missing footage of the Sky Deck. We're shipping the product within the week, and you are our main promo spot. You wouldn't want the opportunity to go to someone else, would you?"

I shake my head. "I'll send the codes, but they're not on my 'site. I'll have to send them separately."

"Do it."

"And I can redo the jump if you give me another chance."

"Just get us those codes."

No smile this time. Yikes. Then the transmission cuts off, and the only thing I hear is Kie's ragged breathing.

"Did you hear that message?"

"Mmmhmmm," Kie says. "When we leave?"

"I don't have much time, so, like, now. I figure we have to boost my tracking signal, see where that guy is hiding."

"I must still be sleeping, because I think I heard you're going to send them your codes. Didn't you say you'd never do that?"

"I'll send them some codes. Just not Cam's."

Kie sits up. "Are you crazy? Don't you think they'll notice?"

"By the time they do, I'll already have her safely in hand, and I can give them the video myself. Say I forgot them, or sent the wrong ones by mistake."

With a good yank, Kie slides off the couch and staggers his way to the bathroom without any thanks.

"Mind if I use some of your music to start today's post?" Maybe I could ask Maglans to look out for the old drunk.

"Whatever."

I queue up Kie's tracks and link up the feed. "Morning everyone, it's time for me to get out into Phen." The laser lights are fired up, the music is rolling.

But I've only got one follower online right now. What the...?

"Account suspended."

No way.

But that's what it says. Right there. Suspended. A message pops up. *"Contact Scitech to re-establish link."* Well, I'm not about to contact them again after our last chat. And there's no way I'm going to post something without any viewers. Who is that one follower?

Scitech.

And I bet they're waiting for me to post any clues about where I'm going, just in case I get to Cam first. I know they only want to help, but too bad. I turn it off. The music and lights fade out and it's just boring old Daj's apartment.

Only a couple of days of this, at the most, and I'll be back in it. My blood pounds so loudly in my head I can hardly think of anything else. A couple of days? What am I thinking? I can't be away from my fans for that long. I'll lose my rankings.

"Think Zaylee found anything?" Kie shouts out from the other room.

Good idea. Scanning over the display in my 'site I get to my messages. One unread from Zaylee, and it's a video.

"Hey babe," she says. That's a good start. *"That was real freaky, yesterday. Sorry you didn't get your jump in. Anyway, I found something on that symbol you sent me."*

My design centers onto the display, and another shape appears, the one Zaylee found. The two are nearly identical. Overlaid diamond and triangle patterns in a wing shape. Is that military?

"Browsed some tattoo shops on my 'site, didn't find anything. Not until I started asking around in the district did someone actually talk to me about it. An older lady. And even then she was pretty tight-lipped. Afraid, almost. She drew the pattern onto a piece of paper. Can you believe it? Paper? Said it was some old religious symbol. Maybe even Eldane. Anyway, that's what I got. Hope it helps."

Zaylee blows a kiss before the message ends.

So, this old nutjob gets thrown into jail, has his robot helper scam me out of some old tech drone, rips it off, and then goes where?

"Think maybe he went to the lower levels?" Kie falls back on the couch.

Chills run up my spine. The lower levels of Phen theoretically go beneath the rings and into the rock. Does anyone still live there?

"It would explain why we couldn't get a bead on that drone." Kie bites into a food tube I had left sitting on the table.

"Maybe if we get down there and ping the drone we'll be able to find it," I say.

Kie keeps sucking down the food.

"Well?"

"That's funny, I thought you said that *we'd* be able to find it," Kie replies.

"Come on, man. I need your help."

"Have you ever been down there? No. Can our 'site work down there? No. Is there a high chance that we'll get robbed or killed?"

"Not a really high chance."

"So *yes?*"

I sigh. "Look, I don't know what's going to happen, but I could really use your help. Think of it as payment for all the times you spent in this apartment eating my food and borrowing my stuff. I wouldn't have any of this if it weren't for my work with Scitech. And if you want to keep enjoying it, you should help me."

"All right, all right. I was just messing with you. Are you going to ask Zaylee along? That'd be a really perfect date."

"Nah, I don't want to risk her getting killed."

"Just me?"

"Just you."

"Aw, that's sweet. Now let's get going before I change my mind."

***

Hundreds of Maglan kids are out on the gleaming lake today. It's a perfect day for it, too. Hovering over the waves on sail decks, swimming, or just lying on the beach. It doesn't seem fair. Why do they get all the fun while I'm stuck hunting down a drunk thief? Soon, the large windows come to an end as the vertical ring nears the base of Phen and all I can see are billboards and bright lights.

Several messages arrive from Scitech reminding me to send Cam's codes. I upload a model schematic for her and send something that closely approximates her codes. *"Hope this is right, I rushed out of the apartment to find her. I'll check back later."*

There. That ought to keep them happy. For a while, anyway.

After 15 minutes, our bench glides to a halt at the bottom of the city and the lights on the walkways dim. It's hard to tell if it's the buildings blocking the light, or somehow the nanos aren't as powerful this far away from the orbital station and satellites.

An involuntary shiver runs through my body. "It's frickin' freezing down here."

The *boost heat* protocol starts up and instantly my extremities tingle with the warmth from the nanos doing whatever they do in there. This place may be cold, but it feels so… alive. There's something in the air, a tangible buzz in my ears, and everyone is moving around with a bustling energy despite their shabby clothes. And the smells. I'm on overload. My nostrils flare as I take in the different foods, burnt out mechanical parts, and even the scents of all the Maglans around me. I close my eyes and breathe it all in.

"Where to?" Kie asks.

There are no signs pointing to the underground. Notifications on my 'site just direct me to all destinations in the rings up above. There's still the bustle of the city down here, but it's filled with more, I don't know, *shady* types of Maglans. Makeshift carts with peddlers selling things from black market shoes to shoddy tech fill the alleyways looking like they're ready to pick up and leave at the first sign of trouble. Not all the tech looks shoddy, I guess. Some of these things are pretty cool. Mag assist stabilizers that strap on wrists, pre-'site era goggles, and an old Mag Disk game set. I hold out my hand and the disk hovers and zips to me.

"Remember this thing?" The disk feels familiar as I flip it from one hand to the other and then behind my back. I pass it to Kie and it promptly bounces off his head. "Come on, get off your 'site."

"You two look like a couple of grade 'A' a-holes just wandering around down there."

"Zaylee?"

"Yeah, I'm watching you through Kie's live feed. It's chopping out, but you look like a yokel, staring at everything. And that mutt is killing the vibe he's going for. You might as well pick it up and adopt it."

There's a starving, pathetic looking yarel by Kie's feet begging for a scrap of something. Kie pushes it away with his boot heel. "Man, I hate these things."

"Don't kick it! What's wrong with you?" I walk past the little black scaled critter whose five good eyes lock right onto mine. A scar runs right across the missing sixth eye. The little guy scampers away through the crowd, stopping once to look back at me.

"I wasn't kicking it. I just didn't want it near me."

I shake my head. What did Zaylee mean about Kie's live feed?

I scan the vid feeds and sure enough Kie is up there, leading the streams today. Not as many followers as I had yesterday, but enough.

There's this annoyingly poppy music track looping over his video as we walk around down here. *"To the dumps below Phen,"* his feed is titled.

There's a recap of me staring longingly at the lake we passed earlier. He's got a caption: *"Fallen hero longs for another dive."* Another remixed video of me flipping the Mag Disk pops up, this one accompanied by some sad nostalgic music and then me making a sad face in slow motion. *"Seems like only yesterday,"* this caption says.

"That's not funny, man." I elbow him in the side and gesture for him to cut off the vid.

"What? Come on. This is good stuff. You should see the number of views and comments I'm getting on this. All right, all right, I'll end it. We're getting blocked down here anyway, and the quality is bugging." Kie clears his throat. "So long, viewers. I'll check back in when we track down our prey. Meanwhile, keep me posted if you know anything about this mark."

I don't see it, but I assume he's showing the world the diamond shaped tattoo.

Not a bad idea.

Kie and I start showing the tattoo mark to every vendor and street bum we come across. "You seen this? I'm looking for an old drunk with a red-eyed, scuffed-up security bot."

We get nothing except dirty looks. Before long, Kie and I lose our bearings and without a sun to see, time slips by. The global locator in my 'site is barely working. It's not like the ring system in the city. Up there you're either on the lateral rings, the central one, or way up on Phen Prime and it's easy to keep track of where you are. Now, I'm not even sure we're on the rings anymore.

It could be the reason why we find ourselves down a dead-end dusty alley showing the mark on my arm to a faded old Maglan woman with a pot of pungent smelling soup.

"You two boys oughtn't be down here."

Kie taps the side of his head, and it must mean his 'site is down. It's way dark and we're far from anything familiar. Still, it feels safe somehow.

"Have you ever seen this before?" I show her the design on my arm, but it, too, fades out of sight. "It's a couple of diamonds." I sketch it out onto the dust on the ground.

"Have a seat," the lady says. She smiles, like I think a grandmother would.

"I'm in a hurry." Still, I squat down and she hands me a cup of the stew. She waves her four hands in the air and begins humming. I take a sip of the bitter liquid and almost spit it out. When I swallow it, my whole body kind of tingles as I try not to puke.

"This is freaking me out," Kie whispers in my ear. "She's crazy. I'm ready to go home, man."

"Just relax, Kie."

"You want soup?"

"No, I don't want your stupid soup." Kie pulls me by my shoulders. "Are you coming?"

I kind of fall back and sit down.

He heads back down the alley. "I'm leaving. Come on, Daj."

"Wait!" I say, I think. No, I didn't actually say it, I just wave goodbye. I'm feeling way more comfortable, like relaxed. That's some good soup.

"Those are nice boots." The voice comes from behind me.

"Yup." I kick out my feet and shovel another bite of the bitter stew into my mouth. "Newest Scitech boots."

"You don't mind if we see them, do you?"

Of course I don't. Why would I? I pry them off my feet and hold them above my head. "See?"

Behind me is a gang of young Maglans, but for some reason they don't care about my shoes. They're running and throwing rocks at me.

"Stupid Ringer," one of them says.

This one reaches back to swing a metal bar. That's an odd thing to do. As the bar comes around toward my head I just laugh and wave at him.

Luckily he misses, but it's like he misses in slow motion. And then he just stops with an expression of disbelief, like he doesn't know how he could have missed.

Something hits me in the back of my head and I hear a high pitched ringing. As I start to fade out, someone shouts, and the last thing I remember is seeing a red light bearing down upon me.

***

When I open my eyes, the first thing I see through my blurry vision is an old piece of machinery propped up on top of metal crates. It's a mag speeder or glider of some sort, but I've never seen one quite like it before. It has a pair of curved, short wings and is big enough for one Maglan to lay flat on. All I know is I'd love to fly it.

Bang.

Okay, ow.

Bang.

No, really, that's loud.

"Stop."

There's a pause in the clanging.

"About time you woke up." It's an old, gruff voice.

Familiar.

And of course it is, because it's the old Maglan drunk I encountered back in the jail cell. He's working on the glider. And so is his psycho red-eyed bot, who flips his hand in a casual wave.

"The mag core is damaged," the bot says. It's the same voice as before in the holding cell, but it's no longer as cold. Must have been an act. "Maybe next time don't do a double roll off the ring on the way up. And down."

"I wouldn't need a core if…" the old guy trails off in some drunk stupor. "Thanks for the advice, Dewey." The old man dismisses the bot with a wave of his deformed hand.

"Dewey?" I say. My head is still foggy from before.

"Yeah, Dewey." His voice drops back to the tone he first had, and he approaches me with a metal tool shoved in my face. "Got a problem with it?"

I inch backwards.

A sound like laughter comes out of the bot's vocalizer. "Nah, I'm just kidding. He's an easy mark. Isn't he?"

The old man nods. This is going to be lots of fun.

"Yeah, those kids stole your boots."

"Not my boots!" I look down to my feet and see some faded leathery scraps on my feet. "Those were Tekkys. You expect me to walk around in whatever these things are? They suck."

"Hey, those are a gift." The old man crosses his arms.

What is going on? Is the whole town going crazy? I quietly attempt to access my Nanosite. Screw what I said about not contacting Scitech. But there's nothing. No displays, no weather stats, no vid feeds. No text asking about Cam's codes. It's just gone. Completely gone. My pulse is racing and I can't quite catch my breath.

"Hey, it's all right, kid. You'll be okay. Now drink this."

He hands me a cup of some liquid, but I smack it out of his hands and it clatters to the ground.

"I'm not a kid. Who are you and what do you want?"

"You are a kid, kid. But my name is Rym. And this is Dewey, obviously."

He slurs that last word and hiccups. Is he ever sober? Dewey picks up the cup that fell at his metallic feet and very delicately dabs a cloth at a few drops of liquid that splashed onto the glider.

"As for what I want, *Daj*, a little thanks would be nice. You ran into a pretty serious gang back there. If it weren't for me and good ol' Dewey, it would have gone a lot worse."

"Pretty convenient, don't you think? Little grandma gives me some drugged up soup, and a group of kids come and attack me. And then, oh hey, there you are to help me out." There's a thudding in my skull that won't stop.

"Grandma," Rym says with a laugh. "She'd love that. As for the gang, you can't just come waltzing off the Rings and think you run the place down here. You two were just a couple of targets."

"Where's Kie?"

"Your *friend*? He ran the second you were in trouble. But don't worry, he's safe back up where he belongs."

There is only one exit out of this work room. Well, only one door. There's also a big window opening out onto some black pit. It's past the glider, a work bench with a neatly organized set of tools, and the security bot. I think I can make it if I had my reflex nanos working, and knew where I was going, and wasn't just a kid. I sigh.

"Look, I know you have my drone."

Rym feigns surprise, looks to Dewey and then back to me.

"Can I have it back?"

Rym shrugs. "There's something I need on it, and you've got that thing locked up tighter than a one-armed, two-fisted," he trails off as Dewey places a hand on his shoulder. "It's just so damn encrypted."

"I can pay you for it. Scitech will reimburse you for the video I took. It's not going to do any good for you, anyway. My video? It's not even edited. I'll get it cleaned up and you can have a cut."

Rym laughs and I smell the alcohol on his breath from here. "Hear that, Stell? He said he'll clean your video up a bit. Make you more presentable." He hits the parts rack next to him and leaves the room.

Who the hell is Stell?

A second later someone drops to the floor and I nearly shit my pants. Spare parts clatter to the ground as I try to steady myself. It's a young female, and she's familiar, too. It's not that girl from the drop, is it? She stands and sizes me up. Can't be. Anyway, she's dead. And this girl's hair is off from the one in the video. And her body is much more... I stop myself from staring and try to ignore the heat rising to my face.

"Hi, uh, Stell?" Good one. I clear my throat. There's another throbbing in my head and I reach back to see if there's any blood, but my hand comes back dry. Something must've smacked me good there, though.

Stell picks up a long wrench and walks to Dewey. She starts tooling with the glider but always keeps an eye on me. Okay, so she doesn't say much. Man, where have I seen her before? It's killing me.

"You spend any time up in the Rings?"

She just rolls her eyes at me.

"So, you were just sitting up in the rafters while we talked." How did I not see her there? Or hear her? "That's not creepy."

I inch closer to the glider and take a look. Man, this thing is old, but I recognize some of the guts of it. Good condition. Except for one thing.

"Your mag core bypass is shot."

Stell narrows her eyes at me, but starts to tweak the connection. A minute later, she nods at Dewey. They shut the engine lid and the glider rises a bit off the floor. Stell smiles.

"No thanks for the diagnosis?"

Her smile drops.

"You're not going to get much out of her that way." Rym comes back into the room with my Camdrone hovering right behind him.

She beeps a hello.

"You're all right!" I jump forward and hold out my hand. The lightweight camera zooms in on my face and locks into place on my wrist dock.

"You doing okay? How are your systems? Everything functioning normal? What about your video storage?"

"Jeesh," Dewey says. "Do you two need some privacy?"

He said that just in time because I was about to hug her. Everything will go back to normal now. Scitech will welcome me back, get me online again.

"So, am I being held here, or can I just go?"

Dewey steps in front of the door, barring the way.

"Hostage then?"

Rym puts his hands on the glider. "We need that video."

"You need money, I get it. Food maybe. The tech is really old down here. I bet you're not even running a version of Nanosite from this decade. Mine's not working at all. You probably lose reception down here. Scitech will give it to you, once I get this video published. They'll give you a reward for saving me. I can tell them you helped."

"Gods, you babble, kid. Scitech doesn't give a flip about your video. Well, they do, but they have other plans."

"No, they're waiting for me, I'm the face of their new Sky Decks, maybe you've seen me?"

"Yeah, HotDaj, I get it," Rym says.

"I have until the end of the day to get this to them. If I don't, I'm sure the sponsorship will go to someone else, and I won't be a pilot."

"I know you don't want to listen," Rym begins. "But Scitech has bigger things than you. Yeah, I've seen your videos. You're good. You're not great."

"Then you haven't seen my vids."

"You're not great." Rym raises an eyebrow. "But you could be better. Them nanos are slowing you down."

I roll my eyes. I've heard this before. Eldane supporters. Think it's better to ditch anything Scitech. "Just because you don't have the tech to do what I do doesn't mean you know everything. Look at your arm nub. You can't do half the things I can with my nanos."

"I can think for myself is what I can do." He grunts and clutches his gimpy hand to his chest.

Maybe I took it too far with that arm comment. But he is a kidnapper, kind of, so screw it.

"You're never going to listen to me, are you?" Rym says. "Don't you remember when you dove off the edge of the city ring with your fancy new deck?"

"Um, yesterday? I remember I was pretty awesome."

"The girl. She was better."

I laugh. "Well, she was certainly better at killing herself. Didn't you see the vid?"

Rym takes a long pull from a flask that somehow appears in his hand. He gestures to Stell.

"Her?" I say. "Sorry, no. I've seen that thing a hundred times now. She looks nothing like her."

"For someone with first-hand experience, you have an awfully poor memory."

"And she died." I know she did. No one could live after that kind of free-dive.

"Get your drone working, and you can verify. Go on."

I cross my arms. Not today.

"Fine. Be a punk. You can just sit in here until you're ready to listen. But you're not going anywhere until you do. Or until you give us the decrypt codes."

My hand instinctively reaches toward the Camdrone. "Not going to happen."

"Ugh, you're just like your parents."

"Wait, you know my parents?" I can't think of anything else now. It all comes together in a second, what had to have happened. My parents are okay! They contacted someone to secretly get in touch with me.

Rym's face screws up like he's trying to think of something. "Nah, I'm just trying to get you to talk. I don't really know your parents. I just assume they're gone. Sorry, I didn't realize it would be that big of a deal."

"It's nothing."

"No really, I'm sorry."

"I said forget it."

Dewey and Stell shake their heads. Stell comes toward me though, and motions something to Rym. He nods to her and gestures to me with a sweeping motion, like a *have-at-it*.

That thumping in the back of my head starts up again. There's a disgusted look on Stell's face as she sizes me up. This time that same pounding sensation occurs in my guts. This can't be random. She has to be doing it, somehow. This is messed up.

"Hey, stay away from me. What kind of nanos is she using? Some new tech?"

Rym doesn't respond.

Somehow she's causing something to happen in me. If she's trying to torture me into giving the decrypt codes, she's going to have to do better.

After a minute she turns to face Rym but she doesn't say anything. So, she's a mute, just like that dead girl. Is she her sister?

"Are you trying to figure out what happened to the jumper?"

"No, you idiot," Rym says.

An alarm sounds over the speakers in the room, a blaring, piercing sound. Rym turns to Dewey and the two run to the door followed closely by Stell.

"What's that?" I yell, but the door slams shut and clicks. "I guess I'll wait here, then?"

No, I won't. I try the door, but it's locked tight. Pounding on it doesn't help, but I give the metal thing a couple more kicks anyway. There's an explosion beyond the door followed by what sounds like gun blasts. He's under attack? Got to be some rival gang down here, and I'm not going to pass up an opportunity to get out of here.

Walking back to the window, I smash my knee into the glider. "Mother—" The smooth black metal machine bobs up and down from my touch. I look to the bolted window, and then back to the glider. Another explosion rocks the compound, and dust shakes loose from the ceiling. And the thick glass rattles in its frame.

"All right, that's it. Cam, scan the room. See if you can find anything useful to get that thing open."

My little drone detaches from my forearm and hovers around the room while I clear the crates and junk away from the glider. "I can fly this thing."

Cam beeps at me.

"It's motivational. Come on, don't contradict me. Just keep looking."

Sure, this glider doesn't look like anything I've ever flown before but I haven't met a ship or deck that I couldn't get to fly. I hop onto it, nearly lying prone, and lace all four hands into the steering straps. My knees click into place. As I shift my hips and arms, each movement turns the glider in that direction. Never seen a steering mechanism quite like this. Now if I could only figure out where to go once I break free of this dump.

Cam lets out a single high pitched beep.

"What'd you find?"

Cam appears from behind a workbench dragging a massive pry bar in her four delicate pincers.

"I like the way you think." Quickly I pop off the glider and grip onto the surprisingly heavy bar. "Whoa, you been working out?"

Cam beeps shyly and then returns to her dock on my forearm.

The pry bar makes short work of the glass in the wide window, and

I spend a few extra seconds shearing off any big pieces attached to the frame. Bright lights flash outside and I finally get a chance to see what's out there. Several gun emplacements hammer the base with explosive mag rounds while troops with mining lasers chip away at the foundation below.

It's Scitech.

And they're firing at me? Don't they know who I am? Apparently not. They seem to think I'm with Rym. Well hell, I'm out.

I'm at least 60 feet up in some rickety looking shack, which appears to be built into the surrounding rock structures. If this glider doesn't fly, it's going to be a real short trip.

In seconds I'm back on the glider with my arms and legs locked tightly in place. My 'site is not working yet, so I can't interface with the control program. But the more I look at the controls the more I think there is no way to do that anyway. This is pre-Scitech, after all. Pre-nano.

"Cam, get ahead of me and make sure I have a clear path." Cam's signal reaches my nanos and I'm able to link her sight to mine. At least something works. She zips out the window and peers down.

There are some troops actually scaling the side of the building. Laser fire glints off their armor. What kind of resistance is this terrorist Rym guy going to put up? And who knew Scitech had this much firepower? I mean, I knew they had a strong security force, but I've never seen anything like this. A hail of rocks releases from above me and showers down onto the troops.

"All right, that's it." I pull up on the grips with my top hands and the glider responds by hovering up to the window height.

The glider keeps rising and smacks my head into the ceiling. I bite back some profanities as I bob back down again. Almost like a joke, a curved see-through panel pulls up and covers my head. Could have used that ten seconds ago. My lower hands twist slightly and a gentle rumble vibrates through the glider. "Throttle. Perfect."

I grip it a little tighter and the whole machine jerks forward, smashing the clear panel over my head into the window frame. "Oops." The screen glints with the fresh scratches. "Those'll buff out."

Once clear of the window, I jam both the throttles. Instead of the flash of speed I expect, the glider shakes and its nose points straight down at the climbing troops. The glider plummets.

"No turning back, now." The throttles, this time, boost me forward and I grip tighter, feeling like I'm going to peel straight off the back. This sucker is fast.

Before I can react, I smack into the first trooper who managed to scale half-way up the building, knocking him off.

"Sorry!"

I don't see him fall as I'm jamming my legs and top arms side to side avoiding the rest of the crew. The glider swerves instantly to my touches and once I reach the ground level, I arc away over the top of all those guns. Images light up my clear display, targets pop up, the entire area around the building highlights. It just did an entire scan of the terrain? Nice. There's no clear way to fly straight up and out of here. I'm in some huge cavern.

There's another set of bars on the display indicating speed and one right beside it labeled *magnetic stack*. That bar is slowly building up, but it's still just above empty.

Now that I'm out of there, I feel pretty much safe. I get a closer look at the troops and see the Scitech insignia. This has to be a rescue mission. I ease back on the throttle and head to a clearing a couple hundred feet from the building, a little away from the barrage. There's a troop transport locked into the ground, I can get some help from them.

"Land your vehicle and stand down!"

Lights from the transport flash onto me. I squint painfully at it. The clear display darkens slightly and I can see again.

I want to say that I comply, to tell them who I am, but my 'site isn't fully up yet. A few flickering displays are showing up, but not my broadcast station.

"You stole our glider?"

The voice comes from inside the clear display, I think. It's hard to tell, as I hear it all around me. Nice speakers. It's a female voice.

"Nice of you to finally start talking. Stell, right? And yeah, you kidnapped me so I took your glider. It's what prisoners do."

"Well, you're not going to want to land there," she says.

"Why not?"

Laser fire glances past the glider and the heat of it sears my neck.

"Oh."

Where's the comm unit on this thing? I've got to let them know I'm on their side. I crank the throttles and twist my legs and the glider wrenches around like some writhing animal. Another laser fires after

me, but I'm already spinning away from it. There's a rear view screen at the bottom of the display on this thing, and I notice two Scitech speeders fly in tight behind me.

"What is this propulsion system?"

"Fully mag," Stell says.

I didn't realize I said that out loud. "Can't be. No mag system can be this fast, or responsive." Several more blasts from the speeders narrowly miss me and explode into the cave walls. Rock fragments pelt the glider.

"Scitech tell you that?"

I bite back a response.

The display shows tunnels through the ground leading several directions from here. I can get clear and then I can find a Scitech base. Better yet, I can probably fly this thing all the way home.

"Watch out!"

I yank on the controls and the glider swerves. A mag shell blasts right through the space I had just been in.

"Are you tracking me?"

"You could say that," Stell says.

I'm outta here. There's a tunnel right up ahead, and I crank the throttle. Luckily my body is locked into this thing, otherwise, I would just be thrown clear.

"Not that way. Those tunnels will be too much for you at that speed."

"You ain't ever seen me fly then, have you?"

There's no response. Well, there is, but it's static. Good thing my Nanosite displays all begin to flicker into view as they come back online. Reflex speed increased ten percent. Metabolism boosted. It's not all back, but this is better than before.

"Slow...tunnel..." the girl's voice cuts through.

"Nope. Fast." That magnetic stack gauge is nearly full and the display is flashing, whatever that means. The speeders' blasts rip past and into the rock up ahead. "Got to lose these guys."

I corkscrew into the tunnel and dive as it starts to curve. An outline of the cave and a projected scan lights up on the clear display and I'm able to anticipate the turns before they show up. An eruption of sound and light from behind let me know that at least one of the speeder pilots couldn't do the same.

The outlines of the tunnel get shorter and shorter until suddenly I can't see what's around the next corner. "Hey what's going on?"

No response except static. Am I too far from the base? The tunnel opens up a little and I twist the throttles to gain some more distance. But nothing happens. The mag system seems to be shorting out. Maybe it's the problem Rym was working on that he never fixed. My glider skims to a halt in the center of the cave, still hovering about fifty feet in the air, but no propulsion.

At that moment another speeder whips around the corner and zeroes in on me like a predator spotting a wounded animal. It doesn't want to kill me though. Four metal legs emerge from the base of the body, and it slowly approaches.

No problem. Once it finds out who I am, it will stop, and it will bring me back to the surface. Daj, the returning hero.

Three clamps lock onto my glider, and a laser drill opens at the end of one of the other legs.

Oh, shit. Are you kidding me?

There is only one light still active on the glider's display screen. The magnetic stack gauge. I don't think. I just slam it.

There's a strange pulling sensation as the Scitech speeder bends and crumples toward me ever so slightly. The metal joints ping and groan under the stress. The stack gauge drops; then two things happen at once. The speeder flings away from me, and I fly like a spit seed in the opposite direction. The speeder crashes into the ceiling and explodes in a brilliant ball of flame. I don't have much time to enjoy the wreckage as I try to avoid doing the same thing. The base of the cave is approaching pretty quickly. And those big, pointy rocks.

With every muscle in my arms and legs I pull back on the non-responsive controls. I dodge one, two, of those jutting rocks, but not the third. The glider hits it just shy of head-on and I spin and spin, hitting the ground with a ripping crash.

CHAPTER 4

"Tell me you got that."

Cam beeps an affirmative. She's still attached to my arm so she didn't get an aerial shot, but at least she caught some of that action. Anything will be amazing.

I brush off some dirt from that spill and check to make sure none of the pains in my body are actually breaks. Better see what the nanos have to say. They can tell what's wrong with me. Probably. Coverage is still spotty way down here below the surface, but for the most part I'm able to get a pretty okay connection.

"Scan body for injuries."

"*Unable to connect to get a full scan. Please find better coverage so we can provide you with detailed information. Do you still want to proceed with minimal scan?*"

I key *yes*.

The display goes over my body and nothing serious pops up. Only some small cuts and bruises. Nothing internal. Hitting the ground in a fall like that should have snapped my bones in half. But this surface is nothing like normal rock. I press my foot down and it kind of squishes into the surface. Like stepping on a sponge.

The glow of the burning Scitech wreck flickers in the massive cavern. I doubt they were as lucky as I was. Yeah, they were trying to shoot me down, but they didn't really know it was me.

"Better check the glider out. That's my only ride out of here."

My 'site scans the machine next and beeps out an analysis. "*No record of any equipment. Please find better coverage so we can update the database.*"

"Yeah, yeah. Is it working?"

"*Unable to access.*"

"Never mind, I'll do it myself."

The glider is hovering, but not very far above the ground, like the repulsor is weak or something. I kneel into the grips and clutch the controls, but nothing responds.

A small rock whizzes past my head and I jump back a step. What the hell? Did someone escape from that wreck? I squint my eyes and then zoom in with my 'site up to the tunnel. There's a girl there and she's picking up another rock. Black hair tied back. Angry eyes.

How did Stell get from Rym's base slash workshop slash kidnap place so fast?

She walks out of the tunnel, gripping the rocks with her toes. Is it a thing now for Maglans to wander around without protective gear and boots? She only comes up to my shoulders and yet she's shoving me aside and kneeling to examine the glider.

Her facial spikes bristle. She doesn't speak, but shoots me a glare with a "WHAT DID YOU DO TO MY RIDE?" kind of vibe.

"Weren't you just talking to me on the comm in the glider? Can't you talk?"

She shrugs.

Maybe it was some sort of computer voice I heard, and she programmed it to talk? It sounded real, though. Man, she's just like that girl up at the Edge. It's a mute epidemic.

Seems a little too coincidental, actually. "How did you get here? I went pretty far, and there's no way you walked. And how did you know I was here? You're not exactly equipped for tracking someone."

My words just bounce off her. She turns the glider over and pops panels open to check inside. She fiddles with a metal canister and pries it out. That's the section I was looking at back at the base.

"The mag core. That robot, Dewey? He was saying something about that, right?"

She nods, still not looking at me.

"I'm guessing that you forgot to bring a spare with you."

She narrows her dark eyes at me over her shoulder before running over to the flaming wreckage of the Scitech speeder. The bulk of the fuel is almost done burning now and she's able to walk close to it.

"There's probably not a mag core there. They don't run that kind of tech."

But that's not what she's looking for. The pilot lays in a smoldering pile of metal near the cockpit. Stell turns him over, but it's clear he's not going anywhere. She leans over him and puts her ear to his mouth. After a few seconds her expression relaxes, and I actually do, too. I mean, wrecking Scitech equipment is one thing. I can explain that away somehow. But killing some guy is different.

The girl stands there for a minute before signaling me to follow.

"No, I'm staying here. They'll be tracking their ships. They don't want to kill *me*, so when they get here, I'll be good. Thanks though. You, however, might want to think about getting the hell out of here."

She points at me and then draws a line across her neck. She then gestures with all four hands so quickly that I can't really see them. I get an idea and click on a bit of software I think might help.

Stell raises her palm out toward me, and the pounding occurs once more in my head and gut simultaneously.

"What is that? That's you, right?"

Her face creases as she scowls at me. The glider bumps into the back of my leg and I spin around to see what's moving it. Nothing. I get out of the way and it floats over to Stell's outstretched empty hand. That's weird. Probably a built-in piece of tech.

It's clear that she's not going to wait for me; she's just leaving with the ride. The only ride. And just as I realize this, a couple of blips on my 'site show some movement away to my right. I try to focus on whatever it picked up, but nothing is there. Just some empty hills.

"What kind of animals live down here?" I ask, hoping Stell might respond, but I also key the question into my 'site. "Anything dangerous?"

Stell gestures with her hands.

A list of potential threats on the underlife of Maglan pops up on my display. I skip the names, but check out the pictures. Teeth. Claws. Wings. Yeah, that was what I thought. I just wished it might have been different.

"How is it that we even see in here? There's no sun." My 'site provides some light by scanning and amplifying the surroundings inside my head, but it wouldn't be this bright.

Stell signs something again but I don't get what she means. Guess the software needs more input.

"What?"

She shakes her head and sighs.

There's a blue glow to the giant cave, but I can't really tell where it's coming from either. Something within the rocks, maybe. When I look closer, there's more vegetation than I first thought. In addition to the spongy mat, there are sprawling, fungal-like bushes. Or maybe they're covering the rocks.

Kie might know about this ecosystem. He's into this stuff. Kie!

I quickly type out a message to him, and to Zaylee, letting them know what happened. I also send a message to Scitech to stop trying to kill me. Send. Come on, send. The message just sits there in my outbox. It's got to be the same interference frigging everything up down here.

Something new must've showed up sometime, a message from Zaylee managed to download. I play the video.

"Daj!" Zaylee's face fills the viewscreen. "You and Kie just disappeared off the map! When you get this message let me know. Scitech has been asking me where you went, and how to find you. I figured you wanted to keep dark, so I haven't said anything. But they really want to know. Where are you now? Stay safe!"

She kisses two fingers and presses them to the screen.

That's my girl.

There are no messages from Kie, though. He did ditch me pretty quickly, but hopefully he made it out.

A rock flies right across my eyes. I don't see Stell's hands move, she's pretty quick.

"Yeah, yeah, I'm coming. Where are we going anyway?"

My head pounds but she only rolls her eyes and shakes her head. I notice her doing the little motions again, but, as before, I'm not getting a translation.

Stell points to the hills and shakes the mag core canister in the air. Refueling. Good. Then we can get out of this dump.

"Hold on." I tilt the last of the water I brought from Phen back into my throat. It's not nearly enough.

Stell points to her own bottle and then to me.

"No thanks. Not after Granny tried to poison me."

She shrugs and begins walking away again with the glider following obediently behind.

It's going to be a long day.

***

"*Hydration levels dropping. Food stores depleted,*" my 'site diligently reports.

"Any other good news?"

It feels like we've been walking for hours. Up and down, down and up. Nothing but fungus covered hills, rocks, and tunnels. Hills, fungus,

and tunnels. Oh wait, look over there, something new. Huge columns of precipitated solids on the ground. What are they called?

A quick check on my 'site.

Stalagmites. I always get those mixed up. I squint up at the cave roof a couple hundred feet up and notice the hanging ones from up above. Stalactites. Don't even need the 'site for that one.

"How do you learn stuff down here? Being an Eldane and all, you don't get something to tell you stuff you want to know."

Stell doesn't turn around.

"How to talk to others? Social interaction? There are lessons on the 'site for that, if you want to upgrade."

Stell turns around and squints her eyes at me, but then widens them and her bristling face spikes flatten.

"What? Is my hair messed up?"

She motions for me to hurry, but I'm not feeling it. "I'm coming, I'm coming."

Something hits me from behind and knocks me to the ground. A small, smooth rock rolls away from me. I reach back to my neck and feel it all slick and warm. It's my blood.

Must be those kids again. Are they after more than my boots?

No, that's stupid. They couldn't have followed me down here.

A quick boost from my nanos pumps some pain killer and blood clotting to the place I got hit, not to mention a shot of adrenaline that gets me to my feet. I clamber up a boulder and scan for my attacker. "See? Nanos aren't too bad, right?"

Two more shots hit me straight in the gut and chest. I crumple forward and roll off to the ground below. Ok, that hurts. Instinctive nanos prop my arms and legs so I don't roll any further, but I can hardly breathe at this point.

I look up straight into the bright eyes of a four-legged creature with sharp, cracked looking teeth sticking out of its jaws. Its mates stalk out from behind several other rocks. They're not very big, but they make up for it in numbers.

"What hit me?"

Almost as one, the creatures scoop up stones in their mouths. I just about laugh. "What the hell? Are they going to—"

Yep. They spit them. Like bullets. My reflexes kick in and I avoid them in slow motion. Almost avoid them. My right arms go numb with the attack and I land on my chest. When I prop myself up again, the rock spitting beasts are scooping up more stones and circling me. Huh. Never thought I'd go out this way.

Stell leaps in front of me with her hands raised up in front of her like some crazed dancer monk. I can't be sure because my eyes are kind of dazed, but the rocks appear to kind of pause in the air. But only for an instant. The creatures all whine at once, as the rocks fly back, thumping against hides, bouncing against skulls, and shattering bone.

Most retreat immediately, but a few are unable to. I can literally see through the hole in a critter's skull only a few feet from me. Eww.

"Uh, that was incredible. How did you do that?"

Stell doesn't answer. She stares after the retreating, limping animals. And the one in front of me. She motions something and a translation pops up on my 'site. She can't be serious.

"Dinner?"

She looks at me sideways for a moment, but then nods. With a single flick of her hand, a stone rips the beast open from neck to tail and the guts and rocks inside empty out.

I promptly empty my own guts.

***

Maybe it's the nanos doing their job, maybe I'm feeling better, or maybe it's the amazing smell of rock-spit beast cooking over the fire Stell rigged up. Whatever it is, I'm awake now. And my stomach rumbles so loudly I'm worried it might alert Maglans to our position. Which I guess wouldn't be a bad thing.

Stell makes eye contact with me over the open flame and her hands flash with some signing.

"Yes, it is about time I woke up."

I'll never forget how the surprise on Stell's face lingers for several seconds. Her fingers race on all hands.

"Yes, I can kind of understand you." A wide grin crosses my face. I point to my head, to the nanos she can't see.

"How? It's language mapping software. It's a basic part of Nanosite. Well, sort of. Me and my friends adapted it a while ago and put it in the system without needing a connection to Scitech. It's taking a while, but it's been scanning your body language and those signs you make to build a database. It's not perfect, though."

Stell signs something.

"I smell like a *large smelly creature*. Is that close?"

She hides her face but I can see a smile there.

Why you make?

My face turns red. "Uh, a class project."

That's not the real reason, but I'm not about to tell her me and Kie made it to help us hook up with girls. Note to self, we should totally market this thing.

What sound?

"You mean, what do you sound like? Yeah, the program scanned you for your age and gave you a voice to match it. Want to hear it?"

She shakes her head and throws some of the dried fungus logs onto the fire. As if to distract me, she hands me a leg from the rock beast and despite myself, I'm gnawing at it like I haven't eaten anything in days.

Is good?

She doesn't need me to say anything to know what I think.

"Now tell me how you did what you did. With the rocks."

You no know. You sick.

"I'm not sick."

Stell only shakes her head and waves for me to eat.

"Do you have nanos? You must have." How else would she deflect projectiles and rip open the guts of one of those things? This is all sorts of messed up.

She shakes her head. *Must go. You no hear.* She points to my gut.

"My stomach is too loud?"

She laughs but shakes her head.

What did she mean? This program needs more data to get a better read from her signing.

There is something familiar about her. About her pushy little attitude. Maybe my memory got twisted up. Could it have really been her up on Phen's Edge? I cue up the video from the news feed. There I am again, way up on the upper Ring peering out over the edge. A news overlay pops onto the screen headlining, *"Terrorist Suicide."* And then there's the girl.

Sad eyes. Flat hair and overall flat appearance.

Definitely not this Stell.

So why do I still think it's her?

My hand slips to the Camdrone on my forearm, but then I see Stell's eager eyes. I'm not decrypting this anywhere near her. If she sees the codes I put in, she'd be able to access Cam without me.

"Let's go." I get to my feet and help her kick dirt into the fire.

She's going through an awful lot just to make a few credits, though. I guess that's what Maglans do when they're desperate.

Ready? Stell holds out her hand to me.

Really? All right. I reach out to take it but she just slaps it away.

No hold. Idiot. Get food.

"Oh, the rock beast. Sure." She had been pointing to the meat skewered by rib bones. I load up the pieces onto the glider. "It also doubles as a floating buffet table."

She smiles at my joke. Good. If she lets her guard down, it will make it easier to escape from her after she tops off that mag core.

***

After walking blindly through a tunnel for a couple of hours, well, maybe less, I lose all track of time in the dark. We finally emerge into another cave but the ceiling is so high up I'm not even sure it's a cave anymore. Maybe if I could get a message through to Scitech they'd tone down the trying to kill me, a little bit.

Connections are still iffy, but I type out a message for them just in case. But the problem is, I can't really tell them where I am, since I don't know where the hell I am anyway. And with this interference, the tracking system in the 'site doesn't seem to be working.

We get close.

"I don't see why we can't just climb to the surface straight up."

You see way?

Good point. But I won't tell her that. I also won't tell her that I'm dying for a spot of water.

"Hydration levels critical. Get a drink," the display says.

Duh.

"What's that up ahead?"

So far it's been lifeless caves, but there's something I might call a small village. A real dump. It's like the residents threw together a bunch of garbage on top of other garbage and hoped it would stick together. The place looks like it houses a hundred Maglans, and maybe has another ten minutes before it collapses. Stell heads toward dump town.

"Wait, we're going in there?"

Stell doesn't reply but just keeps leading the glider to the encampment. A cluster of kids run out to us and shout something I don't quite understand. I clench my fists. They better not be after my shoes, because I don't have a spare if these go.

"Ready to do your thing again?" I wave my hands like she did against the rock beast.

You really dumb.

The children crowd around Stell to touch her arms and hug her legs. She smiles and points behind her. The kids kiss her hands and run toward the glider. There's something off about them. What's up with their faces? They all have some weird deformity, like a missing nose, or an inside out ear. Huge face spikes. Ugh.

"Hey, that's our food!" I shout.

A few kids glance back at Stell but she signals them to eat. She sends me an ice cold glare.

The kids take the rib bones with the skewered meat, but instead of eating them, they run with the food back into the village. Ungrateful punks.

"We don't really have time for this." I've got a date with Scitech.

We make time. This not about you.

Stell leads us into shanty town central where many Maglans have started to gather already. An older lady, bent and worn and as deformed as the kids, approaches Stell. I can't even stomach to look her in the face. She's missing an eye and her ear stretches down to her neck. Yech. She speaks but I don't understand it. I key in to my display to translate, but it doesn't know the language either. It must be a really old dialect, and I just don't have the time to stay here and have the 'site learn it.

The words sound angry though. Why are we even here? Stell gestures to the glider and a small hatch near the rear of it pops open. She removes a small but heavy-looking crate with distinct Phen markings on it, but I can't tell what it says specifically. The old lady sure looks relieved and thankful though, whatever it says.

"All right, can we go now?"

Stell looks patiently at me, like she's my mom, or something. My face heats up when I see the old lady staring at me, as are the other Maglans that are now by her side.

"Hot Daj?"

I spin around to hear a little kid speaking my name. The young Maglan must be about ten. I recognize the look she's giving me. It's the same thing I get from Maglans on the streets of Phen when I walk by.

"Nice to meet a fan." I grip the kid's left hands and then cross over with my rights to hit hers. I try my best not to take notice of her claw-like hands scratching against my skin.

A mile-wide smile erupts on her face and her little friends behind her start to giggle and laugh. The old lady says something to the kids and they run away, but I can still see them peering at me from behind some smashed-up crates. They're swooping their hands in flying motions, probably mimicking my vids.

"See, you've got a celebrity with you."

You act like a child.

"I'm just saying, it's not so bad to be me."

The old lady touches my arm and grunts something to Stell.

No, he's not one.

"This is really interesting, but what's she saying?"

She asks about mark. She points to my arm, to the tattoo that I nicked from Rym.

"Tattoo."

That not tattoo. She wonders if you skywatch.

"Skywatch?" Something tickles at the back of my mind. "What does that mean?"

You not hear before?

"No, I've never heard about it before." I think. Right? "Should I have?"

Stell grips her forearms. *Yes. You should.*

"So...?"

No time. Later.

"Are these Maglans Eldane? Like you?"

Stell shakes her head. *Early tech. Rejects. Made to live down here.*

She makes her way to a shack and lays down on a rickety cot. *Time for rest. I show you real tattoo later.*

Rest sounds like a good idea, but for a while I can only sit and wonder where she has her tattoo.

***

I wake from a nap with a loud rumbling sound emanating from my stomach. And it's loud enough to wake Stell, too.

About time you had some food.

"Yeah, I think you're right." My nanos aren't doing anything for my headache anymore. At least that's what my stupid 'site won't shut up about. "I'll have what these villagers are having, if you don't mind."

Stell stretches her arms. She props her chin up with two hands and blinks at me.

Anything else for you?

"I didn't mean it like that. It's just that you know these Maglans."

All right, I'm going.

As soon as she's out of the shack, and a few seconds later to make sure she's really gone, I activate Cam. It takes me a good minute, but I key in the algorithm to decrypt Cam's backup files. There's footage of me racing away from the speeder. Further back. In Rym's garage. A little more. Cam in lockup. I play it a second longer and see Dewey's glowing red eye appear. Still further back. There. At the top of the Edge, a nice wide shot of me perched on the Sky Deck, ready to jump.

"Good camera work, Cam."

She beeps an affirmative.

And there's the girl. She props her chin up with two hands and watches me with wide eyes, blinking her eyes. No longer sad.

And definitely Stell. But that's not what she looked like in the other vids. I swear it's not.

A shuffling right outside the shack startles me, and I power off and lock down Cam again. Stell comes in bearing a tray of really sketchy looking slime molds and a couple jars of a liquid I think is supposed to be water. But I can't think about that right now.

"That *was* you at the top of Phen."

Stell looks at me funny. *Yes, of course it was. What do you mean?*

"Here, take a look at this."

There's a partially cleared off section of the wall that will do. Cam's projector casts lights onto the wall and shows the news feed of the clearly not Stell Maglan jumping to her death off the Edge of Phen.

"That's not you. Looks like the video was tampered with. But I remember you."

This is what Scitech does. They hide truth.

"Sounds like something an Eldane would say."

Then why they do that?

"I have no idea." I sit there nearly scratching my head at this but my stomach rumbles again. "Can I have some of that?"

Stell scoops up a handful of the mold and scrapes it into her mouth then holds it out to me.

Enjoy.

I'm not about to let her get the best of me, again, so I dip my fingers into the food and gently put it into my mouth. Despite the slimy texture, the strange green color, and the interesting smell, the taste is thankfully pretty bland. I wash it all down with some definitely non-filtered water.

"So, you bring supplies to these Maglans?"

And others. There is great need. Sickness. Hunger.

No wonder she was pissed when I crashed the glider. "They should come up to the rings, like how you did. And Rym. They can make something for themselves."

Stell shakes her head. *You do not understand. Scitech keeps them down here. Hides them. Will kill them if they try.*

I laugh at the hand gesture she uses to signify Scitech.

Something funny about pain?

"No, no, I'm sorry. When you sign for Scitech, it looks kind of dirty."

They need to be stopped. They took everything from us.

Funny, they gave everything to me.

Let's go. We're not far now. Stell gets to her feet and I follow.

Not far now until I'm back where I belong.

***

"You grew up here?" There doesn't seem to be much to this wasteland outside of the village. More hills, tunnels, and huge fungal trees.

Stell nods. *Rym raised me.*

"Is he your dad?"

No. But sort of. My parents left when I was very young. Long time ago.

"Yeah, mine too."

Stell looks at me. I like it when she looks at me like she doesn't want to kill me.

"Some parents do that up in Phen when they go work for Scitech. Flying in the Dust Field. I'm going to do that soon, any day now. I'll get my wings and fly up there."

Look for parents?

"Yeah, I guess that's why."

Whoa. I've never really told that to *anyone* before.

"You know, I never really thanked you for saving me from those rock beasts, before. Or for getting us some food and water."

I guess being a Nonno has its advantages, huh?

"Wait a minute, I think there's something wrong with my translator."

Why?

"It says you told a joke."

Stell laughs.

That's something new. It's like she's a friendly kidnapper now, which makes me wonder if this is all part of her plan. "So why do you and Rym want my camera anyway? I figure you're together on this. Money?"

Stell gives me a double take. *You have the truth. About me. About what Eldane can do. You can show it to everyone.* Stell gestures with all four hands in a wide arc.

I fiddle with the control panel on the Camdrone as we walk. So I've got a video of her taking a dive off the Edge and living. What will that prove?

You could show that Scitech is hiding me. That Scitech is trying to control you.

"Oh man. Are you kidding? You people, why do you keep saying that?"

Stell makes a groaning sound. *You could be so much more than just a pilot in the Dust Field. You could be a protector.*

"Is that what Rym is?"

She nods.

"Some *protector*. Stealing from a city that only wants to help? And where is he now? Drunk, and locked up again, no doubt."

My feet freeze in place and I slowly spin to face Stell. No, I'm not in control. Yes, she's doing this. I can't move, but somehow I'm moving anyway. There's that dull throb in my entire body. My bones are shaking from the inside. My head pounds.

"Don't talk about him that way."

That voice. It's the same voice I heard in the tunnels when I was escaping on the glider. Why am I hearing it now? And why does my whole body feel like it's about to split? I'm looking into Stell's eyes, and she is mighty pissed off. Wait. Damn, it's her. She's forcing those words into my head. But how? My heart starts beating loudly in my ears.

"I'm sorry." I hope I'm able to keep my voice from shaking.

She scoffs and waves her hands dismissively at me. My shoulders slump down, like she just let go of a doll.

"How the hell did you do that?" My hands tremble as I regain control of them.

We're here.

Great. Just ignore my question. At least it's the translator voice again. Whatever she did, it hurt. And it's nice to be able to move. There's something seriously messed up about her.

I kick at some stones and squint at the cliffs in the distance.

"Here, where? There's nothing around." Seriously. There's not even a place for me to hide from this mind-controlling maniac.

Stell walks away in silence, leading the glider behind her.

After five minutes of following her toward a blank canyon wall, a glimmer, like radiating heat waves, passes across my eyes. Is something up with my 'site? Feels like it's been spazzing out all day.

A structure of sorts appears through the fading haze, but I've never seen anything like this. It's carved entirely into the gray cliff face. A multi-level pyramid thing. It's huge, at least a couple hundred feet long at the base. Each level has multiple openings, bigger ones at the base, and smaller, window-like ones near the top. A lot of them.

I don't see anyone around, at least not outside. "Holy… Cam, take an overhead shot of this thing. I can make something of this trip, yet." Cam beeps and begins to separate from her dock.

Stell grips my top right forearm and locks eyes with me.

No vids.

I try to pull away from her grip; it's actually really hurting, but I can't.

"Yeah, all right. Cancel that, Cam."

Cam beeps and locks back into place on my wrist.

"Can you let go now?"

Stell shoves my arm away and finally breaks her glare.

I do my best to not rub at where she held me, but man, it hurts. Who is she? She said she's a Nonno, I mean an Eldane, but there has got to be some tech that's allowing her to do all this. "You know, if you want to work well with others you're going to have to try not to break their arms."

I'm, sorry. This place is special.

Yeah, I can see that. I want to stay angry but my curiosity takes over. "What is it? It's amazing."

A Skywatch temple. And a source of power.

There's that word again. "Doesn't look like anyone is using it."

That's good. We will need some time.

As we approach the temple, the haziness comes back and forth, blocking out the real image. "What's causing that?"

I forget, you can't see through the screen.

"The screen?"

A field used to hide.

"From what?"

Stell smiles and points to my head.

Great, she's cryptic, too. Maybe she's talking about my nanos? I'm drawn back to the temple as we approach and notice tons of those fungal trees growing from the eaves of the building. They're ripe with brilliant red and yellow bulbous flowers.

Stell reaches them first and pulls a few red bulbs from the growths. She sinks her teeth into one of them and a purplish liquid covers her lips. Her eyes flutter.

She tosses the other one to me, and I bobble it back and forth between my hands. My nature ID guide on the 'site does a quick scan of it.

"Name: Fungal spore pod. Region found: underground. Results: do not eat. Extremely poisonous."

Huh. Five bites in and Stell certainly isn't responding to the extreme poison. Maybe the Nanosite database has got this all wrong. All right. I didn't see her switch them, and if she wanted to kill me she certainly had many opportunities before this. The translucent pod jiggles slightly as I grip it and bring it to my mouth.

The second my teeth burst through the fleshy part of the fruit a tingling erupts across my skin. The juice that fills my mouth is the most amazing thing I've ever tasted. Sweet, but not too much. Sour, just enough. Nothing has even come close to its taste.

Before I know it, the pod is completely gone and there are juices dripping off my chin. And Stell is watching me as I stare up at the sky. She's probably going to say something stupid about me.

"Good, right?"

"I know. Wait, you're not signing?" I'm just hearing her voice, her real voice, in my head, like when she blasted it before. But this time my body isn't screaming from it.

"How can I hear you?" My voice is calm, and I feel good. But I tense up and clench my fists. This is like the reaction I had when the old lady gave me some of that soup.

"No, I didn't poison you."

That's exactly something a kidnapper would say. "Then what is this stuff?"

"For once, you're free of the nanos," she says.

I like her voice. It's clear, and slightly musical, almost. My cheeks heat up when she looks at me.

"Go ahead, look around."

Good. She didn't notice that I was staring at her. I look around, and now there's no hazy field in front of the temple. It's perfectly clear. And there's a sky up above, with stars and everything. There was a dome of rock above us before, I'm sure of it.

"There was. Or, you saw that there was. This place is hidden from Scitech."

"Did you just read my mind?"

She smiles.

"How is this possible?"

"You are just beginning to learn what is possible. Come on, I've got more to show you."

Stell leads the way through the first door and I'm actually a little excited. The tingling that spread out over my skin hasn't quite all dissipated yet. I feel small. I don't know how to explain it, really, but my mind is apart from my body, like I'm floating in my own head. I see Stell, but I also feel her presence now. Her energy. Her body.

"All right, keep it clean."

My face turns red-hot this time and I divert my thoughts to the building. She noticed that one. "So, this fruit thing is a type of drug that, what, connects my mind?"

"Not really. It cuts you off from those parasites in your body."

"Parasites? The nanos?" I try to access the 'site, but I don't get any readings on any systems. Literally nothing. I don't remember a time when I had nothing. My heart races and it's hard to breathe. "Are they gone? They can't be."

"Unfortunately, not," she says.

Unfortunately, my ass. When I do get a deep enough breath, I look at Stell. "Wait, is this why Rym is always drunk?"

Stell smiles back at me. "Now you're getting it. This stuff doesn't last long by itself, but it can be distilled into a drink."

"And you don't drink because…?"

"No nanos? Come on, I thought you were getting smarter."

Makes sense. "But, how come I can feel all this?" I wave my arms around me. There's something calling just outside of my thoughts.

"It's what being an Eldane is all about. And you've already tasted a little of that."

"What do you mean?"

"Remember the glider, back in Rym's place?"

I nod. "You were fixing the mag core. But it was empty."

"Right," she says. "And it shouldn't have flown, but somehow it did for you. I'm just not sure how."

"That's crazy. You're saying it came from me, or through me? There had to be some juice left in it."

"Maybe. Or maybe we just give you a little time, and you'll see other things you can do."

My stomach drops. Time. I don't have any time. I've got to get this footage of my jump back to Scitech soon. I'm sure I'm late, or pretty close to it by now.

"Come on, let's go in." I go first into the entrance, and this place sure looks different than it appears on the outside. Out there it looks like a full on temple, ancient stones about to crumble apart. But in here, it's a whole other place. Metallic and functional.

"It's like a base," I say. There are powered down display screens all around, vehicle bays big enough to house tanks and large ships. Except, there are none. "Where is everything? Stolen?"

"Most were taken by Scitech, but some are hidden," she says. "This is a power station and a waypoint for when Skywatch used to patrol the planet. To keep us safe."

"You speak like you remember all this, but you're not any older than I am, and I have no clue what you're saying." Although what she said about Skywatch tickles that part of my memory again.

Stell laughs but says nothing.

"You can't use tech like this, though, you're an Eldane."

"I know how to flip a switch, stupid," she says. "This is all pre-nano tech. Before Scitech even came."

"Yeah, sorry. I guess I don't really know much about Eldane."

"Didn't your parents ever tell you stories?"

After a moment of awkward silence, she continues.

"You know what Scitech wants you to know. About everything. Tell me what you think you know about us." Stell crosses her arms.

The staring makes me uncomfortable. "Well, I read that the Eldane live like savages below the surface of Magla. They have no technology. They need to come get help from Scitech. And, they're pretty mean all the time to everyone around them."

Stell slides her hand over a work station nearby and for a second the screen powers up. She hides her face, but not before I see the red in her cheeks. "I'm sorry I'm angry all the time. It's just that Scitech has ruined everything, and no one knows it anymore. Well, no one up top."

Ruined. It's so much better with the tech. But I don't say that to her. At least she's trying to be nice. Er.

"But," I say, "I'm learning more all the time."

Stell smiles. I guess she's actually not that bad. For a kidnapper, that is. And knowing that's what she is makes the other part of me not feel bad at all.

"I've got to go charge this thing, since neither of us know how you did it before. Right?"

I just shrug.

"Walk around the place. Check it out." Stell waves goodbye and the glider starts to follow her.

I wait until she's around the corner. "Cam." I tap the camera and she powers right up. At least the chemical in the fungus doesn't short out all electrical components. The drone zips right in front of me.

"Go follow her. Record what she does." Cam flies off. "And don't let her see you!" I hear a little affirmative beep in the distance. When I try to connect Cam's live feed to my 'site, however, nothing happens. I'll just have to watch it off her memory later.

Time to find out what this place used to be. And if I can see what's going on up top with everyone, especially my friends. Maybe even send them a message. I bet they're worried sick about me. There has got to be some sort of communications array I can use.

I head to a circular room off of a side hall and run into rows of benches surrounding a central hub. It's got a cool style, kind of retro with plain silver metal and stone built into everything. Lights flicker and hum as I step into the room, but I can't spot the source. It just seems to come out of the walls. All right, so at least this place has still got power. A faint whiff of ozone makes my nose crinkle. Hope this place is stable. Not sure when the last time this stuff's been used, or if it'll last. When I reach the center, a beam of light jets from the hub onto a glass panel and the hairs on my arms stick up with the energy in the air.

It's a blue light outline of the planet, pretty highly detailed for this low tech facility. A signal flashes on the display with some other letters I don't recognize. But there's something like a satellite in orbit around the planet with some red lines over it and I make out the word *Magnus* labeled on there. It also shows the moons of Cadea and the shattered Naglor, but there are no signals coming from them.

"This place is cut off from everything."

The base appears on the map, at least I think it's the one I'm in, and there appear to be others dotted around the planet. There are symbols like Rym's tattoo over them and some text, but since my 'site is offline because the juice is still working, I can't translate any of this stuff. Where's the controller keypad for this thing?

The lights change on the flat display of Magla depending on where I'm standing. Before I can find anything to control it, the lights flicker in and out and the image turns off. The hairs on my arm settle back down again.

It is spooky quiet in here.

"Hello?"

My voice echoes through the room, amplified by the shape of it, or by something else. My shoes click and echo as I leave the room. What is this stuff made of? Doesn't seem like any stone or concrete, but the whole building is constructed of the same materials. Flat, silvery metal and stone.

It's cool to the touch, but there's something else. That same feeling I had when the room powered on seems to resonate within the floor. It almost feels like flowing water. I follow the energy path to the nearest wall and sense a build-up around chest high. When I hold my hand over it, three lit up buttons appear within the metal. Whoa. Cool sensor tech.

For an old place like this, that is.

Of course I push the buttons. What else am I going to do?

The first one activates a glowing path along the side of the hallway that lights up the area I'm in. I take three steps forward and the lights follow me. Cool. Cool. I go back to the panel and hit the next button and only hear a beep. Hopefully, I didn't launch anything or blow Stell up.

"You all right out there, Stell?"

I'm about to hit the third button when a tone sounds from some speaker.

"Yes, Daj. Don't break anything." It's Stell's voice through the same speakers. It picks up her thoughts and transmits them? That is seriously cool.

"Wait, this is an intercom? And I can say anything I want over this and you'll hear me wherever you—"

"Unless I lower your security clearance," she says.

So of course I break out into song complete with instruments and sound effects. After a minute, Stell hasn't responded.

"You lowered my security clearance, didn't you?"

No response. "Your loss. The acoustics of this place are awesome."

The third button doesn't even register a sound when I tap it. A result of Stell's censoring, no doubt. Way to ruin my fun.

Oh well, I'll have to find other ways to piss her off.

Funny, I haven't even thought of running away from her in a while, despite being by myself. She is still some crazy kidnapper who wants to steal my video so she can... what, show the truth? Maybe if I look through that vid of my jump I can see what she's talking about.

Cam is still out there. Being a stealth drone. There are some lights on my wrist control indicating what she's up to. The blue light shows some videoing is going on. That's good. Hopefully she's not getting anything personal. I forgot to specify. Well, I'll just edit out anything if it comes to that. Maybe.

So, on to more exploring. Some stairs, but those look pretty boring. And tiring. It's the lift-looking platforms I want to check out. I grip the rail around the edge of one and step onto the empty panel. There's one of those power panels here, too, so I hold my hand over it and two buttons start glowing. Probably an up and down, if I'm lucky. Time to go up.

Before I can press the button, the panel activates and the lift starts to glide smoothly upward along a track. It's not reading my mind, is it? Once I'm up a couple of levels, the solid wall behind me changes to a transparent material and the center of the building appears. There's a huge open area, a hangar by the looks of it, with multiple landing bays big enough for space vessels. But these are empty just like the other hangars.

No more Skywatch. This is clearly where they used to hang out, though. Where else have I heard about them before? I vaguely remember some crazy stories my parents told me before bed. Stories with insane pilots, rescues, and some spectacular space battles against aliens, but I assumed they were made up for fly-happy kids like me. Who was that one guy my friends and I pretended to be? Commander something-or-other? Man, I can't believe I forgot all about that. It seems like some sort of dream.

Well, whatever Skywatch used to be, they're long gone now. But they appear to have been particularly bad ass, maybe even lived up to the stories. They could get a couple hundred Maglans in here, ships, tanks, and other things I pretended to pilot when I was a kid. Whatever drove them out must've been crazy strong.

The lift keeps going up and up. Oh man, I wish I had Cam here, I'd video it no matter what Stell said. Finally the lift stops above the hangar area, closed off from below. The windows open out onto the valley now, and that sharp pang of vertigo grabs me by the throat for a second. The ground is farther away than I expected. My feet almost feel like they're floating and gliding closer to the edge. A cool wind whips around me, filling my nose with all the smells of the abandoned valley. Soft plants, sharp soil, and the metal construction of the building. They fill me up, and I feel like I'm home, despite the hundred foot drop below. I grip the railing tightly, but there's some irrational part of me telling me to jump. Like I'd be all right if I did.

Splat. That'd be me in what, five seconds? Maybe six?

If only I had a glider or a deck like Scitech's, then nothing could stop me.

I wish Kie and Zaylee could see me up here. They'd die. It couldn't hurt to send out a quick message, right? Make them jealous. And maybe make Kie feel like crap for ditching out on me, and probably leading Scitech to Rym's garage.

I make a sweet selfie of me posing at the very edge of this thing and try to send it. It bounces right back, probably because of some interference from this building or whatever has been preventing me from contacting anyone back home. Too bad. I'll save it and rub it in his face when I can show him. If I ever get out of here.

Well, there's still time to wait for Stell to charge up our ride, so there has got to be something else to see here. A wide hallway leads toward a pair of statues, a male and a female Maglan. They stand about fifteen feet high and are constructed of the same material as everything else. All four arms crossed, like they're standing guard. But over what?

There's a closed door at the end of the hall, but it doesn't open. Or budge. Or anything. The power supply is coursing through the ground and walls here, too, but no matter what I do—wave my hand like an idiot or tap whatever resembles a panel or button—I get nothing.

Too bad, too. This room was shaping up to be something good. Oh well. I'm getting tired anyway.

I head back to the railing by the lift and look up. The sky is filled with the glowing green and purple aurora of night, ebbing and flowing like some tide. Maybe it's because I can't check my 'site and see something else, but tonight's aurora looks particularly amazing. It's safe in here, but I am exhausted. I sit in the lift with my feet near the edge, thinking about what I'll do and post when I get back home. I fade into a dreamless sleep.

CHAPTER 5

"Daj."

Stell's voice jars me out of my sleep. How long was I out? No reading on my 'site to tell me, but it couldn't have been too long. At least I'm feeling a little more rested. But where am I? This isn't the top of the lift. It's all dark.

"Daj!"

"Yeah, yeah, don't yell. I'll be right down. Or wherever."

I sit up with a start. "Cam?" My hearts jump. I'm definitely awake now.

I close my eyes in relief. The little drone had already attached herself to my arm while I slept.

"You're too smart."

I hit the lift controls and start to descend. I twist out the kink in my neck from sleeping on a metal floor until it cracks several times. Needles sting into my leg. I stamp my foot to wake it up faster. I lean over the rail and peer out over the night-covered valley. Lights. Flashing in and out of caves. There's something about them that sends a chill through me.

"So Cam, what do you think of this place?"

I already busted the *no vid* rule so I might as well make the most of it. Maybe she learned something useful. In a second, a projected outline of the building appears on the floor in glowing blue lines.

From the partial projection she's showing, the structure looks like a diamond jammed into the ground.

"*Octahedron.*" The word spells out beneath the projection.

The lift begins to slow as we reach the bottom.

"Cam, cut the feed," I whisper.

The lift settles quietly and Stell's there waiting for me, luckily facing away, and tapping her hands on the rail. The vid cuts just as she turns around.

"This is a really wild place," I say. "It doesn't feel like any building I've ever seen before."

She smiles. "Perhaps it's because it's floating."

"Nice one," I say with a laugh. But she doesn't join in. "Wait, you're serious?"

"Yep," Stell says. "But more importantly, I picked up something on the scanner."

"This place still has access to that sort of tech?"

"If you know how to use it. Now come on. If Scitech searches for us here, the camouflage shielding won't hold up. Maybe we can get out of here before they start looking."

She looks at me with a strange glint in her eye and that pressure hits me again, this time starting at my head and working its way down. I inadvertently cover my privates.

"Grow up," she says. "I'm just scanning you for trackers."

"Whoa, find anything?"

Stell shrugs and starts running. "Nothing yet."

We run through a hall that slopes up and curves to the left. Man, she's fast. I can barely keep up. But her legs don't look like they're moving fast enough for her speed. It's weird, like when I dream and kind of run-float by pulling my feet up before they hit the ground.

The tunnel seems to curve all the way around the building until we're in a circular room with the glider parked in the middle. It's floating about head height in the air, attached to several tubes.

Stell launches into the air and grabs the left hand grip arm. With a twist, she spins through over the top of the glider and parks herself neatly in front of the controls. Pretty cool.

"Where the hell am I going to sit? On your back?" As I recall, there's not a lot of room on this thing.

The glider hisses and clicks and the underbelly shifts. The lower carriage extends with arms and gears, and panels click into place until the bottom mirrors the top half in its design and controls. The glider flips 180 degrees along its length so I can see Stell clinging to the now bottom. She gestures with her chin, and I take it she means for me to get up top.

The vehicle tears free from the cables and whips around in front of me with a dull throbbing sound, kind of like when Stell scans me. I attempt to board it like she did, but I don't think my grab and twist come off nearly as cool. The snickering from below confirms it.

The glider jets forward and I'm jerked along with it. "Wait a second!"

The glider flips over. I lock my legs into position and straps grip me with tightening pressure.

"Wait, you're flying?" I twist the controls and right myself back up. "Not a chance. That's my job."

There's a beep and then I flip back underneath. I try to take control again, but nothing works. I ready my best "I called it" voice, but in my head it only sounds infantile.

"So you like it up top?" is the best I've got.

No response. I guess I won that round.

The glider accelerates and smacks my head shield against the ground a couple of times. Ow. Maybe not.

We shoot out of the temple and I'm staring at the incoming rocks and landscape, all upside down. This is different. Stell tweaks the glider smoothly as we speed away. At first I feel like I'm going to puke in the enclosed space, but for some reason I don't. I'm not freaking out, either. Even when she dips so close to the ground that I could reach out and touch the surface, I still feel safe.

"So, you ready to try flying?" Stell says.

"What do you mean? You're going to let me?"

She laughs. "I'm capable of sharing."

I don't respond.

"Wait, are you scared?"

"No. I already flew it."

"Yeah, and you already crashed it, too."

"Thanks for the reminder. If I had one of my own gliders, I'd be pro."

"I said before, there are some tricks to it. She doesn't handle like other ships you've flown."

I know that.

"You've got to fly like an Eldane. You have to, I don't know, just let go."

"*Let go*. That's all you got?"

"It's in you. You can do it."

I scoff at this. "What are you talking about? Just let me drive."

When I yank the controls the glider fights me. It jerks sideways and twists so that now I'm facing up to the sky. Something's resisting my efforts.

"Not like that. Slow down."

Just when I'm about to try her stupid idea, a bright light flashes right beside us in a huge explosion of rock and fire.

"I forgot to check the scanners. Idiot." Stell takes control back and says some unfamiliar words that I'm pretty sure are curses.

The glider flips over and accelerates so quickly my eyes push back in my head.

"Check the display, see what's out there."

"Shouldn't you?" I say.

"I'm flying, so shut up and get on it."

I bite back a response because, well, she's right. The display down here is just like the one up on the top side, including an outline of our surroundings and the glider's instruments. The mag stack bar is filling up again. I love that thing. There are also a couple of blips behind us, and around us.

"Five marks. Looks like two on the ground and three in the air. Is that a tank down there?"

"Looks like two," Stell says.

She's right, there's one up ahead, looking like it's waiting for us. I press the picture of the tank and some stats pull up. I've never seen one like this before, it's got crazy treads and claws. This is definitely not just a rescue mission. One of the tanks pulls itself right over a huge boulder with ease.

"Yeah, we got speeders behind us." Stell banks to the right and spins behind a pile of rocks.

"Can we outrun them?"

"If we can get out of range of their weapons."

Another blast echoes that thought, and the boulder we just shot behind disintegrates in a shower of pebbles. I crank on my own throttles and we accelerate even faster.

"They really are trying to kill us," I say.

"Just a little farther," Stell says. Her voice appears to be breaking up, though.

"Anything on this glider we can use?"

"Some defensive countermeasures."

Stell swerves from an explosion and rocks pelt the glider.

"Why are we keeping so low?"

"We get up in the air and we'll be an easy target. We have to lose them first. You still got them?"

Two speeders close in behind us and the tank smashes through boulders trying to keep up. The other tank is a half a mile in front of us, standing guard at one of the cave openings we came through to get here. "I can't spot that other speeder."

The glider twists awkwardly to avoid another explosion beside us and my stomach flips.

"Yeah, I see it," Stell replies. "Straight above us."

She veers off to the right, but the speeder keeping pace with us side fires another blast and pens us back in.

How could they have been waiting for us? Maybe I do have a tracker in me… shit. This is my fault.

"We're getting closer to that tank." Two of its claws are embedded into the side of the cave entrance. "You do have a plan, right?"

"Probably."

The glider makes an abrupt ascent until we're directly below the speeder above us. A green light clicks on, and the screen shows us attaching to the Scitech guys. When the speeder turns to the right, we move like we're welded to it.

The pilot tries to shake us off by jerking back and forth, but we're not going anywhere. It takes him a second, then the craft makes a sudden drop.

"Uh, Stell?"

The ground is racing toward us, with those big pointy rocks as the welcoming committee. This guy is going to scrape us off the bottom of his ship like cleaning crap off a boot.

Before we hit the ground, Stell cranks her controls and with a burst of energy spins our glider around right side up. The magnetic locking spins the other ship beneath us with ease. Stell releases the mag grip and the speeder erupts into a fiery spray as it collides with a boulder.

So much for not trying to kill them. My stomach drops thinking of the pilot.

"They would have killed us," Stell says in response to my thoughts.

In the next second, the other two speeders open fire. They're not making the mistake of getting too close to us, though. At least they're not stupid. Well, too bad they're not stupid.

We're almost on top of the tank in the tunnel now and these stupid boulders have still got us pinned in. The glider arcs up again and that weightless feeling hits me full in the stomach.

"Stell? I thought you didn't want to be an easy target."

"Changed my mind."

Both speeders pull up with us, keeping their distance though. A beeping distress signal emanates all around my head.

"We've got inbound." Stell voices the answer to my unasked question.

The glider hums and accelerates.

"Inbound what?"

"Missiles."

"Great."

I glance over my shoulder and see a couple of glowing dots launching up from the tank on the ground. In seconds they're right on us.

The hum in the glider grows louder and we start to spin and glow. Green, like an aurora. The two missiles glide in sync with our spinning.

"Go ahead," Stell says. "Press it."

I don't need to ask what she means. The glowing *mag stack* button is calling to me, and I hit it with a grin.

Suddenly, the missiles launch away from us, exploding directly into the two speeders alongside us. Their burning wreckage continues forward into the cave, knocking rock and debris onto the tank below, and then our glider shoots toward the surface like a rocket.

But not before I spot two more missiles behind us.

"There's no more juice in the mag system!"

Stell doesn't answer. The glider speeds upward, propelled by the mag reversal, and the edge of the cliff is almost within reach. I don't know what I sense first—the shock waves, the fire, or the pain running up my back. There's a huge cracking sound and I feel like I'm being ripped apart. The ledge is not too far off, and the glider grinds along the edge of the rocks.

"Shit!" Some sparking from the instrument panel burns into my arms. But that's the least of my worries.

The cracking sound came from the glider. We both spin upward, but only my part of the glider skips over the cliff edge. I skid to a stop then hear a horrible crunching behind me. I look over my shoulder to see Stell's half of the glider smash into the ledge.

"Stell!" I crank on my controls but it turns so sluggishly I ditch the glider and scramble back to the cliff edge. Fiery wreckage blocks my path, but I kick it out of my way.

There she is, clinging to the rock wall, dangling at the top of a thousand-foot cliff. The skin on her face is singed and half of her scalp is bare and burnt. She struggles to put that casual smirk she normally has onto her face but then her eyes widen.

"Get back!" she says.

I duck, but not before I see a couple more speeders circling down below. Like a pack they cluster and head straight up toward us. The tank turret also points right here.

I stretch out, but she can't reach me. The skin on her hands is burnt, too.

"Hang on, I'm coming down to get you."

"Just take your glider, and stay low," Stell says. "I'll lead them away."

"Are you crazy? What are you going to do, fly?"

Stell winks at me, and even though I don't hear her in my head, I know that's exactly what she's planning to do. She gives me one last smile before taking a backwards dive off the cliff

CHAPTER 6

"Cam?"

She's not there. Okay, all right, don't panic. When was the last time I saw her? Was it in the temple? Nah, she climbed on right before we left, right? My wrist computer dock says she's in range. That's good. I click the *return* button, and get no response. I can't wait for her, not with Scitech coming after me. I've got to get the hell out of here.

The glider jerks around as I nudge the controls to get lower into cover. The ledge gets a little too close and I swerve back the other way. Something feels off with the controls now. I glance at the display screen and notice a speeder hovering way back at the cliff edge. A single pilot leaps out of the cockpit. I guess they're checking out the remains of the glider's other half. And Stell. I'm not sticking around to get caught though.

Stell.

Did she make it? She must have. Otherwise, it'll be my fault she's dead. It's still my fault if she gets caught though, isn't it? I mean, how else would Scitech show up unless they tracked me somehow? If they think I'm helping out Stell and Rym, I'm screwed. No more contract. No more nanos. And forget getting off planet. I can explain it to them. I was kidnapped after all, right?

My glider limps along through the twisting gorge lit up by the auroras' green glow above. Where the hell am I? Maybe I should send Kie a message. But what would I say? And do I even want his help? He didn't stick around to help me when I got taken by Rym. Whatever.

I need help. I send Kie a message letting him know where I'm going.

Minutes fade and slip into a blur like the endless hills. I'm not even sure how much time has passed, I only know I've got to get back home.

What am I going to do about this glider? I can't let anyone catch me with it; can't have them thinking I'm one of the terrorists. But, hell, I'm not going to miss a chance to gut this thing for usable tech. I mean, how can this thing fly like it does? Imagine if I can make something just like it. I could sell it to Scitech and make a ton. Or maybe just get back into their good graces. I'll have to ditch it out in the fields outside of Phen, and maybe get it to the shop after dark. This trip won't be a total loss.

At last, Phen's great rings jut out over the barren rocks, some civilization amidst this desolate place. I circle around the city to approach the old industrial sector from the west because the lake over on the other side would be too busy. I don't want anyone to know which direction I came from.

Abandoned mining rigs overgrown with weeds litter the area. Looks like I've found a place to ditch this ride. And none too soon. If rattling is any indication of system failure, this glider's about to keel over.

The 'site signal is strong now, and the feeds pour in at regular intervals. I scan the news. How come there's nothing about me on there? You'd think a big celebrity gone missing would get some coverage. Whatever. I'll check again later back at my place.

Right now, one of those rusted up rigs will do just fine. The glider eases in under the cab, and once I switch the power down it blends right in with the wreck. Two steps back and I can't even tell it's in there. I tap a dot on my GPS and mark it. Good luck to anyone trying to spot that thing in here.

I turn back toward the familiar rings and my heart freezes.

"Oh, hey guys."

A pack of yarels surround me. Damn. So many beady little eyes staring.

"Hey, I got no food. Go on, get out of here."

They don't move. They don't even make a sound and that's freaking me out even more. There have got to be twenty or so of them. I gulp and eye the glider behind me. If I run, I can probably make it. But then what? The glider'll poop out under me, and they'll tear me apart. I take a step back and the entire pack moves as one toward me. Shit. I stop.

And they stop. How weird. I take another step and stop. They do the same.

A high pitched whining comes through the air, and the yarels cower. A dust cloud forms on the horizon. A bike hovers through it. Not just any bike. Kie's. I try not to wave too frantically. I don't want him to know I'm about to crap my pants.

The bike's flood lights kick on and shine right onto the yarels' heads. Some scatter, but more stay and take several steps toward me. When Kie lands right by my feet, I jump on.

"Wait." Kie pulls out his slug rifle and props it up on his high handlebars. "I'll bag you one."

"Nah, forget it. Let's just get out of here."

The yarels keep watching me. My eyes meet one creature's, and I swear I'll never forget it. I've seen this one before. It's that same mutt with five eyes from back in the city. Must have joined its pack again out here beyond the rings.

A blast from Kie's rifle makes me jump.

Kie laughs. "I got your rescue on vid. It'll make a sweet post."

"Dude, what the hell are you doing?"

"You mean besides saving your ass?" Kie locks the rifle down on the mag grips and tears away, forming another great cloud of dust.

The yarels scatter, and I can't see if his shot got one. Do I even want to know? I look away.

"Thanks, man. Sorry, I'm just a little freaked. I just want to get home." I glance back the way I came. Cam is out there by herself somewhere. I lean back in the seat. She knows to come home. I hope.

"What's with those shoes?" Kie says.

"Shut up."

Kie laughs, cranks the throttle, and makes for home.

***

"Good morning, Phen!"

No that doesn't work.

"HotDaj is back!"

Well, that just sucks.

"Sounds great," Kie says.

"Jeez man, what are you doing back there? I thought you left."

Kie shrugs. "Wanted to keep an eye on you, make sure you were all right."

"Feeling bad about ditching me?"

"Hey, it was pretty messed up down there," Kie says. "I tried to get help. Scitech said they'd send out a search team for you, so I left."

So, Scitech found me because of Kie's call? They sure sent out a heavily armed rescue mission. It doesn't seem right.

"Where did you go again?" Kie says.

"I've told you a hundred times, to the east of Phen. To that temple thing." I wave absently out the window at the rising sun. My head is

spinning. Have I been up all night?

"Wow, that's really helpful. Don't you have any footage?"

I send him the photo I took up top of the temple. "What do you think of this place?"

"Dude, why haven't we heard of this place? Next time, invite me."

I shrug. "It doesn't show up on my system, it's like I wasn't even there. Nanosite was weird out there ever since the old guy and his crazy granddaughter captured me. Nothing on my GPS, either."

Except my glider, but I ain't ever telling him about that.

"And your Camdrone?" Kie says.

"Scitech is probably out looking for her right now. I bet they'll be here with my bot any second and I'll be able to download all my vids."

If they bring her to me. From my last meeting with that Pontane lady, I'm not sure that's their plan. If they don't get some footage they're going to kill me. Or at least suspend my 'site application for my flight upgrade. Right now, I don't know which is worse.

Cam's wrist dock indicates she's still online, wherever she is. At least there's that.

My hearts pound in my chest. I'm sweating all over. My stomach feels like one of those yarels is gnawing on it.

"You know," Kie says through a yawn. "That was weird last night. Me coming to rescue you. Reminds me of when we were kids."

"You're right. Except I was always the one saving your ass from aliens."

"Yeah, but that was a game," Kie says. "From some book, or movie. What was it called?

Images of us playing flit to my mind then fade. "Skywatch." Of course. Why is it so hard for me to remember?

"Yeah! Right! And you always wanted to be that one Maglan, the captain. You'd hate it when I was Captain...?"

"Commander Freewind." There it is. Like a floodgate opening, I remember all the stupid games we played. Running in the streets, gunning down monsters. Jumping off the house thinking we could fly. It sounds stupid now, but we lived for it as kids.

A signal beeps and a tiny light blips in the corner of my 'site.

Incoming call. A few seconds pass.

"You going to answer that?" Kie says.

My mouth goes dry. "Yeah, yeah, I am."

"Mr. Daj." Ms. Pontane's face opens over the full 'site. I can't see anything else.

"Listen, I can—"

"You don't call, you don't message us. We were starting to get a little nervous that we might have to send someone to find you." She pauses for a moment. "We don't have to send anyone to find you, do we?"

"No, no. I'm fine. I just got a little sidetracked down there." So they did know I was down there. Unless she's trying to throw me off. But why would she? Wouldn't she just bring me in for questioning if she thought I was a terrorist?

She smiles at me. "I think we need to have another talk. Why don't you come down to Scitech? Chat about anything you might have seen while you were away."

Great. That answers that. But I was taken prisoner. And Stell hijacked me on the way out. Scitech will understand that. Yeah, I could tell Ms. Pontane everything and there'd be no blame on me. I mean, it wasn't like I did anything wrong.

So why is my stomach twisting up?

And what is Pontane thinking as I'm sitting here staring blankly?

"Uh, I got my camera drone back."

She pauses. I just barely catch the surprise in her eyes as she looks off-screen momentarily. "You did?"

Crap. Why did I say that? Well, Cam's coming back I hope. At least Stell and Rym don't have her. That's what's really important.

"I'm going through my footage now. There's a lot there, and I want to get it all looking good for you."

"Oh, so you do have the correct codes."

I flinch.

"We're sending someone now to help."

"No!" Whoa, take a breath. "I mean, this is an artist's time right here. I can't have anyone watching over me while I make the vid. I've got to concentrate. Give me two more hours."

"One hour." She kills the connection.

"Shit man. Shit shit shit." An hour my ass. I've got ten minutes if I'm lucky.

"What are you doing, Daj? Why did you tell her you found Cam?"

"Good question." I run to my room and change out of Rym's boots. Can't be caught with those. As I grab something quick to eat, I flip through my vid feeds, not really meaning to, just on instinct.

There's Rolun, talking about some new pair of shoes he needs to get. Flit, flit with my eyes and I open another. Crole streaming her new hair colors. Not nearly as distracting now that there's a huge sponsoring corporation threatening to cancel my connection, or worse.

"Did you see anything else down there?" Kie asks from the other room.

My skin crawls. Give it up, man. Flit, flit. A vid rises to the top of the Stream Line, the best of the best. I'm going to throw up. My hearts sting and I can't breathe.

It's Kie. And Zaylee. Riding the same Sky Deck I leapt off the Edge on. I check the time link on the vid. Yesterday. I can hear my hearts throbbing in my ears. Dude, I wasn't even gone for a few hours and Scitech gave them the exclusive ride I was supposed to show off? And now their sponsor cred is growing while I sit around? No way.

I play the vid again to see their faces. It hits me even harder, especially with Zaylee holding her arms around Kie's chest.

A ring starts to swirl around my head, darkness, dizziness. I can't take it anymore. I switch off the 'site for a moment to get a look outside at the city rings in the distance, and at the sky above. The moons and shattered Dust Field orbiting Magla seem farther away than ever.

And my parents do, too.

And there's Kie, sitting on the couch acting worried about me, asking me what I need, but at the same time, probably streaming a vid of me. I'd bet he'd call it the "Fallen Loser." Every sickly sweet expression of concern makes my stomach wrench.

"When were you going to tell me about you and Zaylee?"

Kie falters. "D, it, it just…"

I've got to get out of here. To get away from Kie. To get Cam before Scitech does.

I'm nearly out the door before Kie grabs my shoulder. "Where are you going?"

"Let go."

He hesitates and I pull my arm free to run out the door.

Pretty soon I'm out in the middle of the street. Kids and adults stare blank-eyed into nothing. I stop running and stand amidst the sea of Maglans streaming past me, never bumping into me. It looks like they're going to, but at the last second the 'site alert jerks their bodies away from me and the rest of the traffic follows the bump in the flow. No one looks up. No one sees me. I don't exist.

I wonder if they're watching me. You know, a past me. Some stream where I jump off a cliff on some new Scitech hardware. I want to punch something, but there are Maglans on all sides of me. The sea of them parts again as I plow my way to the side of the walkway. Speeders and haulers bringing crates to and from the city fly by through the morning sunlight.

I barely have time to catch my breath when a clunking sound rattles through the air. What is it? It's getting closer through the bustle of the crowd heading to work. There's a pinging sound now. A small object moves jerkily above me, bobbing up and down as servos and maglevs adjust to attempt to stay in the air.

Cam!

With a final spasm, she falls into my hands.

"Are you all right?" I cradle her to a bench nearby overlooking the street. There's a dim light flickering inside her sensor array. Black marks scorch her side.

"You got this from the escape. I'm sorry."

I don't have any tools. I can't open her up without fear of breaking something else. So I do the next best thing, I hope, and pull up my 'site to scan her. A pale blue screen hovers over her in my eyes and reveals her innards.

"Diagnostics."

Nanos scan over her, making a model of her on my 'site. I pull up the specs for her model so I can compare what damage has happened to her. Hover system, offline. Scan mode, offline. Internal storage? Collating data. What does collating mean?

To gather and put information in order.

"Ah. Keep collating, man!"

The 'site keeps processing as I wait. I've got to get somewhere I can back her up, or at least to my tools, although my hearts rip as I even consider losing her. Back to my apartment? Not with Kie there and Scitech on the way. Some shop? My 'site blips a second and then reports back a list of nearby tech shops I can use. A few are a couple blocks away.

"Come on, Cam, you've got to make it."

Maybe Scitech coming now wouldn't be such a bad thing. They could fix her. The contact icon flashes on my 'site as I just think about it. Another thought and I can send for help.

A series of hisses and sparks jet from Cam's panels. And I think of the message my parents left me inside of her.

I do it. I call Scitech and let them know where I am. I double-think the icon just to make sure.

The sea of Maglans walking past me all of a sudden grows louder. Was it always this loud? A notification pops on my screen and lets me know they're on the way and that I need to stay where I am. I feel better, the weight of it all lifts from my shoulders. It'll all go back to normal now. It'll all go back.

Someone's standing behind me. I can sense it. They couldn't have gotten here so quickly, could they? I spin around, ready to hand Cam over.

But it ain't Scitech. I blink in disbelief. It's that old drunk. With his beat up red-eyed robot. And they look pissed.

"Been looking for you, boy," Rym says.

The robot flexes his fingers and extends various tools. Where was he five minutes ago?

A look of shock crosses Rym's wrinkled face. "Dewey, you see this?"

The bot peeks over his shoulder down at Cam in my hands. Servos spin in his wrist and the tools rotate. "I have seen worse, sir. But not much." His robotic speech sounds surprisingly concerned.

"Good then, get to work."

"No thanks," I grab Cam and hold her behind my back. "Scitech's coming. They're going to fix her up right."

"Scitech?" Rym says. "Are you stupid? They're just looking for that data. We can actually fix it."

"No," I say. "They're looking for you. And I don't need your help. They'll be here any minute, you better run."

Rym grabs my top right arm pretty rough and drags me forward. "No, you come with us."

"Hey, help!" I yell. Not one of the Maglans walking by turns in my direction.

"You don't get it," Rym says. "They're going to destroy that thing and kill you. They almost killed you down below, or have you already forgotten?"

"They were after your girl, not me."

Dewey grips the top of my skull and turns me around. "That look like a tech crew to you?"

A hundred or so paces away, a heavily armored Scitech hover skiff settles down into the middle of the street, scattering the few Maglans nearby in a blast of dust. The others just continue on their way as if nothing is happening. Don't they see the armed guards? Or are they too plugged in? My stomach drops and I glance back at Rym. He sends an awfully loud "I told you so" look in my direction

A Scitech stooge hops out of the craft, trying to hide a large gun near his side. Dewey's right. If this is a tech retrieval and repair team, I'm last week's news. Well, that's already true.

I switch on my vid stream to catch this to show to the public. No way Scitech is ever going to risk doing anything to me if I'm live streaming this. All right, *go*.

I gesture *go* again. And nothing happens. The usual icon in my 'site for starting a vid stream is not responding. Interference? Again?

"You just going to stare at that thug all day, kid?" Rym pulls me away from the approaching heavily armed not-quite technician.

"I'm trying to start a vid, and I can't."

"This is what I'm trying to tell you, they control the feed."

The whole feed? Good one.

Rym points right above the hover vehicle where a red light flashes out of a metal shell. Green 'site connection nodes along the street all flip to red in a ripple effect away from the ship. The crowd stops and looks up, squinting their eyes like they're waking from a nap.

Dewey's front casing pops open with a whir, exposing twin tubes within his chest. "Might want to look away."

Heavy repeating blasts set the streets aglow with blue blurs of light. Terrified pedestrians scream and scatter in all directions. Definitely awake now.

"Damn, Rym. Want to turn your killbot away from my face?"

The blasts center on the skiff but they don't appear to be doing any damage. They just pellet it repeatedly.

"Let's go," Rym says. "Now. And stay in front of Dewey." He drags me by my shirt until I'm next to him. "Keep moving."

"Hey, watch the merchandise."

Rym yanks me forward again.

"All right, all right."

I glance back over my shoulder to see the heavy Scitech agent shove his way through the scattering pedestrians. My ocular lens snaps a shot of him in his uniform.

As I run, the screengrab magnifies in the corner of my 'site. Okay, not a man. Just a really big and strong and scary Scitech guard woman wearing a helmet. A helmet that doesn't quite fit right. There's something weird about her face. It's all misshapen.

"Did you see her?" I look back again. "She's huge!"

Dewey continues to pepper the gunboat, and still, nothing happens. "What's the matter with your gun?"

The guard drops to her knee and draws up her heavy rifle, ignoring the crowd, ready to open fire on us out in the street. Slowly, her arms begin to wobble and the weapon pulls toward the now glowing skiff.

Dewey stops firing and holds up his arms. "Stay there. And watch. You're going to love this."

There's a low groaning sound, followed by the pinging of metal as bolts release from support beams and structures. With repeated clinks, I hear them center on the glowing skiff like metal popcorn popping.

The guard fights the pull of her gun for a second, and then it drags forward. Other metal objects stream through the air and plunk into the now magnetized craft, whizzing past her head. It's a thing of beauty.

Her metal helmet drags her neck sideways and she loses her balance. She falls over and slides to the skiff, sticking to it with a clang.

I'm busy laughing when Rym yells, "Get moving, kid. You're coming with us."

"Why would I go with you guys?"

"They've got Stell, and you're going to help get her back."

CHAPTER 7

"First you kidnap me, and now you need my help?"

Rym shrugs.

"That's it? That's all you have? Shrugs?" I sigh. "So you saw them take her? Alive?"

Rym shakes his head slowly. "It's the chatter on the frequencies. Dewey picked up something about an hour ago saying they found her near our old base down below. We checked it out, but there wasn't any trace of her at the crash site. You don't know anything about that, do you?"

"She told me to go. That she would lead them away." After I led them to the base in the first place.

"And you just left her?"

"Have you ever tried to change her mind about something?"

Rym stares at me.

"Sorry." The image of her hanging on to the cliff is imprinted in my mind, with her face and hands all burned. I rub my temples. *Sorry* doesn't sound real, or right. It sounds lame.

"That's her," Rym says. "Stoic. And stupid." He turns away and I feel his disgust with me.

Dewey's meticulous hands cradle Cam's frame as tiny tools extend from his digits. A micro drill loosens her outer shell and with a quick snap the latch pops open to expose her fried circuitry within. It may be me, but it seems like her sparking and whining servos have calmed down a bit. Hopefully it's not just her shutting down. Hopefully it's the fact that she knows she's being helped.

Rym is over there at the edge of the rent-a-pod repair bay staring at the whole procedure. The window slits are completely shut, leaving the unnatural glow of the humming lights the only source of illumination. Feels private enough, but he keeps checking the door whenever we hear footsteps. His hand never strays far from the pistol at his belt and

I hope that's for any threat from outside, not yours truly. He takes a quick swig from his silver flask in his jacket every minute or so.

"Are you sure you drink that just for the signal blocking?"

He sucks his teeth after the next pull from it and glares at me. "It also helps make you more bearable."

"Fair enough."

Rym tosses me the capped flask. "You got to drink it too, boy."

My tongue curls up at the edges thinking about tasting that stuff.

"You don't want them tracking us in here, do you?"

"How could they? I mean, if I don't ping my location onto the grid or try to contact anyone, like you said, we should just be safe."

Rym shrugs his shoulders forward and stares at me. "They tracked you down under, didn't they?"

I eye the liquid. "Can't Dewey block out the signal somehow?"

"He's got a barrier up, but it only works on some tech. He can jam outgoing transmissions, but as for stopping them from peeking in at us, sorry. Nothing can stop that as much as this drink can, as far as I know. And, hey. It doesn't taste that bad."

"Uh, yeah it does. And the red teeth? That's not the look I'm going for."

Rym shrugs and points at the flask.

"You want to be able to see without your Nanosite, right?"

Only it's not Rym's voice that said it. I nearly dump the flask over, my hearts flip so much. I swear I heard Stell talking.

Dewey and Rym continue working on the drone, they didn't hear anything. I must have just imagined it.

"Why is Scitech after you guys? I mean, I know you're working with Stell, and she's a Nonno living with all those criminals down below. But, has she actually done anything?"

"That's a good question, isn't it, boyo?" Rym grins at me through his scraggly face spike beard.

That isn't creepy. Nope.

"The real question is *who* is Scitech? And what do they want?"

I shrug. "That's easy. They helped us win the war. They're a big manufacturer of the tech we need here to survive."

"To *survive*, huh? You mean to have fun with."

I instinctively scan my 'site for my feed, but of course it still isn't back yet. "No, I mean for learning how to fly, and there's medical stuff. How do you think I got my back fixed up after that nosedive I took last year? You saw me do that, right?"

Rym shrugs again. "Nanotech doesn't fix everyone."

He lifts his lower left arm, crumpled and deformed.

"You could have gone to Scitech a long time ago and had that fixed. Upgrade your nanos. You'd probably get a discount for having fought in the war."

"They don't take kindly to Skywatch." Rym leans back and rubs his face spikes. "Here, let me tell you a story. Back when I was piloting those ships you saw in my garage, the whole planet was under attack by the Cadeans."

"The *Cadeans*? They've been living on one of the moons out there forever." I point up to the sky through the speckled mass of asteroid fragments to Cadea, the blue-hued chunk of rock. "They're harmless. A bunch of weak puny aliens."

"Well, those *puny* aliens were stronger than we thought," Rym says. "Had some pretty desperate soldiers, and were in need of resources since they'd nearly used up their own."

"Didn't Scitech show up then? Help us win?"

Rym laughs dryly. "More like ended our way of life. Skywatch was doing just fine and we had them beat, but then Scitech showed up and made us all slaves."

"I'm no slave. I don't know what you're on about. See, this is why no one believes you. Scitech made us stronger. We won that war. The end."

Rym shakes his head. "They cast out the old order, Skywatch, eliminating the only thing that could hold them back, and then they gave us all Nanos. We lost the best damn pilots ever."

I laugh. "Have you seen *me* fly?"

Rym shoots me a look that shuts my mouth.

"Ever." He emphasizes with some strange two-fingered salute to the heavens. "I went to get help from Scitech for my injuries, and they neutered my ass."

"Huh?"

"They injected me with their nanotech. Said it would help heal me, and that it would increase my edge while flying."

I open my mouth to ask but he gets there first.

"No, it didn't. Instead, it weakened me and the rest of us pilots. And they didn't fix my arm. And then they shut down Skywatch."

"Because they didn't need you anymore is what I heard. Scitech won the war for us, and you don't get it."

Rym shoves his chair back and steps toward me. His face spikes bristle. "No, *you* don't get it. If you could only see what we lost when Scitech took over. The more we forget—"

"Whatever." I'm sick of listening to his gibberish. "How old are you anyway? Wasn't Skywatch a long time ago?"

Rym grimaces. "A lot older than you'll ever be."

"Is that a threat?"

"Hah. How old do you think Stell is?"

I shrug. Stupid old guy. "My age. A little younger."

Rym smiles.

"What?"

"Oh nothing. Just be sure to ask her when you see her again."

"If we see her."

Rym checks on the front door in silence.

Dewey sure is taking his sweet time tweaking with my Cam. I'd say something but the way he keeps glancing at me makes me think he's about ready to use one of those spiky tools on my eyeball.

"So you just keep drinking that stuff?" I hand the bottle back to Rym.

He shows off his red-stained teeth. "All the time. They can't track me. And it slows the aging process."

"Right right. Because you look like you haven't aged a day out of your teens."

"If you could not be a jackass every time you speak, you might be able to listen. I'm telling you, the Nanos speed up your growth."

"And why would they do that, Rym? What is one possible reason why they want us old?"

"Think about it. They keep you working for them, take the best possible years from you, and then run you down. Less drag on the resources here."

"That doesn't make sense. Why not just keep us young if they can do that?"

Rym shrugs. "Better keep that idea quiet. Seems like that'd be a better one for them."

"You don't make any sense. You're just some old-timer who misses the old days with his flying buddies and can't admit that our generation has it better. Why can't you just let us have it? You don't like the tech, so you're against us having it."

"No one remembers the *old times*. No one remembers Skywatch. Don't you think that's funny? They don't teach it in schools, and nanos can wipe memories."

"That's crazy." Although why did I forget about Skywatch? Just me getting older and forgetting about stupid stuff I played as a kid, I guess.

"And what's more, they're draining your mag sense to power their little machines. And without that, you're nothing."

I scoff. "I don't have a mag sense."

"Didn't you see what Stell could do? How do you think she was doing all that stuff? Talking to you in your head? Magic?"

It's not magic. "New tech?"

"No, dumbass, not new tech. *No tech*. She's a Nonno, like you said. And can do more than you'll ever be able to do. But not because she's different than you. No, that's the pisser. She's *just* like you. Only you have those little parasites inside your body. You can make videos of yourself jumping off the Rings. Whoop dee frickin' doo."

"Calm down."

"You don't get to tell me to calm down. We're losing ourselves here, in the Rings of Phen, all over Magla. And if I don't do something about it— I take that back, if we all don't do something about it, the Cadeans are going to end us."

"So you think they're planning another war on us? To take our stuff? With Scitech? That's their big plan?"

"I keep telling you, they don't need to come down here and fight. They know how to get what they need."

"What do you mean?"

"Think about it. They take us up there." Rym gestures to the sky where the shattered moon, Naglor sits. "That's their main base where they broadcast the Nanosite signal. And that's where they have us bring them resources."

That's something I hadn't thought about. And it freezes up my guts. "My parents?"

"Let me guess." Rym sits down and crosses his legs. "They *became* pilots when you were a little kid. It was the best day of their lives, and yours. Because they got to fly and help carry freight to Scitech. And you got a new house, new toys, new tech in your head, and a whole lot of new *friends* following your vids."

I don't respond. I can't.

"Then they disappear. And since then, you've been promised it will be you that goes up there next. Glory. Fame. Money. All that bullshit."

He can't be right. It's just that propagandist line old Maglans feed the youth. Right? The room gets real quiet.

Dewey beeps. "Rym, I think it's working now."

I breathe out a sigh of relief. Cam buzzes around the room like she's fresh out of the foundry.

"Cam!" I hold out my arm and she quickly hovers to it and locks on.

"Is the data safe?" Rym asks.

Dewey nods. "There's some old tech programming still in there, things I've never seen before."

"She seems all right," I interrupt him and inspect the little gears and arms under her wings. I flip through her input screen under her lid. A list of stats appears and scrolls down. "All systems seem to be functional. Memory, too. The data stream from my jump is in here."

I scroll through the storage link and notice a hefty chunk of new footage, too. "Seems like I left Cam recording somewhere. Must have been down with Stell." I don't mention the other footage I always keep on her. That's safe, too.

"Well now you can send out the broadcast," Rym says. "Show your followers what really happened on your jump."

"You're forgetting," Dewey begins. "They'd shut down that feed the second he tried to link it up. Cover it up with something else."

Don't they get it? I don't want to do that. I just want everything to go back to how it was. My instinct kicks in and I flick my eyes to scan my site. I've got to check my feed, even if it's to see what Kie and Zaylee are doing together. But the sour taste of Rym's drink still clings to my tongue, reminding me I can't access anything.

"Say something, kid. When we find a way to send a message, it's your video and you've got the connections." Rym looks pretty uptight. "They've got her. And I'm not sure what they're going to do with her."

"You think a vid of someone jumping is going to change anything? You don't need me."

Dewey is all itchy-like, moving around like he's going to draw those blasters on me next. And Rym's scowl deepens so much there's a huge crease mark on his brow.

"I can't let you just take this footage back to Scitech," Rym says. "They're just going to destroy it. And kill you."

"That's just crazy."

"Where can we go to broadcast this?" Rym asks. "So that we can get everyone to see it?"

Dewey beeps. "Even if you manage to find a way to broadcast the message, Scitech will have no reason to keep Stell alive."

"That's what she would want." Rym doesn't really sound too sure of himself when he says this, though.

"That's harsh, grandpa. You really think that?"

"You don't know her, kid. Stop acting like you're any part of our world. The only thing that matters is shutting down Scitech. Something I should have done a long time ago."

"Why didn't you?"

The silence that follows isn't very reassuring. After a few seconds, he glances at Dewey. "At first, the upgrade seemed like a good thing. I got visual tracking through the Nanosite. I could spot enemies faster, my reaction time sped up, too. And then the war was over. Older ships were marked illegal and confiscated. Newer ships with upgraded security and independent nanos were the norm. And when I tried to get back up in the skies, I was denied access to any of the flight tech. They said I was too *unreliable*. Course, that was because they botched this repair job."

He waves his deformed arm. "They sent younger pilots to head up the security forces and even the mining tugs. Skywatch was killed. And instead, I was offered a part of their R and D for new tech."

"Did you take it? That seems like it would have been a dream job."

Rym looked over at Dewey again. "I went through their interview process here on Magla. I passed their initial screening, and then they said I had to go to their base up in orbit for the final check. And what I saw there scared the shit out of me. Maglan testing facilities. They were messing with the structure of our bodies, installing built-in tech that made us look more like Dewey than Maglan. No offense, buddy."

"Of course."

"I turned them down. Easy as that. Well, then they said it wasn't as *easy as that*. Things got a little stressful, but I managed to get out of there alive with most of my own self. But, I still had the initial base model Nanosite in me; I found out they could track me."

This doesn't make sense. Why would Scitech even want to do any of this? Just to make money? Yeah, I suppose that would be enough. That's all I really want. Besides flying.

"Why are you telling me this? Don't you know I could just as easily turn you in now? Why do you want me to help?"

Rym sneaks another swig. "Because I *need* you to help. I need to make sure that Stell's sacrifice to get you safe was worth something. Don't you see?"

Cam's system boots up a vid file and projects into the room. It's from the interior of the temple when I was sleeping. It sure was peaceful down there. Suddenly the camera pans over to Stell. That same feeling I got from when I first met her hits me hard again. She seems free. Like a young kid without any responsibilities. She is sitting cross-legged and holding her hands across her chest. And yeah, she's floating above the ground. Her eyes shoot open.

"If you can hear me," she says. "Things have probably gone pretty badly."

"Wait, how can we even hear her?" The weird thing is, her mouth's not moving.

Rym covers my mouth and motions for me to shut up. Not just to quiet down, but to full on shut the hell up.

"I've been caught by Scitech. And one of you is saying to come free me."

I swear, her video image is staring right at Rym right now.

"Remember what you said about the mission. About how you would do anything to get rid of the nanos. You must get everyone on our side. Once you spread the truth, the revolution will be easier to start."

Rym settles down hard into a chair and looks down into his lap.

I know just what he's thinking. This girl, who I barely know, is asking for my help. She's not wanting anything for herself. Not even her life, it seems. Her life that I'm responsible for.

And that makes me feel like shit.

"All right," I say. "I have an idea."

CHAPTER 8

"You know how you said that we have to get to a place to broadcast that message? I have the perfect place in mind."

"And where's that?" Rym asks.

I gesture upward with my chin. He looks at me funny so I point up there again.

"What, you mean up in orbit?"

Dewey whistles.

"It's where they broadcast their own signal, and you'd need a place to reach everyone at once. Plus, if that's their main base they probably have Stell there, too."

"First off, that's insane," Rym says. "And second, you probably know there's no free ride up there."

I nod. "You must have access to a ship, all Skywatch-y, right? Something that will keep you off the radar, like back in your repair shop you had that speeder you were working on. With all that sweet tech on it, but no nano integration."

Rym gets up and paces around the room. "I can't keep that equipment in my garage. That would certainly have gained the attention of someone. And don't you remember my story? Your precious Scitech took all the Skywatch equipment. Or most of it." He pauses for a moment. "When you say, 'keep *you* off the radar,' what did you mean?"

"Well I can't go up there. You and Dewey have been doing this your whole life. I'm just a kid. I only make videos of me jumping off crazy shit. I ain't going up against Scitech. I still might have a future. You can take a copy of my bot's memory file and show the video yourself."

Rym stares at me and makes me a little uncomfortable. I can't really tell what he's going for with that look. It's either he wants to kill me, or he just lost a beloved pet. I don't know which is worse, actually.

"You're kidding, right? Stell sacrificed herself just to get a message out there. You owe it to her."

"I don't owe anyone anything." I was fine risking my own life on some new Deck, but having all of Scitech after me because of some Nonno, where's the fun in that? "But I'll still help you plan something."

"Still help us plan something? Oh, that's very nice of you. Kid, you're in this deep now. You're coming along with us if I have to tie you to Dewey's back. Right?"

Dewey chimes a positive response, but he's carrying himself like he's wondering how he could lift me around.

Rym nods sharply. "What were we saying before this kid chicken-shitted himself? Oh right, ships. Dewey? Do you know where some are?"

"As far as we know, Scitech brought them all to their Research and Development center. There's one just outside of Phen."

My stomach is still all sick from the last thing he was talking about. About me going with them. Do I have a choice? I can't do this. "Are the ships all in one piece?"

Dewey's gears creak as he attempts to shrug.

"Any other ship is going to get spotted and tracked the second it leaves atmo, so we don't really have a choice," Rym says.

Dewey pauses for a second. "But if we steal a ship from a depot, that will also be tracked. If it is logged as stolen."

"Then you have to hit multiple Scitech sites," I say. "And make them look like vandalism or just theft. Not you all trying to get off of Magla."

A crash outside makes us all shut up real quick. I try the door, but it's locked.

"Is there any other way out of here?" I say.

Rym pops open Dewey's back panel and pulls out two black pistols. "Take this." He tosses it to me and I fumble it with all four hands. "You ever fire a gun before?"

I swallow hard. "I've never held a gun before." I'd always wanted to. Like in one of those shows where the hero blasts a Cadean stone cold in the face. But now the metal, heavy and smooth, feels oddly wrong in my grip.

"Let's just hope we don't have to use them," Rym whispers and motions us to the back of the small room.

He walks to the door and peers into the outside monitor, but from where I stand I can tell there's nothing but static coming out of it. There's silence for a few more seconds before Rym turns back to us.

"Probably nothing, just a—"

The door blasts inward, crumpling under the force of an explosion, and knocks Rym to the floor. There's no smoke though, so it must have been bludgeoned by something really strong. I don't have to wait any longer to wonder, for some big thing walks in through the door. What the hell is it?

Did I say it's big? Because it's monstrous. I think it's a Maglan, but only because it has the same shape and number of arms as one of us, but after that there's no comparison. It's wearing some body armor, some gray plates covering its chest and head. I can make out its face, but man it's like someone had a fight with a club to the nose and lost brutally.

"Shoot it!" Rym says.

"Why can't you?" My hands are shaking so much, I can't even hold it up to the thing.

"My gun fell somewhere. Just shoot it, kid!" Rym is searching for his weapon, Dewey is not moving. It's like he's analyzing something he's never seen before and can't quite compute.

I shout something and pull the trigger. A flash of light escapes the barrel of the pistol and of course it misses and blasts into the wall. I shoot again and this time the beam strikes its arm that's raised at Rym, and there's a sizzle of flesh and smoke. The thing stumbles momentarily as the arm drops uselessly to the ground with a plop, and then it turns to face me.

The helmet covers its face so I can't see its eyes, in fact there's some glowing under there so I'm not even sure if it has eyes. I yell again and fire repeatedly into its chest, remaining arms, and legs. The heat of the weapon burns into my hand, but I don't let go. Instead I keep firing until smoke fills the room.

When the power drains out of the gun and I'm just dry-clicking the trigger, there's silence. The Maglan's outline within the smoke tells me it's still standing, kind of rocking back and forth. Its four arms lie in a wet pile on the floor and its head is tilted at a weird angle. But the plate armor and helmet have apparently protected its important parts.

It takes one stumbling step into my direction before it comes to a swaying stop on its smoking legs. Its head twitches side to side, almost like a malfunctioning bot.

"What the hell is this?" I pull the trigger once more but it doesn't fire. In fact it's sizzling its way into my hand, overheated, and the pungent smell of my own cooked flesh fills my nose. The gun drops to the floor with a thunk.

Luckily by this time Rym has his weapon in hand and Dewey's chest plate opens to expose the cannons. Before they can fire though, the Scitech agent pitches forward with a whine and crashes into a table. We all sit there staring for a few seconds as it smolders in an unmoving pile. Just to be sure, Rym walks over, places his gun to the base of its neck, and pulls the trigger. The thing spasms one last time.

Rym kneels down and pries off the helmet to expose a grossly misshapen head. I mean, it's nose is wide and flat with large nostrils. "What the hell is right. Dewey, what are we looking at here?"

The bot kneels down and another chest panel opens to expose an arm with a four-inch needle coming out of its tip. The arm jams into the exposed skull of the agent or whatever it is.

"Strange," Dewey says.

"I'm confused," I say. "You mean strange like there's a seven-foot-tall mutant Maglan with a Scitech uniform on? Or something else? Because there's nothing about this thing that isn't strange."

Dewey doesn't respond.

"I've never seen anything like this," Rym says.

"Maybe they just hired a really big and ugly guy."

"I do not think so. There's something about its nanos." Dewey removes the needle from the agent. "They're acting funny. Here, before they powered off, I got a recording of them."

A panel on his chest lights up and shows a highly-focused image of the tiny nanos among the blood cells.

"I see them swimming around. What's funny about that?"

Dewey beeps. "Just because you don't know what to look for doesn't mean there's nothing wrong."

Rym pats me on the shoulder. "Dewey has been analyzing nanos since their arrival. If he says they're acting different, they're acting different."

"So, what, you think that Scitech *made* this thing? From a regular Maglan?" It sounds pretty stupid when I say it out loud.

"They found us somehow," Rym says. "And we're offline. Dewey here even put up that nano barrier so we're not emitting a signal outside this room. They must have tracked us."

"Which means others know we're here."

"Not necessarily," Dewey says. "He would have had to relay a signal once he found us, but this room is blocked. Of course, when he does not report back it won't take very long for them to know where we are."

That nose. That crazy big ass nose. Could he literally have sniffed us out? From my clothes? Did they go into my apartment and find my scent? Great, now I'm the one who sounds insane. But if this one was following us, there have to be more agents.

"They really want to get you so bad they're willing to kill?" I ask.

"I'm not so sure it's *us* they're after." Rym gives me and Cam pointed looks. "But yes, apparently."

Well shit, if they can track me through smell and also my nanos are back online, what chance do I have on my own? A panic tightens my chest and I have a tough time taking my next few breaths.

"Can you two help me?"

"There is one way." Rym swigs more of the liquid from his flask.

I let out a sigh. "Come with you, right? So this sucks. You know there are only three of us? What about your contacts from back then? Your 'best pilots' ever?"

Rym shakes his head. "The old gang doesn't do anything anymore. They're all like me now, injected and infected with these nanos."

"But you stay in touch with them, right?"

Rym scratches behind his neck. "Not really."

Dewey leans closer to him and whispers, "Not even Hira?"

Rym laughs dryly. "Okay, I know where a few of them are. But there's no way they're going to help us out."

"Doesn't hurt to go ask. Come on, you said it yourself. We need any kind of help. And maybe my friends, Kie and Zaylee could do something." When I say it, it stings. Just thinking of them makes me burn up and sick at the same time.

"Nah, I don't trust them. Plus, what are they going to do? Make a video of us?"

I shrug. "We need to break into a high-security base to smuggle out a ship. Dewey, which one of Rym's geriatric friends would you invite?"

Dewey pauses a microsecond and then beeps. "I have managed to procure a list of candidates based on the required skills cross-

referenced with proximity and state of decay."

I shake my head. "Huh?"

"I found who could help, who is close, and who is not dead yet."

"Better. And make sure this Hira is on the list. We want Rym to tag along."

"Done."

Rym grips me on the shoulder. "You are a persistent little bastard, you know that?"

"That's on my bio. And, hey. About Kie and Zaylee, I think I know how they can help."

***

I peek out of the door and glance both ways out into the narrow hallway. No sounds, no trace of anyone else tracking us down. Hopefully this pile of sausage on the floor was a scout or something and didn't have a chance to get back to the others. And also wasn't part of a crew.

A crew. Hah. I look over at Rym and Dewey. A decrepit ex-Skywatch pilot and an ancient 'bot. It's better than no one, I guess, and they're at least willing to stand by me. To suit their own purposes, perhaps, but still.

"So you never shot a gun before, have you?" Rym asks as he hoists his pack over his shoulder. "At least without a targeting array."

"I thought it was pretty obvious, but thanks for being polite. And no, not even with an array."

"Nah, kid, you did great. You could work at the butcher down the street after the precision cuts you made."

That's pretty nasty. But I guess he's trying to be nice. Or make sure I stay with them. "I'm more of a pilot. I'd rather not have to do that again."

"None of us would, but I don't think you'll have much of a choice."

Face more of these things? Or worse? My first instinct is to order an upgrade package for my nanos. I'm not connected right now to any net node because of both Dewey and the drink but I can still see the options available in the offline mode. Mainly because I have Scitech's pilot modification bookmarked ready for the second I can get up in the skies. I hover over the delete icon by glancing at it. Not much chance of getting up there anytime too soon. Or ever.

But Scitech has a complete package of upgrades for different tech jobs, too. I flip through dozens of them I've held onto for a different potential career. Law enforcement, which includes advanced targeting modes. I can't even understand half of what flashes across the screen in the description. Stuff about angles, projectile motion, gravitational accelerated declination modulation. I suppose that would help with something. Mining, either rig-based or with a mining suit. Extra ship-hazard management. That's just some hard-core stuff right there, with the arc torches and—

"You coming?" Dewey shoves me in the shoulder. "Hey, you zoned out for a minute. You're not trying to connect, are you?"

Rym whips around and the gun barrel levels almost imperceptibly toward me. I wave my hands. "No, no, just checking offline stuff I had." I gulp.

"That's good, but you gotta fix that." Rym turns around and leads us down the corridor. "You don't want your instinct to be to always connect up to Scitech's net if Dewey goes down, or we run out of the drink. Phen's rings have enough nodes to pinpoint us in a second if you try to log in."

"Got it," I grip the gun Rym gave me earlier.

"See, I was worried that you came around too quickly, that you were planning to rat on us."

"Aw, thanks," I say.

"But really, why the quick turnaround?"

I shrug. "I'm a sucker for new tech. Or old tech, in this case. A chance to see one of your ships you were talking about."

"Uh huh. And it had nothing to do with your feelings for Stell?"

My face grows immediately hotter. "No, definitely not." I may have answered too quickly there.

Rym smiles. Yup, too quickly.

"That's good, because she is way out of your league, kid."

Hmph. I doubt that. Maybe. Probably.

"Like a couple of generations out."

"Yeah I get it, gramps. Is this really what we need to worry about right now? Where's your closest friend?"

Rym grins and looks side to side as we slip into the street amongst the hundreds of pedestrians. "Well it's not about closeness that we want to focus on first."

"What do you mean?"

Rym nods outside of Phen's rings. "There's a problem with my friends. Scitech never wanted us together again, and they'll know if that

happens. We're going to need our slicing expert first. His name's Neman."

"Why don't we just get your slicer and head out to the base for our ship? Or just skip your pals altogether. Seems like Dewey is pretty good at slicing."

Rym shakes his head. "They'd spot Dewey a mile away, now that they're looking for us. No, our first stop is clear at the top of the central city ring."

"Ooh, that sounds fancy. But we're going to stick out for anyone to see us. We don't exactly belong up there. And when I say 'we' I mean 'you.' Have you seen yourself lately? You haven't shaved in a couple of weeks and those clothes." I wrinkle up my face.

"Just follow me."

CHAPTER 9

I can't believe we have to walk all the way to the top of the Rings and take these dank side streets. I mean I get it, we can't take the shuttles, or walk openly on the main streets with all the cameras and Maglans with their 'sites activated. I've learned to keep my mouth shut, though.

"Don't," Rym says again for the twentieth time when he sees me ready to complain.

"I wasn't going to say anything," I say. Probably. Cam is on my wrist dock, and I'm downloading all the video she picked up since the last data dump. Does that say terabytes? It's going to take hours to sift through it. Still, I'll have it in a safe place. In my head. Dewey watches me closely.

"I could download and prioritize for you," Dewey says.

"No thanks." The less things messing with my Camdrone, the better. "Cam, pick up after that last video you showed us."

Cam beeps once and the feed pops up in my 'site now. I bump into another Maglan wandering these same alleys and she scowls at me.

"Hey, you're that one kid."

"Yeah, that's right," I say and give her my best smile. "It's always great to meet a—" My smile fades though as I see her sort of back away from me. "Wait, what do you mean?"

She trips over herself as she steps away, but her eyes are zipping side to side. She's calling for help.

"Dewey," I say, but before I can finish the bot has already stepped closer to her.

"Ma'am, are you all right?" Dewey places an arm securely around her shoulders.

The woman's eyes dart back and forth faster now. Her call is clearly being blocked. "It's him, from the video, you know? The one they're looking for." She tries to take a step back, but Dewey's grip is locked tightly onto her shoulder. She is staring at me again and Dewey is miming a gun to his own forehead behind her.

"No!" I say.

She's hauling in a deep breath, probably about to let out a scream but a dim blue glow and a few crackles later and the woman passes out. A couple of kids walk by and stop to stare. They're too busy looking at the woman who 'fainted' to notice me, and before they can get a good look, Rym has pulled me further into an alley. From the dark I see them walk away, hopefully without having made any calls.

"We're probably okay," Rym says. "They knew what they were getting into, walking in the back streets."

"What do you think she was talking about?" I say.

Dewey extracts a needle from the woman's neck.

"Wait, did you just kill her?"

"Don't be stupid," Dewey says. His eyes flash for a moment like he's having a seizure. "I just did a quick monitor of her 'site. It looks like you're wanted."

"Wanted?"

"For murder."

"Murder? What?"

"One of your rivals. It seems you could not stand that someone else is more popular than you and you eliminated them. Seems reasonable."

"Who was it?" My pulse races. "Kie?"

Dewey shakes his head and I sigh. He might be a girl-stealing dick, but I don't want him dead. But even if it wasn't Kie, did someone actually get killed? Or is this a cover up? If I could look at the footage, maybe I could tell.

"So now everyone thinks I . . ."

"Yes."

"Really?"

"With a bat."

"With a—?"

"Repeatedly to the head."

"All right, that's enough."

"We've got to disguise you," Rym says. "If we're in the alleys and you're still being spotted, that can't be good."

His eyes dart back and forth. "Dewey, we need a clothing store, quick. And not a sports equipment one for slugger here."

Dewey clicks and beeps for a second. "Right around the corner on the main Ring."

I step to the brighter lit street about fifty paces to the left but not before Rym puts a hand on my chest. "I don't think so. Dewey and me can handle it."

"You'll make it through, and not me?"

"Theoretically they're not even looking for us. Plus, this bot has a few upgrades that will help us out." Rym slaps Dewey on his metal back with an empty clang.

A slim arm extends out of Dewey's back like an eel. There are a couple of thin grabby grabby hands at the end and they click together quickly. Dewey's single eye blinks some sort of freaky wink.

"We'll be right back," Rym says. "Don't do anything stupid."

He hands me his flask and I swig another gulp of the tangy liquid. The familiar tingling sensation washes over me, radiating from my gut and into my fingers and toes. When the two of them leave, I don't sense Dewey's 'site blocker fade, maybe because the liquid is preventing me from connecting.

At least I can get closer to the street, right? This place has a stink in it like week-old dead yarel. I've got to get out into the open a little bit. The subdued lady is still out, breathing regularly, but still out. I place a few strips of garbage over her to hide her from anyone walking by. A slight breeze blows it off, exposing her closed eyes. I stoop to tuck the trash under her neck so it wraps around her. There. That'll stay.

Great. Look at me, I'm hiding an unconscious body under garbage. And acting normal.

Let's hope no one sees me. I can't imagine it helping the murder-with-a-bat image I have online. I get as far away from her as I can and watch Dewey and Rym cross the densely packed street up ahead. Waiting. I hate waiting. My heart races and a burning in my chest shortens my breath.

My eyes flit to the 'site on instinct, but there's still nothing there. This sucks. I check the progress on Cam's downloading. What? Still under one percent? This is going to take forever. I can try to watch it from where Cam left off last time, though. Something has to have gotten through.

But when I queue up Stell's message from earlier, the one where I swear I heard her talk, Cam can't even play it. I surf around until I see the inside of that temple and Stell sitting cross-legged, holding her arms in a meditating pose. She's floating again. Like two feet above the ground. I don't even know where to start with this. Some sort of camera trick?

"You're probably wondering how I can do this." I hear her voice, again with no lips moving. Can that be right? The vid quality isn't the best, maybe I missed it.

"You can do it, too. We all can. You have just forgotten."

Yeah yeah. The nanos.

"Yes, the nanos."

I swear that she's looking right into my eyes now.

"You need to block out the signal from Scitech. Then you need to quiet your mind."

Quiet my mind? What is she talking about?

"Breathe. Listen to the planet."

I glance around to see if anyone is watching. Nope, still in the shadows here.

"Breathe." Stell's voice fills my head.

There are too many Maglans running around. Too many sounds from the street beyond the alley. I can't possibly block out all that. I close my eyes.

"Breathe."

This time her voice is a whisper and sounds just like the wind blowing right through me. I pull in a deep breath of air and hold it, trying to calm the pounding in my chest.

"Hey!"

I shake my head and open my eyes to see Rym taking a knee and staring right in my face. He gently nudges my shoulder.

"You awake? Not a great time to take a nap."

"I didn't nap. You just left," I say.

"Really? We've been gone for a half hour looking for clothes. You've got a strange sense of time." Rym pulls me to my feet with a bit of a struggle. My legs are surprisingly stiff.

"Anyway, here's what we got you."

Dewey drops a load of clothing onto my head. There's a new set of pants, a hood shirt and some dark glasses. I quickly change into them and look at Rym. He's got his new gear on, too.

"Don't forget this." I rip off a price tag he forgot to remove from his brown headgear.

"Let's get moving," Rym says with a glance at the woman still out of it in the alley. "If she wakes and we're still here, she's sure to report us. My guess is when she gets up she'll have forgotten everything in the past hour, considering the shock level in Dewey's knock out. You didn't give her too much, did you?"

Dewey shrugs. "Minimal charge to cause partial memory loss."

Rym stares at him.

"I swear!"

As we leave this spot and the woman behind, I glance around. "Did you all hear something?"

Dewey pauses. "Beyond the street sounds, this woman's regular breathing, and your hearts racing, I'd say it's just your paranoia."

"Nice." But I still keep glancing over my shoulder as we move on and upward. "Can we at least still stick to the alleys?"

***

In between avoiding the streets and any cameras, it takes us an hour to reach the top of the city ring. This is definitely the upper-upper, I mean literally and also because of the upper crusty types that are starting to walk by out there. Even the alley is lighter and it smells cleaner. But that means security is tighter, too. I signal to Rym and Dewey and then point up to an enclosed camera device positioned at the corner of the main street and the alley.

"Nice call," Rym whispers and drags us off to the side. "I didn't even see it."

Dewey hangs his head.

"Apparently, Dewey didn't pick it up either."

"Don't feel bad," I say. "I've been ditching cameras since I was a kid. Kie and me would have to find spots to go jump our gliders off, and we didn't want anyone seeing us. Well, we did want to be seen, but we didn't want anyone to see how we got to our places."

"That'll help. If you keep your face covered we should be good." Rym yanks the drawstrings on my hood tighter. "We're almost there." He points with his chin up ahead.

"These are some pretty classy places." I haven't eaten at any of these restaurants, and I don't think I ever will. "How are you planning on getting your friend?"

Rym chuckles and looks at Dewey. "Well, neither of us can get too close to Neman. That restraining cycle in our nanos will send out an alarm and call the authorities if we get within a hundred paces of each other. Like I said, after the war, Scitech didn't want us seeing each other again."

"Won't the drink cancel it?"

Rym shrugs. "Maybe, but we ain't risking it."

"Well this is ridiculous, how are you going to plan anything if you can't even be seen together or hear each other?"

"Don't worry about that now," Rym says.

"And this will be the same thing for all of your other friends?"

"I said don't worry about the details now. We have a plan."

It finally hits me what he was trying to say earlier. "So you want me to break in, avoid security, find this Maglan who I don't know and who won't know me, and somehow convince him to escape with me to fight some sort of revolution?"

Rym nods. "Yeah, that sounds right."

Dewey pats my shoulder. "You can do it, kid. You're creative."

"And why don't we just wait to get him or her at home? Without anyone watching?"

"Security is actually tighter at home. At work, there's a lot less following around and wondering if he'll sneak off. See, he's a slicer. The best there ever was."

I roll my eyes and keep walking. "You've got a lot of *best evers* on your team."

"No, really. Neman could break into any computer, reprogram drones, anything. Dewey, show him the records."

I wave him off. "I believe you, all right? What does he do now? Does he work in that bank?" I point to the Sol Bank building encased in the ring up ahead. Black onyx exterior. "Probably some high tech trader earning money from buying and selling resources between cities."

"No," Rym says. "There."

I follow his finger to a towering spiral of a building up ahead. "The Mirage? The elite restaurant? That is seriously cool. Does he run their budget? Order food? Manage all employees?"

"Nope," Dewey says. "Dishwasher."

"What? How is that anything he'd choose to do? He could run companies based on what you told me."

"You make it sound like he has any choice," Rym says. "Scitech forced him to not go anywhere near computers or their tech bots anymore, in fear of what he might do if he had access to them. He signed a whole bunch of nondisclosure crap. He had to, or they'd kill him. Or put him in a cage forever."

Seems like they did just that. "And I'm going to go in and what, kidnap him?"

"He'll probably want to come with you, if you show him this." Rym gestures to Dewey. The bot's black arm snakes out toward Cam.

"Don't." I pull my arm away.

"Relax," Dewey says. "I'm just going to upload a message."

"Not going to happen. I'll think of something else."

"We got only one chance of doing this," Rym says.

I sigh. "Dewey said I'm creative. I'll figure this out. But, do you happen to have any rope?"

***

Walking up to the Mirage is harder than I thought. Well, walking up hidden, that is. In this district, everyone wants to be noticed. Not me, not today. I pull my hood down low over my eyes and pass a group of teens near the restaurant pretending to fit in even though I know they're not going in to eat. Not too long ago I was doing the same thing.

Despite it still being day, you can't really tell. The lighting around this place has to be perfect for anyone wanting to make an entrance. The Mirage takes a bunch of vids and makes them available for Maglans to purchase after their visit. Scitech invited me here to welcome me into their family a year or so ago and I remember the video footage I got from it. I watched the vids so many times to get it right before posting, I remember each and every angle from every camera. I'm pretty sure I still know where they're all set. Unless they added more.

Two on the entrance, three across the street, a couple of sweeper cams hovering up above. These things run continuously and when you want the footage, you just ping your 'site and it sends you your feed. For a charge, of course. It will also give you a special editing job with the different angles if you want, but I chose to mess with the stuff myself. You know, to give it the right music and cuts. Plus, I saved a lot of money that way.

As if on cue, a silver hover sled stops right in front of the restaurant. The door opens with an exhalation of fog and a long-legged lady steps out to the cheers and photo streams of everyone there.

Nice entrance.

Luckily, for now even though the cams are seeing me, they're not really seeing "me." They only key in on the 'site and I'm still feeling the tingling sensation from the juice, but it ain't going to last forever. I hurry across the street, not quite a run, but also probably not slow enough, just in case they wonder why they don't have any stats on someone walking past. Like a ghost. I gape up at the structures right above the restaurant, part of the ring's arch extending above. Man, we're really way up in the city.

"Cam," I whisper. "Add those cameras to your map."

I know I don't have to say it, Cam is way ahead of me from her fifth pass of the restaurant. I salute her, up there somewhere. I can't see her, but she's always watching. The direct feed to my link pad on my arm is flashing with the continual upload of her scan. She can't be down at ground level otherwise the security might pick up her movement and take her down. They don't want any other cameras doing their job. They want to make money selling their weak, however full, coverage of the entrance. *Proprietary videoing*, they call it.

In the corner of my 'site, Cam's footage of the Mirage comes together showing the exterior of the building and all the camera points surrounding it. Tons of coverage up at the front, and not much less in the back or around the sides. Security guards are everywhere, too. They don't want anyone sneaking in, much less getting a peek inside.

I try to zoom in on one of the windows, but when I scale in, I get a "blocked" alert. That just looks bad to anyone when you try to post a video showing how you saw someone famous and a floating banner pops up. I guess I can be happy knowing no one else will be able to spot me when I get too close.

So, the street side is not going to be the way I get in. And I don't know anything about sewer and water systems to be able to break in that way. I probably could have asked Rym. He seems to be the kind of guy who would wander around in crap like that.

But I don't have time to ask. My eyes go where they always go. Up.

Cam's map shows a clear entrance on the rooftop. Well, maybe not clear. Less secure than down below, I should say. No guards, but still plenty of cameras pepper the sides and are aligned along some other structures up there. Nothing Kie and I haven't snuck past before.

But how am I going to get up there? The Mirage towers over the buildings beside it. Whoever first built it wanted to make sure both structure and clients would be seen. The only thing taller is what's arching over it.

Well, that's it, then. My way in.

Too bad I'm not going to be able to post the vid once I make the jump off the ring onto the restaurant.

In five minutes, I'm past the buildings and facing the city's rigging. Cam's continual updates to the specs of the restaurant point the way through the camera zones so that I have a clear path. Aw man, how come I never thought of this when I snuck around before? I sidestep around the nearby building and grip onto the framework of the city.

And slip back down, crashing hard onto my heels. My teeth rattle with the impact. I twist my arms over to check them and notice a trickle of blood running down the palm of my upper left hand. Am I really this much out of practice?

"Check status." I scan through my 'site for any irregularities in my system.

Nothing.

"Check status." This time I also manually key in the request with my eyeboard. Man, I haven't had to use this for a long time.

No response again. Just a little flashing cursor in the lower corner of the 'site. I sift through the files onboard the memory system, specifically the support functions of my nanos.

All the programs are there. Agility. Muscle enhancers. But they're offline.

"Oh shit."

I key in the reboot sequence and wait a minute. And then another.

"Everything okay in there?" Rym's voice comes over the secure channel.

"Yeah, why?"

"Because you're still on the ground. Didn't you say you were going up?"

I swing my arms around in circles and take a deep breath. Nope. The enhancement programs are definitely not working. "I ran into a bit of a problem, but I'm all right now."

What would Kie say? Probably something like, "You climb that thing, and I'll stay down here shooting your footage."

Yeah, he'd get some pretty good views from "The fall of Daj: dropping to his grisly death!" video.

A gust of wind rocks the girder next to me and it creaks slightly as it sways. All right, it may be only slightly, but I feel the creak right through my entire body. My hearts skip and I grip on with all my hands and legs and give another try to climb this thing. I swear, if I ever make this climb and come back down, I'm definitely going to get my tech back.

I can hear Ms. Pontane now. "Of course we can help get your system back. You can get your streams online, too."

Maybe it won't be too bad. But what could I tell them? They tricked me? Forced me to do it? I'd get in their good graces for turning in these criminals, right? All would be forgotten and I'd be back in the running to follow my parents.

Who am I kidding? I'm one of the criminals now.

Each grip I make onto the metallic structure I double then triple make sure it's solid. Are there any mag boots around? They have to have a security set around here for any Maglan who needs to go up and replace a light or whatever. No luck, though. This whole area is off limits, probably only tech bots allowed up here.

The top of the ring arches high over the city and right over the Mirage. And that's where I'm going. What was my plan anyway? I'd wipe the sweat off my forehead if it didn't mean letting go of the framework. At least I'm getting up there. I glance down to see how far.

Nope.

I've only climbed about ten feet.

There's still time to go back. Come up with a different plan. Or just bug out completely. But then I remember Stell. Captured by Scitech. Probably scared for her life.

No. Not scared. I can just hear her now, laughing at me to 'trust in myself,' or something. A vision of her floating right off the Edge that first day I met her passes through my mind. How did she do that? Some trick, right? What did she say, that I had to calm down, and breathe?

Holy shit. How long have I been climbing? The city spins in my eyes pretty far down now, I don't even know the distance. I only know I would make a pretty impressive splat if it came to it. My arms ache under the weight of my body being pulled by the planet below me.

Okay, breathe.

A few more dozens of feet ahead and I can be above the Mirage. Not that it's a big cushion for me to drop on, but it'd be closer, and less splatty. I'm almost fully inverted now and my muscles are burning and new trickles of blood make their way down my arm. A few more feet. A few more excruciating feet. My muscles burn and my fingers scream at me.

Down under me, like right below about thirty feet down, is the rooftop. I loop the cable Dewey kept linked into his guts onto the framework. I rest for a minute, but my arms are still shaking. I'm not going to make it much longer, so I slowly begin to let myself down toward the restaurant. Cam beeps and I jerk to a halt.

"What?" I attempt to say, but it comes out as only a pained wheeze. I see what she's pointing out. In the holo map she made there are a couple of cameras panning back and forth over the top of the building and just right next to me. Any lower and they'll pick me up, if they haven't already done so. But alarms would be going off if that were the case, so I've got a few more seconds anyway.

"Rym? Dewey? Now!"

In a space of seconds that feels like an eternity, I slowly rotate at the end of my line. Cheering and whooping from the crowd rise up through the darkening skies to where I'm dangling and I arch my neck to see what it is. A huge group of Maglans cluster around the front of the Mirage as a levitating car pulls up. Not just any car, but a slick black stretch limo hovering above the street level. Music thuds from inside the vehicle as it slows down and it has its own light show. Laser lights flash off its reflective surface in all directions.

I don't have to check to see that all the cameras are now pointing at the newcomer, not that I can, anyway. My arms, almost on their own will, quickly let the line out and lower me to the rooftop. Flashes of light stream past and one catches me in the eye.

"Might be overdoing it now, Rym." It's a good idea though, hopefully blinding the cameras and not just my eyes.

In a few moments, the car will reach the entrance and then the cameras will return to normal. I'm getting closer, but all of a sudden the cable seizes up and jerks me back and forth. I'm at the end of it, and there's still a good twenty or so feet left to the rooftop. I can make it, right?

Rym has only given me a couple of seconds here, since there's no one coming out of the car. I can't imagine him being able to find a big name to do this. It's now or I'm caught. I reach for the cable release clip and vertigo, or something, I've never felt anything like it, grips my chest. I can't breathe. I've got to get back up there, I've got to...

"Breathe."

It's Stell's voice or I'm going crazy.

So I do. I take in a deep breath, and as I start to let it out I push the release button.

Everything seems to slow down. Flashing lights. The spinning in my head. And I'm falling.

And then I slam into the roof, flat on my back, forcing out the air in my lungs.

"Nice entrance." I get to my knees, fighting for a breath. For once I hope Cam hasn't caught me on video. But how did I not break anything? I must have rolled right. Not the most graceful of landings, but at least I'm here. Safe. For a moment, anyway. Right beside my neck a metal pipe is sticking straight up. Damn, if I had fallen a foot to the left.

I stumble to my feet and search for an entrance. Peeking over the edge, I see the limo slowly driving away, its booming neighborhood-shaking music lessens as it retreats. And the sorrow of the onlookers makes its way up to me as well, lamenting the loss of some mystery celebrity who only wanted to cause a scene. A brief image of Dewey sitting in the back of the car cranking the music makes me laugh. Or was it Rym? Nice little distraction, guys.

Oh crap, the cameras.

Those few seconds of being camera-free have to be up, and I'm out in the open. I see a few ways into the building, but I'm pretty sure most would be monitored. Not the vents, though. I scurry over to the grate-covered structure, feeling more exposed than ever. With a few quick tugs, the grating comes free and I climb in. It's confined and pretty steep, but I feel much better in this than free-falling off the ring structure up above.

"Come on, Cam!"

The hovering drone homes into her arm dock and makes a satisfying click. I pull the grate back over my head and begin the next descent, this time into the thick smells of the restaurant. Every food smell I can think of wafts past me from below and my stomach rumbles loudly. The last thing I remember eating was some tasteless bread Rym had in his pack.

Something about Skywatch rations. "We ate it all the time," he said. No wonder they all quit, they never got a decent meal.

With my stomach clenched in hunger knots, I jimmy myself through the narrow conduit. Music also winds its way through the system, which is good because I'm pretty sure I need something to cover up the loud grunts and bangs I make as the metal walls pop in and out. It's clean in here, though. Not much dust. At least I won't have to worry about the laser cleaning service to come through here, as well.

Unless I get jammed and stuck and—

Stop. My breathing has quickened and I'm freaking out, and Cam's insistent beeping reminds me about it all the time. Which isn't particularly helping me not feel claustrophobic. I'm not going to be here when the lasers do their thing.

At least the Maglans down below are having fun. Dancing, eating, making vids of themselves. I peek out through the next intake grate. That was me before all this. I could change it back, right now. A drop from here would make a pretty impressive entrance.

Next time.

Instead, I continue inching my way through until I follow Cam's suggested directions into the next room. The kitchen, if my nose has anything to say about it. The intensity of the spices in the air ups a level so much that my eyes water. One glance through a grate here and, if I thought the dance floor was crazy, the amount of dodging and throwing and maneuvering of chefs and waiter bots tops everything I've seen.

At least I think so until I crawl beyond this to the next room. It's the dishroom. And it's nuts. What look like waiter bots are each tasked with organizing dishes into cleaning racks, removing cleaned plates and dishware, and not breaking a single one.

I crawl to the far side of the room and kick the grating. It pops out and I land on my feet with a thud. In one surreal second, the bots stop what they're doing and scan me. In the next, half of them scurry away like bugs under sinks and counters, and the rest quickly change their posture and pace. Now they look like wait staff who just happened to walk into the wrong place.

In one corner of the room, a hugely overweight Maglan stands up, somewhat slowly, gripping onto the railing next to him to support his bulk. Right behind him, a wall of screens flashes brightly with many images. Games, races, scantily-clad if not nothing-clad men and women dancing around. The Maglan gestures with his head and a wall drops down to cover the screens.

"You lost?" he asks. It's a thick, deep voice. Used to eating whatever he wants whenever he wants. Bits of his last meal sit skewered onto his stubby face spikes.

For a moment, I am about to ask where I could find a master slicer named Neman. But it's all pretty clear. "So they all work for you?"

Neman scratches his chin, wiping the steam of the dishroom from his face. It definitely ain't sweat from him doing any of the work. I still hold out some hope though, if this guy's Skywatch…

"I'm with Rym, we need your help."

A wide grin breaks out over his purple face. "You can come back out."

The bots, as quickly as they disappeared, pop out from wherever they hid and resume their work. Neman settles back with a deep groan into the groove of his well-worn chair. He strokes his face spikes, flicking bits of food off them.

"Not many come in that way," he gestures to the ceiling. "I guess I have to install cameras there now, too. That way I won't look like I have my pants down when someone drops in unexpectedly."

I shudder, glad I didn't have to witness that. "I'm here to bust you out of this place. We need your help."

"I heard you the first time." Neman flips open the screens and resumes watching the many shows and games.

"We're going to break into a base and you—"

"I'm going to stop you right there, kid. I haven't seen Rym in years. Years. Look around. Why would I ever want to leave this place? I've got everything I want. I do what I like, all day long. I come to 'work,' I make money on games and races, I get to slice up bots to do my job. Mirage thinks their bots break down but it's me repurposing them." He doesn't even look away from his screens to talk at me.

"You're kidding, right?" This isn't quite what I was expecting. A little gratitude, a little eagerness to escape, something. But not this. "Scitech put you here. And they're keeping you here. You aren't free. You're just trapped in their little world, you fat piece of shit."

That gets him to look up. "Look, do you want to leave the way you came in, or can I show you another?" He points to the dish line and a wide circular hole making grinding noises and spitting out chunks of bone and other bits. The bots enter a new subroutine and they all stop to stare at me with red eyes.

Okay, that wasn't what I was expecting either. A mean, desperate old slicer. "Come on, can't you see they're controlling you? Stopping you from doing what you do best?"

Hah. Now I'm starting to sound just like Rym.

"Why did you sign up for this in the first place?" I pull up my sleeve and show him the glowing tattoo of the Skywatch symbol. Its diamond shapes light up with a rainbow of colors.

"That's not a tattoo, it's a stupid program." After a second, the tattoo on my arm flashes once then disappears entirely.

"How did you do that?" I ask.

"Hello, what is that?" Neman legitimately hustles to his feet, something I didn't think was probable.

He's got his eyes on my arm and I take an involuntary step back toward the food/Maglan disposal unit. It's Cam. He can't take his eyes off of Cam.

"I can't control it," Neman says.

His fingers twitch, all twenty of them. I don't like it.

"That's an original Camdrone, a Mark I. Pre-Scitech. Do you know how rare that thing is? It is completely off Scitech's radar. They can't touch it. Give it to me."

I hold my arm over the disposal. "Don't move."

Cam beeps questioningly at me.

I give her a little shake of my head.

"Look, I know you're bullshitting me, kid. You know what you've got there. Some family heirloom, right? I just want to see it."

I sigh. "Come with me, and us, and you can see it all you want. *See*."

Neman glances back at his screens, then to Cam. Then back again. Dude, he's like a spoiled kid. An old spoiled kid as wrinkled and gray as Rym. I don't know how he survived this long.

He gives a sigh that sounds like an oversized beast's wheeze. "All right."

"Good. But how the hell are we going to sneak out of here?"

"Don't worry," Neman says. "I'll just do what I do best."

***

Seems like the patrons of the Mirage all like one thing. Making a scene. So when the all-bot dance troupe makes their way across the floor performing their one night only dance number, "Dish Dish," complete with song, light show, and flinging plates, everyone wants to be a part of it.

A few guest dancers from the audience join in as the bots end up on the stage, edging off the live confused singer. I only wish I could stay and see it all, but I'm walking casually behind Neman's bulk trying not to be noticed.

We're almost at the main entrance when I grab onto Neman's shoulder. "We're effed. Look."

Up ahead, just making her way into the restaurant club, is Ms. Pontane. She's all decked out, silvery dress and her hair up. I'd say she's looking good, except she's an evil, corporate bitch. She's with a very tall Maglan female, her smokin' date.

"Well hot damn," Neman says.

"Stop drooling, you're old enough to be their grandpa. And stop taking vids of them." For later, no doubt. Ew.

I'm clutching a plate like some sort of disk weapon, ready to huck it at anyone who makes a move. After a few seconds, I'm starting to think she's not here looking for me or Neman. They're just dancing together, trying to get into the scene like everyone else.

"They're going to see us. Can't you get your bots to do something?"

Neman turns his head back to me, an obvious strain by the grimace he tries to hide, and then he winks at me.

There's a sudden break in the bot dance number as it swells to its crescendo finale. All lights form a line across the dance floor up to Ms. Pontane and the bots push the crowd back. There's another chorus of the song and plates whiz back and forth around Ms. Pontane and her partner as they are escorted to the stage. It's clear that she's pretending to fight them off and finally makes it onstage. Everyone cheers, including a group of onlookers from outside clogging the doorway.

But not us. We're pushing through the door with every last eye and camera on the stage, not on the now silent black hover limo slipping up to the entrance, opening its doors, and hoisting Neman into the back seat. I shut the door behind me and as the car pulls away, I give Rym a wry smile.

"Who's next?"

CHAPTER 10

Rym clasps Neman's arm around his wrist in a strange sort of greeting as the limo speeds away from the Mirage.

"Good to see you, old friend," Rym says. "All of you. Damn, Neman."

Neman settles back into the cushy chair. "They didn't let me out much."

"Apparently. Now have a drink." Rym signals to Dewey who serves up eight shots of bright red liquor and hands them out. The two old men take four each and down the first one quickly.

"What about me?"

Rym raises an eyebrow. "You, *kid*? I don't think you can handle this. It's an old Maglan's drink."

I shake my head and beckon to Dewey to serve me, too. Dewey complies and soon I'm staring into the thick liquid. I don't wait long and upend the contents into my mouth.

It takes all I've got to not spit out the fire drink. The insides of my mouth light up, not to mention the trail of explosives burning down my throat. When I can speak, it's a harsh whisper. "What is this expensive piss?" Because that's pretty much what it tastes like.

Rym laughs. "Pre-Tech Suin. I had to get this special for tonight. They don't make this anymore, or if they do it's done underground. It was found to burn out nanos in some cases."

Neman clinks his glass against Rym's. "Sweet, sweet Suin. Been a long time since we had this."

Great, now along with the fire in my chest, my head feels like it's swelling up, so I grip both sides of it. Wow, this is strong stuff. Through my hazy thoughts, something hits me.

"Wait, wasn't some sort of alarm supposed to go off when you two got close together? That means they're able to track us, right?"

Rym frowns and types something into the pad next to the window. The limo slows down and takes a turn.

"Nah, not five minutes after you're inside the Mirage, I get a message from this piece of shit."

"Hey!" Neman feigns hurt from the statement. "I said I was sorry."

"Bastard debugged that subsystem years ago." Rym sits there with full shot glasses in three hands. "Said he was too ashamed to call me after that." He glares at his old partner who doesn't look back.

Neman just drinks his last two shots in silence.

"Well, this is a great start," I say. "Don't be dicks to each other. You haven't seen each other in years. Finish your sucky drinks, make up, and let's find the next one."

"Yeah." Rym puts the glasses down as the limo glides to a halt. "We're here. Neman, wipe this memory system clean."

"Yeah, who needs *please* anymore." Neman finishes his drinks, tosses the glasses to the floor and pulls a wire from his wrist. From inside his wrist.

"Dude," I say. He's pulling the wire out from inside his arm along with some residual goo. "That shit is gross."

He connects the interface to the pad to the car panel with a little click. "This 'shit' is so I can make a connection with the records in this vehicle. In the Mirage I linked up to the wireless tech to get those bots to do what I wanted." He steals a glance at Cam, still attached to my arm dock.

A few seconds and a couple of beeps later the doors open to let us out. "They won't ever know we were here." Neman hauls himself with loud groans and wheezes toward the door of the vehicle. "I even gave them a five-minute future burn."

"Good, because it's going to take you five minutes to get out of the car," I say.

Rym, despite his argument earlier, gently grips onto Neman's left arms and Dewey onto his right. Without a word, they extricate his bulk from the confines of the limo into an empty alley. We're down near the ground level of Phen and no one is even watching for us, or anything.

"I was able to clear most of the cameras on the way here," Neman says. "But I couldn't get into all of them right outside the club." The black car silently drives its way up the ring.

"How long before they start looking for you?" Rym says.

Neman shrugs. "My bots can cover for me, and my shift lasts for another three hours. Unless they notice something wrong, of course, and then who knows?"

"That should give us enough time," Rym says.

"Time for what?" Neman asks.

"It's complicated," Dewey says. "First we need to hijack a cruiser. Then we will fly to the Scitech main orbital station and send a transmission to the entire planet to start a revolution."

There's a few seconds of stunned silence. "Maybe I should have asked that before I got into this mess." Neman scrapes something from under a fingernail. "Which reminds me. The kid here promised me a look see at his little drone."

I instinctively pull back the arm Cam is settled on. "I don't want your grubby fingers on my—"

"You know, I could just call that ride back here." Neman's eyes flick to the side and the brake lights pop up on the black limo almost out of sight.

"Let him see the thing, kid," Rym says. "He's not going to hurt it."

I know he's not going to hurt it. It's those twitchy fingers that make me nervous. And what I remember about him controlling every bot in that restaurant. "Do anything to her and I'll…"

Neman grins and reaches out with all four hands as I extend my arm. "I know, I know. Don't worry."

The little latch clicks holding Cam to my forearm and she hesitantly hovers. She glances back to me before I allow Neman to handle her. He's giggling like a child now, expectantly awaiting a gift.

"It's all right. Go ahead," I say.

She whines but still drifts to his outstretched hands. He grasps her wings and under-rigging gently, turning her over with this gleam in his eye. A large sigh escapes his mouth, but not without a bit of sadness. "She's perfect. Reminds me of the one I had. As a kid."

"I don't think she's the same one." I hope she's not.

He mumbles something and his shoulders sink a little but only for a second. He holds her in his open hand, palm up and Cam beeps at him, a plaintive little sound, and he smiles at her. With a quick whir, she flies up and back to my arm, clicking safely into place.

"Happy?" Rym says.

Neman nods. "I noticed a bunch of encrypted vids on her. Need them opened?"

"I can open them if I need to." I don't ask the obvious question about how the hell he was able to spot them so quickly without even interfacing.

"Can we go save the world now that you've played with a toy again?" Rym asks.

"Sure, why not? I figure you're after our old crew, right? We're facing west, and that means quarries, and that means Jali."

"Jali?"

Rym nods at me. "Gunner. Marksman. Best on a ship. Best on the ground."

A gunner? An expert sniper? That sounds bad ass.

Rym motions to follow, since Neman is already shuffling up ahead. He can move his body mass pretty quickly. Well, quicker than I thought he would. But who knows how long he can keep it up?

"And you need me to debug the rest of the crew," Neman says.

"We're also going to need to hit different sites around the city, so we don't raise too much suspicion about stealing the ship. In fact, why don't you help me out with something?" Rym falls in close with Neman so I can't hear them talk.

Dewey sidles up to me and hands me a glass of a red liquid.

"I don't want any more of that crap." I push the drink back at him.

"No, you still need this stuff. It is not the Suin from earlier, but I think in the long run they'd have the same effect on you."

All right, I can deal with this. I swig the signal blocking drink and shiver as it does its thing. "Do we have enough of this stuff?"

Dewey pauses. "For now. And hopefully we won't need it forever, now that we have him." He gestures to Neman who is busy linking that interface on Rym's forearm. "He says he can debug the Scitech alarm in Rym. Perhaps even kill your signal for good."

"He kind of creeps me out. Have you noticed how weird he gets around bots?"

"It is what he knows," Dewey says. "When I first met him, he was always good with tech. He really likes to understand how things work. Even if it is, like you say, a bit creepy sometimes."

I pat Cam's chassis and fall behind a step. Did he mess with Cam? Stick that interface wire where he shouldn't have? I'll shove it in his eye if he touched her. With a few quick swipes across the interface link, I run a quick diagnostic scan. Hell, I even punch in a long- term one for kicks. That'll take longer, but I can see if anything was planted.

Data vid log. That ought to be a good start, anyway. Escape ride in the limo, bot dance number in the Mirage, my entrance onto the roof. Wait, what the hell?

There's me, up above the Mirage, grasping onto the ring and looking like a total weakling. I guess that's what I look like with no nano tech. I almost scan forward, but then I start to lower myself on that cable. There I am, at the end of it, dangling above the roof. That's a big drop, man. That should have killed me, or at least broken a few bones.

I'm pausing now, doing that breathing thing. And then I let go and fall. But there's something weird before I hit the roof, something awkward. I scan back and play it again. There's a weird jerking motion in the fall. I play it again and again. Yeah, there's definitely something going on with it. Was there something about the roof? Did they have a mag cushion installed? No, why would they? But what?

Me?

I start laughing. Right. That's Nonno talk. Eldane talk.

But I still can't get my head around it, what I saw Stell do up in the Rings that first day I met her. That vid of her back in the octahe-whatever it was. I did feel something when she was with me. I watch the video one more time.

Nah. Just a stupid glitch in the recording.

"Come on," Rym yells back to me, snapping me out of my thoughts. "We got a slow ride."

An empty mineral cart floats above the surface of the rocky ground, bobbling slightly under the combined weight of Rym, Dewey and Neman. But mostly Neman. Rym reaches out and pulls me up onto the flat bed.

"It's not monitored, or at least it isn't now."

Neman inclines his head slightly, making sure I know that's his work.

"We'll be there in an hour or so. Better get some rest."

A yawn splits my face. Yup, that sounds like a good idea. What doesn't sound good is that pack of yarels squabbling over some dead thing off the side of the road. A pack that size could swarm us and leave behind our bones. If we're lucky. Rym draws his pistol and steadies it on the side rail as we approach.

"No, wait!" I put my hand on his and he frowns at me. "I think I know this one."

"What are you talking about?"

A lone yarel stands apart from the others, staring at us. At me. It can't be, but it has to be, unless there are more special cases like this one.

"Fiver?"

The ragged beastie doesn't growl or approach us, it just stares at me. Me. I don't know what else to do when we coast by besides wave at him. Maybe a him. "So long, Fiver!"

He doesn't look away and soon we're passing a turn and the yarels are behind us.

"Fiver?" Neman says.

"Not the first time I've seen him, or the second." I laugh. "Like it's following me, right?"

Neman and Rym just shrug and get back to their close talk. Me, I'm about to sleep where I stand.

"Take another swig first," Dewey says.

I grab a drink of the berry liquid and make my way silently to the back, kicking up dust as I do. No padding anywhere, but that isn't going to matter since my body is aching all over anyway. I drop to the deck and I flip through Cam's video files, back to the beginning.

"Hey little guy."

That's my dad.

"We love you."

And Mom.

I fall asleep with thoughts of my parents floating and falling in space.

***

"Get up."

Okay, it's not really a voice, but a throbbing pain in my, well, whole body, that wakes me up. Not the best rest, but I suppose that's what you get when you fall asleep on a minecart with an uneven metal grating. It's not just me. Rym grips the cart's side rail with two hands and rubs the back of his neck with his other. His long face spikes are disheveled. Even Dewey, usually ready with a quip for anyone, silently paces across the decking.

The only one who looks to be enjoying himself is Neman. He's still sprawled out across the deck, snoring like an engine. That's what woke me. I thought for sure the cart was misfiring.

The environment has changed since we left the gentle hills near Phen. Jagged mountains reach past the clouds. Long valleys stretch for miles, their sides exposed from drilling, blasting, and excavating for the Mag ore. Dozens of full mine trucks hover past us back to the refineries. Somehow I know this is Mag ore. I can feel it. Well, there are also the carts labeled "Mag ore," but I also somehow know it. That sounds stupid, right?

Our cart veers off to the right from the line leading to the mines.

"Jali doesn't work in the mines?"

Rym shakes his head and nudges Neman awake with his foot. "She doesn't work at all. Lives out here in the wastes somehow. Not much grows out here, can't be a lot of water."

"She?"

Rym nods. "Yes, she. Why can't the best gunner tech be female?"

"They can, I mean, why not?"

"She thought of herself as male, too," Neman says, half awake. "So don't fret yourself."

The mine cart comes to a gliding halt behind a row of mine refuse.

"Come on, doesn't look like we can ride the cart from here." Rym and Dewey jump off and lead the way up the steep pathway through the valley. The moons cast their light upon us, and since it's a Two Full, it's almost as bright as day.

"What about him?" I thumb back to Neman sitting on the cart deck.

"Don't worry about me, pretty boy." Neman stifles a yawn. "I have things I'm working on."

He sure doesn't look like it. But I guess since Rym trusts him, I should. I pat the pistol at my side, making sure I can get to it in a real emergency. Or if I just have to shoot Neman in his stupid smirking face.

***

"How far is Jali?" I'm wishing I did more cardio. My hearts are pumping crazy trying to keep up with the two of these guys through the hills.

"Not really sure," Rym shouts back. "I haven't seen her in years. Been keeping track of her pings whenever I can, and they point to her out here."

"So you're just assuming she's out here."

Rym takes a long draw on his water pack as he waits for me to catch up. "Yes. But it's a damn good assumption. Here."

He hands me the pack and, despite the heavy breathing, I manage to rehydrate, if not respond.

"I never said it, but you did a nice job back there at the restaurant, kid."

"Really? Thanks. You should have seen it. I—"

"Yeah, Neman told us all about it."

Well, okay then. If he doesn't want to hear what I have to say I've got my 'site. I instinctively flick my eyes to access my feed, to see something good, but there's nothing there. Still blocked. Blocked. Blocked. That's fine, I'll play a game. I scan the files I downloaded directly to my drive and hit Flipit. Instantly the colorful lines fill my eyes and the sound pumps directly into my ear nerves.

"You look drunk," Rym says with a laugh.

I don't respond and stumble again as I try to play and maneuver the uneven terrain. It doesn't work. I stub my toe and scrape my hands on the rocks as I try to grab a hold. A little embarrassed and pissed, I turn off the game. I don't want to let Rym know about it, though, so I stay shut up while we head through the quarry.

***

There's more to this place as I walk and look around. Tiny creatures flit here and there. Bulbous, waxy-leaved plants hide in the shadows. Even some lazy, orange-scaled rackards bask in the moonlight. They're a lot bigger than I've seen before. Well, I've really only seen them in science vids before, actually.

"We should be there shortly," Dewey says. "I have calculated our distance relative to her last ping."

"When was that?" Rym asks.

"Two months ago."

So she might not even be out here anymore. Great.

A deep rumbling shakes the ground beneath my feet and the walls of the canyon vibrate. Dust and pebbles fall from above but hesitate in the air, caught by the mag field.

"It seems really strong out here," I say.

No joke, there are a few big boulders suspended and twisting mid-air. A group of the long-tailed orange rackards clamber around the rotating rocks, jockeying for position. When one reaches the top, another rackard already up there jumps off and glides to another stone. Its tail stretches, as if it's trying to catch more of the mag field.

"She chose this place so she could block out any signal."

"You're smarter than you look," Rym says. "We used to all come out here as kids. Sail around on the fields and shoot stuff like idiots. Jali always loved this place the most, though. Before it got tore up to shit, of course."

We walk for maybe five more minutes until the landscape really opens up. That trail we had been walking on had to have been an old mine road, because we're looking at a crazy deep quarry right now. I peek over the ledge in front of me to see the vast pit opening into darkness. Massive boulders float and tumble over themselves in the pit, suspended in the strong field here, too.

"Down there," Dewey says. "The exact ping location originated from below."

"Down there?" I point to the stone staircase.

"As good a place as any," Rym says and begins to descend. "If I was hiding from everyone, seems like it would do the trick."

I click Cam's manual release dock and she takes off.

"*Scanning depths*," she responds on my wrist.

These stairs are narrow, only one of us can go at a time. And there's no railing. Who constructed this? "I don't think Neman would have enjoyed this."

I know I'm not.

I take a few more steps and run my hands over the rough hewn walls. Massive holes spot the wall, probably there for holding cranes and crew. Right now they make this whole section look like skulls with empty eye sockets. It's creepy.

It's getting pretty dark, too. The moons up above aren't exactly overhead anymore. In fact, the last edge of Cadea slips past. This means all the indirect light is gone and the only way to see is coming from Dewey's lamp.

No sound either, except for the occasional rock plinking down the stairs and the spinning, floating boulders crunching into each other. Echoes reverberate down the wide quarry opening. Small creatures flit back and forth across the rocks.

Cam appears out of the dark with an excited beeping and I nearly dump in my pants. She floats toward me, swerving around the debris in the air. A holo projection of the quarry flickers above her dock on my arm as my heart rate slows back down to normal. Man, these stairs just keep going.

"Warn me next time," I say under my breath. She beeps an apology and zips back into the main chamber.

Three little red lights show up on the map where me, Rym, and Dewey are on the steps. Relative to the whole thing, we're not even close to reaching the bottom.

"Guys, I don't think Jali is down here. We're the only things moving around in here. Look."

I show the map to them.

"What are those, then?" Rym points to the other new red images appearing around us.

"I think we had better head back up," Dewey says and the upper portion of his body does a 180 and he marches double time.

"Slow down!" I yell from behind now. The light from the map isn't enough to see the floor, or anything else.

Dewey slows for Rym and me to catch up and he shows his lights on the walls. Onto the holes. He gets closer, props his hands onto the edge and turns his audio inputs toward the wall.

"Dude, I think we should just get out of here." I nudge Rym upward to get him to move.

"Dewey?" Rym whispers.

"Very interesting sounds from inside these—"

A red and very large tentacle grabs Dewey's arm and in one yanking movement they both disappear into the hole. A scraping sound of metal on stone grates in my ears, possibly Dewey trying to claw into the wall.

"Dewey!" Rym yells and points his pistol into the hole. "Kid, get over here, I need that light."

I've got the only light source now, even if it is a weak holo map. But it's Cam that comes to give more help by hovering over my head and shining her light into the hole. The interior of the hole glows slightly, not really enough to see twenty or so feet inside, and not nearly far enough for Rym to be able to shoot anything.

And that's when Dewey comes flying out of the hole. He crashes into Rym who then bumps into me. I teeter on the edge of the steps for a millisecond and then tumble back.

"Kid!" Rym yells.

I flail wildly and grip onto the stairs with two of my arms and Dewey grabs onto another one. I slam my body, face first, into the wall and pain erupts through me. The tentacle, not happy with Dewey's bio content, apparently, now grabs onto Rym. Dewey latches onto Rym's deformed arm, now torn between saving me or his friend. His glowing eye flits back and forth between us.

"What are you doing? I've got this. Save him!" My fingers start to slip from the crumbling edges of the steps. "Save Rym!"

"Sorry!" Dewey lets go and grips onto Rym.

My full weight bears down on my two top hands, straining all my muscles in a fiery grip. I'm going to die here. This is where Daj, sports deck celebrity and stunt master, finally checks out. Stunts. Fat help those are now, with my nanos out of commission.

Breathe.

Seriously? Right now? I'm about to peel off this wall in about five seconds and the ghost voice tells me to breathe?

But I do it anyway. What the hell else am I going to try? I breathe.

It doesn't help me up, but when I concentrate, I can feel something beyond my body. The power in this pit. All around me. Calling to me. Well, maybe that's just Rym screaming as he's about to be ripped in half by that wall monster. Keep it down Rym, huh? I'm trying to listen to the call of the planet here.

There it is. The resonating feeling through my guts, vibrating my every cell. It's like I was born to...

Jump.

And I do, for shit's sake. I jump. Right off the wall, pushing off the rock as hard as I can with my feet and arms. For a moment I'm hanging there, with my arms all outstretched doing a glorious backwards swan dive. They say your life slows down and passes before your eyes right before you die. Well, I must be really dying because everything is slowing way down.

And then there's nothing. No motion. No sound. Am I doing it? Am I flying?

A crunching grinds through my skull as I collide with one of those floating boulders and answers my question with a resounding *no*. With all of my remaining strength and panic, I spin around and try to grasp onto the rock, to anything, with all my limbs. It ain't pretty, but I scramble until I get a grip and when I do, sweet god, I'm never letting go. The boulder, however, has other ideas. My weight starts to spin it, rotating me underneath and I shift my weight and arms to try to hold on.

"Help!" Dewey says, almost with a tone of panic in his computerized voice.

"Really?" I say.

I crank my neck backwards toward him as I readjust my grip to stop from slipping. Even though Dewey's internal cannon panels are opened, at this angle he can't fire at the tentacle with Rym right in front of him. Rym still doesn't seem to be enjoying this tug of war, either.

I've got my pistol, but I won't be able to get a clear shot of those tentacles unless I'm up higher. I'm hanging suspended from this stone about twenty or so feet out in the pit, not close enough to jump to the staircase. I try swimming with a free arm, but it does nothing, except look pretty stupid, I guess.

Another rock bumps into mine, and I spin in the opposite direction. Soon I'm on the topside of this one and I adjust my weight so that the thing stops moving. More rocks surround me, up and down.

All right, Rym, I'm coming.

Breathe. Okay, I'll do that first. That seemed to do something last time.

I leap from the rock toward the large one that just struck me, but I misread the floater. Something about 'equal and opposite' spits through my head, some motion law thingy. Whatever it is, eff physics, man, because I lose my footing without a solid jump. Somehow, though, I'm in the air clutching onto the bigger rock up above.

Okay, never mind. I love you, physics. This one appears more stable. Maybe it's the size or the care in which I'm scrambling up its side. Somehow I get up and I'm on my feet, trying to ignore the burning all over my hands. Hands? Hell, my whole body. I turn around and leap to another boulder. This time I anticipate the flip it takes when I land and I ride it through, tucking my weight below until I spin right side up. I draw my pistol from my belt and look down at Dewey. He's got his head in the hole and I don't have a clear shot.

"Dewey, pull him out so I can shoot at the thing!"

Dewey beeps and he's bobbing in and out, like he's fighting with something underwater. He feints once and the tentacle rips him back in, but that move unbalances it. Dewey plants his feet against the wall and yanks, pulling Rym and the red skinned thing out with him. There's my shot.

I line up and squeeze the trigger. A flash of light jets out of the end directly into the tentacle. The blast cuts right through the flesh and Dewey pulls Rym out with the thing still attached to his waist. Rym pushes it off and waves up to me, giving me a salute at the end of it.

"Look out!"

Another arm slides out of the hole in the wall, but Dewey pulls Rym up a few steps out of the way. It keeps coming out, seeking out its prey blindly. A smaller rock floats past me, and I give it a kick. Yes, I get pushed the opposite way, thank you very much, action reaction, but the smaller rock moves faster than I do. It moves even faster than I thought it would, and when it hits the creature square on, right in the hole, it actually jams right into it. The end of the tentacle falls off, pinched off from the force of the boulder.

As I glide peacefully across the gap, ducking other rocks as they spin nearby, I watch Dewey and Rym stumble up the steps. In this light I can't really tell, but Rym's shirt is darker around his stomach area. That's when I see them.

More friggin' tentacles stretching out from the holes up above. I'm starting to think maybe this Jali set that ping off in this pit as a trap. All I know is I'm going to have a few words with her when I get out of this place.

"Hello down there!"

A bright light flips on at the top of the pit, some fifty or so feet away, shining its light down on us, but also on a Maglan wearing a wide brimmed hat and sporting a hunting rifle. Some of the tentacles respond to this light and retract into their holes, but some apparently aren't too willing to let go of a free meal.

"Jali?" Dewey shouts up.

"Don't come any closer," Jali yells.

"Are you crazy?" I take a few shots at some tentacles that get too close to me as I float by. "Let us up! It's your friends, Dewey and Rym!"

"Yeah, and they know about the failsafe protocol, too."

"For god's sake, it's debugged." I finally make it to the other side and tentatively jump onto the solid steps. I'd kiss them if I weren't trying to avoid getting sucked into the wall. "Neman helped."

Rym isn't looking too good. He falls to his knees, gripping onto Dewey's frame. There still isn't a response from up above, and the creatures are getting persistent. One squelches out of its hole next to Rym.

A cracking sound from a rifle fills the pit with its reverberating echo. I look over to see the shot of a true master marksman. But the tentacle is still creeping out and there's a smoking hole in the wall a good ten

feet from the creature. I guess it's dark out, she'll get it with the next one.

Blam.

And another hole in the wall appears ten feet in the other direction. She must have some plan that involves missing. By a lot.

"Jali, just shoot it!"

Another series of blasts erupts from her rifle. And they all miss. All? The odds are that at least one would have struck something. If she takes any more, odds are she'll hit one of us. Luckily by this time, I've gotten off a few hits so Dewey can pull Rym to his feet away from the thing and up the steps. It takes a good fifteen minutes before we're at the top, in between me and Dewey trading shots and covering our escape. Jali gives up even pretending to shoot.

When we reach the top, it's clear why Jali had missed every single damn time. One of her eyes is completely gone, the other is gray with blindness, and the fingers on each of her hands are crimped at an unnatural angle.

We found our gun expert. But she can't shoot for shit.

CHAPTER 11

The walk back to Jali's house is a long quiet one, especially with Dewey tending to Rym's contusion, or whatever he called it. It's not until we're sitting in her one-room shack at the top of a steep cliff that anyone says a word.

"So, you're not able to...?" Rym says.

Jali stares into the cup in front of her, its liquid untouched. But not for long. After us staring at her for a minute, she pounds it and refills it from an open bottle. I don't know if there's even a cork for it. Her misshapen fingers shake as she grips the cup.

I hesitantly sniff at my own glass. It has that faint odor of the berry extract Rym is always having us drink, but after I taste the smallest sip, the strong burning fills my entire head. And she's already emptied three. Do these guys all have drinking problems?

"I've been nearly blind and crippled for so long." Jali holds two more full glasses in her hands, ready to down them at any moment.

Looks like the answer is *yes*.

"Who is this kid?" Jali asks with a glass to her lips.

"He's all right," Rym says. "Daj. He's with us."

Wow. I'm *all right*. Excellent.

Jali slams a glass down on a small table. "After the war, I took up with Scitech."

"You what?" Rym says, and grimaces from the pain in his gut.

"Don't look down at me. We didn't all have the luxury of being ace pilots, picking up a job anywhere."

"It wasn't always easy for me either." Rym coughs. "I could have helped, you know."

"You could, could you?" Jali crosses all her arms and leans back. "Did you ever try to find me? To find the old squad?"

Rym shakes his head. "I knew where you were but there was the alarm protocol. We'd get killed if we got too close."

Jali sniffs.

"And even if he had decided to find you out here you didn't exactly plan a nice welcome party for him," I say. "We barely made it out of that pit alive."

Rym waves me down. "Best you don't get involved with this."

Involved? I'm already going to be on the top of every wanted list in Phen by morning. Doesn't she know Rym had always kept track of her? Well, apparently not at the beginning.

"That wasn't for you," Jali says. "I'm sorry. Anyway, back when we got separated, I fell back on to what I always knew. Guns. That's it. And Scitech needed me."

She isn't kidding. On the wall behind her there's a rack with some of the nicest rifles, pistols, and other weapons I don't know the names of. They're all gleaming as if freshly polished.

"Whoa, is that a mag rail rifle?" I have only ever seen something like that on some gun heavy vids back on the 'site.

"That's my girl." Jali pats the side of the gun.

"Did you get hurt in an accident?" Dewey stands by her side, scanning her hands and face with a red beam.

"No, I didn't have no damn accident." Jali swats at Dewey until he backs away.

"You know that Nanosite works on the blind, right?" I say. "Prints right onto your retina from the inside, like a monitor."

Jali gives me the stink eye, and it's particularly stinky. "I was part of a nano implant experiment. First gen, so they needed volunteers. Offered me a ton of money."

"Well spent," I mutter and take in the luxurious accommodations.

She smacks me on the side of the head. "It's my eyes that are busted, jackass, not my ears."

Rym raises his eyebrows at me. Right, best I don't get involved.

She settles down into her chair and takes another swig. "Targeting tech. Installed right here." She points to her missing eye. "Reflex accelerators. Here." She waves her deformed hands about. "Worked for a month or two. I was going to be training a new corps of soldiers with these implants. But then, some nights, I'd wake up and not know where the hell I was. Only that I was in the middle of nowhere, and had blood on my hands. And I'd lose track of time. Days went by, and I didn't know what happened. It was the neural upgrades, I guess. Scitech was pissed. Their research was bombing, recruits were misfiring. They were trying to control me, my thoughts, my actions. I didn't know what I'd done. Who I killed. I had to get out of there."

Jali raises another glass with shaking hands and dribbles it down her chin, red like blood. We all just let her speak.

"I took my money that I stashed. All of it. And spent it on back alley surgeons to get this shit ripped out of me."

Then she starts crying. And that cuts the worst. Before I can move, Rym and Dewey are already at her side, comforting her.

"I'm sorry for what I said." I am. I really am. I didn't know what had happened to her. And now I feel like a total asshole.

"You'd best be going," Jali whispers when Rym and Dewey have a seat again.

Rym and I exchange confused looks.

"But you're coming with us," Rym says. "We came for your help. We need you to help take down Scitech."

Jali wipes her eyes and nose with her battered sleeve. "Haven't you seen me? What does a squad need with a broken-down, blind, gunner hack?"

"Let me see," I say. "We've got century old bots, an overweight slicer, a grumpy mechanic with some old stories, and a washed up vid star. Seems to me we've got room for you."

Jali actually laughs. A genuine laugh. "I see why you picked this kid up. Reminds me of someone I used to know."

"Yeah, well don't get all nostalgic on me." Rym gets to his feet and holds his side with his deformed arm. "Get your supplies. We need to leave soon."

"Your arm," Jali says. "Was that from Scitech's implants?"

"Injury from the war."

"I remember that," Jali says. "I think I even helped pull you from the burning cockpit. Let me guess, they promised to help, but only made everything worse."

"Come on," Rym says. "We should get moving."

Jali sits there for a moment staring off into nothing. A slight smile cracks over her lips and she fires down two more shots before getting to her feet, not as steadily as Rym. "All right, now I'm ready. Let's go!"

And she falls back into her chair, drunk off her ass.

"I'll help her get her things," I whisper.

***

Turns out she doesn't have much. Just the guns and they all fit nicely in a portable mag crate.

"Don't nick the plating," she scolds me. "You'll throw off the aim."

She must have already nicked them tons apparently, but I don't tell her that.

"You had some pretty good moves back in there," she says as she bundles more stuff into another crate. Looks like junk to me, but whatever.

Dewey beeps his agreement to her. "I would like to see that again, if I could. My core circuits were routed to freeing Rym at the moment, and could not multi-task enough to record."

"Yeah, I don't get it. I thought I was dead as soon as I jumped off the steps."

Cam pops out of the wrist link and begins to project the whole scene again. Skipping around until the moment I get pushed off the ledge and the tentacle creature grabs hold of Rym's torso. Dewey lets go and then in a few seconds I launch myself off the edge. Just like the vid of my falling to the rooftop of the Mirage, there's a moment of irregularity. Some weird glitch like a skip in the frames.

Afterward, I'm holding onto the floating boulders with all my limbs, spinning around mid-air. And then when I kick the boulder mid-flight, there's a sudden burst of acceleration as it shoots toward the flailing red limb.

"That's some real Eldane stuff you're pulling out there, kid." Jali pats my back.

"What do you mean?" Stell could do stuff like that. Not me. "I just got lucky."

"You say you've got a full nano set, right?" she says. "Then there shouldn't be a way to access the mag source like an Eldane. But it sure as hell looks like it."

"Well, what if it's not me, then?"

Rym stares at me.

"I keep hearing Stell. I swear I keep seeing her, too. It's like she's always here. Maybe she's helping me when I need it. Or maybe I'm just going crazy."

Rym still doesn't say anything.

"Yeah, crazy then," I say. "Thought so. Let's just get out of here and find that last friend of yours. Hira."

Jali starts to laugh. "Hira?"

Rym walks past her and grabs a rifle out of her hands and places the strap over his shoulder. "It's time to go."

"Oh boy," Jali says. "Hira."

Huh. This just keeps getting better and better.

***

As we leave the tiny but sturdy house on the cliffside, someone is waiting for us.

"Jali!" Neman says. He waits until we meet him down on the ground level before clasping his old friend's arm. "You look terrible."

Jali eyes him up and down. "Are we in a competition? Because I think you win."

They give each other a hug and then talk closely as we make our way back to the mine car. Neman pops the wire from his wrist onto her forehead and within a minute he removes it.

"What is that?" I ask.

"Something I worked on while in the dish room. It stops us from being followed."

"Can you do it for me?"

Neman shakes his head. "Not yet. Your tech is newer, or maybe I should say 'evolved.' You upgraded recently. You have way more extra systems onboard. It'll take a while for me to figure it out, if I even can."

I kick a loose rock at my feet.

"I could set up a temporary field, or maybe even something more permanent with your Camdrone. You wouldn't believe the tech that's inside one of those things. Its original code was built to defend against intrusions into its computer system, and even adapt to changes. A precursor to Dewey's model, even." He looks at her like I used to look at Zaylee when I thought we had something.

"How do you know so much about them?"

Neman shrugs. "My father worked on the original model."

A part of me wants to let him take a closer look at Cam, to see if there's something that could help me. But this is all I have left of my

129

parents. I'll never risk those vids getting erased.

An explosion from behind us nearly knocks me off my feet. I turn around to see dust and bits of building settling around us.

"What now?"

I scan the skies, expecting a fleet of Scitech speeders to descend upon us. Then I notice the only one of us not looking around is Jali.

"You did this?"

"Gotta cover our tracks in case they come looking for us, right?"

"Give us some warning next time you want to blow something up like that," I say, trying to settle down.

"She's not the kind of girl who likes to announce herself," Neman says. "Part of the whole *sniping* thing with her."

Jali gives me a wink and pushes on in front of everyone.

We walk until the quarry where Jali almost executed us earlier. Nice memories.

"Get down!" Dewey says from up front.

Oh great, more of Jali's traps? I duck behind a boulder and squint to see what's up ahead, but I got nothing. There's only one moon out now and it's pretty low. I suppress the urge to release Cam up there. For some reason I don't want to let her out of my sight. Jali pulls up a set of trinocs to her eyes, well, to her one less damaged eye.

"What is that thing?" she asks. "Its heat output is intense. And look at its nose."

"Another one of those things sniffed us out here?" The last one that came upon us nearly killed us. But killing us might not be why it's here. "Has it spotted us yet?"

"Does not look like it," Dewey says.

"Can you take it out from here?" Rym asks.

He's asking Jali, and she only responds by pulling the long rifle from her shoulder and laying it across the boulder. She adjusts herself multiple times before settling in. A full minute later and she's exhaling a long held breath. I'm still holding mine.

The head of the tracker twists side to side as he approaches along the path. He must really have our scent now. A few more steps and he'll see us. If he hasn't sent out a signal to Scitech yet, it's only a matter of seconds now. Fire, dammit.

A sudden blast emits from Jali's rifle, but the shot only ricochets harmlessly down the canyon.

"Nope," Jali mutters and primes another bolt in the rifle chamber.

How could she miss? It's literally a straight line to him down a narrow path. I guess she has consumed more alcohol in the past hour than I have in my whole life and then there's the one 'good' eye. Maybe this wasn't such a good idea after all.

"He's running!" Dewey says.

"He's going to upload any vid he's captured," Rym says. He's now limping with every step, definitely in no shape to run after anything.

"Don't worry, I've got it," Neman says. He pushes several buttons on his wrist controller I didn't notice earlier, mainly because it's built into his skin. A beep emanates from my own wrist.

Cam pops out of the arm dock and races through the air toward the tracker. "Hey what do you think you're doing?" I grab Neman's shoulder.

"Let him do his thing," Rym says.

"You know about this?"

Neman shakes free and taps onto the screen on his wrist. "It will block the send signal from his Nanosite. It's a basic function in the Camdrone protocol. I just had to activate it."

"But he'll get away eventually." I grab one of Jali's rifles.

The big Maglan makes it about ten paces when he stops. I squint my eyes and see something atop a pile of rocks near the path, right next to the quarry and the floating rocks. It's a mangy yarel. Braying and howling fills the canyon.

The Maglan glances side to side, like it's trapped. Well, I'm going to make sure it doesn't get out of here alive. He's a good hundred feet from me, and though I'm not sure I can make a shot like this, Jali ain't having any of it, Rym is hurt, Dewey probably isn't able to hold a four-armed long range rifle, and Neman? Hah.

I run down the path to try to get a better range on him so that I even have a chance. By this time, the yarel has engaged him, and by that I mean he's gripping onto his leg with his fangs. There's blood, lots of it, and the Maglan tilts its head back in a howl of its own. Man, that could have been me back before Kie saved me.

I take a knee, right there in the middle of the rocky path. I try to ignore the biting pain the rocks cause when I do so and prop the gun up, taking aim in the scope. Night vision, luckily it's still activated from when Jali last used it. Before I can think, I pull the trigger and the recoil slams into my shoulder. The bolt obviously misses and hits one of the floaty boulders above the quarry.

That gets its attention though, unfortunately. He turns around and locks eyes onto my scope, despite the yarel. I can't believe it. This yarel has five eyes. And, luckily for me, that five-eyed coincidence is ripping chunks of flesh from the tracker's thigh.

There's nothing alive left in the agent's eyes, it seems. They're just scanning. Scanning me. Oh shit. He's got me now.

He'll be trying to upload the vid, and if it goes through, Scitech'll be on us in no time. Cam buzzes by overhead, hopefully still jamming it.

Five-eyes meanwhile is still gnawing at the big sniffer's leg, but it turns to him, clenches a meaty fist around its neck and yanks it off his thigh.

"No!" I scream and reach out.

Things get really weird then. I don't know how it happens, but one of the floating rocks flies into the Maglan. He doubles over, still holding onto the yarel. Are there rock spitters down there, too?

"Did you... throw that rock?" Neman asks.

"Me? What?" There's no way I did that. Right?

But I sense something like a mix between tingling in my hands and a memory. But it's a memory I can sense and control. I feel another boulder, somehow, in my mind. It's bigger this time, but I grab it, yes, grab is the word. Not with my arms, but I've got a hold of it. And then I throw it right into him. This one carries him into the pit along with the yarel. I drop the gun and rush to the side of the pit. The sniffer is pinched in between two floating rocks suspended in the middle of it all, but Five-eyes is nowhere to be seen.

The big Maglan's legs are kicking back and forth, thrashing, and it's trying to pry the rock off its chest with two arms, and also hold onto the other floating rock. I scan down below, but it's too dark to see anything.

With a flick of my mind, I grasp onto one of the floating rocks and swing it at the sniffer's big fat face. There's a squish as the rock hits him and his arms go limp. In the next second, a red-skinned tentacle reaches up out of the darkness and grasps onto his lower body. With a tearing sound, it splits the body in half and pulls the parts down.

Okay, that's a pretty gross way to go.

I lean over and stare into the depths trying to ignore the ripping sounds down there.

"Five-eyes!"

Cam zips over and shines a light onto the stairs next to me, but there's nothing on it. Idiot. Stupid thing, why did it have to go and try to help me? I sit staring over the edge for a minute in silence.

But then I hear some whining and whimpering coming from somewhere in the middle of the pit.

"Cam, shine over there!"

A bright beam lights up the tumbling rocks. Right on the yarel, clutching desperately onto the rock it's on, spinning flat like a throwing disk. A cluster of tentacles reaches up out of the depths, clutching at rocks and pulling them down. They're getting closer to Five-eyes.

"Quiet!" I say, although I don't know if it's sound or something else the tentacles are drawn to. Even more clamber up the wall toward me and a smaller one appears at the top of the pit. I stumble back a step and trip over a rock, landing on my backside.

"Come on, Daj, get out of there!" Neman says.

The tentacle creeps around like a searching finger and something inside of me snaps. I pick up the rock and smash it over and over onto the red thing until it retreats into the quarry.

I run to the pit edge and look down. The yarel cowers from the tentacles that grip the rocks it's on. "Hold on!"

I take a breath and I feel the power filling this place. It's easy to pick up the stone Five-eyes is on, tear it out of the tentacle's grasp, and lift it out of the quarry. As soon as he gets above solid ground, he jumps off and runs away. He pauses for a moment to glance back at me, but only for a second before disappearing in the darkness.

"Ho-ly," Rym says when the group finally reaches my side.

"And that, kid, is how an Eldane do." Jali whistles. "Well, maybe not what you did to that Maglan's head, though. Sheesh."

***

I keep telling myself there's no way that could have been be me. But I could definitely feel something, and I still can, even though it's fading away like a dream. A part of me wants to ditch these guys and go mess around. And get Cam to record it. She probably got some great footage of that anyway so I can piece something together later.

"They still might get information out of that, whatever it is," Rym says.

"I'm calling it a Sniffer. And if the Maglans at Scitech can pull enough from its head to get an image, they earned it. Besides, they might just think he got pulled into the pit like we would've if we followed Jali's signal."

Rym sighs. "Maybe. But if not, that doesn't give us a lot of time before they connect what we've been doing and start a real focused search."

I take a few more steps in silence. "What is going on with me? I can't do that again, what I did in the pit." I twist my hands around, but I get nothing.

"Certain places are focal points of energy on our planet. We're moving away, so you can't sense it as easily as before. You're new to it all, as well, so you don't really know what to do." Rym looks at his own hands.

"Wait, could you do the same things like I did?" Was this really something Maglans so easily forgot?

"The nanotech," Rym says. "It takes away your connection to it. For me, when I got my first set of upgrades, I didn't realize what I was missing until it was too late. No, I could not move things around like that. Well, nothing that big. It was different for me."

"But it's the drink you gave me. It cleared my head. Doesn't that allow the connection?"

Rym nods. "It inhibits the nanos, yes. But for you there was a big leap. I mean, we don't know many Maglans who can do that. Stell, yes. I'm not certain, but perhaps Scitech was grooming you."

"Grooming?"

"Like they knew something about you, and have made everything easier for you."

It makes sense. They've given me everything I ever wanted. Money. The best tech. But not a family. Is that why they want me off the planet? Shit, I was all lined up for a big promotion to get my pilot's license. To follow my parents.

"Maybe you're right."

Cam flies overhead in a zipping fashion. Her lights make cool streaks as she does it, but then I think about where that came from and that gets me pissed again.

"Neman, she went out after that Sniffer without my control. If you ever touch her, or make her do something like that without me knowing…"

Neman snorts. "She's old tech, kid. Like I said, she has old protocols. What I mean is a yarel's gonna howl."

"She did it all by herself?" I'm not buying it.

"Okay, I'm not saying I didn't *encourage* her to follow those protocols..." Neman scans over his wrist pad with his fingers. "But for what it's worth, I'm sorry. I knew we needed to do something."

I shrug. It's crazy, she's got a mind of her own, almost. No longer mine. She took right off and hovered right over that Sniffer. I didn't even know she could do things like that. And is she going to keep doing them?

"Do you think that maybe now that we're running low on the drink, she can block any Nanosite traffic, in or out?"

A light sparkles in Neman's eyes. "I can do that. It's probably going to be localized to just you. She doesn't have a big mag cell in her. Speaking of that, we need to charge her up, I'm sure. And then—" He sort of trails off and types madly onto his screen.

I walk next to Rym, who starts to fall behind a little bit. "I'm starting to think that maybe Stell didn't just accidentally bump into me when I was jumping off the Edge."

Rym smiles. "We did need to get on your vid feed, but you weren't the only kid we were watching. Plenty other Scitech brats are all over Phen, and other cities. You were just a means to an end. With that many Maglans watching, we could start everyone thinking there was another way. An older way. A revolution. And then, as you might say, shit turned sideways. But, other than a few bumps, I'd say maybe yes, it was no accident we chose you."

"A few bumps? Stell is missing, maybe dead, or at least being tortured. You got mangled by a crazy tentacle thing. Your friends are not turning out to be aces."

"And like you told Jali, she fits right in with the rest of the crazy. We're doing fine." Rym doubles over and clutches his stomach. He coughs, showering the ground with a spray of blood.

"Dewey?" I hoist Rym's arm around my shoulder and help him sit. The bot hustles over and runs a quick scan over him and injects something into his stomach with a needle atop one of his fingers.

"He'll be fine."

I look Rym in the eye.

"Yeah," he says with a groan. "Fine. Let's go. Hira isn't far from here."

I'm not so sure he's going to be fine, but he's not having any of it. That tough old bastard. He is starting to grow on me though. Who knew all this could start with a little kidnapping?

The mine cart is a welcome sight. I'm going to need a rest, and I'm pretty sure Rym won't be able to even move without it. I help haul him onto the flat bed and try to make him as comfortable as possible. He grunts in response.

When we're all on, Neman hooks his wrist port into the control station and soon lights are flashing and we're moving away. I take this time to slide next to Rym and keep him talking. There were times when I was pretty beat up from some jump gone to shit, and if it hadn't been for Kie or Zaylee to keep me chatting, I'd have fallen in shock. But it didn't take long for me to get better, not with the nanos to fix it.

"What version are you running?"

Rym's eyes lose their focus and he doesn't respond.

"Hey, come on, wake up. What version?"

He shrugs. "Early. I haven't updated my tech in years."

"So you probably don't have the updated health nanos."

He coughs and wipes the blood on his sleeve. It's tough to know where the clean begins and the blood ends on that thing. "I removed all those subsystems. I didn't want Scitech trying to assassinate me, or something. So I'm running next to nothing. If I could get the rest of them out of me, I would."

"But you could die if we don't get you some help."

"There are other ways," Rym says.

Dewey raises a hand to Rym's forehead and takes a reading. "Elevated temperature. Blood pressure lowering." He injects Rym with something and he begins to breathe a little easier.

That seems to help, but I can't imagine it will last long. Maybe Neman can help.

"Neman. Do you have any health subsystems you can get running in him?"

"I offered," Neman says, wiping the sweat from the long walk off his forehead. "But he didn't want it. Although I'm not sure what I can do. He's tried to fry his nanos, so I don't think I could get them to work again the way we want. I'll keep trying, though. It's too bad you don't have training, you might actually be able to help."

Jali snorts. "That was a fluke. A fluctuation in the mag field. He probably can't do something like that again. Not with the nanos powering back up in him."

"Eldane can do that?"

"Wasn't much the Eldane couldn't do. And we just turned our back on that connection. And it turned its back on us."

I can almost feel the nanos powering back up inside me. I haven't had that drink in hours now, and I'm feeling like my old self again. And being my old self sucks a little.

"Why did you activate a ping off your 'site?" Neman asks Jali. "You know we picked that up a while back."

She shrugs and sips some liquid from a metal flask. "Hope, I guess."

"Next time keep your hope away from the center of a damn tentacle pit, all right?" Neman laughs and grabs her flask from her hands.

***

An hour passes after we meet up with other mine carts, these probably full of ore bound for smelting and export. Before any check station, Neman reroutes us toward a smaller outpost. The rings of Phen are clear on the horizon now, but it's not time to head back there yet. Once we get Hira, I should say 'if' we get her, since there've been a lot of misfires with getting new crewmembers, we're going straight for the research base. And who knows if I'll ever get back home again after all that.

"Hey kid," Neman says. "It's your Camdrone. Do you mind if I try something out?"

I reach for Cam, still on my wrist, like I'm pulling her back from some line of fire. Neman's been working on something for a while now, although that doesn't make me feel better. Plus, I'm like my old self and more connected to my Nanosite, so that just puts me right on edge. Scitech could pop in if they wanted to. So I release her from the dock and reluctantly hand her over.

"I did some research on her model. I keep a rolling database, you see, update it when I can at any historical library that hasn't been erased or updated with Scitech propaganda. There are tons of subsystems she has that might have gone out of use, with updates and all." He slips the wrist connector up to her access port under her chassis.

"It looks like you've kept her off the grid, too, nice. She's still running an older firmware so there's hope." He mumbles for a good thirty seconds as his eyes flutter and roll back into his head.

I reach for him, but Dewey interrupts. "You do not want to do that. He is focusing on the data and systems that are running, as well as any dormant ones. Break him out of that and he could go comatose. Or if that does not motivate you, you might lose your Camdrone's memory."

I nod.

Five minutes drag on and finally Neman lets out a deep breath and his eyes go back to normal. "Go ahead. Give her a try."

He flips her back over and in a second her lights flash on and she hovers about. She seems to be all right.

"Is the signal blocker running?"

Neman nods with a super smug grin. "Try to access something."

My Nanosite display in my eyes lights up when I pull up the controls. Music? A steady stream of my stored beats for my vids pumps out of the internal speakers right into my skull. But when I try to access any online music sites, I get a 'no signal' notification popping up. The same goes for any messages when I try to access them. I see a full list of my saved content, but I got no live signal.

"You're welcome," Neman says.

It's none too soon. We've been out of that drink for an hour at least and I was starting to feel the nanos again.

"What's the range on this?"

Neman shrugs. "I wouldn't push it past a couple hundred feet, probably."

That's awesome, but I'm still not ready to thank him for this yet.

I glance behind the cart to see if Five-eyes is tailing us, but there are only empty rolling hills in the bleak landscape. It had to be the same yarel from before. I mean, what are the odds that another five-eyed creature is going to show up?

But what are the odds that a creature is going to try to save me anyway?

I try to check on Rym, but his little cluster of friends won't let me in. Dewey keeps a near constant watch on his vitals. Sometimes Neman crawls over, moving awkwardly on the cart as it moves, and places his wrist wire onto Rym's forehead. I'm sure it's a scan, or maybe trying to jump start the internal nanos into some repair sequence. Dewey and Neman shift turns at the controls of the mine car, but Jali never leaves his side. She holds Rym's hand and recounts stories from their old squad in Skywatch. She keeps him talking and laughing, and if his eyes start to close she gently pats his cheeks.

They're his family. They'll stick together now.

I suddenly feel cold and alone.

I used to think Kie and Zaylee could be that way for me, but what are they doing now? While I'm off trying to straighten things out, they're back home making videos. Together. They're still my friends, though? Right? My family?

I have some old vids, partials, that I never got around to putting together. With a flick of my eyes, I scan and sort through the file labeled "K and Z." I hesitate to open it. I steal a glance over at my companions. Jali winks at me with her eyeless eye. It's pretty weird, but I still crack a smile.

So I close it. I don't want to spoil it. You know, the memories I have of them. I'll keep that all golden and happy until this is over.

"We're close," Dewey says.

Good. Worrying about whether or not I have any friends can wait for later.

The mine cart creeps to a halt as we come out between a set of hills. Up ahead, the lights of a small village peep out through the dark.

"What does Hira do, exactly? And will she mind us popping over for a quick op?"

Rym, who appears to have stabilized a little, cracks a smile. "It's late, but not too late to drop in on someone. I'll let her tell you about herself. But, we best be careful on our way to her house."

"Hmm, yeah, maybe we should call first?" Jali asks, fiddling with something she brought along for the ride.

"Does she have some sort of booby trap set up?"

"I haven't seen her since the old days, but she'll want to see us. If I remember her." Rym tries to get up, but can't do it without a lot of groaning.

"You should stay here and rest," I say.

He slaps away my hand and gives us both the 'back off' look. So instead I offer to help him to his feet, and he's too weak to argue that. This is going to be a long walk with him on my arm.

"This place looks quaint." I look around and see fences and tall plants growing alongside the small huts. "Was your friend a tactical gardener?"

Neman lets out a snort. "Good one. I'm going to use that later."

We end up at a hut, no different than the others we passed along the way. Friendly warm lights glow from little posts along the dirt pathway. They're organic, it looks like, but also with some metal components. Pretty clever design.

"You doing okay, Rym?" I help Dewey carry him to the door. He's not making a sound, even after Dewey and I jostle him around.

"Any chance someone's watching?" I ask. The nearest house is within sight, right across the gardens.

"Hira would never get close to any tech like that," Dewey says. "This place will be as far off the grid as—"

A bell chimes once from the small house and the lights on the pathway brighten. I glance down to see the plant-like tops of the post unfurl, as if alive. Like little eyeballs, the posts follow us as we near the door.

"That's not creepy." I keep to the center of the path. Cam jumps off her dock station and zooms into the air. She sets up a system scan and soon an outline of the house and surrounding area begin to form in a holo map on my 'site. It even starts to predict the inside of the place from whatever scan she's doing. Did Neman uncover this subroutine in her? I guess it's kind of cool.

Neman reaches the door first. Yeah, he's faster than Dewey and me trying to bring Rym along. He knocks softly with two hands, a soft patter that sounds rhythmic. Has he got a musical side to his bot centric life? Or is it some sort of code?

The lights inside the house come to life and a massive flood light shines over all of us outside. Jali tenses and draws her rifle, turning around and scanning for something. If anyone's looking, they'll be able to see us.

A slow steady pacing, I can hear it through the door. There's no lock being unlatched. The door simply opens revealing an older looking Maglan woman. She's old, but not as worn out as Rym, nor as mangled as Jali, and not even close to as obese as Neman. She looks like a pleasant typical grandmother. Or, maybe what I think a grandmother would look like, since I don't even have parents to make any connection. Just from shows.

"What are you doing?" she asks.

The anger and surprise on her face melts when she sees Rym in my arms. Something flashes behind her back in one hand and then she reaches out with all four to help Rym into her house.

CHAPTER 12

We quickly bring the now utterly quiet and unmoving Rym onto a couch in the center of the room. Wooden and stone carvings of different styles adorn the walls. It's chill in here, like time has stopped and the stress from outside seems to have slid away. I step over a pistol lying on the ground, probably what she threw to help get Rym inside.

"What happened to him?" she says.

Oh yeah. Rym is dying.

That's got to be Hira, although no one introduced her. Anyway, she brings a small black bag from a closet and opens it up.

"Internal injury," Dewey says. "Not sure about the extent."

"Why not?" she says, with a tone of judgement hanging on her words. She pulls out a metallic box with a monitor on it and flips on the power. A bright light and Scitech's logo bounces across the screen along with the words *Medical Assessment and Repair System*. She goes to hook the port up onto Rym's forehead, but not before Dewey grabs her wrist.

"We are trying to avoid contact with Scitech," Dewey says.

Slowly, Hira returns the link module to the case. "I see." Her eyes flit back and forth.

"She's accessing her 'site?" I say.

"He just said we can't call for medical help." Jali says.

Hira's eyes slow down until she focuses back on Rym. "You can't be here."

Neman scoffs. "We're here, Comm— Hira. And we need your help.

141

He needs your help."

A door slides open at the end of the room exposing a staircase. It's not just a one-bedroom domicile unit like Jali's. Vid frames line the wall back there showing small children playing, swimming, and Hira with them in every one. She didn't go silent. She didn't go dark after the war.

"You got hooked up and had some kids?" Rym coughs out. Blood spatters onto the couch and his eyes quickly flutter back shut.

All eyes fall onto Hira. Well, not mine. I'm looking at the two kids that just popped out from the stairs. They take a look at me and their eyes go wide. I've seen that look before. And a sense of pride swells deep in my chest, but it's fear that crushes it as soon as I look at Rym.

Hira glances over her shoulder. "Rito, Jama, back to bed. It's late."

"Now?" the boy says, glancing back and forth between the blood spurting old guy and me.

"Now!"

They leave, but like I said, I've seen that look. They know me. There's something not right about this. How have the kids seen me? If Hira was half of what Rym was like, you know, never touch nanos, the kids would never have seen a vid with me on it.

After the two kids retreat down the steps, Hira puts two hands on her knees and the others on her forehead. "I can't believe this. We all disappear for years. And I mean *years*. I'm sure you all got on with your lives and now all of a sudden you want to get together for what?"

"That doesn't matter now," Neman says. "We need to fix him."

Neman slowly lowers himself to sit on the floor. He reaches out his arms until Jali clasps the one next to her, and places two on Rym. With her free hand she reaches to me.

She motions for me to sit next to her and do the same but I back up. "What? Why? This is really weird, like some…"

"Eldane Nonno voodoo magic?" Jali says.

Yeah, that sounds about right. I tentatively hold onto her hand and place two on Rym, just like they did. I hold my free hand out to Hira.

"I can't believe you brought this into my house," she says under her breath as she links up with me and completes the circle with Neman.

"You look good, girl," Jali says from across the circle.

A slight half-smile twists Hira's mouth. "You look the same as always."

"Hah! Just a few more miles on me." Jali winks her blind eye.

As I look out at the group in front of me, I see the distinct diamond shapes of Skywatch tattoos on their upper arms. Under each is a different symbol, maybe a rank insignia or something. The strange thing is now the marks are all slightly glowing, and I can even see some other light coming through their clothing, like they've been covering more marks. My own digital tattoo seems pretty stupid right now, and I shake my sleeve to make it slide down a little to cover it up. It works, but not before everyone looks at me.

"This is ridiculous," I say when their eyes fall on what I'm doing. The whole thing just feels wrong, and embarrassing. What do I have to offer their little seance anyway?

Neman gets my attention with a little nod of his chin. "You're doing fine."

"But nothing is happening." Nothing is. I'm just holding onto Jali's mangled grip in one hand and some lady I just met in the other. I swear, if someone tells me to—

"Breathe."

That's it. I stand up and break the circle. "You don't need me for this."

No one says anything as the circle closes right up from where I left, like I wasn't there at all. See? I don't belong. I walk away to where Dewey is standing guard near the front door.

"What are they doing?"

Dewey scans through the small glass on the door and then replies. "Checking his vitals. Assessing the situation. Repairing."

"Okay, but how? They're just sitting in a circle and holding hands." I didn't get any assessing or repairing vibes.

"I am not able to participate when they do this."

Seems like he's kind of bummed out about that, but he doesn't say anything else. Several minutes pass before he speaks again.

"You should help them, the more Maglans connected will speed and strengthen the healing process. I will not feel remorseful, in fact I would appreciate it very much. Rym is my friend, and it would be most unfortunate to lose him."

I don't know what I'd do. I'd just be sitting in the circle like some idiot. I fidget around with Cam's dock, just flipping switches and turning dials. Over on the couch, Rym starts twitching like he's being prodded. The others are full-on glowing now, marks that were hidden within their skin light up the room. I guess Dewey's right, I could try to do something. I head back to the group with a hesitant smile. Will they let me back in, after I just ditched out on them?

But when I get there, Jali pulls herself to her feet and Hira rocks back and stretches her arms out. The faint glowing of their tattoos has disappeared. They all look exhausted but meet my questioning eyes as I approach.

"He's going to be all right," Jali says. "It was close there for a while."

I smile, but something eats the inside of my guts. "I'm sorry I left."

"Hey, don't worry, kid," Neman says. "We did it."

Without me. I feel that's what he just left hanging. In fact no one is looking at me anymore. Hira gets up and checks on the children still watching from the stairs. Neman struggles to stand, so I rush to his side and grip under his arms to hoist him to his feet. He doesn't refuse my help, but he doesn't thank me either.

Shit, what could I have done? They did it without me. Are they just pissed at me for not trying? "I should have stayed."

"The good news is he'll be all right," Neman says. "And don't worry, there'll be another chance, considering what we've got planned."

"Don't post it," Hira's voice rises from the stairway.

Who is she talking to? I edge closer and see Rito and Jama standing with their heads down. They don't have any cameras or drones to take any footage. Why would she be telling them not to post anything?

When the boy, Rito, maybe, sees me his eyes light up and he nudges the girl. Hira turns to face me and walks up a few steps to see me eye to eye.

"The twins know who you are," Hira says. "They watch your channel all the time."

I smile. Any other day I'd take the opportunity to meet and greet with any fan, but not now.

"They even watched the footage of you killing someone."

My mouth dries up and the pit in my stomach deepens. "That wasn't me."

"I know," she cuts me off with a sharp tone. "I know. That scared the piss out of them though. Kids shouldn't see something like that, even if it is fake. I can spot a hacked vid stream even if it is really good. Someone wanted to set you up. Someone with the skills and money to get the word out."

"Scitech. So your kids are hooked up to the Nanosite, huh?"

She's just about to answer when she gets interrupted.

"Why the hell do they have nanos in them?" Rym says, but his voice is so weak and raspy I barely can tell it's him. He strains to prop himself up to a sitting position and I find myself by his side in a heartbeat.

"Are you all right?"

He brushes me off, but he smiles a little bit. "I'm good now. Except for this nano bullshit." He's pointing at Hira.

Hira directs a killer glare at the twins behind her and they scurry downstairs.

"I can't believe you got them nanotech. They're your own family, your grandkids."

"*Great*-grandkids," she says.

"What?" How can she have great-grandchildren? She doesn't look that old.

"I wanted them to have a normal life," she says.

"Normal?" Rym says. "Their lives will be cut in half. At least. Haven't you noticed that you look the same age as their parents?"

It's true. All the frames on the wall have Hira in them and she looks exactly the same age. The kids don't. They just keep growing and she doesn't change a bit.

"Yes, a normal life. To have fun, and to be with friends. And to do what they want to do, and enjoy it. Not live in the wastes like animals. How exactly is that working out for you, Rym? How did that work out for my sister? Living amongst the filth of the underground? Diseases? This family has had none of that. And which one of us shows up at the other's with some injury because they're still holding some grudge against new technology?"

"It's our true life. None of this is real." Rym gestures to the air around him. "You're not free, you're a slave to them. To Scitech. Even if you didn't get full nanos like the rest of your family. One day you're going to wake up and everyone you care about will have grown old and died."

Her eyes seem to glass over, but I can't tell if it's in anger or sadness. Or her 'site.

"I've made sacrifices," she whispers. "I promised my husband years ago I would protect our children. I promised I would always be there for them. And I did it. I've been there for all the tough times. I was around, and I will continue to be around."

"But the connection," Rym pleads. "To Magla. Didn't you just feel it there? It's still in you. You reached it to save me. Don't you want your kin to have that, too?"

I wish I had. Why didn't I stick around long enough to see what it was? To help out?

"Come with us," Rym says, locking eyes with her. "We can stop it, Hira. Commander. And we need your help."

Hira grips the edges of the chair she's sitting in. Whoa. She was their commander? Their squad leader? I glance back at Jali and Neman, and they're actually saluting her. It's a strange salute, their lower hands grip the elbows of their upper arms with two fingers held up. I can see their Skywatch tattoos on each arm, even though the glow is completely gone now.

This feels like some game I played as a kid. It's weird. She's going to come back to her squad. She'll lead them again and this is going to be one last kick-ass mission.

"I can't."

"What?" I say.

"I have to protect my family."

That's it. That's all she says.

And I really can't believe it. Not even as we're walking out of the house without her.

CHAPTER 13

It's a quiet walk back to the mine cart through the hills. Rym, looking better after the crew fixed him up, seems to be lost in some deep thoughts more so than anyone else.

"So we go and do the job without her," I say. "We don't really need her, do we? Oh yeah, speaking of that, what was her specialty? Besides being a bitch, that is."

Dewey breaks the silence. "She was our commander, as you know from Rym trying to remind her."

"I thought you were in charge, Rym." I pat him on the shoulder, but he doesn't respond. "You've been putting everything together so far, and look how far we've made it." I wave around to us all.

"That's not helping, kid," Jali says as we load up onto the cart. "And hey, whose bag is this? It's in my seat. Move it." She points to a duffel bag sitting near the control panel.

Rym hoists himself aboard and slumps onto a seat. Neman sits at the flat control panel near the front and fiddles with a lever. Neither of them say a word.

"No, seriously," I continue. "If someone could get a screwball like me to take on the entire tech company that pretty much made me who I am, then I'd say that Maglan is a pretty good leader. We don't need her."

Rym still doesn't say anything.

"Bring it down a notch," Neman says. "This wasn't going to happen without her."

"Hey, stop programming that to go back home. I can see what you're doing from here. Stell. What about Stell, Rym? We can't leave her, wherever she is, to be tortured, right? Can't we just find someone else to join us, to lead us, if you're so desperate? Someone else from your dream team?"

Dewey beeps. "Location and skill requirement scan yields no

positives. Not with the subsequent time frame before Scitech begins their searches for Neman and possibly Jali. And then with the projected security upgrades after learning what we're doing, it will be impossible to break into a Research and Development facility."

"Huh?"

"There's not enough time."

"Then we've somehow got to get Hira to help," I say.

"She has her own family to take care of," Rym says. "There's no way she's going to drop them for us."

Something hits me then, as if it didn't quite register when Hira was talking back in her house. "What did she mean by what happened to her sister?"

Rym gives a sad smile. "Her sister was forced to go her own way, like the rest of us. But she didn't get nanos and went completely off the grid. She saw the storm that was coming at the end of the war and headed deep underground. Some disease took her, is what the story is. But it didn't take her daughter."

Wait a minute. "Stell?"

"Good guess," Rym says.

"Does Hira know that?" That can't be right. Stell would be frickin' old is what she'd be!

Rym shakes his head.

"And you didn't think this was useful information in trying to convince Hira to join up? Family? That seems to be what fires her."

"She has her own to worry about."

That doesn't make a lot of sense. Wouldn't some remnant of her own sister's life be enough to make her want to help? "Look, screw her. If she's not coming, we've got to save Stell. What do you say?"

"Yay," Neman says, twirling his fingers in the air. "Our new commander is here."

"Shut up, Neman," Jali says. "We've come this far. I'm with you, kid."

Dewey beeps, like he had never doubted the journey. Neman smiles, I guess he was just being an asshole about it. I can appreciate that, it's usually my job. With this group of misfits, how can Rym disband? He doesn't say anything, but if flipping me off with a grin on the side is his only protest, I'll take it.

***

"We'll be at the research base in an hour," Neman says, clicking a few buttons on the nav panel. "Time for part one of the plan."

Rym takes in my confused look after pulling his head out of a duffel bag. "Scitech is going to be looking for us damn soon if they haven't started a search already. If we get caught with our pants down at this research facility they're already on high alert, which means screw what we want to do next."

"What he's saying is that we need a distraction," Neman says. "Luckily, over the years I've gotten close with the security systems in and out of Phen. How's this sound? I trigger multiple events around the city to coincide with our own break in. Stage one: security bots at a mining tug station will report a break in. Reckless teens attempt to steal a tug." Neman looks around, obviously expecting us to say something about his plan. When we don't, he continues, his voice a little flatter and quicker.

"Just about the same time, more of my bots engage different stages at high profile locations in and around Phen. These places were chosen so that when we hit the station out here, Scitech'll be so preoccupied elsewhere that we'll encounter a lighter resistance."

"Huh," I say. "Maybe I can help, too. I know I'm Scitech's biggest target right now, so maybe I can use my friends Kie and Zaylee. I've got unused footage from jumps and runs off of many illegal areas. Ever since Rym mentioned my 'loser' friends, I wondered how they could actually help."

"You're thinking of using them to post it for you? What if they're working for Scitech?"

"They might be, but I don't have to say what it's for. I can just ask them to post a vid I made. Maybe say that Scitech has me shut down, but I still want to keep my fans happy. They'd post it anyway, or turn it in, which is what we want to do."

"Not a bad idea, kid," Neman says. "I can help you get it to them through a scrambled site."

I smile my thanks.

Finally, something I can feel good about. I only want to do my part. I'm still feeling guilty about bailing out on the healing circle back at Hira's, especially when I hear Rym hack and wheeze a bit.

"Let me construct a send code. I'll have it ready soon and we can bomb the network with all sorts of distractions." Neman busily begins to type away on his arm panel with a huge grin on his face. He's having a bit too much fun.

"Is this what it was like back in the day? Jali is your gunner tech, Neman is the hacker/slicer, Hira was supposedly your commander and something else you won't share with me. What was your part in all of this, Rym? You weren't just the mechanic, were you?"

"I don't want to talk about it."

"Good memories, huh?" He's still bummed out after our visit with Hira, that's pretty clear. I thought talking about what he did best would pick him out of that hole. Oh well, too bad we even went to Hira's. Could have saved a lot of time if he had just sent a message through and asked first. But that probably would have caused some problems with Scitech. And then there was the fact that he was dying. I guess she helped with that.

Was he a mechanic? I've seen him working on old tech, and he sure has kept Dewey in good shape. I wish I had seen them all together back then. Just hearing the stories now makes me sad I never knew more as a kid. History seems to have been wiped, thank you very much, Scitech.

Just like the Eldane's connection to the planet. Our connection. What could they possibly gain from shutting Maglans off from that? Money, no doubt.

"How could this have happened? Scitech, I mean. Skywatch must have been big, and how could Maglans forget about what they have? No one can just forget they can float around like Stell."

Rym shakes his head. "You underestimate the power of ignorance. But whoever created this sure as hell didn't. It made something that appeals to everyone, even me. The more we forget, the stronger they become."

"Just to make money?"

Rym shrugs. "Maybe you can go ask them."

"Huh?"

Rym points ahead. There's the base, about a mile ahead, on the other side of a chain link fence. It's not a huge facility like I thought it'd be. Pretty nondescript. Just a couple of buildings, one of them with a pretty big hangar door.

"This is it?"

Rym points beside the building to a couple of massive holes into the ground. "Hangar bay access tunnels. I'm guessing it goes down a few floors. They don't want to appear too conspicuous, maybe. But we still have to get through this fence. Run a bypass, Neman."

The mine cart glides to a halt. "Help him out, Dewey."

The team hops off the flat bed as soon as he says it, but Neman lingers by the vehicle after he disconnects. "Thanks, cart. Stay close enough in case we need you."

"In case we need a really slow getaway?" I say.

Neman just smiles and pats the bed of the cart. "Don't listen to him, sweetheart. Thanks for your help."

It's almost sweet, the tone he sends the cart off with, if it weren't a machine. "Do you always thank your machines?"

"Of course," Neman says. "They'll remember me when they take over."

Sounds familiar.

Jali scans back and forth across the line of the fence, holding a high-powered scope. "No cameras. Maybe this facility isn't as high on the Scitech list as you thought. Are you sure it has a ship we can use?"

Rym nods. "Dewey and I did the research. Tracked down several atmo-breaking ships, and this has to be the place. As far as how much they've dismantled them, that's another story."

"I trust them," I say.

"I didn't say I didn't," Jali says with a snort. "I just like to know everything I can. Is that the ridge you showed me?"

Rym nods. "You ready?"

Jali smiles at him. "Yes, sir." She throws a couple packs on her back and straps the big ass railgun over her shoulder.

"You're leaving?"

"Don't worry. I'll be keeping an eye on you."

"You have more than one?"

"You'd be surprised." She hands me a small bag, and when I shake it, small metallic pieces rattle around.

"What's this?"

"My extra eyes. Hold onto them, will you?"

"Ew. Thanks, I guess."

She salutes me and leaves at a trot toward the nearest ridgeline.

I check the pistol at my side. It's got a full charge, but for some reason I feel really uneasy about this whole thing. Maybe it's the fact that I've never broken into a high-security research facility before? I just wish I had something more to bring to this fight than a pistol.

What would Stell do, if she were here?

She'd try to use some of that mag sense to help her out. I take a deep breath and try to feel it like I did back at the pit. Cam zips overhead, still blocking the nano signal from me, but I can't feel anything. I don't like it. I was getting used to that feeling, of having something else kind of watching over me. I don't know how to describe it, but now I just feel cold.

I almost call for Jali to come back so I can take a swig of that drink, but I'm worried it will screw up my nano reflexes or whatever. Well, I can at least access my offline 'site programming now. I scan through the options. The familiar red lights of the 'site bar fill my eyes, and it feels good. Like a huge weight taken off me.

Reflex enhancer, check. Optical zoom, check. Strength boost, it's a go. That's more like it. Now I'm feeling ready for anything.

"So this place, it's a what again?"

"Research facility and storage depository," Dewey says. "Decrypted files say they test new equipment, weapons, and ships. And they study older materials, too. We'll find what we need in the hangar. Neman boosted a partial map of the facility. Here."

Dewey projects an image on the ground of the facility, including the wide ring of fencing around the whole thing. I spot the ridgeline to the west. I think Jali is heading up there now.

"You really think Jali's going to do any good up there?"

Dewey gives a short bark of a laugh. He doesn't respond with any words though.

The base sits in the center of the clearing. Blue lines of the holo map show some outlines of floor plans for a couple levels below the surface, but it's not very detailed down there. There are four big gaping holes in the landscape in front of the recessed entrance to the base.

"Those are hangar doors," Dewey says. "We go in, get our ship, and fly out of there. And pick up Jali before anyone even sees us."

"Right," Rym says. He points to a smaller building outside the main one. "This has got to be the hardline Scitech access point. Neman hits this first, cuts security, then we go in."

"That's where I can do my business," Neman says and pats me on the back. "We ready?" He looks to Rym.

No response. Rym checks the duffel over his shoulder.

"That's not the bag you had," I say. "What is it?"

"Hira left a package on the cart, somehow managed to get it on there without us seeing." Rym smiles at Dewey.

"Wait," I say with a smile. "Did you have a thing for Hira?"

If it wasn't so dark out, I'm pretty sure I would see a huge blush on Rym's old face. As it is, he doesn't say anything.

"And you let her go. Damn, dude."

"Watch it," Rym says. He gently adjusts the pack on his shoulder.

"What did she leave us?"

"A way out, if we need it. Now will you get this fence open? I want to get this op rolling."

***

A small building lies about a hundred feet past the fence. It's about twenty feet tall and wide. Just a plain gray shack, or it looks gray anyway in the security lights as they shine down on everything.

"That's mine," Neman says, pointing to the building. "That's got all the uplink capabilities we need. I'll upload your vid, start the other acts of needless mayhem around Phen, and we'll be good to go."

"What's their security?" I say.

Dewey scans the area. "A drone flies through this field but it's pattern is highly erratic."

Neman settles in with a heavy sigh. "No, it is not. I have been trying to explain this to you. It comes by at fifteen, ten, seventeen, eleven, eight, nineteen..."

Dewey cuts him off. "That's random."

"You haven't analyzed it enough. Aren't you a robot with a computer brain? You're supposed to be able to read patterns."

"I can if there is a pattern to read."

"There it goes." Neman points to a blinking object as it hovers past the inside of the fence. "That was seventeen, next eleven, nineteen…"

"Enough!" Rym says. "How much time until the next pass?"

"I already said it, eleven, eight, ninet—"

"If the bypass is complete, we go now." Rym waits for Neman to acknowledge that yes, the bypass has indeed been completed. "That will give us two minutes for Neman to get into the shed there and plug in. Right?"

Neman gives him the quadruple thumbs up. "Just don't shoot anything until after I'm done in there, right?"

Dewey's forearms extend and his pincer grips open wide. There's a glint of the security lights on the metal grips as he twists them around on the fence. With a smooth motion, he carves through the links without any resistance. That one sweep opens up a space big enough even for Neman.

He doesn't waste any time and jimmies himself through. "And that's why you do the heavy lifting and I do the heavy thinking around here." Neman salutes the bot and ambles off toward the shed.

Dewey waits a moment and then kicks sullenly at the ground. "I can think, too."

"I'm going to send Cam off with him," I say, clicking a control button on my wrist dock. "She should still be in range to block me if what Neman says was true."

"I'd trust him," Rym says.

Dewey nods begrudgingly.

Cam first zips around my head and then follows after Neman.

Dewey looks at me and I can tell what he's asking in his single eye. I grant him access to Cam's dock, at least the video portion, and immediately five little orange dots appear on the map he's projecting on the ground. There's one moving almost out of range, that's got to be Jali heading up to the ridgeline. Three dots together, that's me, Rym and Dewey. And finally there's Neman slowly making his way to the security access shed.

"Thanks," Dewey says.

"Well, we've all got to start trusting each other sooner or later, right?"

Inside though, I'm still a little tied up worrying about letting her go away with Neman, but also with Dewey. Breathe, isn't that what Stell said?

The little blips creep across the grounds as I sit here. Man, he's slow. It feels like forever, being exposed next to the snipped open fence, but soon they're at the building.

"Security is just as weak as we thought," Neman whispers through his comm unit, a little out of breath. "There's nothing out here. I'll be inside in a minute."

"Just hurry up," Rym says. "They'll pick up on your bypass before too long. And that drone will be here any minute."

"I said eleven, remember? Then—"

"Just get in there," Rym says.

The connection closes, and we're left to wait again. I heft the bag Jali left with me. She never said not to look inside, right? I pull the magnetic seal open and Dewey's dim light flashes in. Looks like he's just as eager to see whatever's in this thing as I am.

There are fifteen little metal disks, each about the size of my hand.

There's a dial on them, too, like an activator or timer. But for what? I pull one out, it's got a good heft to it, and touch the dial.

"Don't," a voice calls through on the comm. It's Jali. My hand relaxes. "At least not yet."

"Did you give me a bag of explosives?"

"No, that's not my department. This one's a bit more fun. You like surprises, don't you?"

"I guess."

"Then you'll just have to wait and see. You'll know when you need my help."

Man, couldn't she just tell me? That would make things a little easier.

My silence must prompt something in her. "Okay, if you want, there's a link button on the back of each disk. You can hook it up to your 'site."

"Will it alert Scitech at all? Having that connection?"

There's a pause. "It shouldn't. Neman and I put these together on the mine car, and he made sure to back off the current 'site software."

They did this on the cart? Where was I?

I'm about to ask, but Neman interrupts me.

"I'm in," he whispers. "Of course. There's hardwire access to the entire base."

And none too soon, I see a little flitting shape in the distance scanning the grounds with a blue beam. It's got to be that drone, and it's on its way here. I drop the disk back into the bag and click it shut.

"What's that beeping?" There's an insistent beeping in the background on Neman's comms device.

"Nothing. Well, nothing I can't handle."

The regular scanning of the drone stops and a red light replaces the blue one. It immediately makes a straight line toward the security shed where Neman and Cam are.

"You're about to have company," Dewey says. One of his chest cannons extends and a small whine emits from it.

Rym puts a hand on him. "You might miss at this range."

"What about Jali?" I say.

No one responds.

The drone gets closer, he's almost there. "Cam, be careful."

Rym clenches his fist and is about to say something when the red light switches off and is immediately replaced by the blue. The drone changes directions and begins scanning again.

That was close.

"I got it," Neman says. "Not to worry. And that fun little guy out there? He works for us now."

Rym pats Dewey on his back as the chest cannon retracts. "Nice work, Neman. Keep your eyes open for any news on Stell."

No time to waste. I throw the packs over my shoulder and hustle after Rym and Dewey already running into the compound. I veer toward the shed.

"No," Rym says. "Neman will keep tabs on security and stay in there as we head inside."

He's talking about the central building, or maybe even the four hangar access ports in the ground. Something thuds against my mind and gut, just out of reach. I've felt this before, down inside Magla by the pyramid, or octahedron, whatever Stell called it.

But this time I can't reach it. It's those nanos. I don't have any of that juice to block whatever they do to my head and body. But that's all right. I'm not going to get caught climbing without them again, like back on the Mirage. As long as I don't try to communicate with my nanos, I should stay off Scitech's radar. I flick on the night vision on my 'site, and zoom in on the ridgeline, knowing Jali is up there somewhere.

Even if she can't aim for crap.

"You coming?" Rym asks over his shoulder.

I guess that's the real question. There's no going back to Scitech after this, is there?

I nod. My reflexes tighten up; my strength builds. I sprint out after them, ready to bust this ship out of storage. Cam zips by and hovers in front of me. She's really quick, quicker than I've seen her before, except maybe down in the caverns with Stell. That just confirms what I thought about this place being another magnetic upwelling. She's harnessing it. Cam's mag vanes sweep into her body and she locks onto the wrist dock.

"Go ahead straight for the main building," Neman says through our short range comms. "Security is light. The only things outside are the drones. Our drones, now. And I've got access to the inside. Mostly cameras and motion detectors. Nothing I can't hack. This is going to be easy."

Did he really just say that? In any of the movies I've ever seen, that's pretty much a death sentence. An open invitation for anything to go wrong.

"Can you open one of these launch tubes?" Rym asks.

"Someone would surely notice," Neman says. "When we do that, we're only going to have a few short minutes to get the hell out of here with a ship."

"Then we go with plan B. Right in the front door. Can you clear us a path there, too?"

"Yup," Neman says. "And I've just coordinated our other attacks, and sent your message to your friends, Daj. Sent it through four or five back channels so we can't be traced, either."

This is the real stuff now. Kie and Zaylee are getting a message with me jumping off a roof somewhere in the middle of Phen City. In my message, I told them I couldn't stream my jump, and asked if they could help out and do it. No doubt they'll post it, even if they're compromised, like Rym claims they are. There's no way they'll miss an opportunity to get more views on a vid like this.

"I'll keep you posted about news stories around, and listen for anyone making a move on you." Neman really is in his element. He's not even gloating. "You're coming up on an entrance now. Once you're in, use Dewey's map function and I'll live update it with the data from here."

Maybe he's right. Maybe this will be easy. Shit, now I'm saying it, too. "What is that room?"

"It's a security hub. Not normally accessible, but I know the right way to get into it. That doesn't mean there aren't other stations around the base; in fact I know there are at least three. But I don't want to go poking around so much that they detect me here. I cut off the fence and drones. I sent the message. I'm going to check to see how far I can go without getting detected, but it might be a good idea to hold back."

"So he can't put everything on our map," I say.

"Not yet. But hopefully soon."

"Well, *hopefully soon* we need to be the hell out of here," Rym says. "Dewey, keep your sensors up and let us know what Neman can't see."

Two huge doors loom in front of us. They look like they could let in some smaller transport vehicles or larger if the two doors open together. To the left are a couple of smaller doors. A red light flashes against some sort of scanner next to the door.

"I think they're—"

The light quickly turns green, accompanied by a short hiss and the door opens. All three of us draw our weapons and aim inside. But there's nothing there, just a nice wide open mouth welcoming us in. Not a pleasant image.

"Unlocked," Neman says over the comms.

Another green light skips over the wall and door in front of us, a tiny little dot.

"That you, Jali?" Rym asks.

"I'm a watchin'," she whispers.

"Some good she's going to do us inside," I say as Rym and Dewey pass indoors. I take one last look at the night sky and see the brilliant colors of the aurora. I never get tired of that. I sigh and step inside. The cold night air is replaced by a relatively warmer and drier environment, and a blue glow of industrial lighting flickers down on us in an empty hallway.

"Those things I gave you..." Jali says.

She doesn't say more, so I extract one from the pack on my back. "Wait, these are actually extra eyes?"

"Mmm-hmm," Jali says.

"And your rail gun?"

"Mmm-hmm."

I spin the disk around in the air. Maybe we won't have to rely on her aim so much after all.

"She's always thinking of something," Rym says.

"Seems like we've got a pretty good team," I say. "Makes me wonder what Hira could have brought."

Rym creeps further into the facility toward the hangars in the sub levels. "We're just going to have to trust ourselves on this one. Come on."

CHAPTER 14

Large lift pads sit just inside those big doors to our right. Looks like all the ships and equipment are down below. Too bad. I thought we'd just be able to jack a ride right when we got in.

Thud.

I hear it again, and feel it in my gut. Like someone knocking on a door three levels below my apartment. What is this place? It's loud in here. Cam is sensing it too, I think. Her activation lights swell with each pounding blow.

"Do you guys feel that?"

Rym nods. "The magnetofield. It's strong here."

Cam's repelling flaps creep out of her central housing unit, but I push them back in. "Just stay close, it's not time to take off."

No matter how much I insist, Cam keeps flexing her wings as we walk down the abandoned hall. It's like she can't keep still and wants to head further into the facility.

It doesn't look like there's anybody in here. It's kind of creepy. Must be more of a day research facility.

"Cameras in the following hallway," Neman says. "I'll shut them down, temporarily."

We'll have to take his word for it. The black globes on the ceiling up ahead have to be cameras, but there are no lights to indicate they're even active.

Up ahead on the right must be a cafeteria for the staff. Rows of tables with floating stools parked beside them. All gray, which fit in with the rest of the cold sterile work environment. The place is empty, too, except for a cleaning bot delegated to scrubbing the floors. It bops up and down as the floor buffer does its thing. Rym motions us to sneak past the room. Even though it's a janitor bot, it might still have security protocols.

It's not until we reach the offices up ahead that we see our first non-robotic staff. Dozens of work techs are programming something, and in some cases hooking Maglans up to wires and other interfaces. Come to think of it, I can't really tell if this is an office or a medical facility.

Probably a mix of both. Luckily, it's not during the day. This place would probably be crawling with staff. And security.

"Just stay low," Rym whispers back to me. "We've got to find out if there's even a ship here to steal."

My hearts race a little more. "There might not be one?"

"Our intel is good," Rym says. "We just have to see how good. There will be ships here, but in what condition is the real question."

Down to our right past the cafeteria is a wall of computer screens. It must be some sort of database for the entire facility. "Can we use those to find out?"

Dewey beeps a positive. "That interface is hard wire only. They use a computer like that to back up and store everything that goes in and out of here."

"He's right," Neman says. He sounds a little upset, like he wanted to share that first. "I can't access it from here. Part of their security protocol."

"Cam can do it." Before anyone can argue, I release the lock and Cam's wings extend. She hovers right above the floor silently cruising on the mag waves pumping from this place. "Look for Skywatch ship tech."

In an instant, she zips along the floor. She blends in so well with the bland tiling that I just about lose sight of her. The only reason I know she reaches the computer is the camera hooked up to my minimized 'site. With a green light on the indicator, she's ready to start downloading info.

Before I can ask how she's going to access the database, Neman pops in. "Yes, I added a few files to her so she can crack their login. Sorry. Again."

I wonder if Neman will ever come clean and tell me exactly everything he installed in her.

Charts and images zip past the screen showing me what she is up against. "Don't download all of that stuff. Just find information on the ships."

After some exasperated beeping, the info pops up on my display.

"Sub level two, in the hangar area. We'll find Skywatch ships there."
Several schematics pop up of various ships. Speeders, troop transports,

a sled like the one Stell and I totaled. Maybe it is hers.

"Rym, that glider we rode, there's one here like it, recently logged in."

"Maybe she's here," he says. A slight smile flickers on his lips. "Neman, run a scan for any new prisoners."

"You got it."

Rym looks back at me. "Any ships we can use to get out?"

"I think so. Look." I point to a beauty of a ship, sweeping lines, and diamond-shaped just like the tattoos everyone has.

"I'm not sure they're ready to just take and go," I say. "They might need a little work."

Rym looks over at my display screen on the dock. "You let me and Dewey worry about that." He grins over at the bot. "It's a Skywatch ship all right."

"So no one's going to notice it's missing?" I say.

"Let me worry—" Neman starts.

"Yeah, yeah. Is anyone going to let me worry about something?"

There's a stairwell next to the lifts, so to avoid any cameras we sneak down the steps to sublevel 2. When we make it down and crack open the door, I nearly drool. This is it, the mother of all hangar bays. Everywhere I look there are Scitech skimmers, hover cars, and even some bigger tug ships hooked up to various monitoring equipment. And those are just the first things I notice. It was one thing to see their schematics on Cam's display, but face to face it's something completely different. This room spreads out beyond what I can see, and it is jam packed with tech.

"Here, take these," I say to Rym and Dewey. There are tech headgear, mag-linked work suits, and tool carts right by the stairs in a cubby.

Rym takes the clothing and steps back into the stairwell to put it on. I follow suit, but Dewey doesn't take anything.

"If anyone asks, I'm just a bit of old tech you're working on, all right?"

Not a bad idea. I put the uniforms on and the mag seals cinch themselves tightly across my chest and legs. This doesn't feel right on me. Meanwhile, Rym looks like he's one grease stain away from being a master mechanic.

"Has Cam sifted through that data file yet?"

Cam's wings pop and droop out to the sides. She's acting kind of, well, full, is what it looks like. Seems like she grabbed a bit too much for her memory. Initial reports pop up overlaying info on different vehicles over the floor plans.

"New tech is up front. Mainly repairs. A tug with a faulty power system. Mag cores and solid fuel replacements needed in some speeders, ones that look similar to what chased me and Stell out of the caves."

"Yeah, yeah," Rym says. "What about our ship?" He arches his neck to try to see past the hundreds of different vehicles around us.

Showers of sparks pour into the air in the distance. I think that's the disassembly area. I point to it.

"Pretty sure it's back there prepped for gutting. I think parts are being scavenged and researched here. I don't know how many whole ships we're going to find."

"There better be something, or we're not getting off this planet. Let's hurry."

I'm not sure we even need to be wearing these clothes. The few techs that are working tonight are dialed right into their stuff. And the ones that occasionally glance up, do it briefly and quickly and get right back into their work. This is the gutting crew. They're not paid to keep an eye on intruders.

"I got a mag core!"

Two other techs scramble away from their torches to give a hand to the one who called out. A Scitech researcher, by the look of her data pad and lack of dirt and grease on her, scans in the device the man is holding. Dewey grabs me by the collar and pulls me out of sight behind another line of vehicles, this time a series of gliders.

"We're not invisible," Dewey says.

"Oh, man, these are the new gliders, like the one they lent me." I reach up to touch the smooth lines, but Dewey drags me away.

"We've got a job to do."

"And you don't want me screwing it up. I get it."

Dewey glances back at me and when he turns about he nudges a part from a nearby shelf. It begins to roll and falls off the edge, but I grab it with two hands before it can clatter.

"We're not invisible," I say in his robotic speech tone.

Dewey keeps on walking. Hopefully he heard me. He hasn't had enough of my sass lately.

As I follow behind, my neck kinks up from staring up at the ships and parts all around me. Back in the city, we'd see outsiders come visit the Rings and they'd all look just like I do right now. The cities don't draw me in. I mean, the buildings are cool 'architectural wonders' according to Kie. But I don't need anything more than this right now.

Mechanical arms mag-linked to the ceiling haul massive freighters and engines across the hangar bay. Repairing and flying. I wonder if they need any extra help around here.

"Come on," Rym whispers from up ahead. He's weaving his way around parts jutting out into the middle of the aisles.

Seems like they could be better organized.

Rows of parts, another of ship frames, and finally we get to some of the older tech. It looks like it, at first, anyhow. Rym traces his hands along an obviously older wing segment fused onto the frame of a new speeder. He spits on the ground.

"Old is best," he mutters.

He does have a point. His old tech had the better designs, but Scitech sure has a way with squeezing the most speed out of an engine. I'm not so sure a mash-up of the two isn't what might be best.

I don't tell him that though, as he seems to have a lot more spit left. And we definitely need the old tech to fly undetected into the moon belt. Although from the looks of things around here, I wonder if anything is in one piece.

In a minute, my question is answered. And, dear gods, there it is. A real beauty. She's got the smooth lines of a classic Skywatch freight craft, not as compact or pointy as one of the partial fighter classes next to it, but there she is. One of the arms from the ceiling is still attached to it holding it upright, but there's also landing gear supporting it.

"A Skywatch FT-200."

Rym stares at me. "How do you know that?"

I shrug. "I don't know. From when I was a kid, I guess."

His eyes go back to the craft, and I wonder if he's starting to tear up. But I can't tell for sure as he runs around, checking on various parts. "She's missing some things, but from what I've seen around here, Dewey and I can fix her up. I'm going to try and get in the cockpit to run a diagnostic. Come on, baby, let's hope they haven't gutted you."

Rym slaps a button on the side of the ship but nothing happens. He hits it several more times but still nothing.

"Dewey, come here. I need you to provide backup power to get me in."

Dewey hustles over and plugs in.

An FT. Freight transport. Its wings sweep back from its prominent front half, but it looks like there are pieces missing from up top. It's got a massive mag plate on its base, useful for producing the lift here on the planet. I step around to the back and start to chuckle.

"Those are some big boosters."

No joke. There are two big atmo busting mag repulsors sticking out its back end. Hopefully the mag core hasn't been drained, although by the sound of those workers back there, there's at least one core around.

With a click and a hum, the gangway opens like a yawning mouth from under the ship. Rym pats Dewey on the back and the two of them hustle on board. I've got to see this. Something tugs at my memory, some sensation of playing with a toy ship, a smaller version of this.

There's a little scoring around the edges of the outer hull, damage from some old battle. But from the inside of the sealed walkway, it seems to be a solid ship, still I pound the wall just to be sure.

There's a real strong similarity to the glider Rym had been tooling with in his workshop, not in size at all, but the material is pretty much the same, I think. It also has the same smooth lines. Scitech is all about the industrial packaging, abrupt boxes and edges. These ships, however, seem to have been made for sailing in the air.

"How's the power back there?" Rym shouts from up front.

"Negative." Dewey plugs into the consoles in the cargo portion of the ship.

These things could haul troops or materials anywhere on the planet or offworld.

"I'm able to run the circuits back here though, so they haven't been gutted."

There's a built-in mini mag lift arm in the cargo hold, so I sit down and grab the controls to help clear out some of the parts taking up space.

Nothing.

"And I bet you'll get nothing," Dewey says. "You have too many nanos in you to operate anything on this ship. They get in your way of controlling the basic components. You could say you're not compatible with this hardware."

I examine my hands. He's right. I can't sense anything about this ship other than the distant thudding of the mag field around here. This sucks. I was able to use the glider with Stell, though, right?

"You don't have any of that drink left, do you?"

Dewey gives me a shrug of his shoulders and gets back to checking out the ship. "Go tell Rym I'll be checking out the engine and mag repulsors next."

Sure. I guess I have to be the useless messenger boy.

Thud.

"You hear that?"

Dewey ignores me.

It's that call again. There's something going on in this place.

By the time I get up to Rym, he's hard at work running through different consoles in the cockpit. Seems like one Maglan can pilot this whole thing.

"Dewey says the circuitry is working back there, and he's going to go look at the engines next. I think the main power core is depleted."

"Yeah, that was my guess, too. That's not our only problem. Did you see that space up at the top of the ship?"

"You mean the big gap, like something's missing up there?"

"That's where the weapon components should be. We're not going to make it very far if we can't shoot anything."

"It's got mag capabilities though, right? Defensive? I've seen what something like this can do on a smaller scale. Your glider had something like it."

Rym smiles, finally. "You know your stuff. Yes, it does. But we'll need as much firepower as we can get."

"What's the rig look like? I can go through the files Cam ripped. There are tons of parts. There has got to be something."

Rym flips open another console and tweaks with it. "Well go on. Go find it!"

"I'm going, don't worry."

"Stay close. We need to get out of here in less than an hour, and maybe sooner."

"He's not joking," Neman says over the comms from the ship. "Oh yeah, I patched into the system there. You'll never guess what ship this is."

Rym keeps working as Neman strings out the wait.

"It's the 'Peace Hammer.'"

I laugh. The name suits it.

Rym snorts. "Are you kidding me? We actually flew this thing a few times. What are the odds?"

"Unbelievable," Dewey says.

"Neman?" Rym asks. "Any word on Stell, yet?"

"Negative. But there's a lot of stuff here to go through."

Rym looks at me. "You still here? Find that weapon. Watch your bot for any sign of Stell, but stay out of sight, and out of trouble."

"I guess you don't need me here," I say under my breath.

Still, I salute him and walk out of the ship's cargo hold watching Cam's downloaded feed. The schematics for the FT pull up and, yeah, there it is, I see where the attachment goes. Apparently, different things can plug in there including an interchangeable weapons modification unit, an advanced sensor array, and orbital mining equipment. There are some other additions, but I can't access them right now, and according to the log of the parts and ships, there's something in this room that will work.

I take it all in, the huge underground bay. I bet I could spend days sorting through this material and still not find what I'm looking for.

"Cam, give me a hand, will you?"

She zips off as soon as I make the request.

While I wait, I pick through different piles around the ship hoping to see anything that might be able to help. Various parts, belts, gears, booster boxes. Nothing weapon-like, but old and rusted is the general look of things. I wonder if we'll find anything that'll work.

"I'm going to go over here," I call out to Dewey. He doesn't respond.

Whatever. He's busy with his thing.

After two rows of more of the same tools and parts, I lose my crap.

"You are kidding me." It can't be.

There's something, sleek and narrow, about twenty feet long. My hearts pump wildly when I think what it might be.

It's covered with boxes and sheets of metal, but I make short work of them despite what Rym said about being quiet. It's a silver color with two dark red fins jutting out from the front sides. And yes, it definitely is what I thought it was, a vintage Skywatch recon fighter with multi-tiered engines. It's definitely made for speed, but it also has enough firepower to put up a fight. I think this model was called a Dagger.

Okay, I one hundred percent know it is.

"Cam, get over here! We need to get this running."

Even if this isn't the weapon Rym needs, I can fly alongside him and give him cover. I run to the back and pull aside tarps and parts to expose the booster jets. Dude. If these things work, they can break atmo, too.

Cam settles on the hull near the cockpit shield and plugs in. A dim light blinks on the ship, definitely running underpowered. The cockpit shifts an inch and then stops. I have to pull it the rest of the way, but it opens to a well-worn padded seat with a helmet resting on the floor.

I tentatively hop in. It's like a dream I've always had.

There are four control sticks right next to me. I instinctively grasp them, click their buttons and move them from side to side.

"Nah, it's mag core is drained." Not like I had much hope.

The array of buttons and screens is a little daunting. I've never seen this kind of thing before, up close anyway. Cam displays a holo projection over the instrument panel in front of me indicating where targeting systems, power supplies, and a whole slew of other controls are located. I reach for the mag core switch, flip it, and hold my breath.

Nothing. Not even a spark or a flicker of energy.

I sigh. "Rym, I found us a ship, an old Dagger."

A second later, Rym responds. "A Dagger. That's good. That'll do. Is she working?"

I flip more switches but still nothing. "No, but I think everything is here, just a power supply is missing."

"That's not much help, unless you can scrounge a core for it. Keep an eye out and—"

"Help, Daj."

What's that? Who's calling me?

But there's only the thudding sound shaking my body.

"Did you hear that?"

Both Rym and Dewey ignore me. I strain my ears to listen for the call again, but nothing happens. There are only the distant machinery sounds in the hangar. But I heard it, I know it.

And it came from down below. Could it be Stell?

I can't ignore this, and maybe I can find a power supply as well. I mentally request the part through Cam's interface and she stores that info. Maybe there's some other weapon or tech that could really help us out, but I really, really want this ship to work.

That sound. Wherever it is, it's not on this level. It's down there, somewhere. And if there's a chance that it could be Stell, I've got to help.

I glance back at the behemoth, the Peace Hammer. Rym and Dewey are hard at work doing what they do. They'll be fine without me. I'll be back soon, no worries. I check my pistol just to be sure I've got a little protection and then I pat the side of the Dagger.

"Don't worry, I'll be back for you, too."

Man, I sound like Neman. He'd probably say the same thing, or worse.

I duck and follow the line of equipment back to the lifts. The other Maglans in the hangar are hard at work on whatever project they're still doing, no matter if it is way late at night. Early in the morning? Whatever.

A wave of exhaustion washes over me reminding me of how long a day it's been, and that I'll probably be awake for a lot longer. Another deep rumbling reverberates through me, but this time it comes from my stomach. There are some food bars that Rym packed for me, so I tear into one. Mmm. Flavorless and no texture? Delicious.

Cam lifts off from my arm, still a little slow, but she hovers above me as I walk. It's pretty awesome that I don't have to tell her what to do. She seems to know what I'm thinking. I reach the lifts and the stairwell without any problems, and in seconds I'm down to the next floor.

I peek out of the door into the long hallway here at sublevel three. This place is a little busier than up above. The lift opens and lets out a group of researchers carrying boxes. They're armed, too, or at least I think they are. There's a device attached to their lower hands that looks like some sort of energy emitter. They're not talking to each other or really looking at anything as they head down the hall. I know that look. That's the 'site. They must be hooked up and following orders or researching as they walk.

There's a large door that first beeps and then hisses open as they approach. There has got to be some sort of scan that's letting them pass, so I quickly follow without following too closely and slip through as the door hisses shut behind me.

"Daj?" It's Neman, but he's cutting out.

"I can barely hear you. Hello?"

No reply. My gut tells me to contact him through my 'site, but of course that would set off all sorts of alarms if I even got close to activating that signal. I hesitate and turn around to check on the door.

Damn, it's locked. Probably nano-linked to the researchers. The control pad next to the door blinks its lights in a merry *eff-you-I'm-not-going-to-open* kind of fashion. The hall is at least ten feet wide, but has no place to hide while I wait for someone to open this door.

Guess I've got no choice but to keep walking and see what is going on down here. The hall keeps going for quite some time, though, not a door or window anywhere. Cam flits off to go check things out just in case any researchers come back down the hall.

"Stay close." She checks back every thirty seconds or so, but still keeps zipping up ahead. After one more minute, she sends an image of a wide open room.

When I finally catch up to that point, I see how large the room is. Dang, that's a big flipping room. The ceiling isn't very tall, and the lighting is way down low, but the banks of lights extend way back, a couple hundred feet maybe. The lights are shining down onto long rows of tanks filled with liquid. Some researchers walk past them, some reaching in to extract some of the liquid, others just standing by different control panels, possibly verifying the measurements. They're all wearing heavy coats.

I check the door, not holding much hope for it being unlocked, but to my amazement, it slides open. Apparently once you're down here in the secured area there's no reason to lock anything up. When I get inside, a cold blast of air cuts right through me. What are they keeping in here that needs to be sub-zero temperatures?

Luckily, there's a rack of jackets with hoods, and I throw one on. A breath mask pops up over my mouth. Built-in goggles slide down over my eyes and a series of lights flash, informing me of a link-up error. A message pops up saying that the thermal-insulated jacket will remain nonfunctional until connection can be established. Crap. It's cold in here. At least this jacket is better than nothing, and can possibly provide me with some cover.

There's a single data pad next to the coat rack, so I grab it just in case anyone asks. It makes me look official. Again, I'm met with the same connection error message, but this flashes once and then displays some information.

'Magnetotroph monitoring protocol.' What the hell is a magnetotroph? Something hits me, back when I was in school, about some microscopic early life forms. I can't place it though, maybe it's something to do with these guys. If I could just pull up the 'site I'd be able to remember something about the proto life forms on the planet.

I walk past a tank and stare into the glass at the dark liquid. The data pad registers the temperature of the liquid. It's a balmy near-freezing inside. The digital label of this says '*magnetotrophs v 1.7.*' It looks like normal water, but for the shine of tiny particles moving around in there. There's a tap next to a small bench and a pile of clear poly tubes.

A series of lights appear on the tubes as I approach and the data pad alerts me that I need to grab a sample. I grab the cold container and hold it to the tap. In a second the thing fills up with liquid.

Thud. The deep pounding outside my ears resonates again, but this time there's a much crazier reaction. Whatever is in the container swirls as the pounding repeats. The tops of the tanks beyond me splash up in tiny droplets and suspend in the air for a few seconds before trickling back down. The critters align themselves through the glass in a weirdly symmetrical pattern with microscopic specks of silver all glowing slightly when they line up.

The pounding fades away and the water settles back down. That was cool. Way too cool to put back. I think I'll hold this, and bonus, it fits nicely in my pack.

I hurry past this tank to another row to see what the data pad says about them. Another stock section. And the next one. Are they all the same? I swipe through the data pad to see if I can glean any other information about what is going on, but this seems to only be a monitoring station.

"Why do you think they do that?"

I almost crap my pants right there.

I am too busy looking at these tanks to have noticed that someone else was monitoring them, as well. And she's standing right next to me. Asking me questions. She's just someone else dressed just like me, with her goggles pulled down.

"You know, the alignment thing?"

I am dumbfounded so I do the only thing I can, and that's shrug.

"Same. It is weird though."

She doesn't sound very much like the upper level scientist I thought everyone in here would be. Nor some evil bureaucrat like Ms. Pontane. Do they just hire a bunch of interns to scan in simple data? I don't want to get caught up in this conversation, or even say one word, so I wave and move on to the next bay of tanks.

This section is different. There's no sign explaining what's in this one. But when I hold up my data pad, I get a brief description. This one says *"Magnetotrophic nanotech research 3.5."*

"It's been a busy day. Did you hear the report?"

It's that researcher. She's followed me over here, too. Can't she take a hint?

"What report?" I say in a low voice. I feel that if I don't reply she's going to get suspicious.

She does pause for a second and tilts her head slightly. Is she going to bust me? Is she already making a call? I wonder if I can even turn on my body language reader on my 'site. Would that get picked up? Nah. Better to stay off.

"The one about the local terrorist? Turns out some old Skywatch fanatic in a neighboring village was discovered. It was pretty crazy. The lady apparently had her whole house rigged up to explosives waiting. Scitech got her though."

I can barely breathe. Hira? That has to be her. And her great grandkids? Are they actually all dead?

Maybe I can get the feed on the data pad here. I tweak a few buttons and try to access the news, but it's easier than that. There's a direct line sequence to the actual raid, including multiple vids of it from different angles.

"Is there something wrong with your 'site?"

"Uh, yeah, I've been having, uh, connective issues all day."

I hope she buys it. I don't have any time for more questions. I watch the vid from the beginning, see the troops and the skimmer approaching the little village with their augmented night 'site.

Scattered dialog, but it's pretty quiet. The security squad is focused and tight. There's a text bar scrolling past: *"Report of a blocked Nanosite feed on a known insurgent."* That's all it took for Scitech to prompt this attack? Seems like there has to be more, like maybe footage of me or something.

The skimmer touches down just outside of the house. The lights along the walking path lock onto the camera. I remember those creepy little eyes. What I don't remember is them rising out of the ground. And I really don't remember them starting to flash. The feed is killed in a blinding light and a howl of static.

This is followed by the vid of Maglans running for cover and finally losing their shit.

"Hit the house!" a Maglan shouts.

There's an intense whining as the skimmer powers up and rises through a swirl of smoke from Hira's security system. Explosions go off, rocking Maglans to the ground and killing their 'site feed. This goes on for ten more seconds until the feed completely severs.

"Did they capture the terrorist?" I turn around to face the researcher, but she's not there. Just an empty aisle.

"Shit."

Time to get out of here. Even if she didn't see who I was, it won't be long now until all of Scitech is on to me. And all of us. I look up to the way I came in and there she is talking to a security crew. An armed security crew wearing body armor. They've got rifles.

I duck so fast and start hustling down the long row of tanks. Away from the front entrance. There's got to be some other way out of here. Right?

"Neman?" I whisper into my comm unit.

Nothing.

"Cam? You got anything? A way out?"

Cam lifts from the dock and zips away down the aisle. There's no chance of getting out the way I came in, so I start to follow her to the back.

That tech didn't see who I was. I'm just someone breaking into the base, or escaping from it. Not Daj on the run from Scitech to hijack a ship. Nope. And if there's any luck on my side, security will just think she's nuts. Lost her mind. You've been on shift for too many hours. Why don't you take a break kind of thing.

Why didn't I just stay in the hangar and find that weapon Rym asked about? I pop my head up and look back. Bad idea. They've got drones of their own flying my way with bright lights scanning the rows. Ok, go faster. I duck back down and sprint.

My breath comes out in big steamy puffs in this cold room. This is one long row. Same thing, though. It's filled with liquid and the shiny magnetotrophs. I'm still clutching the data pad in one hand and catch the words, 'stealth chromatophores' on it. That sounds cool.

The next row contains a completely different ecosystem. Glass walls pen up fungal trees, bright red flowers, and plenty of those berries I saw when I was with Stell. Those things were good. Anyway, it looks like they're trying to keep these environmentally controlled with different colored lights, moisture, and temperature. My data pad reveals them to be slightly warmer than the sub-zero temps from before, but not by much.

My stomach rumbles as I eye those red berries. That bar Rym gave me a while back didn't knock much of a dent in my hunger and these would help. A quick glance over my shoulder shows no one's running in my direction yet.

The clear glass door swishes open as I approach and I reach out for the berries. They pop off the fungal plant with ease. They've got to be perfectly ripe. My mouth waters right around the edges but before I can eat one, Cam flies back in front of me and a light flashes on her arm dock. She found a way out of here through the back, a security hatch or a ventilation system or something. Well, there's another poly tube here, too, so I stash a couple handfuls of the berries into it, and seal it with a slight whooshing sound. Cam bumps into my head, gently.

"All right, I'm coming!"

She leads the way through the aisles and I run after her, low and hopefully out of sight. There's no calling out from the guards. I can still hope they think the technician is crazy, right? But there'll be evidence from her Nanosite, for sure. If she's like everyone else I know, she'll have run her vid capture all the time, hoping for some cool thing to record so she can post for views. Luckily my face was mostly covered. They can't get a partial from that. Right?

What does Scitech want with these fruits? And what experiments are they doing with the nanotech and magnetotrophs? The fruits cancel out connection to the Scitech server, and essentially all nanotech. They certainly don't want to do that.

Finally, at the end of the huge room, Cam comes to a hovering stop right in front of a grated wall panel. I grab onto the edges with all four hands and yank. The grating comes loose with a couple pings and little metal fasteners skitter across the floor. It's dark back there, but I flip on my night 'site and instantly pipes, wires and other conduits come into view.

This is going to be a tight squeeze, but I can make it. And it's better than the alternative out there with security getting closer. As if to remind me, the sound of approaching footsteps grows louder.

The panel is tougher to pull up from this direction, but I stick it into place as best as I can. It wiggles back and forth when I leave it, but it's probably solid enough that they might not notice. Now, if I had only thought about sweeping those fasteners away.

Amidst those thoughts, I knock my skull against some low hanging pipes.

"Dammit." How much lower am I going to have to scooch to get out of this tunnel? Any tighter and I might not fit. The dim light behind me starts to fade as I inch my way through the wall, metal bits and things jabbing into my side and face and pretty much everywhere else.

Cam doesn't stray too far now. She disappears for a second and then comes right back to check on me.

"Still here, girl."

She gives a plaintive beep and then inches past my face hovering away behind me to go check on the security team. I freeze up and listen and try not to make any sound someone might hear. Cam's speaker pops on in my comm unit and I hear what I hoped to avoid. Footsteps approaching, only twenty feet away. By the sound of it, there are at least two guards.

I'm so cramped up, and I draw in a few deep breaths to help not focus on the walls closing in on me. I've never been claustrophobic, but I'm guessing I can learn.

The footsteps get louder, louder, and then they stop.

"Are you sure he didn't double back?"

"Pretty sure."

Cam extends one of her filament-like fingers and settles onto some wires. Like some gigantic insect, she injects the fang-like finger into the wall. A series of lights flash and her central servos spin as she accesses some inner working of the facility. I hear a faint sound of sizzling electronics coming out of the corridor.

"Did you hear that?" a voice says through Cam's audio receptors.

"Yeah, this way."

There are more sounds of footsteps but this time they move away. I let out a breath I didn't really know I was holding and jam myself forward.

"Nice distraction, Cam." I pet the top of her frame when she returns. It's kind of like her head. "Did Neman show you that one?"

She releases another string of beeps. Seems like she set something off in the hall for those guys. I don't know what I'd do without her.

Rip.

I bite back a string of curse words as a metal protrusion catches my pants and tears a nice long gash across them. And it's back to pulling and squeezing through this maze for the next twenty minutes before I reach another grate.

I don't even listen or ask Cam to do a scan for what's on the other side. I'm getting out no matter what. I can't breathe anymore and sweat is dripping down my back.

"Help us."

There it is, that voice, or voices again. I'm closer to them now. Like, really close.

With one big kick, I shove the grate outward into the dark room. Even the night 'site is not letting me really see what's going on. There must be very little light to amplify in here. It smells weird though, like dirty feet. Like a huge pile of dirty feet. I'm not going back in the tunnel, so this room and its stinky feet will have to do.

I walk a few paces and kick some solid things, like fist-sized stones. They scatter and roll away. Then I brush up against something damp and cold like a huge slab of meat. It sways away, but then it comes back and bumps into me knocking me back a pace. I stumble and actually hit another something just like the first one. This time something wet and slimy drips onto my forearm. I instantly swing my arm back and forth to get it off.

Cam gives a pathetic little beeping sound. I don't like it, either.

Okay, calm down, and find the way out of here. I wonder if there is any information on my data pad about what the hell I just walked into. The dim glow from the pad illuminates the space around me, but I focus on the words on the screen, "Neural disruptor research." That sounds normal, right? But what is in this room?

I slowly lift the pad up to light whatever keeps bumping into me. A sick feeling in my stomach starts to bloom as the wavering thing next to me materializes. There's a leg, and arms, and a head. I think it's a Maglan, but I can't really tell because the size of its limbs are at least twice what they should be. But it's the head that comes next. A thick line of drool hangs from the distorted mouth.

I back away from it only to bump into another. That's when I start to freak out. How many of these guys are in here? And why are they stuck altogether in the pitch dark? A soft moaning surrounds me and I shine the light up into their oversized, bulbous eyes. They don't see me, or if they do, they don't do anything besides let out a low moan.

Is this the result of the neural research? I don't care. I just need to get the hell out of here. Keep calm. Don't freak out. Don't bump into the brain-fried meat bags. I step directly onto one of those stones on the floor and twist my ankle reaching out for anything to stop me from falling. I grab onto an arm, cold and wet, probably from that drool.

"Shit!" I manage to keep my balance despite the dark and not wanting to touch anything.

Thud. This one's so loud my whole body shakes. Even the things in my backpack rattle around.

"Help us."

The call is much louder now. I must be really close. If I can get out of this place maybe I can…

Wait, the voices, are they these guys?

There's some sort of feeling in the air as I seek out the entrance to this place. It feels like a bunch of angry Maglans, but they're not saying anything. I just sense it. Forget it, just hurry and find the exit, man. Hell, I'd even go back into the wall at this point if I could find it.

I slide myself through the milling Maglan nano zombies as if I were back in that tunnel trying to avoid any contact or anything to keep them from noticing me. Cam responds to my thoughts and flits overhead to get a better view of the room. In a second, she transmits a 3D image into my head detailing the room edges, the tunnel entrance we went through, and the door. Luckily this room isn't too big. It's maybe fifty feet deep, but man did they try to cram in as many of these guys as they could.

The ones closest to me grunt and turn to face me. I disable the image Cam sent and they return to their normal, pleasant groaning selves. Wait. I flip the communication back on and the ones nearest to me swing out with their limbs. I flick the com off again and the Maglans stumble a bit. Their feet make a clicking sound as they shuffle along the floor kicking stones, too. I look down for the first time and notice gratings and spigots sticking up. Is this a cleaning station? There's no water dripping anywhere, but there is a faint smell of some chemical. Strong and familiar.

Wait a second. My heart pounds in my chest as I lift the data pad up to read the display. Fully this time. *Neural disruptor research.*' And below that? *Test subject disposal and bio-metal collection room.*'

That smell? It's fuel, or something else similar. Whatever it is, they're going to torch this place, these mutants. And me.

A flashing light begins to reel around crazily in the center of the room and I hear a pounding all around as if panels are dropping in place. The horde sways back and forth, smashing into each other. They're going to burn me, dammit, and take the metal in my gut for some sick research.

"Neman?" I yell through my comms channel. The whole room erupts with a loud scream. The channel seems to have tripped them up. There isn't any way I can get through this, so I turn it off. If I couldn't reach him before, there's no way I can get through now.

"Cam." I stay off the frequencies so these poor bastards don't hear it on their oversensitive neural receptors. "Get to the side of the room and make some distraction so I can get through here!"

Cam's little lights flicker and she zooms away over the tops of their heads. She must know what I'm trying to do, as I pick up a really low-frequency transmission over my comms channel. There's not a lot of movement in the horde, just enough so that half of them move toward her with a groan. That leaves me barely any room to move, but it's enough.

I've got to get to the door.

It's still a squeeze, but much easier, and I finally reach what I think is the front of the room close to the exit. But panels drop down to the floor, something to seal us all when the fun begins. And those grates? My dust will go down there when I'm done.

Nope. Not going to think about it. I'm getting out of here.

The data pad displays a little helpful message in the corner of the screen. *Two minutes until conflagration.*

I'm guessing that's referring to my crispy death.

"Cam? Any help?" My voice is a pleasant couple of octaves higher than normal.

Maybe I can piss off this group and they'll tear the walls down.

And me at the same time. Next.

Cam attaches herself to the wall right in front of me and I can see an overlay of the mechanics underneath it all. Glowing green and blue lines representing parts and electronics. And it's all centered around one section. A control panel?

"Can you short it out?"

Cam beeps once and begins to prod at the wall with her tiny fingers. She pries and sparks with her digit, but nothing gets through to the circuits. I hold the data pad up trying to find some way to remote control the lock. If only I can get that to disengage. It should reset the power to this grid and stop the process.

"One minute to conflagration," a calm voice says. A sharp whoosh comes out of the grating, and I see a blue glow of priming fire warming up.

Yeah, that's very motivational. I shove the pad into my pack and as I do, I run my hands across a bag with small disks in it. It's Jali's. I'd forgotten about that. Didn't she say she was always watching? I hope to hell she is now. I remove one of the small disks and turn it over in my hands. It's got a dial on one side. One way says *timed* and the other way says *targeting*. I twist it to targeting and the unit powers up with a small hum and a green light.

"Attach unit to target," a small computerized voice says.

I line up the disk with the holo projection of the control panel and put it against the wall. It locks into place and a series of red lights emit from it. They look like control arms and trajectory paths incoming. That's hopefully Jali's location they're coming from. I touch the four beams and they respond like a holographic control stick.

"Thirty seconds." A thin hiss surrounds me, and the smell of fuel grows stronger.

I get it, I get it. I tweak Jali's targeting beacon so that it lines up with the box. For a brief second I applaud the control function on these things. Very detailed and receptive, but then thoughts of my upcoming incineration bring me back.

I let go and the control beams disappear, hopefully letting Jali know. What's this green beam of light pointing into my head, though? I shift my head away from it and turn behind me to see the projected light continue past me.

Was that thing Jali's targeting—

A white hot sizzling projectile whips out of the ceiling through where my head just was, and into the wall. Yes. Yes it was her targeting beam. The alarm lights immediately turn off and the walls retract upwards as the system resets. There is a hole in the wall with hot, melted, metal around it. The shot also continued through it, exposing the hallway beyond this room with a gaping hole in it as well.

The door slides open and I'm free to go. As are my new friends, the traveling zombies.

"You're free! Now help me get the hell out of here!"

CHAPTER 15

Alarms blare with flashing lights, too. I'm praying it's for the busted doors on the incinerator murder project they had running, in which I had almost been an unwilling participant. The crowd of nano zombies follows me into the hall in a stumbling fashion, free, for the moment. I don't think they can hear me, or see me, but they're moving out of there anyway. Like water spilling out of a tipped bucket.

Thud. The pulsing is louder now.

In the echoes, I'm pretty sure there's a faint whispering. I can't understand what it's saying, but it's not 'help us' anymore. And it's definitely not Stell saying it.

Someone's on the way here, that's for sure, and our little mission will be toast if I'm caught. I only need to find some stairs up, and then I can get back to the ship, screw the guns.

"Don't follow me," I yell at the horde. "I freed you from the room, you go figure a way out of here yourself. Go on."

But they can't even think. They can't move right. Hell, they got themselves caught up altogether in a room that was going to torch and harvest their gut metal. Maybe it would have been a better idea to just leave them to that fate.

No. The thought sickens me as I let it sink in. I'm not a monster. But what can I do for them, anyway? Besides die along with them in this hole. I sprint down the hall with a nagging guilt riding in the pit of my stomach. A quick look over my shoulder shows that the huge group of mutated freaks is following. Or they're just spreading out from the fire room. Either way, they're going to bring security right onto me.

The data pad blips up an announcement. *"Neural research breach. Test subjects need immediate redirection."*

Yup, security right down on me.

The hallway turns the corner and up ahead is the sliding door I came through before, or it certainly looks similar. Either way, there are lifts and stairwells beyond. It's a way out.

I give one last glance over my shoulder to see my followers tagging along like sad, mutilated pets. Right in front of them, straight out of the ceiling, a massive metal panel drops down. It's like a corral or something, a moveable piece of the maze to get them to turn around.

But it's more than a wall panel. Gears within the wall twist and spin as it moves further toward them. I can still see through gaps in the structure to the Maglans on the other side. When the wall meets them, a series of sparks erupts and the low moan becomes a collective growl. They're shock prodding them back to their deaths.

That's it. Enough of this bullshit. I run to the prod wall.

"Cam?"

She alights onto the wall in different locations, scanning the surface, ready to help. When she settles onto it, portions of the wall spin around, screens that have to be cameras. The goggles and breath mask still cover my face, so I should be safe. Let's hope they don't try to run Cam's image through their database though.

If the cameras weren't enough, the sparks pop up on this side, too. Cam yelps in an electronic whine and limps away in the air.

No, no. You don't do that to my Cam.

I leap at the wall. Well, it's really more of a careful advance considering the metal arms that are extending from it. But I'm going to stop this thing. One more step and an arm pulls up and points at me.

"Return to your post," a robotic voice says. "Situation being handled."

Through the windows on this floating wall I see the mass of Maglans herded together. Those that wander too close to the wires suffer a series of shocks and fly backward into the crowd. They can't think for themselves. This is just sick. How can Scitech be doing this?

I obviously don't back away; instead I take a few more steps forward. The arm responds by opening up and exposing what looks like some sort of dart. From the sparks coming off of it, I assume it's for precision incapacitation.

"Return to your post," the voice repeats. "This is your final—"

"I heard you the first time." I throw a targeting disk I had been cupping in my top right hand. Little flickers of yellow light spit off the targeter, different from before. I had turned the dial to instant lock this time.

The disk magnetically clicks into place near a panel from which circuitry seems to emanate. The yellow lights change to solid green after it fastens onto the wall. A green beam of light twists around, hopefully aligning itself with Jali's position. Luckily, this time my skull isn't in the target path. The metallic arm powers up and the dart spins in its shaft. I duck and cover my head with my hands, as if that might help protect me.

A searing white beam of light cuts through the ceiling and slices the wall right through the control box. Yeah, that's definitely what the box was; I can tell because the wall powers down almost instantly, creaking as it topples back toward me. It isn't until I see the group of zombies that I realize they pushed it over and are rushing my way.

Thud.

Well shit, there's my cue to go.

The security door opens without needing a verification from this side, and I make a dash for the steps. I'm still clutching the data pad in one hand so I jam it into my pack.

Some static chirps in my ear for a second, then is replaced by a voice. "Daj? What the hell is going on down there? Are you all right?" It's Neman.

"I don't really have time right now. Just tell Rym I'm almost there."

"They're going to take off without you, kid. It's too hot in there."

"They're what?" They wouldn't do that, right? He's just saying that so I run faster.

And I do. Like I've never run before in my life.

***

I don't really care about the pounding of my feet on the steps. It sounds so loud that I'm sure I'll attract anyone in a one-hundred-foot radius, but screw it. No one's leaving without me.

"Neman? Neman come in."

"I've got to leave, kid," he says. "I'll see you on the other side."

So that's it. Everyone for themselves here? Are they even certain Stell's not down below?

I feel the clink of Jali's disks at my back, and I wonder if she's not looking out for me anymore either.

"Cam, you have to confirm, is Stell here?"

The bot cycles a few seconds and sends a definitive 'no.' Well, at least I can just save myself now and not worry about her. When I break into the huge hangar, lights are flashing and computerized voices are blaring. Freaking chaos. Good luck saving myself.

"All personnel evacuate. All personnel evacuate."

And there's a nice screaming alarm to go along with that pleasant voice. I don't see any of the techs running around with parts anymore, but down one of the long corridors between the ships there's something worse, some sort of large four armed lumbering mech. Two of its hands are glowing and carrying a shield that floats along the ground, not directly touching the bot. It's got to be some sort of mag tech.

At least it's not running in my direction.

There's also the sound of an engine powering up in the distance, like from a ship. It's a deep thrumming sound. Maybe it's the Peace Hammer getting reading for a launch boost. They haven't left me behind. Not yet.

That mech has probably got friends, and probably cameras on all sides of its body. I sure wish I had those stealth chromatophores right about now, but I'll have to figure it out on my own. There's a way through the parts and wrecks that's not on the main aisle with this bot thing, so I push through. It's a tight fit, but nothing like the tunnel.

"Rym?" I call through my comm.

No reply.

The whining from the distant ship intensifies. That's not a good sign. I scramble a little faster, but I end up knocking over a container of parts that scatter across the hard gray floor. Without moving, I wait to see if the bot's stomping continues in the direction it was going. There is no change in its gait, but there's a soft whumping sound, like something getting shot into the air.

I'm not going to wait around to see what it is though. I push my way through a pile of scrap, but not before Cam zips up in front of my face, stopping me. And none too soon, either. A grid of green lines scans across the aisle right in front of me. After it passes, I glance up to see a small black shape hovering past. Great. Tracking drones. It did hear my clumsy ass.

Now I've got security bots looking for me, my friends ditching me, and nano zombies about to break the door down probably. I guess I'll have to be extra sneaky.

One of the huge magnetic arms slides past overhead, empty. Probably returning to the side of the room after delivering something. Huh. I wonder if…

I pull out the data pad and watch its screen recalibrate to the room location *'Main hangar repair bay,'* scrolls across the top. Different functions appear on the clear panel in blue lights along the side. Maintenance. Lighting. Parts delivery.

There, that one. I press the button and a list of options pop up including the one I'm looking for. Arm lift controls. Got it. Now to reach the ship so we can get out of here.

Closer. The next aisle brings me closer to the sound of the engines, but I still hear the clunky movement of the security bots beyond the next pile of scrap. My hearts are pounding so loudly I wonder if they can hear me as I approach. Around the next corner of parts I finally see it. The Peace Hammer. The panels are all closed up, the engines are definitely firing, and it's hovering a few feet above the floor. Rym got the mag repulsors to work after all. And there he is, right through the cockpit glass, busy at work, flipping some control levers and switches.

But the ship is surrounded on four sides by those loading security bots. Their arms are pointing at the Peace Hammer, and also at each other. A pulsing sound fills my ears. The Hammer revs its engines, but something holds it in place, some sort of force barrier. It's got to be coming from those bots. Each of them is mag clamped to the ground for support.

Cam beeps in my ears and a message pops up. Reinforcements are coming to help deal with the situation. With no guns, it doesn't look like Rym will be able to fight back. This is it. I heft my pack with Jali's disks in it. There aren't a lot of them, at most five, but I can make this work.

I edge closer to one of the bots, making sure not to make any sudden moves and knock something over again like an idiot. I consider my targets as I heft a disk. With a thought, I flip on my agility enhancement nanos. My muscles tense up as the tech engages then just as suddenly they loosen. A shot of adrenaline pumps me up and then I let the nanos do their job.

I'm running faster than I ever have with a disk dialed to *timed* flashing in my hand. The bot looms up in front of me and I leap up to the wiring along the back of its right leg. With another jump, I reach above its waist for a metal bar and hoist myself up. Cam projects a holo scan onto its back, and I slap the disk to the bot where I hope Jali will be able to target.

The telltale yellow lines project Jali's trajectory; luckily it comes in from behind and above my head. The light turns green and I'm off to the next bot, luckily still focused on the ship in its magnetic grip. This time I'm up at its lower back in fewer leaps with the disk primed and locked onto its back. Again, the green trajectory is free from interference. Luck is still holding.

A loud sizzling of electronics and some bright lights lets me know that Jali has taken her first shot, and that the target was solid. A smoking hole in the floor shows where the projectile continued after shattering its core. The first bot I tagged drops to its knees, face planting into the hangar deck right over the smoking hole. Before I can cheer, one of the bots I haven't targeted yet focuses right on me. Twin cannons flip up from its side and open fire. Luckily my nano-assisted reflexes already jumped me to the side and I avoid the barrage.

Now, all three bots shift their gazes to me as I run behind a pile of scrap. Come on, Jali. Take the shot.

It must take a little time to prime and charge up her rifle. Time I pretty much don't have. The bots seem to deliberate, and I can imagine it's about whether or not to pursue me, or to stay behind and lock down the ship. It doesn't take them long to decide, and they make the smart move, which is to stay put. After all, what trouble could I do to three big robots with backup on the way?

Another sizzling white beam of light pierces the guts of another bot, ending it. That's what kind of trouble I can cause. When the bot falls in a short circuiting, frying mess, the Peace Hammer wiggles a bit and the back end swings around. Two more bots to go, and we can get out of here.

The two remaining bots position themselves away from me and let their cannons blast out laser rounds in my direction. These shots have tracked me down even though I'm pretty well hidden. The metal in front of me sizzles and begins to glow orange from the continual blasts. This isn't going to give me cover much longer.

"They're tracking your nano use," Dewey says through the comms unit.

It's sure good to hear his voice again.

But my nanos? The agility enhancers? I don't even know how that's possible, but it seems to be right. I shut it off and immediately my muscles relax and I feel absolutely weak. The firing lets up for a second, and I take that opportunity to make a dash for the next aisle through the scrap. Dash is an overstatement. I'm absolutely laggy compared to how I was moving a second ago. Sparks erupt next to me from incoming blasts as I slide under a metal sheet.

Time to get them off my back. I swipe the data pad's screen and access the massive arm up above. There's visual scanning on and it shows the Hammer and the robots. I activate the arm with a single button press.

Another hail of blaster fire pelts the metal sheet. This one melts a lot quicker than the last cover I had, and I yelp when a spatter of molten material hits my skin. I hold my breath, but then the firing stops and is replaced with a groaning creaking sound. I venture a peek to see the robot dangling from the arm as it slowly retracts it to the ceiling.

Got you. I key in a request that the bot be dragged to the trash.

The robot on the ceiling freezes in place. I hit the command again, but it doesn't respond. Well, it does, if you count shutting me out of the controls. Shit. It didn't take them long to figure out what I was doing. The mech is still up there. At least that's better than being dropped on my head.

I hear approaching footsteps. The reinforcements are getting closer. How can I stop them from tracking me? Cam's blocker doesn't seem to be working. Would that fruit I took help out? If it's anything like what I ran across underground with Stell, then maybe.

Stell, I wish I knew where you were.

I don't waste another second and pull out the clear canister with the red fruit in it, unscrew it, and pop a single, delicious berry into my mouth. The memory of when Stell picked those fruits off the fungus flashes through my head as the amazing tingling sensation runs down my arms and legs. The UI on my 'site flashes and disappears. I feel more alive, and even though I'm cut off from everything I've ever known, more aware.

Thud.

Except this time it's not just a thud far away; it's threatening to smash my head apart. I've only felt this power in one other place, at the Eldane temple, the octahedral pyramid. This place has got to be a center for mag power, but so much stronger than it was there. It feels like I could just burn myself out as I sit in it. And the voices. I hear all the voices calling as one. They're the same ones that called for my help before, but that was faint. These voices are right inside of my head now.

"Daj!" Rym yells.

Well, my comm unit in my ear still works.

"That arm won't hold it much longer. You've got to help us get out of this thing's grip."

The ship's engines strain as it tries to pull away from the bot, like someone trying to yank a tooth out. The Peace Hammer spins around one axis point where the remaining bot is holding on. Two arms are still powered and locked upward, but the remaining two are sweeping the hangar with the gun arms. Three more drones pop out of the thing spreading out to head in my direction. They project the green grid lights and systematically check around every corner.

There's no hiding from all of them, but I scramble away as quickly as I can. Too late, another wave of drones is returning from their scans and a bright green grid passes over me. I hold my breath and freeze. I swear I feel the little lines crawling right over and through my skin.

But it continues past me. It doesn't even slow down. That was weird. Can they only detect motion? I'm pretty sure I was shaking something fierce. How come it didn't sense anything?

No time for that. It just didn't, and that's freaking good enough. I need to get some sort of weapon to help Rym and Dewey.

This area looks familiar. This is where Rym worked on the Hammer. And over there is... that's weird. The Dagger, the thin ship I saw earlier without a power source is now wide open.

"Rym, did you...?"

"No time, kid," Rym shouts back. "A little busy here."

There's a sound of guns firing from the ship's direction. The bot has now turned its arms upward and is firing at Rym and Dewey. I think it's gone past the point of peaceful resolutions. For now, the hull seems to be taking the blasts, but that's because Rym seems to be keeping the armored bottom of the ship pointed downward. Other equipment up top might not be able to withstand the fire.

Some memory flits in my mind when I look at the ship in front of me, but I can't place it. I jump in the cockpit of the Dagger, and as soon as I do, the consoles flicker on. All right, Rym, thanks, you did get a mag core installed. I knew they wouldn't leave without me.

I clasp all four controls and the ship vibrates as the engines cycle on and onboard systems warm up. Cam zips in and clicks onto a panel on the main console just as the cockpit screen locks down. There's no turning back. No time to download a schematic or a tutorial either, if there even is one for a Dagger. And I have no connection to any 'site capabilities anyway. But at least I won't have to jump or climb anywhere, I just have to fly.

And I know how to fly.

I push the back two controls and the ship bucks forward smashing into a large wing leaning up against five others. The resulting impact knocks each one over, one after another with large resounding clangs. So much for stealth. And the nose of my ship? Is that a scratch? Dammit.

Well, I think I know how to fly.

"Cam?"

Cam interfaces with the central console and beeps at me.

"Get me some shields. We've got shields, right?"

An affirmative beep from Cam and a glowing halo forms around the ship. I glance over the console to see other basic systems, but I can't focus on them now, considering the drones clustering outside the cockpit with their green grids plastering my ship. They couldn't track me, but they're able to get the ship.

Alarms blare and two more security bots stamp down the aisle toward me.

I grip the controls tighter and gently pull back on one and twist the other. The Dagger rises and turns to face Rym and Dewey.

"There's a good ship."

The Dagger powers up and the engines whine as I flip a switch. I knew that would happen. Now where's the weapons system on this thing?

"Cam? Guns? Weapons? What do we got?"

A beep and a quick message on my wrist. Weapons charging. Perfect. This ship wouldn't carry any type of weighted ammo; it's built for speed. These shields look pretty tough, though.

The Dagger jerks forward under the slightest nudge, but I think I'm getting the hang of it. And good timing. The bot aiming all arms at the Peace Hammer is lined up in front of my viewscreen. A glowing ball of plasma circles in front of its chest, ready to puncture a hole through my friends.

My own weapon is just about charged, at least for one shot but before I can fire, a shower of sparks pelts my own cockpit and throws me off course. The shields hold, for now. It's that bot suspended up above by the lifter arm. Another blast and the Dagger staggers a little more.

Well then, I've only got one shot.

I crank the control sticks forward and fly straight at the mech on the ground. With a twist, I sideswipe the bot with the back end of the Dagger and fling it head over feet along the floor. With another move, I line up the suspended bot in my sights and pull triggers. A rapid firing beam of red plasma peppers the bot, the ceiling, and most importantly, the arm itself.

The bot may be armored, but the metal on the arm easily slices in half causing the bot to plummet fifty feet into the other bot now directly underneath. The two erupt in a fiery mess of metal fragments.

Perfect. I did mean to do that.

More blasts hit my ship and flip me into the nearest junk heap.

"What was that? Didn't I just clear our way out?" I grip the controls and twist them around, but nothing happens.

Unfortunately, two more bots are angling in on me from a distance. They keep firing, but also their other two arms are pointed at me. I'm guessing whatever held Rym down is now keeping me pinned. They're not waiting any longer to see if we're going to go down quietly. More fire hits me, and an alarm sounds. Cam beeps and the words *'low shields'* appear on the heads up display.

Man, this is a sucky way to—

I'm momentarily blinded by a glowing shape that flies past my cockpit viewscreen right toward the two approaching bots. In a strange smashing motion, not unlike that of a hammer, the glowing shape crushes each bot, leaving piles of molten scrap behind.

"That's the magnetic defensive measure I was talking about," Rym explains over the Dagger's comms.

"The Peace Hammer," I say with a shit-eating grin. I jiggle the controls and the Dagger quickly responds by ascending to the Hammer's level. "Are we ready to leave yet? I got your guns."

"Try to keep up, kid."

The roar of the Peace Hammer's engines rattles my ship as it passes by. Something catches my attention as the wide, swept shape of the ship flies through the hangar tunnel to freedom. There's a commotion at the back of the hangar where I came through the stairs. I squint and make out a swarm of my old friends, the nano zombies, shambling their way out into the bay.

I can't afford to get caught by any more security bots, not with Rym gone. I can't help these guys. I tug the controller to get out of here.

"You did what you could."

This is what I hear, or I think I hear. It's the voices within the thudding of this place. But I can hear them clearly now. And they need help, despite what they say.

Just leave. Go out the hangar bay tube, it's open. Save yourself. Those are my thoughts. And I sound like an asshole.

A great grinding and screeching sound cuts through my cockpit. Oh perfect, let me guess. I waited too long and the doors are closing.

"Daj!" Rym shouts over the comm. "You better hurry your ass out of there. Ain't no time left."

I crank the controls and the ship's back end spins around so I'm facing the way out of here. Yup. The massive forty-foot tall doors are sliding shut, but I've got time. I gun the throttle and I'm thrown back into my seat. The mag belts ease me slightly so I'm not pressed back so hard.

Gunfire rains down behind me. There's pelting against the walls and who knows what else. What are they firing at? No, they couldn't be. One more twist of my wrist and I swing back around to face the horde. I zoom in on the carnage through my panel sights. Piles of unmoving science experiments litter the metal floor. Scitech security is trying to herd them back down stairs by blocking their paths with their own dead.

I eye the hangar doors and check the level of my weapons again. Not quite fully charged up, but just enough for what I have to do. I drop the Dagger down until I'm at floor level and then gun my throttle. I can't see the mech, so hopefully they don't have eyes on me either. But I have a good idea where they are. The aisles fly past as I approach. We're all getting out of here, or none of us.

The plasma blaster charges up one more pip on the gauge. That's a few more 'Tech goons I can paste before I check out.

This place is a maze. I turn left and right but don't see the bots. I don't want to gain altitude or they'll be able to shoot me out of the sky or trap me. Suddenly an image appears in my mind; I'm not quite sure how it got there. It's like I can see ahead, sort of. In that vision I can see where the zombies and security forces are.

One more left swerve, and then I am right behind the one remaining bot. I open up the guns and lace into it, draining the charge completely. Its head pops off, severed from its frame in less than a second. Toast.

"This way, come on."

The horde seems to respond and they amble over the wreck of the smoking bot toward me.

I do a quick 180 and gun the engines, lifting slightly up above the aisles so I can see my way to the exit.

Boom. Both hangar bay doors slam shut.

This whole looking out for other Maglans isn't really working out for me, is it?

The horde continues to push into each other like a gelatinous blob but more or less make their way to the hangar bay tubes.

"Daj?"

The tone of Rym's voice makes me realize things are going to be worse.

"We just picked up Neman. He said he put a bug in their system, meant to scramble their security for a bit. But that won't last. He also says that they have a magnetic floor safety protocol. He disabled it for a time, but it looks like that's warming up."

Yeah, much worse. The nose of the Dagger dips toward the deck and I fight to keep it level. Plink. The charge level of the weapon system is barely moving, yet I don't think any weapon onboard would be enough to crack those huge metal doors. No missiles, plasma bombs. Nothing like that.

Do I have to abandon ship? Trust my luck to get out of this place on foot? Not with security tightening up, and whatever it was Neman disabled. Too bad he couldn't have stayed hooked up, but I guess it was getting too hot in there, too.

Well crap.

"Uh, Daj? Make sure you're away from the big doors."

"Why?"

An explosion bursts from the left hangar bay tube, a brilliant white light that sears my vision and leaves a mark that I still see after the blast dies down. I blink several times and then realize there's a gaping hole near the base of the door. I don't even question if it's big enough for me to fit through. I'm already hauling ass out of here, nose pointed directly at the exit. I try to keep the ship level, but the magnetizing floor pulls me down closer and closer, making me have to continually readjust my flight path. I plow over rack after rack, spraying parts all over. I can't afford to touch the floor. If the magnetic grip grabs me,

I'm not sure I'll be able to get free.

Closer, closer, oh man that hole doesn't look wide enough.

But then I'm through. The cold lights of the hangar disappear and I'm surrounded by blackness. The perfect night sky appears at the end of the tube with the brilliant aurora lighting the way.

CHAPTER 16

"We did it!"

The Dagger soars out of the launch tube and I'm free. Where are the others?

"We're at the ridgeline." It's Dewey.

I aim the ship to the ridge and spot a blue dot on the heads-up display. A bunch of readouts clutter the corner of the screen, but I only look for the Peace Hammer's specs and location.

"We've got Jali," Rym says. "You ready to rendezvous?"

"I'll follow, but are you okay?"

"Yeah, not a scratch," Rym says. "Not big ones, anyway."

"I have enough firepower to cover you." I'm loving this ship. I have never flown anything like it. I only ever dreamed I would as a kid. She's fast. Real fast.

Rym laughs. "Just come over here."

Tracking shows the Hammer lift off the ridge and I plot to intercept. Well, I don't do much, I just tap the screen and a green projected holo line shows me the path. In ten seconds I'm behind them, watching their booster rockets warming up.

"Now what?"

My ship suddenly jerks a bit, and a light flashes requesting docking access.

"Sure?" I press the light.

The Hammer gets closer and closer, but I no longer have control of my ship. I'm locked into a docking beam or something. The slot on the top of the Peace Hammer? Is that for me? Landing lights blink until I'm right above the ship and then there's a clank and a hiss as the two connect. Before I can even marvel at this, my seat drops and I'm lowering into the Peace Hammer's hold.

When the chair stops at a stepping platform, I jump out. I'm shaking all over. I can't believe we made it. Can't believe any of this.

"Are you all right, kid?" Rym asks over the internal comms unit of the Hammer.

I glance around the interior of the ship here and smile. This is way different than anything Scitech advertised I would fly once I got my flight pass. Matte green walls, minimal circuitry, solid chunky components. This thing is perfect.

"Yeah, I'm good. Nice work getting out of there." I don't say it, but I'm thankful he didn't leave without me.

"Not a bad job yourself," Rym says. "You had us scared for a hot minute after you disappeared like that. What'd you go back for?"

"That's a fun story. I needed to let out some friends."

"Friends?"

"Yeah, I thought once the hangar bay shut I was dead. How did you blow the doors down? I thought you said this thing didn't have any guns?"

"I think you better come down. Just follow the steps and you'll be right here."

I turn around quickly to glance at the chair for my ship, just poised and ready to pop back up. There's nothing I'd rather do than go take it out for another flight, this time in space, but I'm also super tired. I can't remember the last time I slept. It's been a big ass day. And I've got to see Jali, thank her for saving my butt.

The stairs are narrow and I have to duck so I don't hit my head on the low ceiling. This isn't a spacious ship. I guess it's more built for function than for comfort. But, man, it's perfect. The door at the base of the steps slides open when I approach.

And there's someone I didn't think I'd ever see again.

"Hira?"

The old ex-leader of this squad is here, and her troops stand around her smiling.

"I thought you were dead, I watched the vids…"

"Scitech is good at fabricating those things. As soon as you left, the kids posted a vid of what happened on the couch. I knew it was only a matter of time before Scitech came. In fact, it was quicker than I expected. My countermeasures along the path went up as the troops approached, but luckily I had an escape system of tunnels below the house. Got the kids out safe, and then I figured I had to come make sure you were, too."

"It pays to be paranoid, huh?" Rym says.

Hira nods.

"So, the hangar door?" I say.

"Come watch," Hira says.

I sit down at a row of monitors and Jali stands behind me giving me a reassuring pat on my shoulders. I turn and flash a smile of thanks.

A link up of Hira's vid feed plays on the ship's screens. I see the hangar tunnel, but this time from on the ground outside the base. The lights under the tunnel begin to fade as the door closes. It's weird to think at this point I was on the other side getting drawn to the floor and almost trapped. The vid continues and what must be the mine cart we rode here on descends through the launch tube at an accelerating rate. Hira's hands appear in the vid holding a controller which begins beeping rapidly. She clicks the button on it and there's a brilliant flash of light. I only saw that on the other side.

"You're a bomb tech?"

"Well I'm not a tactical gardener," Hira says with a smile.

I catch Neman's eye with that one.

Hira continues. "That package was one I sent you away with. Stashed it under the cart. Luckily you hadn't found it, since I wasn't able to bring any supplies from home after I was evicted, in a sense."

"So you planted explosives on us?" That's not very comforting.

"I got one package." Rym pats a pouch on the floor outside of the cockpit. "I'm assuming the other was a backup. It was a backup, right? Not for when we might have turned around and tried to ask you again to help?"

Hira shrugs. "Either way."

I check out the room. Neman is curled up at a monitor, Jali is standing in the corner of the room with her rifle propped next to her, and Rym hovers near the entry to the cockpit like he doesn't trust Dewey to pilot this thing himself. Who's leading this crazy gang? Hira used to be in charge, right?

She seems to read my question. "I may have been the commander once, but I'm past that. I'm just here to blow some shit up."

Rym shakes his head. "I doubt that. You never were one to have things out of your control."

"Oh I'll still be in charge, I just won't be commander." Hira laughs.

A jaw-splitting yawn erupts on my face.

"We're a couple hours out from a waypoint, you can snag some sleep down below."

I begin to fight the offer, but another yawn happens. "Maybe just a little."

"Hey, what did you find down there?" Neman asks, not even looking up from the monitor.

"It was really messed up. There were some mutated research projects, Maglans, and they were going to be torched, and harvested."

"Going to be?" Jali asks. She rubs her gnarled hands, remnants of a time when she was a research project.

"Yeah, you saved me, and them. I don't know if you knew what you were firing at, but you helped free them. I only hope they got out of the hangar."

I don't know why, but somehow I know they did.

"What do you mean, *harvested?*" Neman says.

"That was the weird part. I mean, it was all messed up. In that incinerator room there were a bunch of metal lumps on the ground. I think they were going to collect them. Are they really that desperate for metal?"

"That is messed up," Neman says. "What would they want with our dantoliths?"

"These things in here?" I point to my gut. "I thought that was just some buildup of metal bits that we eat. And that some Maglans have their fortunes read from them."

Neman laughs. "It's more than that, and you're going to want an Eldane to explain it all to you. Interesting." He turns back to scanning the onboard computers.

"I also got this stuff." I put the tubes of fruit, magneto whatevers and the data pad I lifted onto the table near the monitors.

Neman stares greedily at the pad and picks it up to drool over. He taps on the screen so quickly I can barely see his fingers move. "They shut you out of the control sequence, but there's a chance I can still get something out of this." He links his wrist port up to the screen and begins to scan through the info packed in it. I don't think Scitech would want him to get his hands on something like this. He'll be busy for hours.

Jali meanwhile picks up the two tubes. "I'll get these scanned and see if they can be of any use. Nice job, kid."

I nod to her, and take my leave. I don't head straight to the beds, instead I take a detour over to Dewey locked in to the controls. My eyes widen as I take a look outside the window. I've seen vids of the planet before, but nothing could have prepared me for this. The dark blue, purple planet below me is absolutely breathtaking. Wide oceans, cliffs, mountains. And the auroras. I'm lucky it's still night so I can see the wavy lights covering the horizon and extending up into the sky.

"What are those?" I point to strange shapes undulating in the green lights.

"Zeplogs," Dewey says without pause. "They live up there."

"Wait, they're alive?"

Massive creatures, they must be creatures to move like that, float among the sea of lights cascading in the sky. They're flying, but it looks more like swimming. Is this for real?

"They ride the magnetosphere," Dewey says. "Seeking out minerals and magnoplanktonic life forms."

I just nod with the name he just dropped. I'll have to just believe him. A cluster of the bigger zeplogs gather around a tiny one and they bump it up so it can reach a ring of dust. I have to clamp my mouth shut because it's hanging wide open. I had no idea things like this existed, or if I did, I forgot it in the flood of images and vids I watched every day. We fly past the cluster and a few trail off from the main group to tag along as we pass through the night sky into the stars. Their deep-set eyes reflect the stars, and they hold some deep knowing, or understanding. I sound like an idiot, I know, but I don't think I'll ever forget this.

"Now go catch some sleep. We're going to need you soon," Dewey says.

I reluctantly get up from the bucket seat next to the robot and give the zeplogs one last look. I stumble down to the lower level bunks and I'm asleep before I even lay completely down.

***

I wake up to an alarm sounding throughout the ship. It's not loud, only insistent, but ugh. That was definitely not enough sleep. And that was definitely not a comfortable bed. My neck is killing me. And my back.

"You're almost here."

Stell? That's definitely her voice, but it can't be. There's no one in the bunk room with me, no one but Cam.

The chronometer on my 'site says I was out for a couple of hours. I yawn and stretch as I stand up. Time to go check where we are, and what everyone's been doing. The cold of the staircase railing cuts into my hands as I pull myself up to the cockpit. Isn't there a heater on this thing?

Dewey is alone. His mechanical head shifts back and forth scanning the wide viewscreen. I plop into the seat next to him and stare at the instrument panel and control sticks.

"What's the alarm all about?"

"The waypoint is coming up."

"Hey, I think I saw something like at the underground Skywatch base. Is this it?"

Dewey nods. "If you saw Magnus Base, this is it. We lost its signal weeks ago, but hopefully we can alleviate that."

"Are you sure it's safe?"

Dewey nods. "Of course. We can rearm and refuel there, if it's still in one piece. We're still about an hour out. Rym also wants to meet and plan soon." Dewey flicks off the alarm with a button press.

"Did you hear anything about Stell down there?" Dewey asks.

I just shake my head. "Other than Cam saying she wasn't there, nothing. No word about where she might be."

"That was the consensus Neman came to, as well."

It's nice to know they didn't just ditch that place wondering if Stell was there.

"You need anything?" That's kind of stupid, asking a bot if he needs anything. What would he need?

Still, he cocks his head at me. "No thank you."

"Think you can show me how this thing flies?"

Dewey straightens himself after I ask this. "We should meet with the others soon, but we have a little time. I'd be honored. The flight controls are here." He points to the thruster and control yoke. "They're on auto now; well, actually it's running through me. But I can remove that so you can try."

"Really?" I just wanted a tour. I didn't think he'd offer me to fly this thing.

The control gear in front of Dewey clunks downward and then shifts over to my chair. The steering mechanism is similar to the one on the Dagger. I tentatively grasp the controls and feel the ship respond to the touch. An energy surge ripples through the hull. I let go and glance at Dewey.

"It's okay, it does that. Try it again."

When I grip all four controls the ship reacts again. I can feel the ship. Yeah, that's the best way to describe it. The engine, the power source, the weight of the ship as it skips across the upper atmosphere and magnetic fields. I feel it all. And it almost feels alive.

"We want to keep it within base magpulse, anything faster and Scitech might pick up on it. The magpulse skips us along the planet's magnetic field, so we can go pretty much undetected. If we don't go too fast."

Only then I realize I've crept the engine up, the speed gauge is pretty spiked right now. I let off and resume the cruising speed Dewey had us set at.

"She's a beauty of a ship." I relinquish the controls and they slide back over to Dewey's side of the cockpit. This only makes me think of one thing though.

"I'm going to go check on the Dagger. Thanks for the flying lesson."

"No problem. You're a natural."

"Thanks," I say. This time I think I straighten a little. "Where's Rym?"

Dewey gestures up and behind him. That's the docking bay.

I climb up the narrow flight of steps back to my ship and my heart stops. There's no seat! Did someone take it? Is the ship gone?

Before I can take a step onto the docking platform, there's a sharp hiss as the ceiling opens up and the chair silently descends. With Rym in it.

I don't know whether to feel like it's nothing, or like I'm seeing Kie and Zaylee together. The two emotions teeter in my brain. He must read the confusion on my face, though.

"I was just checking it out," Rym says.

"Everything okay?"

"I was wondering what had happened. You originally said there was no power supply for the ship, and then when you came back it was open and all powered up."

"Didn't you put a mag core in it? I figured that's what happened."

Rym shrugs. "No, it was empty. I put one in there now, but I'm not quite sure what caused it to even fire up for you."

"Maybe it's linked to the Hammer?"

"Maybe. When we got this old heap running, it could have done that."

That certainly is a better explanation than me eating some fruit to charge up a ship.

Rym pats the dropped down chair. "She's a real fast ship, the Dagger class."

"I know. She maneuvers like nothing I've ever flown."

"She sure does. We're going to need it, and soon."

"Hey, what's this waypoint Dewey told me about?"

Rym starts to head back down the stairs. "One of Skywatch's old orbital stations, it's hidden away in the debris field. Hopefully, still hidden away. We can learn more about what we're up against there. It has more advanced tracking capabilities than we do on this ship."

I look up and see the stars through the Dagger's cockpit. I wonder how she'll fly in space.

"Come on," Rym shouts. "Everyone's on the bridge going over our plan."

"Plan?"

Rym just waves me on. I know we're going to hijack the nano signal broadcast facility and try to convince everyone that Scitech is just using them. But really, what is Scitech's reason for it? I mean, science is good, right? It's what gets me brand new decks each month so I can make my vids.

They're blocking something in our bodies, the connection to Magla, like Stell said. I believe that now. Looks like Rym was right all along, about everything.

Jali, Hira, Neman, and Dewey are waiting for us when we show up on the bridge. It's a good-sized room, with display screens and holo projectors for whatever battle they used to plan for back in the war. News updates from around Magla are displayed on different screens, but nothing looks like the destruction we just left at the research facility. Just running vids of weather patterns, life in the city, interviews with leaders. Normal boring news.

"Didn't you send out your bots around the cities?" I say.

Neman nods. "They did their jobs. All of them."

"A cover up," Rym says. "They don't want the Maglans to know we hit them."

"And we hit them hard." Neman is still tweaking with the data pad I lifted. "I coordinated several attacks and other break-ins around the major cities, not just in Phen. Here, look. These are some bits of the footage before Scitech blocked them."

He flicks some vid feeds through, presumably from the bots he programmed for the attacks. Graffiti sprayed on government buildings, Scitech signs destroyed, vehicles stolen from garages. You'd think that this would be all over the 'sites, that at least they'd be looking for some help tracking down the perpetrators. But nope, everything is fine all over. The government is doing its job, everyone. Nothing to worry about here.

"What about Kie and Zaylee? Can you get a lock on their signal?" I type their stats onto the screen for Neman to track. Funny, I can think about them and not freak out anymore. Weird how a crisis can make certain things less important. I mean, it still sucks, but it's not in my mind right now. I guess a global takeover trumps shitty friends.

It takes a moment, but soon a report vid pops up.

"Fugitive Daj is now being tracked to a site in Phen," the feed says.

"Daj sent us some footage of his latest jumps," Zaylee's voice reports. She is good. Well, actually, I don't know if she's betraying me right now, or just helping to distract Scitech from finding me. Either way it's good for us. The vid follows her and Kie through the back streets of East Ring, scanning the potential jump spots where I might be. The vid I sent had me wandering around this area, and the two of them are visiting them all.

A Scitech warning with my face pops up listing all the offenses I had made. And yes, murder is definitely still on there.

"Be on the lookout for Daj, known to most as HotDaj," a newscaster says. "Report all suspicions."

The video continues to show Kie and Zaylee looking for me, but ending up shrugging their shoulders and giving up.

"Your friends, I didn't think they'd be able to help." Rym pats my back.

"See? Vids can be helpful. That ought to keep them off our trail for a while."

"Maybe," Hira says. "Will they be able to track these ships?"

Neman shakes his head. "I've bought some time. I would have been able to fully scrub our presence from that place if I had maybe even five more minutes. It's going to take them a long time to figure out it was us there, unless they have some really smart Maglans."

"Or those Sniffers," I say.

Neman groans. "But this is why we took these ships in the first place. Skywatch ships like this are very hard to detect."

"Back in the war," Jali says. "Who's to say they haven't upped their research? I mean, look at these things." She holds the tubes I brought along. "Stealth nanotech? Neuro blockers? And they had these ships in that hangar for years. Maybe they cracked the codes."

Neman groans again. "I erased all record of these two ships from the inventory. I blocked transmissions while I was there, so those scrapped security bots shouldn't have footage of you leaving."

Rym taps his fingers along the table in the center of the room. "What have you found? Did you get anything about Stell?"

"Stell? Who's Stell?" Hira asks.

Rym and Dewey catch each other's eyes. "Someone who got captured because of us."

Hira doesn't look satisfied with that answer but Neman continues before she can say anything else.

"Still compiling. I got a lot of their research. But you wouldn't believe how big that place was. So much research going on there. Daj stumbled across the neuroblock test subjects. Nice job freeing them, by the way, kid. I'm particularly interested in this energy consumption research with the nanos. And the nano removal protocol section, too. I'll let you know when I find something worthwhile."

Hira gives him a strange look after those rambling thoughts.

"Hira, how's our supply of weapons?" Rym asks.

"Other than Jali's rifles and a few others, we're running low."

It seems to keep her from asking more about Stell.

"I'm working on some more helpers," Jali says with a wink. "There's not much to work with in the garage, but there are some."

"We only have a guess about what to expect. We'll have to do some recon from the outpost, either with telemetry or get someone to fly out there." Rym looks at me.

My face heats up. He wants me to do this?

"You're one of us now, kid," Jali says. "Which means we'll have to do something about this little light show." She points to my nano tattoo that I constructed at the beginning of this whole thing.

Hira laughs. "You call that a tattoo? Come on. I want to show you something in the hold."

I go with her, but the look Jali gives me makes me think I'm being sent to my own funeral.

***

"Holy sh...!" My words turn into a garbled scream.

"Baby," Hira says with a smirk.

"That's what a tattoo is? Are you nuts?"

The inking press pops off my upper arm with a searing sound. Hira wraps a bandage around the new addition and smiles. "Now don't mess with it."

Don't mess with it? It's simultaneously burning and itching like crazy. How am I going to not mess with it?

"Yeah, okay," I say, but I'm afraid it only comes out as a weak mumble. I don't want them to think I'm not part of the team anymore. "I'm going to go check on the Dagger."

Secretly I'm going to go whine about the pain in my arm in private. And avoid everyone's laughing.

"Be careful."

I look around the room, but no one here said that. I know I heard her this time. Stell. Careful about what? About my tattoo? No, that's stupid. And she's got to know we'd be careful heading to the moon base. No need to tell us that.

The Skywatch hidden base then?

It's got to be. I stop by the cockpit to tell Rym all about it. Is he going to think I'm crazy though, hearing voices? Maybe I really didn't. At least I can ask them to do a scan of the area, see if this is a trap.

"I hear Hira gave you one of these." Dewey clangs his fist against his own forearm, right against his own tattoo of the diamond shaped Skywatch symbol.

"Yeah, and I bet that didn't hurt you any, did it?"

If Dewey could smile smugly at me, I'm sure he'd be doing it right now.

"What is it, kid? Something bothering you?" Rym sits back in his seat keeping an eye on the instruments.

"It's this base. Do you think there might be a trap for us there?"

Rym and Dewey look at each other. "There's no reason for us to think so. It's been hidden since the war, I'm sure of it." He points to a blip on one of the panels. "Long range scans are not picking up anything else there. Nothing to worry about."

"I don't know, I've just got a feeling."

"Don't worry about it," Rym says. "Scitech couldn't find it before, they ain't going to have found it now."

For some reason it's not Scitech I'm worried about.

"So just go back and rest. We'll be there shortly."

I'm just about to open my mouth and tell them about the voice, but I can't. It sounds so stupid to even think it. But something still bothers me, anyway. So even though I leave, I don't head to the bridge but walk back up the narrow steps to the Dagger's docking bay.

"Cam, you ready for some recon?"

The little hovering drone, never more than a few feet from me, zips onto my wrist dock with a few beeps. Her little wing legs curl and click into the mechanism.

The Dagger's lowered seat is just as welcoming as I remembered from the last flight. The second I settle in, it hovers up into the ship above and I'm brought to the stars. This is for real. I am actually in the absolute black of space now. Well, maybe in upper orbit but still this is farther up than I've ever been. And now I'm about to go out on my own.

Cam lifts off my arm and plants onto the main console. The panel lights dance when she links up.

"Think you can not let Dewey know we're going away?"

Cam pauses for a moment and beeps an inquiry to me. I get the gist of it.

"No, I'm going to be all right. We don't want to bother them on this. We'll just do a quick check up ahead and be right back."

Cam reluctantly beeps, but she'll do it.

Power is up and topped off, and with the extra mag cell in here I'm feeling more comfortable. I don't want to get stranded out in space without any of it. My feet kick something on the floor. It's the helmet. I remember seeing it when I first got in, but didn't have time to put it on. It looks pretty clean, as does the rest of the instrument panel. Like someone gave it a once-over recently.

The helmet fits nicely on my head, and several lights and system stats boot up on the glass screen in front of my eyes. Weapons charged. Life support. Oh, yeah, I guess that's a good thing now that I'm out of the atmosphere.

I have no connection to my 'site, but something tickles the back of my mind, like I should bring more of that fruit with me. But I'd have to get it away from the others, and that would draw attention. Plus, I'm already in the ship. I might not be able to get away if they saw me.

I reach for the ship's controls and the engine begins to whine. Cam beeps once and the connection to the Peace Hammer breaks free with a reverberating clunk. Hope they didn't hear that inside.

"Cam, project the flight path and plug it into the nav unit." She better know how, it's not like I know anything.

Sure thing, a path lights up on the cockpit window, a holographic projection made by the internal computer. I engage the engine, remembering to keep it low enough that I won't be detected, and I'm pushed back into my seat. It takes me a few seconds to keep the ship on course. In order to stay on manual I have to keep readjusting the flight continually.

And it is amazing. I wish I had access to my music for this first time flying by myself. I'd be cranking it for sure. I imagine the lights and sequences I'd string together making a vid of this, aw man I'd have so many views of this thing, I'd be...

Cam beeps to warn me that I'm veering way off course.

"Yeah, I meant to." Not true, but I say it anyway. And then I readjust the headings to match the holo path.

Things act differently out here. I'm used to the continual battering of the air in the atmosphere. Slight adjustments cause the internal magnetic pulses to quickly maneuver the ship. It takes some getting used to, but after a minute of fiddling with the controls I feel pretty good with it.

Up ahead in the debris-filled Dust Field, not too far now, is the final destination marked by a larger green outline on the holo display.

"I'm going to cut around behind it first, you know, to check to see if anyone else is here." I say this to Cam, hoping for some sort of approval but I get nothing. At least she isn't openly arguing with my decisions.

The area ahead is packed tight with chunks of floating rocks. I can see now that the flight path enters the area through some hidden breaks to reach the base. But I've got to check if there's anything waiting for us around the other side. I can always hope there'll be another way through from the other side, or at the least I can swing all the way around and come back here.

The Hammer is a good distance behind me. I figure I've got at least ten minutes before they arrive. Enough time for me to prove I can do things on my own and still be a part of this team. I ease the throttle up and begin my circle around the base.

"Can you do a scan of this?"

Cam beeps, as helpful as ever, and a visible ping radiates from the Dagger's scanner. There's a great deal of static and shaky imaging as the scanning wave does its thing.

"See if you can clear that up. Please."

Cam beeps once and begins to work. At least that's what it sounds like from the internal chugging and lights flashing. Looks like I'll have to keep visually scanning this place for any sign of trouble, yet so far the only thing I have to worry about are these rocks. Most everything seems pretty stationary, but some debris spins in and skips against my cockpit.

A particularly large rock tumbles right in front of me and I jerk the controls. The lateral repulsors engage and I drift to a relatively safer place. Still, maybe this wasn't such a good idea after all. Instead of finding whatever trouble I imagined, I might only damage this ship for real. I prime the weapons system and another hum vibrates throughout the ship. Just in time, too, because another volley of rocks pelts my hull.

The ship weaves in and out of the incoming projectiles, almost as if it's doing it on its own. I don't take my hands off the controls to test that theory, though. I'm almost halfway around the debris field and I veer to my right to get clear of this for a minute. Take a breather.

Then I hear a clunk and the ship skews off its flight path slightly. Did I just hit something and screw up a thruster?

"Cam, check the system status. See what's causing that."

Clunk.

This one is a little louder and when I try to turn around the ship feels like I'm trying to steer through mud.

"Cam?"

She sends a report through the monitor, saying that all ship systems are unaffected.

"Well something's wrong, what's hitting us?"

Clunk.

The ship slows down considerably this time and the back end begins to drift around. I arch my neck and look behind me at the rear panels of the Dagger to see something attached to the hull, something round and metallic.

"What the hell is that?"

Cam runs another scan, this time an external one. I get a readout of the entire hull on the monitor. Four objects are stuck to the ship and now I can see an arcing energy beam leaping from the ship to the four objects. Is this something of Rym's old defensive system around the base?

"Cam, do you recognize these?"

Her reply pops on my visor. *"Nothing in data file."*

Suddenly the energy levels on the ship begin to drop and the lights flicker. The control sticks don't respond to any motion and the ship begins to drift. What is this parasitic thing? There's an audible buzzing vibrating throughout the hull and Cam flashes out a warning.

"Hull breach. Life support system failure imminent."

Shit. Perfect.

I crank the controls and try to get this ship to move, to edge closer to a tumbling rock so I can bash these things off of me, but the Dagger moves so slowly that I'm not sure I'm even doing anything. I guess I picked a bad day to not pack space gear into my ship.

"Send a call for help!"

Cam emits a sad beep. Another message appears, but weakly this time. *'Magnetic field disrupting communications.'*

Magnetic. Is that how the mines attached to me? Something flashes through my head, lessons about poles, or something. Man, why didn't I pay more attention in class? Sucks when I don't have the 'site to check any bit of information I might need to survive.

"Any way to reverse our magnetic... polarity?" Yeah, that's the word.

Cam can't even respond this time. Looks like they're drawing her energy too. She sits there motionless and with lights fading fast.

Breathe.

I can't believe it. It's Stell. In this cold, dead space, it seems like it's going to be the last thing I ever hear. I hope it doesn't take too long. You know, to run out of air, or freeze first. Or will I boil?

I said breathe, you idiot.

All right, all right. I'll breathe.

I try to forget about all the, you know, impending doom around me. Okay, that's not helping. How can I not think about the thing that's about to kill me? Breathe, right. I try to remember what it was I held on to back at Jali's quarry. How did I control those rocks?

I didn't. I didn't try to control them.

I just *breathed.*

And then I feel it. The rocks around me. The field that is blocking our communications. Those pieces of shit metal things attached to my hull. And I push.

I push the energy that is connected to the Dagger away. I don't know how I do it, but I can feel the energy outside my body and it is strong. And I shove, as hard as I can.

Four separate pops later and the metal parasites spin away from me, as do several floaty rocks that happened to be too close. The mines collide with nearby rocks and burst with a blast of light. That's my ship's power! I reach for the nearest pocket of crackling energy like a mental arm grabbing hold. Like a swirling vortex, the beams of energy or plasma or whatever stream back to the Dagger. I pull harder until the glowing blue bolts slam into me.

As soon as they hit me the power systems come back online, if only a little bit. The levels are barely minimal, but hopefully enough to get us back to the Peace Hammer. Or maybe enough to boost our transmissions?

For some reason the grips of the ship are pleasantly warm. Were they always this way? Why am I just noticing it now? My arms tingle and my tattoo under the bandage feels like it's also heating up. Now the radar display lights up with clear images of the surrounding space, all interference gone. Tons of rocks, a massive one in the center of them all, and Rym's ship all the way on the other side of the mess. And they're wandering into a potential minefield. They won't make it if those things attach to them.

I've got to have enough power to get this ship over there and use my cannons, or at least warn them. I gun the throttle and the Dagger boosts ahead.

"Keep an eye out for any more of those things, will you Cam?"

Her lights have come back on, too, and I let out a sigh.

A couple minutes and I'll be back to the other side. The Peace Hammer approaches the rock field and pauses for a second as new signals appear on the radar. The rock field opens into some sort of pathway right in front of the Hammer aligning with some flashing pylons. This must be their old way of clearing a path to their base. Maybe there won't be any of these mines over there, or perhaps they were Rym's all along.

Well, that's wishful thinking. As I carve my way through the rocks in a long, looping arc back to the entrance, I catch the Peace Hammer's trajectory begin to degrade and spin. Just like what happened to me. Oh crap, crap, crap.

"Rym? Rym? Come in!"

Nothing but static. I twist the controls and dodge out of the way of a quickly rotating boulder and then jam the throttle again.

"If you can hear me, reverse your polarity. It will boost those things off you!" Fat chance getting through, but I say it again. They've got to hear me.

That's when three other ships from Rym's own base approach from inside the cluster of rocks. Two ships move closer to the Hammer, while one, the larger one, stays back.

Blips on my radar show the main ship charging up its weapons. The two smaller ships appear to be mining rigs, possibly Scitech, each with little claw bits hanging from their front end like mandibles. Deflated sack-like things hang behind the main structure. Are those scrap collectors? Those bastards are going to gut my friends' ship.

Not while I can still fly.

They're not moving to intercept me as I finally make it around the circular area into the cleared pathway. I take another breath and still feel that connection to whatever power surrounds me. The Dagger seems to hum with that same energy.

"Cam, power down all lights. We've got to get in there without them being able to spot us on their visual scans."

Cam responds by immediately dousing all outboard light sources and even dims the interior ones. The smaller ships slowly approach the Hammer and the bigger ship holds back. Frickin' scavenger. That ship bounces several encrypted comms to the smaller ships, or I guess that's what's happening with the data transfer on screen. Probably warning them to just wait until the vac seals have popped on the Hammer.

That ship has got to be in charge of the mine parasites. I ease my finger off the weapon trigger. If I blast it out of the sky, who's to say the little things will be disabled? I've got to get in there and make whoever is in charge turn them off. I repeat my last comm to Rym, hoping he'll get it, and urge the throttle up a little so I can jet in behind the lead ship.

"What else do we have for weapons?"

A short list appears on my visor. Apparently this ship is meant to get in, pelt the enemy with pulse blasts and get out of there. It's got moderate shielding, but speed is the real deal with this thing. Don't get hit. One thing catches my eye, and it's a category labeled link systems, but I don't have time for that. EMP ammo? That's more like it. I click the button to access it and a whir vibrates within the hull.

My ship cuts through the standoff without anyone noticing me and I halt in space right behind the trapezoidal ship. It's an ugly hauler, all boxy.

"Scan ship?" Cam asks on screen.

"As long as they can't detect it, but hurry." I eye the Peace Hammer and see sparks emitting from the parasites on it. Drain the power, then cut life support. They've done this before, apparently.

A quick scan of the ship appears on the radar screen. Engines, weapons, communication arrays, and nav systems. No time to waste. I target the engines first and open up the EMP weapon. A purplish blue stream of energy blasts from the cannons and plasters the two huge engines in a swath of sparks. The engines cut out and immediately the ship sways off kilter.

Their side cannon facing me comes into my viewport and I lace into that one, too. I'm hoping the clouds of energy arcing away from it signify that it's unusable for now. There's the other side, though, but I open a hailing frequency before I make a move.

"Pirate ship, I order you to cease attack upon that vessel, and remove the mines on it."

There's no reply.

"I will destroy your ship, and your other two puny rigs if you do not comply."

A light on my console indicates that the lead ship is attempting to scan for me. They also target the Peace Hammer, something they can actually pick up on their visual scanning.

All right, they're not taking a hint here. I flip the weapon systems back to the pulse cannon, target the left side engine, and release a stream of superheated beams. They pummel and slice right through the engine, erupting the back end of the ship with brilliant blue flames.

"I swear I will tear a hole right through you if you do not pull off your attack."

A rain of incoming fire comes right at me from a topside turret I didn't spot earlier. Stupid. Luckily I rip the controls and the Dagger sidesteps the attack in time. They must have been waiting for me to fire again to zero in on me. I peel off from the incoming fire and approach from a different angle.

I'm about to open fire, my finger wants to jam down and fill that turret with fire and vent those assholes into space. But this isn't Scitech. This is just some pirate ship out here, full of Maglans, like me.

I move my thumb away from the trigger.

"Stand down, I repeat, stand down. We don't need to fight. This is no good for either of us. Just let my friends go." My hands shake on the controls. I hope my voice sounded confident.

There's a brief pause, and then a click on the comms channel. "Copy. Ceasing attack."

I glance over at the Hammer and run a scan on it. The little parasitic mines disengage from its hull and return to the lead ship. The two smaller rigs return to the main ship, too, and fly around to its engines.

"Perhaps we can meet on the installation behind us?" the Maglan says.

"Let me check on my friends first."

"Daj?" Rym's voice calls over my personal comm unit. Oh man, he sounds pissed. "Get back here. Now."

I have a retort, some fantastic excuse fresh on my lips, but I bite it all back. I screwed up. I sullenly rev up my throttle and head over to the Hammer's landing bay. If I had a tail, it would be hanging between my legs.

CHAPTER 17

"Are you stupid?"

Well that didn't take long. Not ten seconds after the docking mechanism hisses and lets me into the Peace Hammer, Rym laces into me.

"You endanger the entire mission by flying off alone? There are more Maglans to think about other than yourself."

"But I was—"

"I know what you were doing." Rym busily checks the hull of the Dagger and runs a scan over it while he talks at me. "You were bored and you wanted to fly around in your fancy new ship and get a video of it so you could post it for all your fans around the world. Isn't that right?"

"I wasn't doing that." I can see why he would think that, though. It wasn't too long ago that's all I wanted to do.

Rym is practically boiling over right now. He's clenching his fists pretty tight, and I wonder how long before he uses my face as a punching bag. I open my mouth to say something harsh, but I change my mind. The only thing that comes out is a mangled, "I was trying to help."

"Help." Rym spins around and begins to walk down the stairs to the main hold. "Now we have these pirates to deal with." He practically spits the word *pirates*.

Better you're alive to deal with them than having me mop up their bits. Still, I change my mind again about saying that, too. Rym mumbles something but I don't catch any of it. Probably cursing me out. Hira meets him at the bottom of the steps.

"You know, if he hadn't gone out there in the first place, we'd probably be floating around there and our ship would be a bunch of scrap parts on those pirates' shelves."

"You're not helping," Rym says. "We would've figured out the polarity thing sooner or later."

"Any later and we'd have been dead." Hira waits for me to follow down the stairs and slaps my shoulder. "You screwed up in a good way, kid."

"Rym'll never see it that way."

"He does," Hira says. "He's just trying to maintain control around here when it's all starting to fall apart. And did I say thanks? Thanks for saving my ship? I've always had a sweet spot for this one." She bangs her fist against the hull.

I smile and shrug.

"Well, I mean it. And you had him worried about that ship of yours, too. If you haven't noticed, he really has a thing for old tech ships. Especially that one."

"I noticed."

"And these pirates, they're really messing Rym up. He's wondering why you didn't blast them right out of the stars. And now we're going to meet with them on our old base. We don't know how many there are, or who they work for, or if Scitech is going to show up in five minutes."

Rym glares back at her over his shoulder as he sits down in the cockpit next to Dewey. I stand there, watching the little ships guiding the still crippled bigger ship through the debris. Man, I got that thing good. I get to see the base for the first time and... it doesn't look like much, in fact I can't even tell it's a place. The center of this whole circle of rocks is a big pitted asteroid chunk.

I approach the cockpit, but Rym gives me a cold glare over his shoulder. Man, I'm like the pet that puked on the floor and they don't want to let me back in the house.

"Kid!" Neman calls out. "Get back here."

I hadn't noticed him and Jali in the back of the hold. Neman is still preoccupied by the data pad I lifted from the research base, I wonder if he even noticed he almost died.

"Hira is right," Jali says. "Without you out there doing whatever you thought was a good idea at the time, and it wasn't, at the time, by the way. Anyway, we were just about to be popped open and left to vent. I still don't know why you let them live."

I don't know why I did either. I think it was to make sure the parasite mines were off the Hammer. But it also felt like I wasn't quite ready to kill anyone. I mean, is anybody? I glance over at Jali, checking on her guns. Well, maybe she is.

"And who knows what tech is going to be left at our old place," Neman says. "If these are pirates, they've probably gone through it all. We should be salvaging that tech."

Jali throws a small metal part at him and turns to me. "That was a neat trick, to switch the polarity like that. What made you think of it? And how did you do that? I didn't know that was a thing Daggers could do."

"It wasn't the Dagger." That gets Neman's full attention. They both wait for me to spill it.

I gesture to the container of berries locked onto the table in front of them both.

"Remember what I did back at the quarry?"

"That's hard to forget," Jali says.

"It was kind of like that."

"I want to get my hands on that mine tech," Neman says. "If you don't mind, I'd like to take a look at what your ship and Cam learned about them."

Something tickles inside my head. "They're parasitic mines. They sucked the energy out of my ship, just like Rym said these stupid nanos do in us."

Suddenly, I feel claustrophobic. Like there's another life form invading my skin, trying to take over and I can't stop it. I can only hold them off for a little bit, while this supply of berries holds out.

"That's funny you should say that." Neman waves the data pad in the air. "I was able to find some interesting information about energy consumption within the nanotech. Scitech is trying to find a way to permanently mod their nanos so they are impervious to the effects of whatever we eat. They want to make it so no one can block them."

That's why no stores in Phen have any food like that. It's banned, outlawed even. Nonnos are evil, and not having the 'site is wrong. Man. I was so stupid.

"This tech is stealing our life away. Literally." Neman taps the data pad and focuses on it with full attention now.

I feel itchy all over. "How do I get these things out of me?"

Jali shrugs. "Look at what happened to me trying to get the cyber implants out. I don't think I'm ever going to recover from that. Once those nanos go in, they ain't coming out."

There has got to be a way.

"Crew, we're almost at the base," Rym says over the comm.

He sounds a bit nervous. I've never heard him this way before and I don't like it.

"Are we worried Scitech will pick us up off the pirates' communications?" Jali says.

"I don't think so," I say. "When I was out there, I couldn't pick up anything. It's like there's something scrambling communications."

Neman grunts. "That is why we chose this place back in the war. Damn Cadeans were hunting us down once they began working with Scitech. We needed a place to hide, and this worked nicely. A bunch of Skywatch techs hid out for months carving a hole in this rock so we'd have a place to stay."

"I helped too," Dewey shouts back from the cockpit.

"Yeah, you too."

"I still don't get what's happening between Scitech and the Cadeans," I say. "This is all really new to me."

"Rym didn't go over this?" Neman says. "I guess it isn't in the history classes nowadays. That's the whole problem, right? They say we won the war. I say we lost. And we're still paying tribute to the enemy."

"So, Scitech? They don't want to just make money? You're saying that they work directly for the enemy?" I've heard the rumors.

"Running supplies, stealing food from Magla," Jali says. "That's what I heard."

"And we've got to figure a way to shut them down." Neman pats the data pad gently.

I turn back to the cockpit and see the asteroid base filling up the viewscreen. A landing bay opens up like a gaping mouth. The two smaller ships spin the main ship around like tug ships and begin their descent. Are we really going in there? I'm starting to have mixed feelings about following these guys into their lair. What if it's a trap? I don't know how much more crap like this we can take before we actually infiltrate the Scitech base.

"Don't worry," Jali says as she stands behind me. "We just need to get in, get our stuff, and get out."

"You don't think the pirates have scrounged everything yet?" Neman says.

"Some of the stuff," Jali says. "Not everything. We hid it pretty good, remember?"

I clear my throat to try to get Rym's attention. "Should I stay out here with the Dagger? To keep an eye on things?"

"Oh, he's asking questions now, and not just running off on his own?"

"Come on," Hira says almost at a whisper. "He knows he made a mistake, which kind of worked out in our favor."

"That's not the point," Rym says. "If this team is going to work, we have to be just that. A team. You get that, don't you? We can't afford to lose anyone."

Jali nudges me. "Aw, he doesn't want you to get hurt. That's sweet, Rym."

Rym turns back to the viewscreen and readjusts his grips on the controls. "Shut up, Jali." After a few seconds he talks again.

"We'll stick together. We're not sure how many of these pirates there are, and how much they've infested our old place. They just want to talk, they say, but they could also be trying to lure us in. If Captain Pacifist had just blasted them out of the sky, we wouldn't have to worry about this. Either way, we need to grab our supplies and go. Dewey here has a list of what we need. We may need to split up so they don't see us."

"So about the *stick together*, you didn't mean it? You just don't trust me?"

Rym sighs. "You're a good kid, but no one goes alone."

Jali whispers in my year, "See, he does like you."

The Peace Hammer follows the other three ships into the docking bay. Clamps have already locked on to the smaller rigs and are pulling them in. The main ship waits while its engine sparks from when I laced it with the EMP rounds.

"Did they change up the codes?" Rym says.

Dewey nods. "But I can still retrieve them. It will take some time, though."

"Get Neman to help you out. It'll be faster with both of you on it."

Dewey stands up and heads back into the briefing room of the ship next to Neman. The two of them link with Neman's wrist cable and sit silently working their digital voodoo.

"Should I bring along Jali's disks? She can cover us just in case." I shake my pack with the few remaining targeting gadgets in it.

Rym shakes his head. "We risk breaching the integrity of the walls with that weapon. There's no atmosphere out here and that would just pop holes. We got this place sealed up, but it's not a real fortress. We never had time or resources for that. There are some other things we can fall back on if Dewey and Neman can get this to work."

Jali pats her sides with her gnarled hands. "I've got close quarter weapons and a few other surprises, too. Don't worry."

"Of course, your plans are all contingent upon them turning on us," Hira says. "They might actually be..."

"Nice pirates?" Rym says.

"They might just be really pissed at Scitech, like the rest of us. They might join us in our fight."

Rym adjusts the controls but doesn't answer.

"We're also not sure about how many there are." Hira reviews the initial scan of the facility. "We don't have access to our computers yet. And I don't think we can secure our communications. We don't want to tip them off to anything."

"There are another two ships docked there." I point to the ships clamped along the docking platform. They're sleeker than the big box that came out to greet us, faster looking. I get a little dizzy looking at this whole place. We're heading to what looks like the floor, but since we're in space, it's hard to tell what's up or down. "Are they manned, or bots?"

Rym shrugs. "Not sure. Whatever they've got, they have the drop on us. For now."

A large clamp arm reaches for the Peace Hammer and latches on. The hull shudders and we're pulled inexorably toward the landing pad, no longer under our own control. Rym cuts the power to the engines and they wind down. I almost ask if this is worth it, but we're in it now. Maybe blasting them out of the sky would have been a better decision. Captain Pacifist, indeed.

The ship comes to a rest, and an airlock attaches to the side. Rym stands up and Hira follows him to the exit. She turns and looks at me.

"Are you coming?"

"You want me to come with you?" I thought they'd sit me out for this one. Leave me behind to watch the ship.

"Whoever's in charge will want to meet you," Rym says. "If they can see who spared their ship and their lives, that will probably work to our advantage. Our goal is to get in, ask nicely for some of our old stuff, steal it out from under them if that doesn't work, and hopefully walk out of here alive."

"Daj," Neman says. "Your Camdrone unit would be perfect to keep an open line of communications with you. But in order to do that, I'd need to set up an access port in her."

I know what that means. One step closer to not being just mine. But he's right, she is the best way to communicate. And if I'm ready to be a part of the team, Cam should be too.

So I lift her from my wrist dock and place her gently into Neman's hands. That light shines in his eyes again, like a kid who just won some great prize and can't wait to play with it. It still freaks me out a bit, but I know he knows what he's doing. In seconds, Cam's frame pops open and he's busy working with her insides. All four hands are doing something. Installing software, checking connections. I can barely look at her opened up like that.

As he preps Cam, I glance over at the jar containing the nanotech blocking fruits and wonder if I should eat any before leaving. I'm heading into an unknown base with a possible enemy presence, though. Maybe I should have access to my upgrades. The reflexes, aim assist, right?

Not sure how much lifting rocks I'm going to have to do inside. My hand hovers over the jar as I consider. I place the jar into my pack and seal it up tight, just in case.

Neman grunts softly while handling Cam and double-checking everything. Finally, he secures the top back on her.

"I'll be able to check on your progress through her now." Neman slides his chair over to the monitoring station and flips on a switch. "Thanks."

"No worries," I say. I don't say that I'm worried a bit about Cam's autonomous nature possibly being gone. But she hovers from Neman's hands over to the dock with her familiar beep and we're good to go.

"So just follow our lead, and be nice," Hira says. "Oh, and bring a gun."

Jali tosses me a pistol and I catch it awkwardly. I check its charge, and it's topped off. "To be nice with, right?"

"To be nice." Hira checks the cargo door panel and then clicks in a code. The door opens slowly and I'm greeted with a gust of processed air.

A strong burnt fuel smell drifts in. This is going to give me a headache.

Rym gives Hira a look expressing his disgust. Probably because of the state of disrepair the base is in. It does look a bit shabby.

The door lifts all the way up and three of the pirates greet us on the other side. They're dressed in drab uniforms, not the flamboyant garb I expected from all the stories I heard when I was a kid. I guess I'm a little disappointed.

But they're armed. Rifles, pistols. The leader, a young male with a smile I don't really believe, stands in front of the other two. They've both got their pistols drawn, and even though at first I think he's unarmed, I notice the butt end of some weapon jammed in his belt, right in quick draw range. Something hits me then. If they've got Nanosite technology, they could record us. Yes, they can't transmit right now through this rocky ring but they could save it for later and sell us out. They are pirates after all. Rym had to have thought of that, right?

Rym extends two arms in peaceful greeting and the leader reaches up to clasp them.

"Welcome!" the man says. "My name is Rancelon. Welcome to my base."

Oh, crap. They don't even know this was Rym's. Luckily I didn't spill any of that earlier. This is good. Really good. I can almost sense the same feeling oozing off of Rym and Hira.

"I'm Rym, and this is part of my crew, Hira and Daj. The rest are staying behind."

Rancelon's eyes dart back and forth over all three of us, weighing his odds, perhaps. The smile returns. "And who do I have to thank for sparing my ships?"

Not his crew. His ships.

I open my mouth to speak but Rym cuts me off with a sharp glance. Apparently he is going to say everything.

Rancelon seems to have caught that exchange.

"This young one, huh? And what is your name?"

I check with Rym first, and he nods.

"Daj."

"Nice piloting, Daj. We didn't see you sneak back around us, but it's a good thing you did. Your friends wouldn't have made it out of that without you, and where would we be now? We certainly wouldn't be able to have this conversation."

You'd be in a smoking pile of space dust, you smug bastard. I give him a small smile.

"Can't be too careful with Scitech's patrols and other ships flying through here," Rancelon says. "Speaking of which, what are you doing up here? In old tech like that?"

"Surely you have a place where we can sit and talk?" Rym says.

"Oh, my manners, where did they go? Of course, please, come with me." Rancelon beckons for us to follow him through the tunnel.

There's gravity in this place. That's strange. I always thought we'd be floating around up here in space. I fall in beside Rym and Hira. They don't say anything, they only keep on walking with smiles on their faces. I'm not quite sure what our plan is. Would've been nice if they actually told me something other than to follow their lead. I guess you keep the new guy, the one who saves your butts, in the dark, right?

Lights kick on as we walk through the tunnels. Some sort of motion sensing tech so that energy is conserved. Smart. We pass an intersection of walkways, but I only see more tunnels going out both ways. It's dark down each path, so I'm guessing no other pirates, or whatever these guys call themselves. In a minute, we reach a door and Rancelon welcomes us into a nondescript meeting room, big enough for us all to sit around a central table. There are two others in there, a male and a female dressed in the plain suits the other two armed guards are wearing. They're casually not casually sitting on tables and holding their weapons.

Is that all these Maglans do here?

"What can I offer you? Food? Drink?" Rancelon offers us to sit at the table.

"Nothing, thanks." Rym takes in the room. "How long have you been up here? This is a well-hidden facility."

"Not too well-hidden, apparently," Rancelon says.

"We were lucky to come across it."

"And what brings you up here, if we can get right down to it. And who are you going to tell about us?" There's an edge in Rancelon's voice.

I don't like it.

"We're just smugglers, trying to make our way," Rym replies. "You'll never see us again. Unless you want to do business, of course. And we hope you won't pass on our specs to the authorities, either."

Rancelon pours himself a drink in a tall metal cup. "You won't mind if we check your 'sites, do you? We'd love to scrub any record of us in there. Just to be safe."

"I don't think that's necessary," Rym says. "Like I said, we're here to do business with you. There's no reason we'd want to report you. If I did that, Scitech'd be on this facility in seconds and wipe it out. We both don't want that, right?"

Well played, Rym.

Rancelon takes a drink. A long drink.

"Mind if we take a tour of your facility?" Rym asks. "I'd love to see how it's built."

"Sure, sure," Rancelon says.

I think he might mean it, too.

"Come with me," he continues. The armed guards behind him stand back, semi-relaxed, but showing enough weapon to let us know they're not even close to relaxed.

Rancelon walks beside Rym and Hira, and I follow. I can still hear them talking as we walk, most of the words at least.

"Where'd you pick up that old tech?" Rancelon asks again. "I haven't seen ships like that before. Only in my research."

"We recently acquired them off of some dealers who didn't know what they had," Rym says. "It was a steal."

Rancelon smiles. "Looks like you're a fellow who knows how to get the better end of a deal, huh?"

Rym nods. "We do what we can."

We walk down a long windowless hall. I guess I haven't seen any windows here; it's probably too dangerous to build those into a place that needs to be airtight. We end up in another room, this one with two more guards in it. They're not smiling, either. I'm not getting a really strong positive vibe in here, and I'm finding we're getting more and more outnumbered.

"This is our main area where we plan out our next jobs." Rancelon waves his hands around like he's some sort of salesman. Rym nods approvingly.

On our way out of the room, Rym turns to look at me. "Didn't you say you needed to relieve yourself after flying around in that ship of yours?"

"Uh," I say, almost followed by a 'no, what are you talking about?' And then I see both his and Hira's eyes. "Yeah, I shouldn't have drank all that water before we left Magla."

Rancelon eyes us. "Of course, in fact it's right around this next corner."

That's a little too obvious, Rym.

The hallway branches off in two directions in ten more paces. There's a strange arc to the facility as we progress. I can't see more than thirty feet or so ahead as the hall bends to fit over the rock we're on. It's not a very big facility, and it makes sense we'd have to adjust to fit on it.

"This is it," Rancelon gestures to a doorway. It opens to a standard if not low frills water closet. Everyone sort of stands around the door.

"You're not all going to wait for me, are you? I'll catch up to you. Which way are you heading?"

Rym smirks slightly.

Rancelon's smile falters again. Whatever he's working at isn't quite going like he hoped it would. "We're going to the warehouse beside our ship docks. The next right."

"I'll be out in a second."

Rym begins to walk, to lead them away, and Rancelon hesitates. "I'll leave an associate to help bring you back to us."

"Not too close. It makes me nervous."

This time it's Hira who has to try to hold her smile back.

As they walk away, the 'associate' with the gun stops about ten paces away from the door. I give him a thumbs up and get into the small room. What the hell does Rym want me to do in here? Come to think of it, I do need to relieve myself. Was it that obvious?

Static clicks in through my comms unit, but no one speaks. Maybe they're worried the pirates will pick up on whatever we talk about. Should I try to talk through Cam's auditory unit? Maybe the pirates have this whole place bugged. So what do I do?

Before I can think of doing anything, or worse, to go back out in the hall, Cam pops off my wrist and attaches to the wall on a peculiar grating. After a second and a beep, a panel clicks loose in the wall to the right. Looks like whatever Neman programmed in her included finding secret panels.

The static in my ears clicks twice this time. Clearly someone is communicating with me. If the plan is to keep me in the dark as long as possible, it's working perfectly.

"Cam? Can you help?" I press a button and she hovers in front of my face as I peer into the wall. Another passage? This one doesn't look as claustrophobic-y as the last one we crept through, so that's a plus.

"What do you think, Cam? Think we should go through?"

She beeps once at me and zips ahead. This must be what Rym wanted me to find here. And maybe Neman is watching after me if he did unlock the panel. Kind of creepy. I hope he wasn't watching in the water closet. I step in and close the panel behind me.

The tunnel continues straight through the facility in darkness. It's still pressurized like the rest of the place, so that's good. Breathing is a good thing. And Cam is emitting a little light of her own so I don't trip on anything.

"Thanks, Cam."

There's knocking on my door, way back down the passage in the water closet. Crap. They're going to bust in, or wonder where I am.

"Cam! Can you head back into the bathroom and link up to my comms?"

She dips her frame slightly in acknowledgement and disappears into the bathroom behind me. I keep walking forward, although this time it's in complete darkness. In a few seconds Cam's beep comes through my wrist dock.

"I'll be out in a minute," I say. "Don't worry about me."

The pounding stops, but I hear a voice through the door. "Hurry up."

I push forward as quickly as I dare, holding all four hands in front of me to make sure I don't get a face full of metal. After thirty or so more seconds though, I run into a wall. The static in my ear pops once and the panel responds to my presence by sliding out of place. I shift it aside and poke my head into the next room. It's dark in here, too, not as dark as the passage, but the lights are definitely dimmed. Only a few computer screens are illuminating the room.

Cam zooms past my head and scans the room before I get too far.

"Always looking out for me, huh?"

She brings a little light with her, but I really can't see much beyond the row of screens next to me. Cam does a once-over of the room, but immediately returns to the screens and the ancient keyboard next to them. A blue light on her frame flips on and she immediately heads straight for the panels.

I guess this is what happens when Neman takes over her flight. It seems wrong to have her controlled like this, but it is what it is, I suppose. She clicks right onto the screen with her little landing pads and immediately the screen floods with images of attempted logins.

They must have some sort of encryption on this system. I can almost hear Neman cursing as he works through Cam to obtain control of the base.

Or maybe he's really enjoying the challenge of it. Yeah, actually that's what I imagine is going on back there, he's got that crazy look in his eyes like he's about to uncover some great secret.

Hurry up, Neman. I don't have all day to pretend like I'm taking a leak. It won't take them too long to notice I'm not in the room anymore. Trying to wait patiently, I sit down at one of the other screens next to the one Cam is working on. Just let Neman do his job. We'll have control of the functions of this base soon, right?

What is this? There's an image on the screen, a picture of the Peace Hammer. No big deal, I guess. The pirates had to have taken a scan of our ship. But there's more. There's a detailed list of the crew members. Hira, the captain. Rym, lead pilot. Neman, systems specialist. Jali, weapons tech. There's also a list of other Skywatch members that I haven't heard of.

Wait, Hira the captain? She's not the captain. There'd be no way the pirates could know that. How old is this list? I push a button and a series of pictures pops up including a much cleaner ship, and a crew I don't recognize.

I squint at the first picture and there's a girl pretty much my age. Her hair is cut way short, military buzzed, and her face spikes are adorned with metal tips. The way she's staring at the camera is badass. Those eyes. Wait a minute.

I swipe over the screen and prompt it to list her name.

Come on.

"No way."

It's Jali. Weapon proficiencies, sniping headshots percentages, hand-to-hand combat. She's a beast. It also shows where the crew was stationed, Magnus Base. I look up at the wall and see a name inscribed into the wall.

"Magnus Base."

Oh, crap. If the pirates have access to all these records, they don't just know who we are. I scroll down the screen and see a log from before Neman's hacking to see what the pirates were looking for. Access warehouse, failed. Unlock weapons stash. Failed.

They've been trying to gain control of this base for a long time now. And they know what crew was stationed here. If they capture Rym, or anyone, they'll be able to run this place one hundred percent. And they won't need us alive anymore.

I don't want to break Cam's concentration on trying to access the base, but I really need to talk to Neman. He'll call for a retreat, maybe get everyone back to the Hammer and we can blast off this rock. But it's more important for Cam to finish doing her job. Just a few more seconds, hopefully.

Suddenly I hear something else in the room. Something alive. I grab onto my pistol and hold my breath. Whoever it is has been in here this whole time and hasn't said a word. Maybe it's a pirate waiting for me to crack into this system and then steal it from me. I power up the pistol and it gives a sharp whine.

There's breathing, ragged and short, like whatever it is is hurt, tired, or both. There's a switch near the wall so I hold my hand over it and a dim glow warms up slowly until the room is bathed in a pale bluish light. And that's when I see the energy cage.

And the freaky thing behind the bars backed up against the far wall. It's about half my height, I think. I can't really tell from it cowering back there. I've never seen any creature quite like it. They must have dragged it up from some depths back on Magla, or maybe it's another science experiment. It has a strange diamond shaped face with a long set of shoulders, except the shoulders don't have arms below, instead they're long articulated legs. And a pair of shorter arm-like appendages hanging beneath its face.

But the strangest things are the dark large eyes that take up a big portion of its face. Okay, I take it back. That's not the strangest thing. It has a messed up mouth. I mean, most mouths have a side to side slit, like every other creature I've ever seen, but this one has a wide line that extends from its pointy chin to the top of its head. The whole head splits open to expose its mouth as it takes in a raggedy breath.

This is disgusting, but I can't look away. It seems so pitiful, all backed away in the corner and shrinking away from me. But this thing is trapped here by the pirates and there's no way I'm going to let them keep it locked up. I wave my hand over the panel by the energy cage, but nothing happens.

A bottle of liquid, probably water, sits outside the cage. There's none in the prison, so I carefully slide it between two bars, trying not to singe my arm in the pure energy coruscating up and down. The creature doesn't move so I back away, holding my four hands out in a gesture of peace.

"I'm not going to hurt you, buddy. Just get the water."

It doesn't take long for it to do so. It must be really thirsty, or it can sense that I don't mean any harm. What I thought had been the arms were just another pair of legs, or leg arms. I really can't tell. The big legs do the walking, but the leg arms kind of help guide it forward, and keep it steady. It covers the distance in a few strides and a tiny pair of what are definitely hands right under its face reach down to clutch the bottle. In a second, it pops the lid open and tilts the bottle to pour the water in its mouth that has now fully opened. Sideways. Man that is weird.

"I'll try to get you out of here. Maybe there's a key around or something."

The creature tracks me with those two large eyes after finishing the water, but then moves to the back of its prison again. The ragged breathing seems to have evened out a bit, though. That's good.

Oh crap, I forgot about what's going on in the rest of the base. The pirates know who we are, and I'm the only one who knows they know. Cam is still engaged with the decryption process, but I've got to get word to Neman and the others as fast as I can.

"Cam, I need to contact the ship, warn them."

Cam continues to spin the data but I heard a faint beep as a connection is established. There's some static in the channel, but I can hear someone on the other end.

"Neman?"

There's no answer.

There is another sound though, like voices muted in the background.

"Neman! You've got to warn Rym and the others. The pirates are on to us. We've got to get out of here."

There's some shuffling of feet. I guess that someone is approaching the comms station. Hurry, come on. The mic clicks on and there's someone on the other end.

"Neman? Jali? You've got to send word to the others. We have to power up, we have to—"

"Hello, Daj."

Oh shit, I know that voice. It's that douche Rancelon.

CHAPTER 18

"Congratulations on figuring us out, but it's time to give it up, kid. We've got your friends on the ship and on the base. It's just you. And we know you're not in the bathroom anymore."

They might not know where I am right now, but there's only a few places they can look. Unless this place is bigger than it appears. For a second, I think about just giving it up. How am I going to free all of my friends by myself? They could be dead for all I know.

Remember the last time I tried to help out? I nearly got us all killed. Nearly. But it also saved everyone.

Come on Cam, hurry up. If I've got any chance to figure this out, it's with Cam's help. If I can get her to pull up the plans for this place, crack the code, be able to control things.

Wait.

"Cam, are you going to get control? Or is it going back to the Hammer?"

She lets out a small beep, and I guess that she's going to relinquish control over to where Neman was, or is. But if Rancelon is there, he'll have access to the whole base first.

"Cam, if you can disconnect the uplink back to the ship, do it now. Now!"

A series of beeps and flashes emits from Cam's body and the connection is dropped.

"Keep trying to crack the code. Neman gave you enough to go on without his backup, right?"

The flashing of numbers and images on the screen lets me know she's still trying. In just thirty seconds, the beeping comes to a stop. Did she finish the decryption?

A series of words lights up on my wrist lock. *"Partial access. Not all systems on Magnus Base engaged. Need to maintain connection at this point to finish."*

She can't leave here? Crap, that's going to cut down my mobility. "What do I have access to?"

A list of systems comes across the screen. System status. Lights. Doors. Power. Defensive countermeasures.

Ooh. That sounds perfect. First thing I need to figure out is where the hell I am, and how this base is laid out. I wish I had looked at some blueprints back on the Hammer. At least I have Cam's map downloading directly to my wrist station. She might have to be connected here, but I can access the facility via my minicomputer in the dock. If anything, I can distract the pirates by leaving so she can stay connected. But let's see what I can do for now right here.

The map shows the room I'm in and the main entryways. I know there should be the tunnel I came through on here, but that's not showing up. Apparently Cam couldn't download everything or perhaps it was meant to stay hidden. I tap the door on the screen and engage the lock for it. A fraction of a second later, the actual door to this room clicks locked.

Other things in the room populate on the digital map, including controls to the energy cage. I hover over the disengage button but don't push. Something about those freaky eyes really gets me. Although it doesn't look too dangerous, maybe I could...

There's a crash at the main door. I jump so much that my finger accidentally presses the button and the energy bars fade to nothing. I could just as easily press the lock again and seal the thing in there, but I don't. It's like, now that I've gone ahead and done this thing, I kind of want to see what this guy is all about. Maybe it can even attack the pirates if they come in here. Rabid trapped monster seeks revenge on its captors.

Or me. I reach for my gun just in case.

There are more sounds coming from outside, someone obviously doesn't believe the room is locked and abandoned. I turn from the door back to the cage and the creature in there. It's not moving. It's just backed into the corner staring out with those bulging black eyes. So much for an enraged captive.

"Come on." I beckon to the critter.

For a second it huddles even further away and tucks its long legs behind it.

I don't want to hurt this thing. I'm not one of those asshole pirates. It takes just those thoughts and the microsecond to think them and old Legs here twists its triangular head at me.

"Wait, can you understand me?"

Nothing.

Aw man, I just want to help.

The sideways mouth cracks open exposing long filament-like teeth. What is going on in there? Is it gonna eat me? I have no idea. But then there's a sound, a tiny, high-pitched whine and a buzzing feeling in my skull. It fades as quickly as it began, but right after it does, the creature walks to the mouth of the cage, right at me.

I hesitate and almost flick the lock back on, but something stops me. Pity, or something like it, I suppose. There's another bang at the door and I turn away. This thing isn't going to rip my head off if I look someplace else, right?

"Stay quiet, Legs!" I whisper. I think it, as well, just in case.

"Cam? Is there another way out of this room?"

A quick scan of my wrist dock shows the bathroom and all its functions, and even though the tunnel isn't showing up, there's the panel that I went through and it appears fully closed. Hopefully that means no one's checked on it.

There's a small video feed symbol on the map from the hall outside of the bathroom and I click it. Several pirates walk past the camera and one goes right in. The pirate looks everywhere in the small bathroom, around corners, up at the ceiling. He pounds on the walls, but luckily the hidden panel doesn't open for him.

"So, anything, Cam?"

This one we're in, the one labeled the *auxiliary closet*, links up to a hallway which extends to other sectional rooms embedded in this rock. So far, I've got no other way to go. There's got to be a vent or something getting air from the central air processing unit. Legs now moves freely around the room, seemingly investigating every feature, not only with its eyes, but also sniffing and feeling every surface. I think it's sniffing, but I can't really tell if it has a nose.

I look back at the map, right at the hall. There's at least one asshole sitting outside our door. Do I have access to cameras and other monitoring equipment, or that defensive countermeasure thing? Maybe it's somewhere in the blank menu along the list of systems on my wrist screen.

I've got to do something. The longer I wait, the more pirates will get here, or even threaten my crew to get me to surrender. The least I can do is block the way here as best I can. I press the screen on the door icons and they activate, shutting off the hallway to my room. There's a pause in the sounds outside the main door, I guess that whoever it is is checking out what's going on behind them.

There's a click from a speaker in the wall. "I guess you think you're pretty smart," Rancelon's voice calls over the intercom system. "But if you don't give yourself up, we're going to start jettisoning your friends out into space."

These guys suck.

A plan starts to form in my mind, at least how to get the one (hopefully one) pirate outside my door. I check the gun at my side, not knowing how good my aim is versus someone who actually knows how to shoot. There's not a lot of cover in here. There are the chairs next to Cam's link up station, the secret panel on the wall, and then there's the cage. It was roomy enough for Legs inside.

As if in response, the strange creature pull-walks itself over to my side with an inquisitive tilt to its head. I'm still slightly worried it's going to just bite my arm off. What are they holding you here for, little guy? Research? It's not like this thing is intelligent, right?

It bares its filamentous teeth.

"Back up, I'm trying to think," I whisper. Do they really know I'm in here? All right, all right.

I wave and point for Legs to get into the hidden tunnel, but it's already in there before I know it. Okay, ready. One swipe of my finger on the screen and all the lights in the room go down except for a few on Cam's console. She's still there attached to the screen. That should do the trick. I step in the tunnel in front of Legs and the door starts to close, but I hold it open a few inches to keep watch on whoever enters.

Another touch on my wrist panel and the main door to the room beeps and slides open, letting the pirate walk in. I sense him moving past me in the dark toward the computer screen where Cam sits as bait. That's right, a few more feet. I draw the gun up and hold it steady with two hands. I've never shot someone like this before, not in cold blood. But they're forcing me to, right? They took us prisoner. They're going to blast us out into space if we don't give up and give them access to the base. Rancelon would shoot me without a thought. Screw Captain Pacifist.

The pirate's back is to me, and he's almost to the computer screens. If I'm going to shoot, now's the time. The trigger feels cold under my finger. It's either him or me, right? Man, it always sounded so easy to just shoot someone in all the action vids I used to watch.

But I can't do it. I don't know what it is. I click the gun off and it powers down. I'll figure something else out. As I start to shut the door, the pirate cocks his head back.

"Daj?"

But it's not a guy, and it's not a pirate.

I can't get the panel open fast enough. "Hira!"

She turns around, and even in the darkness I can easily tell it's her. I reach her and wrap my arms around her in a hug. She hesitates a second, I don't really know her that well after all, and then pats my shoulders affectionately. I can't believe I almost shot her.

"How did you get away? They told me they had everyone on the ship!"

"After you went into the bathroom, Rancelon made his move on us. He took our weapons, neutralized Dewey. He let his guard down for a second, and I ran."

"And Rym?"

She shakes her head. "They're still alive, but hostages now. These pirates haven't been able to hack half the things we set up in this base and they want it. To set up their operations, with weapons and some materials we stashed. Rancelon talked about some ransom they were in the middle of. But that's over now; they don't know this place like we do."

"They knew we were coming," I say. "They got into some of your systems. I'm sorry I couldn't warn you."

"It's not your fault. And like Jali said, we'd probably be dead by now if it weren't for you."

Jali. Her gun. The one I had powered up and pointed at Hira's back. I almost killed her. "I almost killed you!"

Hira freezes for a second and then pushes me aside, grabbing my gun out of my hand. It takes me another microsecond to realize she is pointing the weapon at the tunnel behind me. At Legs.

I yank her arm and she fires into the floor. The big-legged, short creature scurries back into the tunnel and out of sight.

"Why did you do that? You're letting the bastard get away!" Hira pushes me and heads into the tunnel.

"What are you talking about? Do you know it? I freed it from the pirates. It's just some—"

"It's a Cadean. Don't you know that?"

A Cadean? Is she kidding? One of the aliens that waged war with Magla? That little, pathetic thing? Why was it in the cage, and not just executed? Doesn't every Maglan want the whole race dead? Unless the pirates don't know what they've got. Or maybe they do. I run in front of her even though she is still aiming into the tunnel, and stick my head in the dark.

"Is this what they meant about the ransom? Maybe this little guy is worth something to someone."

"It's the least of our worries, unfortunately," Hira says. "Just shut the door. That'll keep it out of our business for a little while, anyway. We can think about the ransom later."

Come on back. She won't kill you. I hope.

No response.

"We've got to hurry," Hira says. "I don't think they were messing around with the killing."

"They're smarter than we think. They hacked into the computer and found evidence of the Peace Hammer and crew."

Hira scans the screens that Cam is attached to. "Maybe. Now that you sealed us both in here, it won't be long until they know where we are. If they don't already."

"I know we're trapped, but I managed to get some systems from Neman's hacking."

Hira turns to me. "What systems?"

I gladly share the info from my wrist screen.

Her concerned expression grows a slight smile. "Oh, that's good. There's lots of fun stuff for us to use. Nicely done, kid."

She smacks my shoulder and I cringe. That tattoo hasn't healed up yet. Ouch.

"Looks like we don't have full cameras," Hira says. "That's going to make tracking them difficult."

Something triggers in the back of my head. A memory of the motion sensors when we first walked through the tunnels.

"We've got access to the lights here, which includes the motion sensors. Maybe this will work."

I sit in a chair and Hira parks next to me. On the screen, there's a map of the base and the lighting protocol, which registers five different areas as being active. Hira grins.

"We installed this to conserve energy. I never thought we could use it for something like this. Good thinking." She types something onto the screen. "I've reduced the time it takes for the lights to register inactivity. That'll give us a better idea of movement."

This room, the hangar bay with the Peace Hammer, two hallways near us, and a command center are currently in use.

"We've got to get them to take our friends over here," Hira says and points to an empty room on the far side of the rock and highlights it on the map.

"Why?"

"It's a good tactical area." Hira winks at me.

What's a good way to clear the hangar? I scan through the systems list and settle on the docking controls. Hira smiles like she's impressed that my good crazy ideas just keep coming. I pull up the list of that room's functions. There are multiple ships clamped to the platform, but not for long. In a few button presses, I release the clamps to all the ships except ours.

I imagine there are some sounds of the clamps disengaging and some general wondering what the hell is going on. By itself, this isn't going to freak anyone out too much, but I've got plans.

Rancelon clicks on the intercom. "I will kill one of your crew if you don't—"

I switch the comms to my channel and cut him off. "We have control of the hangar. Get our friends on the ship and then I will vent the air out. You have thirty seconds."

Rancelon laughs. I interpret that to mean that's not going to happen. "Not with your friends in here."

"Five seconds then." I hit the button to manually override the airlock. There's a blaring warning alarm, and I'm sure a lot of flashing lights are accompanying it as well. Funny, Rancelon isn't laughing anymore. Man, I wish we had cameras.

The main door begins to open, while a red light flashes a warning asking me why I'm doing this and if I'm sure I want to go on with the mass space exodus. I shut the airlock and wait.

I don't have to wait too long, because in five seconds the doors back into the facility open and the motion sensors trip in the hall. Did Rancelon bring my friends with him? He's not going to leave them in there, right? Ten more seconds pass. Twenty.

And finally the lights turn off in the hangar which could mean a few things. Rancelon brought everyone out, or maybe he left them in the ship. I try not to entertain the idea that he might have killed them. Lights kick in, indicating motion in the halls.

"Nice work," Hira says. "I'll take it from here." She pushes a few more buttons and a pathway opens through the tunnels while other doors lock along the way.

The lights continue to activate toward the tactical spot Hira plotted, sometimes veering away, sometimes branching, but always leading back onto the target location. At least they know there's more than one way to go, but also that the 'best' way to go is our way. Finally, they reach the empty storage room. The door closes and locks.

"Are any of their own crew in there with our guys?" I ask.

There are other monitoring systems besides cameras, like temperature, and life support. I hear a high pitched whine in the distance. Is it a drill or something? Are the pirates trying to get through the locked doors here?

"Cam? Can you do some quick math? Can you determine how much the temperature is rising there? Cross check it with the rate of air consumption?"

Whoa, that sounded really smart of me. Maybe it's being surrounded by all this tech, or the pressure of it all, or…

"Keep it out of here!" Hira shouts.

My eyes go to the tunnel opening, and I see Legs sitting there staring at me. I urge it to hang back with some hand gestures. Apparently Hira needs to concentrate and this thing isn't helping.

Cam beeps back after a few seconds and gives me the number I was waiting to hear. Three life forms based on air consumption. Four life forms based on temperature raised. Which could mean a couple things. Either Dewey is in there giving off some residual heat, or Neman takes up two life forms in one. I tell Hira.

"Good enough for me." Hira clicks a few more buttons on the storage room, locking the door and accessing other systems I can't follow. "Okay, now your turn."

I take the controls back and release the hangar door into space. There's no one in the hangar area so it doesn't hesitate this time. I imagine a major amount of air pushing out into the lower pressure. That will get the pirates to hurry up and try to save their ships. And as predicted, the lights to the hangar bay pop on. Cam, now tuned in to the heat and air strategies, well at least heat, since I vented the air, indicates that four pirates have entered. Perfect. Now to encourage the ships to leave. I extend the docking arms and something else I've been waiting to release.

Another alarm flashes. *"Are you certain you want to disrupt the base's internal gravitational system?"*

Oh, yes I do.

On the whole base? Yes, indeed.

There's a sound like the winding down of power, and then things get really strange. I'm no longer sitting in my chair for one thing, and neither is Hira. Tools that had been sitting casually on desks are now floating in front of my face as well. This is the craziest thing I've ever felt. I'm halfway between feeling like I'm flying and throwing up everything in my stomach.

"How long do we wait for your plan?"

Hira twists around as she floats and then she shrugs. "A little longer. So tell me about yourself, Daj."

"What? Are you serious?"

"We're not going anywhere. And you look pretty nervous. Thought this might get your head straight."

I shrug as I slowly rotate in the air. "Before coming on this vacation with Rym, I used to make vids." Sounds pretty dumb when I say it out loud.

"I knew that. I meant where are you from, family, all that."

"I've lived in Phen ever since my parents left. They flew for Scitech. They went on a flight one day and never came back."

"Did they leave any word?"

I shake my head and my hand involuntarily reaches for Cam. "I'm glad your family is all right."

"That was close, but nothing I've never dealt with before. Now your parents, I know what that's like. My parents died early in the Skywatch wars. And my sister died near the end of it all, some sickness. She was all I had left of our family. Damn, I miss her." She salutes the air.

I gulp. It's what Rym told me about Hira's sister. And Stell.

"Now's the time you say something nice to me. Right?"

I hold my breath for a few more seconds. "What if your family weren't all gone?"

"Huh?"

But before I can say anymore, something happens that we weren't expecting. The lights in the nearby hallway start to flip on in sequence, closer and closer to our room.

Suddenly, I hear the whining again, this time a little louder. The door vibrates with the sound. It's like a drill or some sort of saw. How did they get through the doors in the halls? They still show up locked. Could they have access to systems we thought they didn't?

I plop to the floor as gravity reasserts itself. Apparently they do.

"Get into the tunnel!" Hira shouts and scrambles to her feet.

"What about Cam?"

Hira pauses and looks at me funny.

"She needs to be connected physically to maintain the connection, if we take her, we lose that."

Hira grabs me by the shoulder and pulls me toward the hidden tunnel. "So what's the problem? Leave her!"

"I'm not going to let the pirates get her information." I don't include that she's my one possession I really can't leave behind.

But screw it. I rip her off the screen and place her on the wrist dock. Her little legs curl up around my arm and then the screen with all the connected data fades away.

"You better be right," Hira says as she disappears into the wall.

Yeah, I better. At least I know I'm right about one thing, and that's saving Cam.

The whining increases to an almost painful level, but as I shut the hidden panel behind me, it dies right down. I hear the intruders outside, but I don't have time for it. I'm pushing my way through the darkness to the bathroom. I really hope Hira isn't flattening Legs as she barrels along.

Muffled cries erupt behind me and the whine picks up again. This time I'm sure it's aimed at the panel into our tunnel. Hira makes a disgusted sound up ahead.

"Get out of my way, slime," she says. In the darkness I can't really see what's going on, but the scaly skin shoved into my legs gives me an idea of what Hira did to get ahead. There's a slight increase in the pitch of the whining. They probably are about to cut through the door now.

"Come on, Legs," I say to urge the Cadean onward. I still can't believe this is the enemy.

A bright light appears as Hira releases the panel on the wall to the closet, and the room is blessedly empty. I cram in beside her and pull the gangly little creature with me. Hira holds a finger up to her lips and readies the pistol. I check my wrist screen just to make sure, and, yeah,

there's nothing going on there. We're on our own. Good thing I've got Hira with me, she can tell us where to go and—

The bathroom door opens with a hiss, and there are three pirates with rifles squared right on us, and of course it's Rancelon standing right in front. Hira doesn't even put up a fight, she drops the pistol and raises her hands.

"Not good enough," Rancelon says with a sneer.

Well crap, he's going to kill Hira. And then me.

But he doesn't. A blast of energy collides with Rancelon's face and expands from there to cover his entire body in a coruscating pulse of blue lights. Did Hira have another gun? Did Legs do that somehow? Whatever happened, Rancelon falls to the ground in a twitching heap.

"Pirate intruders," Rym's voice calls out from the intercom system. "We have taken over *our* base. Lay down your weapons and proceed to the hangar."

The two other pirates with Rancelon glance at each other, obviously confused. Another pulse of energy hits one of the pirates and he too collapses.

"It's not a suggestion!" Rym yells.

The remaining pirate throws his gun to the ground and raises his hands.

"Maintenance to the bathroom in the 1A hallway, there's a bit of a mess." Rym chuckles over the comms, and I finally let out a breath. "Are you two all right in there? It's a good thing you had your little drone with you, I couldn't have tracked you otherwise. What in the…? Is that a Cadean?"

Hira shrugs up at the camera in the corner of the room.

"Wait, there's a camera in the bathroom?"

The pirate leans over to his fallen comrade, stunned, not killed, and pulls him to his feet. He puts his arms around his shoulder and carries him away leaving Rancelon face down in a puddle of his drool and other bodily fluids. What a shame, he was so close to the toilet, too.

CHAPTER 19

Ten minutes later we're all assembled in the hangar staring at the pirates, fifteen of them, sitting in a circle, looking like a depressed group of teens who just got busted at a party. I mean, it was great. The pirates actually locked up the actual owners of the base in a back closet and expected them to not access the controls. What was worse, for them, obviously, was that Hira had directed them to the secret supply room where all the weapons were stashed.

Win win.

For us.

"We can shove them in escape pods," Jali says. "We've got enough for them. Or maybe we just vent them in the airlock. What do you think?"

She's got one of her large assault rifles leveled at the berated pirates and they duck away from it. Maybe it's because she has that gnarled up face and can't see straight. And she looks a little crazy.

"That's what they were going to do to us, right? Just vent us out? And then along comes Daj here, and makes a little truce so we can talk nice. He could have just dusted your ship, Prance-along." Jali shoves the barrel of her gun right into the lead pirate's face.

"You would have done the same," Rancelon says under his breath.

Jali presses the barrel against his forehead. "We didn't do the same. And we had the chance to, many times. Moron."

"That's enough, Jali." Rym walks up and places a hand on her shoulder. "Maybe we just let them go."

Jali spins to face Rym. I know she's feigning anger, but the pirates don't. "We can't! They'll just come back. Or lead Scitech to us. They'll do anything for money."

There's a squeaking sound from behind me, and it's coming from Legs. He or she or it is spinning on one of the chairs. If I were closer, I'd stop it. It's kind of taking away from our intimidation factor.

"We won't go to them," one of the pirates says weakly.

"Shut up!" Rancelon says.

"No, you shut up," a female Maglan says.

Rancelon drops his eyes.

"This is all your fault," she says. "We could have let them go. Or warned them or…"

It hits me that these pirates are all right around my age. Like by a couple of years. "Where did you come from? Are you mining pilots?"

"We—"

"Enough Pran," Rancelon says.

Jali levels the rifle at Rancelon's face. "I think we should hear what she has to say." He doesn't make another peep.

"We are," Pran says. "Or, we were. That's where we got these ships. Most of us left Magla within the last year to fly for Scitech. You know their big spiel, right? Get the upgrades, leave the planet and fly the mine ships? The big fancy ones that leave from Phen?"

I know that all too well.

"Anyway, we realized that their deal wasn't all they said it was. Sure, we got to fly. But we were flying all the time. And in terrible conditions. Exposed to radiation. Some of the older miners tried to warn us."

Other pilots start talking. "It's worse than anything you can imagine. Do you know what we're hauling up there? All of Magla's resources. Food. Water."

"These rocks in the Dust Field?" Pran says. "That's all that's left of old moons."

"What are they doing with all the resources?" Rym says. "They can't be just using it on Scitech's station."

Pran shrugs. "Some of it is. The rest though, they're not keeping it there. Processing it, and then it goes away. They take it away, but it never goes back to the planet."

Legs spins again on the chair, making one long squeak. Everyone stares until it stops spinning.

"And where did you find this thing?" Rym says.

"It was being held there, on the moon base. Locked up as some research project, so we took it. Rancelon thought we could use it as a bargaining chip. We escaped on a mining run one day, came across this place, and tried to hide here."

"So you hate Scitech as much as we do," I say.

Pran fixes me with a look. "More, probably."

"Aren't you afraid Scitech will track you down?" Neman says. "Use your nanotech against you?"

"That's why we're hiding up here," Pran says. "They can't get a bead on us in this area. But it's only a matter of time before we get caught."

Rym laughs. "Well, looks like someone's ready to join our resistance, huh?"

The pirates murmur to themselves. I think they were set on being ejected into space, not being asked to join up. Rancelon sits quietly off to the side with a few pirates, wearing a deep scowl.

"You just want to be used by another faction?" he says to his pirates. "These guys are worse than us."

Jali feigns a punch into his face and he flinches.

"So, stick him in the escape pod then?" she asks.

There's some hushed laughter among the pirates.

Rym waves everyone to silence. "We're offering you the chance to join us. We're a group of old soldiers trying to make a dent in Scitech's reach."

"They're Skywatch," I say. "And screw dents. They're trying to end Scitech, and give the power back to the Maglans."

"You mean we, right?" Hira pulls up my sleeve and shows the tattoo, pretty much healed now and only moderately painful.

Murmurs of *Skywatch* finally break the silence. They're looking at all of us, even me, with different eyes.

"You're obviously good pilots," Rym says. "And can manage to stay off the radar, so that means you've got some good techs among you."

"Not to mention some good munition experts." Jali pulls Pran to her feet. "Who came up with that parasite mine? Brilliant. Shitty, but brilliant."

Pran smiles and pats her chest.

"Well, you and I got some things to discuss then." The two of them begin to talk together and the other pirates stand, as well. Rym begins to speak to them, going over our plan of sneaking onto that Scitech base, where we can broadcast a signal to the whole planet. Looks like our party is about to get a lot bigger, and thankfully, too. These pirates should know a lot about the base we're aiming for.

"It's a good thing we didn't kill them all after all, huh?" Hira says.

Rym nods. "Captain Pacifist, I guess I owe you an apology."

"Forget it." This kind of stuff makes me uncomfortable.

Rym settles down at a computer terminal and begins cycling

through the systems. "Never thought we'd be up here again. Magnus Base."

"Yeah, I ran into some comms when Stell and I were in the old Skywatch temple." I flinch and glance at Hira when I mention Stell's name, but she doesn't react. "It mentioned this base, but couldn't connect with it."

"We kept it offline when we ditched," Rym says. "I'll try to reestablish the connection with it. That could actually be useful. Thanks, kid."

Thinking about losing connection tickles my brain again. The claustrophobia of this nanotech in my body makes me want to scratch the buggers out of my eyeballs. I feel them sucking the life out of me, like the parasite mines sucked the life out of the Dagger.

I could eat more of that fruit. I could block some of the 'sites capabilities, right? I hear them spinning around in my head, draining my thoughts.

"Hey, where's Rancelon?" someone shouts.

Everyone looks around, but there's no sign of the pirate.

Dewey plugs into a computer outlet and accesses the system. "Escape pod launched."

"Can you track it?" Rym asks.

"It appears the beacon on it was disabled."

"Shit," Rym says.

"Anyone know if he heard the entire plan before he left?" Hira asks. "Or just some of it?"

"Shit, shit." Rym punches the wall. "Well, that moves our timeline way up, doesn't it?"

"What if we went back to Magla?" Pran says. "To try to help everyone down there?"

Hira shakes her head. "Scitech would tear us a new one, have us pinned down all over the planet. We have to do it now."

"Let's pool our resources," Rym says. "We get to the base, hijack the signal, and get everyone on Magla on our side."

"That base you're talking about?" one of the pirates says. He's not much older than me. "That's where all the food, water, and ore goes. It's pretty high security, but you could get through with a quick update to your creds. Tons of ships go there a week."

"But before you can use that broadcast station, there's a redundant system you'll need to crack." Pran knows a lot about this operation, apparently.

"Where is it?" Rym says.

Pran pulls up a map of the quadrant and points to an area above the base we're aiming for. "Here, somewhere. It isn't an official location, and they obviously don't want to tell everyone about it. I only know about it because of stories and catching sight of it a few times during transport. This thing acts as a watch on the broadcasting. They turn it off, you can't send out a signal. I think we'll have to coordinate an attack on this place before you get the message out."

Rym paces with his hands on his hips. "Can anyone confirm this? Neman?"

"Sounds right. I figured the filter system would be on the same base, but this makes more sense. You know I'd have to be there to do this."

Separate the team? We can't do that. My hearts begin to thump extra loud in my ears.

Rym shakes his head. "We don't know if this intel is legit. Maybe Scitech is spreading false info just to cloud everything. We can't afford to split up like this."

Neman settles down into a spinning chair next to Legs. "It's what I'd do, you know, put up a redundant system like that."

"Pran," Jali says. "Do you think you could get us there? The others will be going straight for the main base."

"Wait, you wouldn't go with us?" I say.

Jali flashes me a crooked smile. "You're going to be broadcasting a signal to the whole planet. I ain't the most photogenic one of us, right?"

I don't know how to respond to this.

"We'll be all right," Jali says. "They'll need some firepower and know how, that's all."

"She's right," Rym says. "They can shut it down, draw eyes away from us and the real plan. You said this base is a major port, right?"

Pran nods. "Ships and supplies in, empties fly back down to Magla. Processed materials and other supplies are flown off somewhere else by drone pilots."

"Somewhere else?" I say.

"To the Cadeans, no doubt," Rym says.

I glance over at Legs, who is still sitting in the chair, seemingly oblivious. "I don't think so. You say we went to war with them, but why? They seem harmless, and pretty unintelligent."

Rym grunts. "They're craftier than you think. Sure, it can't talk, but it's always listening. We ought to kill the thing now, it could be planning to give all this information to its kind."

"They don't speak," Hira says. "Not the way we do, anyway. But they can get into your head. Plant ideas with their neural suggestions, if you're not careful."

That's messed up. But then I remember what happened when I stumbled upon Legs in the first place. I had some pretty inventive ideas, ones I don't know how I came up with under all that pressure. I remember it looking at me, opening its freaky mouth. Could those really have been its ideas?

"How do they communicate? They must, right?" I'm starting to feel a little uncomfortable with it possibly being in my thoughts.

"Some say it's a different wavelength," Neman says. "Like a radio wave, or something similar. I think it's more than that, though."

I hear a high-pitched whine like from before. Maybe now that I'm aware of what's happening, I can block its thoughts. Great, now I'm paranoid.

"How did something like this nearly win a war with our planet? Look at it. It's nothing really that strong, right?"

"It's smart," Rym says. "Really smart. Like intelligent, and tech smart. And they can make Maglans do things they don't want to. For all we know, it's making us do this plan. It might have fed you this information about the other base just to split us up."

Different wavelengths, huh? If I could hear Stell talk to me, even though she had no voice, maybe I've just got to listen to this thing a little better. And then I can figure out what it's up to.

Breathe. Yes, I'm going to do this. Like Stell taught me. I tune out the voices around me, of the pirates discussing what they know, and I just listen. First off, I get the feeling I'm floating way above everything. And I guess that's right. I am in this base in orbit around Magla, but I can really feel it. There's a pulsing energy around me, and it's a familiar feeling, warm and welcome.

And then this sensing, this hearing or whatever, I turn it to the leggy creature spinning around in a chair. There is a sound, I'm sure of it now. A warbling whine with lots of variations to it, not only the high pitched tone I heard before.

And I slow it down. I don't know what I'm really doing. It's like tuning a dial on an incoming transmission, but I'm using my mind to do it. It happens almost on its own. And then I get it, like a picture coming into focus, I get what it's saying. Not words, not really. I'm listening to images, feelings, and it's coming in fast. I can't understand it all completely, just pieces here and there. It's like a dream, or trying to remember a dream, anyway. Little bits pop into my head and start to unravel.

It's not a linear form of communication. The images cycle around, come back to what I first heard, but this time as the language spins, I pick up on something else and it makes sense as it builds upon itself. I'm not quite sure, but I think the creature is telling me its history. I catch glimpses of itself in different ages in its life. Is this its name? Something about rolling hills, puzzle solver, seeker. I don't get it, it's all jumbled.

But there's a sense of pain in everything I'm receiving in every image. I don't think it's internal, or some sort of sickness. I think it has something to do with this place. Or not necessarily this place, but everything around me, and below me.

"I think there's something about this base, or Magla, that is making it sick, or killing it slowly. Poor little guy."

"Poor little guy, my ass," Jali says. "These alien bastards attacked us first. They've always wanted what we have down here. If we didn't win, they'd have come down and killed us all."

This guy doesn't seem to want to kill us. And why would they want what we have? From what I learned in school, Cadea is big enough that it has its own atmosphere and resources. I'm pretty sure that its creatures evolved up there and they're doing just fine.

More images cycle around in my head. I forget that I'm still tuned into Legs' mind. A desolate terrain. Plasma storms bombarding the landscape with energy. Maybe these are images of its home, but it doesn't seem very friendly to me.

"Pran, where did you find it again?" I say.

"On Naglor, the broken moon. On Scitech's base. It was in a cell looking like it was about to get deported somewhere. Maybe testing, who knows? There was a bunch of scientific equipment near its room."

This wouldn't be the first time Scitech would test on a living thing. I mean, look at what I ran into at the underground research facility. Huge nose sniffing Maglans, neurally disrupted big-brained ones, too. Maybe that was a by-product of Cadean communication, although it felt different at the time.

"It's probably best if it comes with us," I say. "If not for a bargaining chip, at least to get it away from here and whatever is causing it pain."

Legs looks me right in the eyes and tilts its head slightly. I'm not fully listening to its voice anymore, but a slight warbling pulse comes through, nonetheless. If I didn't know better, I'd think it was thankful.

"You're a better Maglan than I am," Rym says. "But it's staying locked in the hold. Got it?"

That's better than a no, or just Rym blasting it.

"Even though Rancelon is out there, we can afford a little sleep," Rym says. "I take that back. We *need* sleep. The moon with the main Scitech base is circling Magla, pretty much on the other side of the planet from us now. Dewey, how long to get there?"

Dewey responds immediately. "Three hours at minimum burn if we're trying to avoid detection, and I'm assuming we are. If not, two hours. The base Neman and Jali and our new friends are heading toward is near that, as well."

"Perfect," Rym says. "Load up what gear we have stashed here, split up what Neman and Jali need. We can get some sleep, and then use these stims to help us after we get there. We leave within the hour."

"Rym." Neman hustles back into the room. "She's there. On the moon base. I got it out of the data pad Daj picked up."

"Who's there?" Hira says.

"Stell," Rym says and walks out of the room. Neman pretends to work on a computer.

Hira looks at me and my insides go cold. It's that same look she gave me when we were trapped. She wants to know what I meant about her family. I gesture for her to talk to Rym and she follows him.

I'm not quite sure how this will end when she finds out she has another living relative out there somewhere and that Rym hid her. Dewey and Jali tilt their heads away as if expecting a bomb blast. Before I can hear the fallout, Rym places an arm on Hira's shoulder and leads her down the hallway. I let out the breath I was holding.

Pran walks side by side with Jali going over the schematics for the parasite mine on a data pad. Neman and Dewey go over the inventory here at the base and begin to order pirates to start packing it in ships. I hear them talking about setting up a Nanosite blocking protocol for the pirates. Dewey has that built in, but Pran will need more coverage with their group, and a bot or transmitter to use it. If not, Scitech could pick up on their movement.

I pull up a spare data pad lying on the desk to see what Pran gave us on the base. Flight paths, some rough maps and protocols for entry. She and her friends didn't do more than make deliveries, but they must have caught on to some bad stuff going on before they split.

This base is crazy. It's situated smack in the middle of the debris field on what's left of the moon. According to the maps and recon photos, it appears to be almost growing out of the rock. I guess it's like this base, but on an exponential scale up. The transmission facility is huge, and must project signals to orbital stations all around Magla. We've got to break in, hack into it, and then make a plea to the entire planet without being shut down.

And find exactly where Stell might be. Unless she's in the same room as the broadcast station, we have no idea where to look. Well, that certainly gives me something to do on the way over, since I have no intention of sleeping right now.

Hira storms out of the hall where she and Rym were talking. By the look on her face, I can't tell if she killed him or not. She doesn't meet anyone's eyes, but she busies herself about, picking up weapons and gear and hurrying them into our ship.

Rym walks out of the room a short time later and starts ordering us about. It looks like he just got the talking-to of his life. In minutes, we load up the Peace Hammer and I make sure the Dagger is ready to go, too. Jali has an especially curious look in her eye as she brings some crates onto the pirate's main ship. When I inquire, she only smiles that crooked smile.

"Time to go," Rym says on his final check. "Hira? Which group are you going to go with? Neman and Jali, or with us?"

Hira crosses her arms. "I'm going to find my damn niece."

She looks at me and narrows her eyes. "I've got a few things to talk to you about."

"All right." I gulp and force a weak smile.

Neman and Jali stand at the door to the Hammer and talk quietly to Rym. Hira and Dewey crowd around to give hugs and final words.

"You just blow up the relays there, Jali," Hira says. "We'll need your assistance when things get thick."

"Pran there has some good ideas." Jali points to the young girl loading up her own craft. "And we're bringing some of those mines to slow down any interference."

"Speaking of interference," Neman says while adjusting a boxy device. "I believe that everything is monitored up there so we're going to have to be comms silent. Only the Hammer and Dagger are undetectable, for now. That's the main reason we stole them, was because Scitech couldn't detect us, right? That means the other rigs will be picked up the second we get there. I've crafted some permits similar to what other mining and transport rigs have, so we should be all right, for a little. This has got to go quickly."

"What if there were a better way to communicate?" I say. "Like how this guy does?" I gesture to Legs who has kept close by while we packed.

Rym looks at me. "You mean like how Stell talks to you? She did that to me too, but I never really figured out how to do it. She's not clouded up by nanos, I guess."

"I can *hear* her, and she can hear me, if I use these." I show him the canister of berries. "Take some, I think we can learn to talk like that."

Rym rubs his hands. "We don't have time, kid. It's great you want to come back to your roots, but we're going to need every ounce of our skill, and that unfortunately comes from the tech inside here." He points to his skull.

He's right, I think. But it's tough to hear him say this stuff. I mean, wasn't he the one who first told me to get rid of it? And now he can't let go. "You're a Skywatch pilot. You can't tell me that you're better off now with more nanos than you were in the war."

"Things slow down, and yes I'm talking about my body. This is too big for any one of us."

I laugh. "I'm not quite sure how this is going to go over when I try to tell everyone to ditch their tech because they're being manipulated. 'Sure, we'll believe you, especially with your main crew still connected.'"

"Kid, it ain't that easy."

"Someone once told me the more we forget, the stronger they become."

Rym laughs but only pushes past me into the hold and preps the ship for launch.

I flip the canister over. Neman and Jali just shrug at me. I give them both hugs and wish them luck.

"I've packed a few things away for you," Neman says. "My research and a data hack for getting through the computers on the station."

"Thanks, Neman. And I never got to say thanks for saving Hira and me back in the bathroom. I heard you were behind that."

He smiles and shrugs. "It was your bot that led us to you. I followed her signal because the cameras weren't booting up quick enough."

"Good thing." And it's a good thing I brought her along, even though Hira told me to leave her. Not that I ever would have.

"This isn't exactly how we used to say goodbye back in the war," Jali says. "You take care, kid, and watch over those three."

I look over my shoulder at Dewey, Hira, and Rym.

"Wait, what about that Suin?" My mouth curls just thinking of that liquor again. "Seems like something you'd have before every op, right?"

Rym walks behind me. "He's right, we can't jinx this mission."

Dewey's chest opens and produces five shot glasses in his extended arm.

"What, were you a bartender bot in another life?" I ask.

"Nah, these guys just went on a lot of missions."

Rym smiles and fills all the glasses while we stand in a circle. "Skywatch," he says, and raises his glass. He looks at Hira.

She stands still for a second, not meeting his eyes.

"Skywatch." She pounds the Suin with a grim smile.

"Skywatch," we say together.

This time the liquor doesn't burn nearly as bad as it goes down my throat, but it tastes like piss just the same. Every op they do this? I guess I'll get used to it.

I just hope we all get the chance.

Jali and Neman salute me with their two right arms crossed over their chests. I return it as best I can and walk aboard the Peace Hammer as it powers up its launch cycle. The whining cycles and the ship vibrates. I close the main hatch behind me, clutching the canister and weighing my options.

CHAPTER 20

"Daj?"

Man, there are only so many places I can hide out. It took her a while to track me down, though.

"Hey, Hira. Just checking out the systems on my ship."

"You've been in there for a long time. Everything all right?"

The Dagger's chair retracts back into the main hold. I guess I can't keep avoiding her any longer. "Do we have any food or water onboard? I'm dying."

Hira crosses her arms and raises an eyebrow.

Well, it didn't hurt to try, anyway.

"Please." Her tone softens. "Tell me about her."

"Didn't Rym have anything to share? He's known her forever."

"He did, but he's not the most eloquent Maglan..."

I get it. She wants to know more about the family she thought she lost forever. I'd want to know what someone had to say if they knew my parents, too.

"She's like you, a bit."

That eyebrow raises again.

"She's direct, and strong. And connected. You know, how you care about your great grandkids? She's that way about Magla." I've never really sat down and thought about her this much. Really, I went from being kidnapped to saved by the same Maglan.

"You both helped me out when you didn't really need to."

She smiles. "Seems like something my sister would do."

"What was your sister's name?"

"Sarissa. Sarissa Freewind."

My hearts skip. "Wait, you mean *the* Commander Freewind?"

"Well, we both were, but yeah. I thought Maglans forgot about us."

Aw man, that's right. They were sisters. "I used to play Skywatch games when I was a kid, and we all wanted to be like you guys."

Hira's face spikes droop. "That was a long time ago. I just wish I could talk to her again."

"Hey, we'll find Stell, right?"

She pats my shoulder. "We will."

"So your sister, she was a Non… I mean an Eldane?"

Hira nods. "Kid, we all were, until we got the nanotech."

"Something's been bugging me for a long time, ever since the research base. That room I found, the incinerator? There were a bunch of our bio metal stones, dantoliths, I think Neman called them. What do you know about them?"

"The dantolith is our center, our core. It develops as we grow. The Eldane say our connection to the planet stems from this part of us, and it is very sacred. Families would honor their ancestors by keeping the dantoliths in a shrine, and this way they could maintain a connection with their spirits. That tradition is now forgotten."

"Any reason why Scitech would want to collect them?"

Hira shrugs. "This is sacrilegious. And disturbing. There is power within the stones, extracted over the years we are alive. I hate to think of them being harvested."

That is really creepy. I reach for my gut and try to sense my own dantolith.

"All right, about that food." Hira pats my shoulder. "Were you serious, or just trying to hide from me?"

"A little of both. I've been starved since two minutes into the Dust Field."

Hira leads me down the stairs and nods in the direction of the meeting room behind the cockpit.

"You sure this stuff is still good?"

Hira shrugs. "Should be."

There's a row of nutrient distribution devices tucked behind the screens and I grab a bowl and a cup. Ration bites and a protein rich gel pour out of the wall like some sort of pet food dispenser. Damn, this stuff looks nasty. But my stomach is grumbling no matter what it looks like. I try a bit of each, sniffing first to make sure it isn't spoiled.

Well, I don't throw up. I guess that's good. My tongue curls up enough from the bitter taste, though. I raise the food up in a toast to Hira and she laughs.

"I'm going to get a bit of sleep," she says. "You should too."

"Can't."

She yawns and starts to walk down to the bunks. "I can."
I wave and take another bite, spinning in my chair.

"Oh, hey, Legs."

The long-legged Cadean is in another chair on the other side of the room, spinning around, too. It's got to be bored being locked up in here.

"Want some?" I toss a bit over and it grabs the ration piece in its small front hands.

Its face opens vertically and in goes the food. There's a slight pinching of its large eyes, possibly signifying disgust, but other than that it finishes eating. Strange how an off-world alien life can eat the same things we do.

We both finish and I serve up another bowl for Legs (I'm starting to feel bad about calling it that knowing I should be calling him something like Traveler or Finder, but Legs just sticks). It pumps its back two legs up and down to spin a little faster in the chair. The bank of monitors shows the cabins. Rym and Hira are already asleep, having run their 'site programs to engage deep sleep. Always a useful tool for falling asleep so quickly, and I'm kind of wishing I had access to mine to get this trip over with.

But instead I twist back and forth and watch the screens and the chatter from Magla scrolling across. The vandalism across the globe has Scitech puzzled. From graffiti to stolen equipment in at least ten different places. No coverage on the research facility that we all hit, though, and that's just weird.

There's also no deaths on any of the attacks; that's good. None reported, anyway. And it's enough to keep Scitech off our backs while we sneak up to their main control facility. Then we send a message to the world, and find Stell. Sounds so crazy. I still can't believe we're about to do this.

"Cam, you ready to broadcast?"

She beeps and a *"system positive"* verification pops up on the wrist screen. There are hundreds of vids I can use to transmit from the base, I should probably get them organized.

"Compile a list of vids for me. Flag anything with Scitech recently." It's been a while since I've made up a vid for views. I wonder what music I should splice in with this. Hah. It isn't quite the same, I guess.

Cam busily gets to work with the vids she collected in the past week. It'll still be a bit before I can see what she's gotten, so I flip to other screens.

A strange feeling of longing or sadness steals over me. Like I'm leaving my friends, or even worse, like my parents are going and never coming back. It's so strong and sudden that I reel and have to grab onto the table so I don't fall over. Am I just exhausted from the lack of sleep and a good meal? I don't remember the last time I *really* slept without worrying about being tracked down by crazy Scitech goons.

I breathe deeply and try to relax. I can't be like this and still be able to fight, or fly, or even walk. But as soon as I start, the weariness fades. Not completely though, unfortunately. It sticks to me, like being hung over the few times I partied after a good viewing of my vids.

Legs, on the other hand, spins around with increased fervor. Little bastard. It's like it's rubbing it in. Maybe I'm too tired and everything seems faster and more irritating.

I spin the canister of fruits around on the table and contemplate taking them. Not only to fill me up, but for what they could do to my nanos. Man, they sound so good right now, especially after eating the ship's version of food production. How long has that food been sitting around? I'm surprised and at the same time relieved I'm not keeling over from some sort of bacterial infection. Food poisoning. That would be great if I got in front of the whole planet only to puke all over the camera. Special incoming message, folks.

Still, I hold off on the berries. I'll still need access to my 'site, right? I miss that connection. My friends. Plus, even Rym doesn't want to go full 'site blind.

To get my mind off of all that, I flip through the screens to see what the Peace Hammer is connected to. Maybe I can catch a show, or play a game.

Ship status. Check. Everything nominal. Boring. Flight path. Unrestricted.

Dewey created a flight lane that would avoid the major shipping lanes so nothing appears on the radar, not even the other ships that left the base with us. The plan is to remain off the grid from everyone.

One of the screens shows cameras off each side of the Hammer. It takes a little adjustment, but I spot the five ships following closely behind us. I only catch the glint of the sunlight off the hulls of the mining rigs and the trapezoidal hauler. They'll be with us until it's time to split up and attack the other relay station.

Ventral cams show us getting slightly farther from Magla and the fading auroras. My hearts slip again but this time it's from me watching the green and purple lights fade away. Never been this far away from my home. Somehow, I always pictured this escape from gravity to be more triumphant and epic. Don't get me wrong, this is amazing. I'm in space with my own ship and all. But I'm nervous, too.

I kick my feet up onto the table and lean back in the chair. What do I do? I scan the rest of the room and see a clear box containing some canisters, some familiar canisters. Are those the ones I lifted from the research facility? I stomp my feet down on the floor and get up, startling Legs in his seat. Sorry, pal.

Yup, those are definitely the things I brought back, including the data pad. This must be what Neman was talking about. Indeed, there's a tube with different interface equipment sticking out one end. That's got to be the data hack Neman mentioned. There are a couple extra containers in there as well. Looks like someone put the materials from the canisters into them, mixed them up maybe.

I pick up the data pad and activate the screen. Words, images, tables, charts… these all flip past as the power comes on. Man, Neman was busy doing a whole bunch of testing after I gave this stuff to him. There's even extra data spooling going on, so there's possibly even more to uncover. I want to find out what he's figured out so far though about these nanos.

Test case 1. *"Nano live connect. Failed."*

Test case 2. *"Magnetotroph reaction. Minimal motion and response time. Possible problems linked to temperature and/or magnetic dispersal."*

Makes sense, I took them out of that subzero research chamber.

Test case 3. *"Possible stealth nanotech. Scitech tried to fuse stealth tech and biotic subject but failed. Inability to activate field protocol?"*

I flip through more of his research, including one with my name on it. For a second, I wonder if he's found some info on me, like about my parents. But it's only a reference to something I said comparing the parasitic mines to the Nanosite.

"There's a connection to the nanotech that I've long suspected, and it's how the little things are powered. Daj made me think about it after we befriended the pirates. Our lives are connected to the 'site, for sure, and it must be that they are draining our own energy. A lot of it. So much that our bodies age at an increased rate."

It goes on like this, comparing Stell's age and mine, dantoliths, and into some stuff I can't even come close to interpreting. Does Neman think Scitech is stealing our energy and transferring it somehow?

I'm definitely going to have to get into this one later. The list goes on, including weird notes I'm sure that only Neman can translate, and mostly ending in failure. That's science, I guess. But stealth tech? That would be amazing. The last entry he put in sounds hopeful though.

Test case 15. *"Good news, I got them to work together. But only briefly."*

Something in the box shifts.

"Whoa!" I leap back from the pile.

The extra canister, the one containing the mix of materials, rolls to the side. By itself. I double check to make sure Dewey hasn't made any course corrections or that the Hammer hasn't been struck by anything. Nope.

And the vial that moved? It's the one labeled *'Test case 15.'* Well that's interesting. Both Legs and I approach the box a little more apprehensively and peer in. The mixture of purple liquid sloshes around in the glass jar as it keeps smacking up against the walls of the box. Right toward me.

Okay then. Strange life form trying to eat me. Maybe I can type that into Neman's notes for future reference.

Glancing at the pad one last time, I see that Neman put a note next to his research on Test case 15. Stealth nano hybrid failure. Initial response indicates light bending, but now only a dead batch.

What did he mean by dead batch? This stuff is flipping out. I pick up the vial and hold it up to the light and something weird happens. The thick opaque purple goo in there twists about when I touch it but that's not the weirdest part. At times, I see *through* the stuff. I'm going crazy, I must be, but the stealth tech seems to have adapted to the magneto-whatsits that Neman brewed up. But why is it activating now?

I've got room for it in my pack. Maybe, just maybe, I could use it on myself. Right. I'd be just a purple sauce covered Maglan. That would totally not stick out. But then if it's not meant for me, maybe it could work on the ship.

The Dagger. I've really missed being in there considering my last joyride got cut short. I could go out and scout the area, since we can't send out a ping to scan for drones or check stations. Last time I went out on my own, though, I kind of screwed things up. Sort of. It's still up for debate.

"Dewey?"

"Use the inter channel," Dewey's voice pops out of the comms. "That way we don't alert all of Scitech to our presence."

His passive aggressive function is working properly, I see.

"Yeah, sorry." Maybe it wasn't a good idea to ask. Or maybe I've just got to get used to being verbally abused like this. It does remind me of riffing back and forth with Zaylee and Kie. Man, they'd flip their crap if they knew half of what I've done in the past couple of days.

Zaylee.

Huh, I really thought I'd be missing her more than I am right now. I thought we had something special, but I feel disconnected, I mean, more than being thousands of miles away and in space. Maybe that's why she and Kie hooked up. There are a lot of things going on down there.

Why am I thinking about this right now?

I smack my face lightly to help keep focused and awake.

"I think it might be a good idea to go do a scouting flight around; you know, to go look up ahead."

"You mean like last time?" Dewey says.

"Yes, like last time." Jackass. "And just like last time I might be able to spot problems before we get there."

I don't tell him about the stealth nano goop in my pouch. Best to skip that part. It's silly anyway. How would this even work? Was Neman planning on drinking this? Wiping it on the ship?

"Stay in visual range at all times," Dewey says.

"Wait, really?" I was pretty sure he'd say no, or wake the others and they'd say no.

"I'm in charge when they're sleeping, so get out there before I change my mind. It's actually a good idea."

The *for once* is left hanging in silence, but I can hear it. He's good.

"The others are planning to head off to the other relay station soon, if not already." Dewey gestures to the viewscreen in front of him where a lone blip on the horizon appears. Our destination is further to the right. Still in range of each other, but far enough to help boost or control the signal.

"Keep an eye on Legs. I mean the Cadean."

"Really? I have enough to do to watch the screens here."

"What, your robo-connections with the cameras of this heap are too much for you? I thought you could multitask? Are you getting too old?"

Dewey slinks into silence. What, did I say something that hurt his *feelings*? Ugh, I can't believe I'm worried about hurting a robot's feelings. I could leave Cam, right? But I've only ever flown the Dagger with her on board to help out with running the systems, tracking, whatever. Will I be able to do it all without her? There's probably an onboard computer I didn't use.

Getting out there feels important. I don't know why, but it does. Or else I'm just getting really bored. Either way, it looks like there's only one way around it.

"All right, you can have Cam to keep you company."

Dewey's head slowly twists all around (especially creepily) and I swear there's something like a quite pleased expression on his normally expressionless, dead-eyed face. Cam shifts around on her wrist dock, like she's excited to spend a little time with him, too. Sheesh, I hope they'll be all right together. With a click, Cam's legs curl up and she hovers right next to Dewey's head. I'm starting to think that Dewey had this in mind all along.

"Okay, maybe not to keep him company, but to keep an eye on Legs, right? And to keep working on our vids."

Cam's nose dips down almost imperceptibly, but flies obediently past me into the room where Legs is still spinning around on that chair. Man, those guys are easily amused.

So I guess that's it. I'm out of here.

"Daj," Dewey says.

I turn and he crosses his arms with the same salute Neman and Jali gave me. I guess that's a Skywatch thing. I return it and turn to the stairwell for the Dagger. My ship.

That's right. Mine.

My boots clunk on the metal steps as I climb up. I kind of wish I was videoing this, you know, the epic hero walking to his ship in slow motion. Settling into the lowered seat and pushing the button to retract up into the waiting vessel. The helmet locks into place. Life support engaging and airlock hissing with separation. Lights on the panel flicker to life. The gentle rumble of the engines begins to whine and grow in pitch until it fades into the darkness surrounding him.

I mean me. Sometimes I forget I'm not always narrating my vids.

Systems pop up all over the display. Full power. Course nav syncs up to the Hammer's destination and comes up as a little glowing line directing me to the base. Weapons ready to go, just in case. Shields, full. Those are the important systems. Well, I guess comms is too, but I'm restricted from using that, at least the outgoing portion of it. As the engines finish their warm up cycle, I just take it all in.

And also that view outside. We're flying nose up to the stars and my jaw just hangs open. Stars forever. At this altitude the aurora is visible in the distance, flickering purple and green. I crane my neck to the side to see Magla's curved surface veer off, pockets of auroras cluster at different spots around the globe.

"You're cleared," Dewey says over the connected comm. "This is our last communication until you return, so stay in visual range."

"Got it." Am I supposed to say something more to confirm this? I don't know what their lingo protocol is. "Over?"

"Copy that."

I push the release button and a small thud reverberates through the hull as the ship disconnects. The Dagger hovers a few feet away from the Hammer's topside and then I grip the throttles, edging them forward a little until the engines cycle up. The ship gently cruises forward and I'm free. As close to space as I've ever been. Only for a second does my breath catch in my throat as I consider how long this ship was sitting in the research facility. What if the seals are shot? Much less any circuitry.

Well, too freakin' late now.

I jam the sticks forward and am thrust back in my seat. Damn, this thing has got some go. It's weird, I have no frame of reference so I can't really tell how fast I'm going. Sure, there's the speed readout on the display, but the only way I can tell is when I feel the acceleration.

With a small twist of the control sticks, the ship spins quickly on the horizontal axis. My eyes bug open as I hold on for my life. The seat reacts to my actions, tightening up when I turn, and allowing me to settle when I accelerate. I love this thing.

The pirate ships veer off away from Dewey's flight path now, just like he said they would. I steer the Dagger toward their convoy and fly behind them in a wide arc.

"Proximity alert," a lifeless computer voice says in my headset as I approach the ships.

"Thanks, uhhh? What do I call you?"

"Proximity alert."

Stupid name.

This time lights flash on the screen and an alarm sounds making sure I know I'm getting close. So this computer isn't going to be the same as Dewey or Cam. Oh well.

"Turn off the alarm."

"Proximity alert." There's much more beeping and flashing this time.

I search the panel to switch off the damn thing myself. After pounding several lights and switches, the thing finally shuts down, either from me or the onboard computer pitying me.

"Thanks for the help, P.A."

When I'm right behind the ships, I crank the throttle up to see how fast it can really go. The inertial dampening seat kicks in and I barely feel the acceleration. The little mining rigs turn to a blur as I pass and even the big trapezoidal ship is gone as I buzz them. Without even thinking, I twist the controls and let off the throttle so that the Dagger spins around 180 degrees, the engine lets out a blast of ionized energy, and I'm pretty sure I come to a standstill to face the oncoming ships.

Okay, that was bad ass.

What isn't, is the bottle of purple goo that Neman cooked up. At least that's what I think cracked up against the seat as I spun to a halt. The cold liquid drips down my leg, soaking into my pants and skin like I've wet myself. Great. This isn't uncomfortable, really.

As I look up from the purple stain growing across my legs, the big pirate ship lumbers by. Pran and Jali are staring down at me with big smiles on their faces. They're only there for a second and are gone as they fly past. Great. At least no one is recording this.

Although that fly by was pretty amazing.

By the time I look down again, the purple stuff isn't just on my legs, it's now expanding across my chest and onto the seat. The thickness is spreading out as it does so, and I swear I see little waves of light passing through it. It thins out until the color fades, but they dance on my skin like little bugs all over my body. I have an irrational thought to open up the cockpit and jump out of here, much like the feeling I had trapped in that tunnel back on Magla.

But it goes away like the fading nano tech that just covered my ship. In the back of my mind, I feel that thought sitting there, though. A mining tug casts a shadow over my ship as it passes by and I look up to see the pirate pilot staring at me. They must think I'm some sort of jackass. Well I thought the move was cool.

There's a tickle in the back of my head, one that is starting to become familiar since Stell left. For some reason the pull or connection I normally feel is not as strong. Maybe it's because my 'site is starting to come back online. Some of my old interfaces are fading in, including a chronometer which is acting kind of weird. Probably because I'm flying past different time zones as I circle the planet. I'm even considering flying back to the Peace Hammer to dose up on those berries, although I know it would take a while for Scitech to be able to locate me. This should give me some time to still check things out. With Dewey's signal blocker nearby, I'll probably be safe.

I hold on to the tickle in my mind as much as I can and feel something else, kind of like I did when I lifted those stones back near Jali's place. The attraction is much closer this time. In fact, I know it's right inside the cockpit with me. The feeling of those little nanos crawling all over me begins as an itch but then I start to imagine them burrowing into my skin.

The last of the tugs flies by. I've got to look crazy as I'm brushing off my skin, so I at least wave to the confused pilot as it passes.

There's more to this specific connection than I've felt before. I can almost sense the little mechanisms churning and spinning around. It's like there are tiny little nanotech thoughts flipping through my mind.

Well I've got a mission to do, so I can't focus on this right now. The flight path is glowing on my display panel, and I'm facing the completely wrong direction. The Dagger responds with little hand motions and soon I'm facing the Hammer's aft side, increasing my speed. I press forward to sidle up alongside Dewey. Well, he's not too interested in my fancy flying either, it appears; he's just staring straight ahead monitoring the flight path.

Some of his warnings go through my head then. Keep within visual range. Don't fly too fast. I know it's in our best interest to not push that last request, but this ship is way too fun. I better not though.

"P.A."

No response.

"Hey, P.A.?" I ask in a sing-song voice.

There's a pause. "Standing by for request," the monotone voice replies.

"That's better. I can't use radar at all, but can you help magnify visual sensors? Nothing that will appear on someone else's scopes. Please?" I'm not sure how to talk to this thing yet. Does it even need manners like that?

"Affirmative. I will also open a scan including other wavelengths. IR. UV. Radio. Gamma—"

"That's good, thanks." Sounds like the computer is just warming up and I don't need to hear the whole spectrum. The display screens amplify their range giving a wider scope of what's around. If anything pops up, I'll be sure to spot it.

"Let me know if you see anything out of the ordinary out there."

"Affirmative."

With the extra scanning underway, I bring up the Dagger's speed and shoot ahead on our flight path into the debris field. Huge tumbling space rocks pass next to the viewport and I twist the controls to avoid them.

"Proximity alert."

Yeah I got it. Man, this ship is perfect. It's like it was made for me. Every move I make is exactly reflected in the Dagger's flight path. The throttle twists easily and I'm weaving in and out of the rocks with barely a thought. Before I know it, a large rock spins right into my path.

"Proximity a—"

But the computer cuts off the alarm with a pulse blast, shattering the rock into thousands of bits. The pieces shower the Dagger with pelting sounds thumping against the hull. If P.A. hadn't fired, I would have had a collision and probably been killed. But it did fire and now I have to deal with it.

I power down the engines and come to a halt relative to the floating space rocks. If anything is anywhere around, it would have picked up that energy blast. Dammit. What an idiot. I can't even keep it together for ten minutes. Well, maybe nothing is even around. Maybe nothing spotted it.

But something does appear on my screens. A slight signature of varying frequencies. But that could be normal radiation, right?

"Scitech craft in the area," P.A. says.

The screens triangulate the changes in signal to get a location on whatever it is. Some information pops up on the screen and, yes, it is Scitech. A drone, not bigger than my ship, patrolling the area. It's got a long, narrow back section, making it look like a tail on some sea creature. The stumpy wings up front look almost like fins, finishing off the animal image. It probably would never get much action out here, out of the normal flight routes to the base. But we're trying to sneak up from this direction and I had to go and screw it up.

"Did it notice us?"

P.A. pauses. "Affirmative. It is approaching. It must be investigating the flash of the pulse weapon I needed to discharge."

"Don't worry, I'm not blaming you. It's my fault that happened."

"Affirmative."

Great. I'm getting shit from all sides.

Now what? Do I make a break for it? Risk getting spotted on the way out? Stay put? Hope I avoid detection? I guess that's it, and if it comes down to it I can blast this thing to pieces.

"Power us down as much as you can."

The engines cycle down and then we're just floating out here in the open. I instinctively flip a switch on a panel and we move downward. In a second, we come to an abrupt stop. The ventral camera shows we're butted right up to a large rock. If the drone flies by, it might not even see us, right? No, that's stupid. Stupid. It will have better scanning equipment than us. This is its job, after all.

That tickle in my head runs up and down my back this time. The purple goo. The stealth nanos. Neman said this stuff didn't work, didn't he? Still, I breathe. Slow down my thoughts and try to reach out to those little things to get them to turn on, or whatever they do.

A wave of energy touches my skin and a warm sensation passes over my arms and legs. It's like I'm feeling embarrassed or something. There's a ripple extending from my mind that pulses with my breath and extends beyond me. The light twists and reflects and begins to wrap around the hull of the ship. Well that isn't going to help. Those lights will draw in any eyes watching. And like I just called it over to hang out, the bot drone ship appears, scanning the rocks with a green light.

It's getting closer.

Almost time to bug out and get a bead on this asshole before it spots me.

But when I grab the throttles and try to power up, the ship refuses. Maybe because the whole ship is shut down, or P.A. is making a conscious choice. Either way, I'm just sitting here waiting for the drone to pick us off. It's going right overhead now. I can see the individual rivets used to piece the thing together. And I read the word, 'Scitech' on its underside.

But when the green lights flicker off our surface, the drone doesn't even slow down. I sit tight, thinking it's going to make another pass, but it only does one sweep of the area and goes back around the way it came. I watch as it retreats out of visual range on the Dagger's screens.

It didn't see me? That's impossible. It ran its scan right over the ship, didn't it? I look out at the hull and there's a rippling effect over its surface. I don't remember the color of the metal exactly, but I don't think it was dark gray and speckled with shadows. In fact, it matches the rock we've backed up to perfectly.

The stealth tech? Neman did fix them up, right? No way. This is going to change everything once we get to the base out here. But there's still the Peace Hammer to think about. There's no missing that thing if you get anywhere close.

"Positive lock on the ship energy signatures," P.A. says. "Scanning field."

A few blips appear on the display screen.

"Wait, are those all drones?"

"Affirmative."

"And they didn't detect our scan?"

P.A.'s silence makes me think it doesn't have time to deal with my ignorance.

"We can use this to steer a path clear through the entire field now. I've got to get this back to the others."

There's little chance I can give info to both of us, though, not with the speed at which the Peace Hammer is approaching this place. Plus I don't know how to get back to the other ships, and sending a transmission is out of the question. This sucks. I don't want Neman and Jali to get identified, but I can't let the Hammer wander into this mess.

The Dagger begins its power up sequence and thirty seconds later I'm heading back as fast as I can without being detected. I'm going to leave it and hope that Neman and the others will be able to avoid any similar encounters on the way to their station. We've been lucky so far, and I'm not ready for it to run out yet.

CHAPTER 21

The Dagger locks onto the Hammer and there's a hiss as the pressures balance. My seat starts to descend into the other ship, but I'm already tapping the comm unit.

"Dewey! Stop! You've got to stop the ship. Stop them all."

Almost immediately there's the sound of retro thrusters firing and I feel the ship decelerate. "Copy."

I'm too nervous or excited to really let the fact that Dewey acted on my report without question sink in. And when I'm greeted by Hira and Rym at the bottom of the chair's descent, I can only wonder if they're going to rip me a new one. Their expressions don't give me any clue as to what to expect.

"Report," Rym says as he salutes both arms across his chest.

Good. Not pissed. And Hira's not either. All right, what did I do wrong? When are they going to throw me in a holding cell or something? But they just wait for me to tell what happened out there.

"Drones, on patrol." Why am I out of breath? And talking so fast? "P.A., uh, my ship's computer, has data we collected on their signatures. Says we can spot more in the area if there are any."

Rym nods and turns down the stairs toward the cockpit of the Peace Hammer. "Hear that, Dewey? Plug into Daj's ship and get that info to plot a new course."

"Got it, boss."

"We need to get this information over to Neman and Jali," I say. "I can fly to their ships and tell them."

Rym looks back at me and scratches his chin. After a moment he shakes his head. "They're too far out of range now. Anything we send might get intercepted, and that goes for you, too. Plus, it would take too long to track them down, and we need you here for the next stage. We've waited too long as it is and can't risk having Rancelon reporting what he knows."

Rym and Hira walk down below and sit in the main room behind Dewey. Hira stays silent regarding Rym's decision, but whether or not she agrees with it I don't know. I follow and sit next to Legs.

"Nice job out there," Hira says and Rym nods.

That's it? I thought for sure there'd be some reprimand.

"Neman was working on some stuff, some of the tech I brought from the facility back on Magla. I grabbed some of this stealth nano research and got it to work out there on my ship."

Hira picks up the data pad and scrolls through the notes. "What did it do?"

"I'm not one hundred percent, but I think the nanos redirected the light and other EM radiation, somehow. Bent it around the ship to project an image of what was around me."

"How did you get it to work?" Hira points to the pad. "Neman says here that it dudded out."

I shrug. "Maybe it was activated when it touched my ship." I'm not really feeling like talking about how the nanos entered my mind. In fact, I can still almost feel them on the edge of my thoughts.

Hira doesn't break her stare and it starts to make me feel uncomfortable. It's almost like she's trying to prod around in my head with her eyes. Can't everyone just stay out?

"Are you sure they're just on your ship?"

I unconsciously wipe my arms off.

Hira hits Rym with the back of her hand. "He got some on him!"

"So?" I say.

"Try to do what you did out there," Hira says. "I couldn't sense anything just then, nothing active that is. But you must have done something to get them to work."

Rym and Hira look at me expectantly like I'm some kid just about to take his first steps. Even Legs seems interested. It twists its head to a 90-degree angle. Whoa, creepy.

I take a deep breath and slowly let it out. I reach out for that feeling that Stell always told me about, to open up. But this time it's clear there's nothing there. It feels cold and empty in my head. On the other hand, all my Nanosite systems are populating my eyes, not just the clock anymore.

"That's it." I reach out for Neman's data pad and flip to case 15, opening it up for edits.

"What is?" Rym says.

But I'm too busy typing, running a test for how much of that system blocking food is in my system still. The screen responds and a scanner lights up at the end of the screen, which I promptly point at myself. It takes a minute, but the scan pulls up my body systems, including my circulatory and endocrine ones. I don't even know how I know these words, it's like all my years of schooling are coming together for this moment.

I type in some time variables into the research tool, guessing approximately how long ago I activated the stealth nanos, and cross reference it with the average time my body takes to cycle through the berries. A simulation quickly runs the time back in direct relation to my body's processing speed and I figure out the endpoint.

"What concentrations of the berries would I need to eat in order to maintain this exact point?" I ask the screen while pointing.

The pad processes the question, taking a bit longer to finish up the analysis.

"How are you doing this?" Rym asks. "You certainly are channeling your inner Neman on this one."

This isn't the first time I acted smarter than I know I am, and have thought things I never could have before. Like planning out the attack inside Rym's Magnus base when I was trapped in the room with Legs. In fact, I'm pretty sure that Legs has been staring at me this whole time.

The Cadean places one of its stumpy hands on my arm. What was it Rym told me? That the Cadean weren't the strongest, but they could manipulate others? Did they do it with their thoughts? In this case, I let the thoughts continue. I feel like I could shut them out now that I know where they're coming from, but I need to get this figured out.

Or do I? Is Legs forcing me to do this? Or just helping? Why would it want to help me out at all? I guess I did free it from imprisonment, and we're heading back to where it was captured. But maybe it wants to get back, maybe its friends are waiting there for it and it only wants to help itself.

No. I want to help you.

The words aren't actually words, but I sure do understand them. And I am utterly convinced that it wants to help. I don't know how I know, I just do.

Beep.

The data pad arrives at a concentration estimate of the few berries I have left. If I can keep this amount in my system, I should be at the proper balance between the two forces, so I can control both things at the same time. The nanos in the stealth package, as well as the abilities I have when I'm fully away from my tech.

"This is Neman's lab station, right?" I say.

"I can't believe you did that," Hira says.

I smile, but don't tell her it's all faked data manipulation skills.

The pad uplinks to the computer monitor and begins the protocol. I take the few remaining berries and place them into a glass analysis chamber connected to the lab station. The panel shuts and the process begins autonomously. The only question remaining is whether I want the dose in pill or injection form.

I guess injection would get the dosage right into me, but damn I hate needles. Pills it is.

Neman's lab station takes over the process and the pad continues on with its own data unraveling. I'm about to stand up when something catches my attention from the screen. Something about research on a test subject Scitech has in custody. A pure. An Eldane.

"Stell!" I say. It has to be her. Hira hurries to my side and looks over my shoulder.

I quickly press the tab and a string of info pops up. Date acquired. Location acquired. Transfer location protocol. Current location. I press that one.

'Subject transferred from Magla. Initial nanotech injections failed. Possible failure due to magnetic field strength and subject's connection to it. Recommended to move subject as far away from planet as possible. Currently on Naglor to resume testing.'

Then it shows a detailed map of the building she's in. Perfect.

I slump back in the seat and hand the pad over to Rym. The two of them, make that the three of them, look at the screen. It takes a second for Rym and Hira to notice Legs staring intently at the results. Can that thing read?

"What is your deal?" Rym takes the screen away from the Cadean. "We fought your kind years ago, you ruined your planet, or moon, or whatever you live on, and you wanted ours. You lost. Remember?"

"I don't think it wants to hurt us." Really. It hasn't shown any hostility toward me or anyone. "It just wants to survive."

"You don't know anything about it, kid," Hira says. "Or what it would do to survive. We spent years fighting them. Sure, it wants to survive, but at what cost?"

"It's watching what we do so it can get back to its kind." Rym eyes the room, possibly looking for some place to lock Legs up.

"I don't think so." Everybody looks at me. I take the data pad from Rym's hands. "And I don't think you want to kill it. Something is holding you back."

Rym opens his mouth but hesitates.

"Right?" I say. "It can't be sending strong enough thoughts to trick us entirely, can it?" I don't know if it can, but it just doesn't seem possible.

I hold the data pad out to Legs, who stares at the screen bug eyed. There's a video file of the test subject, so I click it open. It's Stell, all right. She looks tired and beaten down, but seemingly all right. Rym and Hira see her and look relieved, too. But it's Legs' response that gets us all.

Its mouth opens wide, but since it's a different species, I'm not sure entirely what it means. The thoughts that float through my head, however, let me know for sure.

"Legs knows her." But that's crazy, right? How could it know who she is?

"The pirates said the Cadean was a prisoner there. Perhaps it was near Stell." Rym ponders this. "It could have been a test subject as well, right?"

I shrug. Legs looks up at me expectantly and back again at the data pad. "Looks like they became friends, somehow."

"Great," Hira says. "Let's be best friends with our enemies."

Legs responds with what looks like should be a smile, but the vertical mouth twisting to the side just looks plain weird.

Ding. The lab equipment spits out six gel-like tablets, bright red. There's a circular receptacle below the screen and the pills rattle around in it until they spin to a stop. I swallow one and pocket the rest. How long before it kicks in? Oh weird, in a few seconds the HUD within my 'site starts to fade and wink out.

A message flashes on the screen. "Take one pill every hour to maintain equilibrium."

Excellent. I sync my chronometer to the time I took the initial pill and set the hour timer. Equilibrium, huh? I guess that's the point right between the Nanosite and whatever I've got without it.

A tone sounds on the inter comm channel. "We're there," Dewey says.

The Peace Hammer decelerates and then stops. We all move to the cockpit and stand behind the controls to look out the viewscreen. The shattered moon, Naglor, sits just beyond the debris field that Dewey has us parked in. I'm not really sure if this place is a moon, or just a bigger chunk of the Dust Field. Maybe it's an asteroid that got held in Magla's gravity. But the jagged shape of the place looks almost intentional, like it was carved out this way, or blasted.

A near constant line of mining ships funnel toward the base from the planet below. The moon's surface is covered in factories billowing smoke. According to the notes in the data pad, the place has its own atmosphere, despite being so small. Must be some sort of localized gravitational amplifier.

Thanks for that thought, Legs. I know it's not mine.

The little guy is taking turns staring at the base and back at me.

If you've got an idea on how to break in, you should probably let me know.

"The advice your onboard computer gave us was helpful," Dewey says. "We managed to get here without notice."

Good ol' P.A.

"But there's more." Dewey points out the viewport to a string of drones surrounding the base, tagged and glowing red through the holo displayed screen. "I've positioned us where we can go in undetected."

"Didn't we get this ship to deal with this problem?" I ask. "To not worry about being detected?"

Dewey nods. "Radar, other scans, we're fine. It got us this far. It's the visible spectrum we need to worry about. And the security shield."

"Didn't the pirates give us codes to get through? To pretend we're just a mining rig with a delivery?"

Dewey shrugs. "Theoretically. I have a way to falsify our cargo. However, we altered our flight path to avoid the drones, and to get back to the line of other ships, we need to pass through the shield here." He points straight ahead. "And reintegrate there. The problem is that the shield doesn't open where we are. And we can't exactly fly through it."

I feel a tug at my shirt from behind and turn to see Legs looking like he needs to be let outside to go to the bathroom. "Guys, I think Legs has something."

The little alien pushes past us and sits at a computer terminal next to Dewey. Its two tiny front arms reach out and tap onto the screen. Rym draws a pistol and aims it at the creature's head.

"Stop." Rym readjusts his stance. "Seriously, *Legs*, stop now."

I stand in front of the gun and hold up my hands. "No, look."

Legs continues typing without even looking back. The speed at which it's typing is insane. In thirty seconds, it looks like it opens an access channel to the shield frequency.

"It should work," Dewey says slowly. "But any drop in the shield will be noticed."

Legs types some more.

"You're right." Dewey grabs the controls and accelerates the ship toward Naglor and the Scitech base.

"What's right?" Rym says.

"Not *any* drop. According to this calculation, we should have a two second gap before anyone notices."

"But that means…"

"Correct. I will need to be flying both close enough to activate the signal and pretty fast to pass through."

"Those seem like two very precise variables," Rym says. "Is it worth the risk?"

"I can't see another way through," Dewey says.

"It's not like it wants to get killed," I say.

Rym looks at me, confused.

I thumb over to Legs.

"I wish you'd call it a he or she," Rym says. "This 'it' thing is confusing me."

"Don't you know anything about the race you were trying to terminate? They've only got one sex type, hermaphro something."

Rym laughs. "You got me. Okay, 'it,' let's get moving."

Legs stretches its fingers and closes them until the knuckles crack. It continues to clack on the screen, accessing ship controls hopefully in a non-traitory kind of way. Dewey follows along with the plans, and the ship accelerates again. Either it has a natural skill with technology, or there's something else going on.

"I can't see anything out there." I really can't. I thought there'd be a laser beam screen of death waiting for us.

"It's there." Dewey points to the monitor. "Even if your eyes can't detect the wavelength of the energy, mine can. And I daresay Legs' eyes, too. Interesting creatures. So different from Maglans."

There's an image on the radar screen showing our distance from the protective barrier. I think maybe Dewey prompted that to give me something to see.

We're fast approaching the line and an alarm starts to blip.

"Adjusting speed," Dewey says. "You got that code ready?"

Legs doesn't respond.

"Hey, you got that ready?" Dewey says again, much louder. If bots have an emotion simulator, Dewey is running the latest update for *nervous*.

Still, Legs doesn't do anything to indicate we're about to splat up against a shield. It hits me then that the Cadean doesn't communicate like we do, or even how Dewey is programmed to. We're just about at the line, and I start to sweat. Huge rocks flash by as we jam at a speed we've never gone before.

"Legs?" I say, fully thinking the thought as loud as I can.

Its head tilts slightly, it clicks its mouth together in a chompy fashion, and then it pushes a lit up portion of the screen. The barrier flicks off just at the moment the ship reaches it and then in two seconds, just as advertised, it comes back on. The ship fires braking thrusters and I lurch forward into Legs.

"Oh yeah, sorry," Dewey says. "Forgot to mention we'd have to do that."

I don't take my eyes from the radar screen. We didn't end up a blot on the protective shield, so that's pretty good. Now, we've got to see if any drone picked up the excessive speed boost.

Seconds pass, then minutes. The ship rocks, buffeted by the light atmosphere trapped in by the shield and whatever gravity system they have in place. I'm holding my breath waiting to see one of those red lights start to zero in on our position. By ten minutes, Dewey begins to tap the engine sequence back on, and we all release a collective sigh. Maybe it's a trick of my ears, but I swear Dewey sighs, too.

Rym pats Dewey on his shoulder. "Nice job."

I gesture in Legs' direction.

"Really?" Rym says.

I gesture again.

Rym pats Legs on his back like he's trying to avoid a disease. "You too."

Rym looks at me like I better not suggest anything else.

"We will have to find a way to disable that shield when we need to run our asses out of here," Hira says.

Rym raises an eyebrow at her. "Sounds like something that might need to be blown up. Know anyone who can do that?"

"I'm on it, *sir*," she says with a smile.

"We have possibly thirty minutes until Jali and Neman reach the relay station," Dewey says. "Once they neutralize it, we should be free to broadcast whatever we want through the satellite network."

"And when he says 'we' he means 'you,'" Rym says, looking in my direction.

"Just me?"

"We're going to be distracting Scitech."

"And finding my niece," Hira says.

All right. No pressure.

"Don't worry," Rym says. "You have enough footage of Stell back when you did your first jump off the Edge, right?"

"I remember." It seems like we've moved past just a quick video about the Eldane, and that this runs deeper than we thought. Stealing resources from the planet for some reason, I had thought it was for their own research, but something else looms over everything. And freakin' murder? What about all those test subjects just about to be torched? How many more *were* killed before I could stop them?

Scitech runs the planet with their technology, and we have to shut them down, despite Magla's dependence on them. Just a week ago I was crapping on Rym's ideals and as stuck inside my own world as anyone could be. But I've been in and out of the life-enveloping technology I was born into, and now I'm finding my own abilities. If only everyone could just have a life-changing encounter like I did...

But they could. There's more footage beyond just Stell's jump on Cam. The little bot is more important now than ever. And even though the need to stop Scitech is what I should be focused on, I am more worried about Stell than I have actually admitted to myself. She's been captured for days now, been injected with nanotechnology, and even moved off world to get away from the planet's magnetic field.

Whoa, is that why I'm feeling weaker lately? Those waves I've felt as we've flown from Magla? There's a distant ripple of that emptiness, or loneliness; I'm not really sure how to put it. But it's there, and I know it's been deepening ever since we left the planet. I hope Stell's all right, because if this is happening to me, it must really be affecting her, too.

"You okay, kid?" Rym says.

I look at the grizzled old Skywatch pilot, someone I thought I would never try to get to know. And now I'm going up against the governing technological body of an entire planet with him at my side. And he's trusting me, too.

"Yeah. I got this."

The Peace Hammer is close enough to the cracked moon to pick up features like the different buildings peppering its surface. As they appear on our screen, Legs types until words pop up next to the structures. The biggest building has the words *unloading and processing* next to it. The building next to it says *control,* and the broadcasting station I need to get to is behind it.

"So Legs, you know our language?"

"I told you those bastards are smart," Rym says. But I can tell Rym is disturbed at how quickly the Cadean accessed this old tech ship. At least it knows what's on the Scitech moon once we get there.

"If I'm heading there," I say and point to the broadcasting station. "Where are you going? Where is Stell?"

"That's a good question," Rym says. "Hey, Legs, where do you think the research station is? We're looking for someone."

Legs, still typing as the last couple of buildings come into view.

I pick up the little screen and point to the data referring to Stell. Legs' wide eyes grow a little wider and it continues to type. A red outline appears over a building with the words *'research and holding'* over the top of it. It's off to the side of the admin building. Rym pats the little alien on its back and Legs jumps at the touch.

"Sorry, I didn't mean anything by it," Rym says. "But we'll put down over here."

There's an empty zone he's pointing to next to the research building. "We should be able to make it there undetected. The place is not on lockdown. See the ships?"

Mining rigs fly in and out of the unloading and processing area as they always have, I'm assuming. And that looks like a suitable place for everyone else to go. Me on the other hand...

"I don't think I can make it to the broadcasting station on time if I leave from that landing site." Around fifteen minutes now. "I'd have to cut through the buildings, dodge security." A thought hits me.

"I'm going now." I back out of the cockpit. "Dewey, can you port this info to the Dagger?"

Hira looks at me, questioning me.

"I can slip through with the stealth tech." I've got plenty of time, still nearly a full hour of time before the next dose, although I don't feel as strong as I did before back on Magla.

"The information is on your computer," Dewey says. "Good luck."

Rym salutes me. "We'll get Stell, and hopefully draw eyes away from you."

"Thanks. Mind if I take this?" It's the data pad. Seems like I could use something from it in the broadcast.

Rym nods. "Find yourself a secluded terminal, use Neman's data hack, show whatever you've got, and get the hell out of there." He pauses for a moment before continuing. "Stell chose you for a reason, kid. You're stronger than you know. I joked before that I knew your parents, and I'm sorry. I wish I had known them."

I don't know how to reply to that, so I just salute by crossing my right arms over my chest like a member of Skywatch. I tuck the data pad and the metallic hacking device into my pack and, with a heavy feeling, head to my ship.

CHAPTER 22

The chair pulls up into the belly of the Dagger and Cam twitches on my wrist.

"You ready to plug in, huh?"

Her tiny fingers move a little faster. Yeah, I'm excited, too.

"Initiate startup sequence." I tap out the buttons to power up and Cam flies toward the console.

"Acknowledged." The lights on the panel flip on before Cam can settle in. The ship begins to hum as the engines activate.

"Oh, yeah, Cam, meet P.A." I forgot about this. Awkward.

Cam looks at me then back at the console. She looks almost hurt, if that's possible.

"Don't worry. The onboard computer knows what to do, you just, uh, you prep a video for us to show, all right? Include any footage from when Stell interrupted my jump."

The little drone stamps her tiny legs up and down, but she cools down and hops back on my wrist, silently collating data, or whatever it is they call it.

The Dagger separates from the Hammer and I grab the throttle controls. The ship responds instantly and makes me wish I could fly it without the threat of a full-on incursion about to happen. The atmosphere rocks the ship back and forth as I fly side by side with the Peace Hammer. Rym is sitting in the cockpit instead of Dewey. I guess the old Skywatch pilot needs to take things into his own hands. I know exactly how he feels. I wave and he returns it with a salute.

Time to see if this stealth tech is operable or I'm going to have to find another way in. Okay Stell, help me out here. Breathe, right? I focus on that slight tingle in my head and relax. The connection feels very far away right now, but I reach out for it anyway. I imagine the little nanos on my ship bending the light, but mainly I just picture myself hiding.

The tickle stretches from my mind outward and a myriad of tiny flecks of light cascade across the ship's exterior, just like last time. But does it actually work? Rym has looked away, but I don't know if it's because he is focusing on his own path or if he lost sight of me.

So I steer right in front of their ship to find out. Yeah, so maybe I fly a little too close. The Dagger's proximity alert goes off and I jerk away to get some distance. Yup, too close. P.A. doesn't say anything, but I get the feeling it's had enough of this pilot who ignores its warnings.

When I settle back in line beside the Hammer, Rym just keeps looking forward like nothing happened. Well, that's enough for me. Now, can I keep the stealth going? That's another question.

The same red lines that Legs projected back on the Hammer are on my screens, too, and I search out some landing spots on the broadcasting station. There's a perfect one right on the rooftop. My hearts wind up and the stress of the mission settles in my head. Ten minutes, that's about how much time I have to get into that building.

Help is coming, Stell. Does she know? Is she even still here? Or alive? I push that thought down and focus on the plan. Get in. Get the whole world to stop using their 'sites. Accuse the government of treason. You know. Easy.

The closer I fly, the more this moon looks like a shell of what it used to be. Cavernous holes litter the surface, and when I think of the thing as a whole, it makes me think this was carved out for resources. Could all the rocks around Magla be remains of this moon? Maybe it was pummeled by some asteroid or something?

Smoke rises from the mile-wide processing plant, painting a picture of what lies beneath the roof. Maybe it was something else that gutted that rock. And maybe that same thing is beginning to gut our planet.

Focus, Daj. Everyone's got a job to do.

I tap the viewport, right at the place where I want to land and a full trajectory heading pulls up on the screen showing me the flight path. P.A. beeps in, inquiring with some text if I want it to do the landing cycle.

"I've got it. But, just make sure I don't crash into anything, all right?"

There's a fraction of a second pause. "Affirmative."

Again, despite the monotone reply, I feel a hint of its irritation that I ignored the offer. Cam, on the other hand, taps around on my wrist, doing a little dance of joy. Vindictive little thing.

The Dagger swings around upon approach and I activate the repulsor landing system. It doesn't seem very loud, a hum and a whine, but I scan the rooftop for anyone who might be watching or listening. No one around. The ship should still be under stealth cover as it hovers above the surface.

"Be ready for a quick takeoff, P.A."

"Affirmative."

"And update your vocabulary while you're waiting."

"Aff— all right."

"That's better." I pat the console a couple of times and lower the chair. Hopefully, P.A. wouldn't hold a grudge and not tell me if the atmosphere outside wasn't breathable. I remove my helmet and take a few tentative breaths. Despite the processed smell, it's breathable.

When I step out onto the roof and look back at the Dagger, I freeze. There's nothing there. A slight shimmer in the bending of the light, I guess, but it's like I can see right through it. It's there, though, when I raise my hand up and smack the hull. Now, will that stay active as I move away?

"Hey, P.A. Move the ship over there if you notice the stealth cover fade, all right?" I point under the cover of some scaffolding.

"All right." P.A.'s voice emits from my wrist dock making me jump.

I guess that's pretty awesome, being connected to the ship like this. But did the ship automatically connect to me? I never really told it to. Old Skywatch tech assumes a lot. I salute the invisible ship, or at least I think I do.

"Come on, Cam."

Cam disconnects, extends her hover pads and flies above my head. The lights of the facility illuminate the rooftop with a bluish glow as we're still on the night side of the planet. The wrist screen lights up with Cam's viewscreen, highlighting points of entry up on the building. Not for the first time, or last, I assume, do I wish that I had full connection to my 'site. It would make this a whole lot easier.

A glass door waits for us at the corner of the building, and surprisingly it's not locked. Well, maybe not surprisingly. I mean, who do they think is going to break in? I'm lucky they aren't expecting me. I hope. The door slides open welcoming me into the broadcasting facility's cold, dimly lit hallways. There are no computer ports here, nothing I can use for Cam to hack into to figure out a layout of this place, but she's looking.

She's already storing data and predicting a floor plan based on outside scans and whatever she's picking up now. The results that map onto my wrist dock don't show much, but hopefully it will populate as we progress. Neman's jumpstart to her onboard systems didn't feel right at first, but they're turning out awesome. I hope I get a chance to thank him.

This is a long, empty hall. According to Cam, there's a bank of rooms at the end that should be good enough for a comms hack.

I glance at my chronometer. Forty-five minutes until the dosage runs out. Five minutes until Jali and Neman theoretically complete their task. But how am I going to know? I guess I just get in there, try to send my message until it works. Man, there are a lot of loose threads in this plan.

Cam zips up ahead, and more of the floorplan materializes onto the map. Portions of predicted lines get rewritten as she autocorrects. But still no ports, and no place to plug in. Didn't Rym say there'd be stations everywhere in here? I guess he wouldn't know, for sure. Neman would. I wish he were here right now.

An upper level appears on the map. Cam must have gone up some stairs. A green light blinks over a set of rooms that pop up on my display. That's a good bot. I pick up my pace, but not too fast that I make any noise. It's creepy quiet in here, and any sound I make echoes in the long hall. Still, there are no Maglans on the scan.

The stairs at the end of the hall are empty, just like everything else in here. The constant thought of being watched hangs over me and I skip two steps at a time to get up to the next level as fast as I can. The room Cam found contains a bank of twenty or so desks, each with a dedicated workstation and computer terminal. This will do nicely. A huge window overlooks the rooftop, and I can see where I landed. No ship of course. I mean, it's there, I just can't see it.

In the distance I spot the building where Rym and the others must have landed to find Stell. I sure hope Legs is helping to track her down.

"I'm going to use Neman's data hack, so get ready with your video."

Cam settles onto the port at a workstation near the window and begins dancing over the interface like some strange insect. I face the door, pull out a chair and sit down with Neman's slim metal device ready to go. I give a quick thumb press. The stick lights up, scans the interface and with a few spins, the device chooses the correct connector which extends from the end. I stick it into the port and the hack tool engages with a series of clicks, whirs, and beeps.

The workstation powers up, but the screen only shows a series of symbols scrolling about. Probably Neman's device doing its job. And good thing, too, there are only a few minutes until I have my window. I tap my fingers against the tabletop. As I do, I hear another tap, tap, sound, this time coming from outside the room.

Cam perks up from the panel and zips over to the door. She takes a second to scan back and forth and then an image appears on my wrist. Shit. Security guards are approaching, two of them. They're not moving fast, so I don't think they're onto me. Maybe they're just doing their normal rounds. No alarms, either. I can just hide under the desk.

No that's stupid. I sweep my hands over the pistol at my side.

No, that's even stupider.

Sweat trickles down my back. Man I didn't know I was this nervous. Do I have Cam make a distraction? Try to talk my way out? Hah. Good one.

Breathe.

Oh crap, Stell's voice is right in my head. But it's louder than it's been in the past. She's got to be close. The footsteps are closer though. I scramble back away from the door and the workstation with the hack tool still spinning and hopefully doing its thing.

Just breathe, idiot!

What am I going to do? Fling chairs at these guys? I don't think that's going to help much. But I take a breath anyway, and when I do that tickle in my brain skips around. What, do I get the ship? Maybe P.A. could blast something outside and... no, I don't want the whole base on lockdown.

That feeling of bugs crawling around my skin intensifies. Wait, is this what she wants me to do?

I focus my thoughts onto the stealth tech, this time on me. The connection is weak, very weak now, but I still reach for it. I close my eyes and picture the nanos working. Hiding me.

When I open them, I see the two helmeted Maglan guards walking toward me, a male and a female. Cam flits by overhead, ready to dive bomb them. But she holds off. The guards scan the room, walk past the first row of computers and pause. A green light shoots out of the female's helmet, sweeping the room. Then the light scans over me.

I hold my breath.

The light shuts off. "Visual scan, nothing here," the female says. "I guess you're seeing things. Again."

The male walks to the door. "I swear there was something here. You're not going to tell command, are you?"

"That depends." She walks up to the other and wraps one arm around his shoulder, another on his waist.

Am I going to have to watch this play all the way out?

He goes in for a kiss, but she slaps him with her opposite hand. With a laugh she walks out the door, and he stands there stunned for a moment. After a second, a stupid grin crosses his face and he follows her out.

I finally exhale.

It worked! The stealth tech wasn't just on the Dagger. When I spilled it, it must have stayed on me too. I hold up my arms, or at least I think I do. I can feel them raise, but I can't see anything besides a slight shimmer of light. A beeping goes off inside my head, indicating the first timer is up. Jali's relay station is about to go down, and I need to get moving.

I start to walk, but I stumble all over myself heading toward the hopefully hacked computer. With a thought, the stealth tech deactivates on me and my skin ripples back into existence. I don't have time to learn how to walk without seeing my body; I just need to get that message relayed.

"Cam?"

The little drone pops back in through the door and races to the workstation. When I get there, the screen controls light up with a big 'broadcast connection ready' across it. The entire planet. Connected to everyone's 'site. This is it.

"Adjust profile image?" my internal AI prompts.

"Are you kidding?" I flip the option off and focus.

I've never really been nervous before when making my jump videos, but I am freaking out now. I mean, according to these numbers, there are more than three billion Maglans online that need to hear what I'm about to say. I take a breath before Stell can remind me.

And I hit the broadcast button.

"Some of you know me. My name is Daj and I'm here to show you some things you never thought possible. And I'm going to tell you how you're being used and drained by the technology we were pretty much born with."

If I wasn't sweating before, I'm soaking in it now. My voice is shaky, as shaky as the first time I went live. I'm used to doing edits and having flashy lights and music behind me, and now I feel naked.

"Kie? Zaylee? If you're watching, you need to help me get the word out in case I get cut off. I know this probably won't make sense at first. But watch. And listen. And record it. That's all I can tell you to do. It's the truth."

I nod to Cam.

"Ever look up into the sky and say, 'That's where I belong?'"

Those are my words, but I barely believe they came from me. It seems so long ago, from a different Maglan. The video starts playing, the one of me up on the Edge. Most Maglans have probably heard about or seen this thing already. But they haven't seen the whole thing, only the edited version. Not this one from Cam's point of view.

Cam fast forwards to the actual jump with Stell hanging from the suspended rocks without any safety gear. A pang of sadness and some fear hits me. Now, I'm sure everyone has seen my old video with Stell's fake face on it. They need to know the actual her.

"This is Stell. The real Stell. You only saw what Scitech wanted you to see, and that was someone who was depressed and took her own life. This is her. I only hung around with her for a few days, but she was the first *real* Maglan I ever met."

The 'me' in the vid grips the Sky Deck. Before I can head down, though, Stell leaps off the Edge in that amazing swan dive. And then I'm racing after her, thinking somehow I can get in front and beat her. I had no idea.

This is where my own feed cuts off, so I don't even know what happens next. Cam stays tight on Stell's fall, although it's not quite a fall, is it? She steers her body back and forth avoiding rocks and parts of the building with ease. At the very bottom of the drop, she pulls up quickly, and just sort of hovers there. And she's waving at the camera.

Show off.

Cam's feed clicks off for a second and I'm pretty sure it's over, when the screen pops on again, this time focusing on Stell. Where is she? I don't remember this. Oh, now I do. This is Rym's garage. Somehow she got a hold of Cam and recorded something else. Or Cam just found her. This is her, and it's enough to prove she survived that flight off the Edge.

"This is a couple days later. Alive. Yes, she actually flew."

The video cuts again, and this time we're down below the surface in the depths of Magla seeking out the charging station for the glider. Stell spins like a warrior monk and fends off those rock spitters by deflecting their own shots.

Next it shows the small village we ran into.

"Here's where we witnessed Scitech's first wave of tech rejects. These poor little children, deformed and abandoned. Barely surviving on scraps and what Stell brings to them."

Cam then jumps ahead to the Scitech research facility, to the dark incineration room.

"Then, there were more test subjects that didn't work."

The nano zombies bump up against me as the burning lights warm up in the grating.

"And Scitech just burns them in here."

The test subject Maglans mill about, but also move aside to let me get to the door. It blasts open with a shower of sparks as Jali shoots it with her mag rail gun.

"I was only able to save these few. But there are more. And many more that they burnt."

In the next cut, Cam goes back to the huge octahedral temple. She shows me sleeping in the depths of the place and then flies away, this time finding Stell. She is sitting near the very edge, overlooking the valley. Well, she's sitting, but not on the surface. She's floating with four hands pressed together peacefully and she has a serene look on her face.

"This is what we used to be. What we were forced to forget. We are all Eldane."

"I do think that is quite enough." That voice. I know it.

Connection terminated fills the screen. My hearts race. When was it cut off? Did anyone on Magla actually see anything?

"Don't you agree?"

I turn to face the Scitech employee standing right behind me and I stare into Ms. Pontane's sharp features. With a couple of those huge nose sniffing goons behind her. Instinctively, I reach for the stealth tech power and for a second the cascading lights flip on my arms. But Ms. Pontane points a device at me and suddenly I'm shaking with an electric shock coursing through my body. Next thing I know, I'm on the floor looking up into her unhappy and irritated face.

"You can't use our own technology against us." She stoops down next to me. "Clever use of the nanos. We could not get it to work this well. And this, we've been looking for this for a while."

She picks up something, I can't really see since my eyesight is all blurry.

"You have certainly been busy, haven't you?"

I'll show you busy, you corporate bitch.

But I'm pretty sure all that comes out is some drool and coughing.

She laughs. "If you're wondering how we knew you were here, it was a smuggler we finally tracked down. I think you know him."

A channel opens on a speaker on the panel beside me. "They'll be approaching Scitech with stolen Skywatch ships. And these mining rigs as well."

My hearts drop.

"Thank you very much, Mr. Rancelon," a recorded Ms. Pontane says. "Here is your payment."

There's a scuffle and a thud followed by three gun blasts. Ms. Pontane smiles slightly. "Unfortunate turn of events, but he helped to track down a known terrorist, so it all worked out."

Yeah, she caught me. But there's still hope for the others.

"He gave us a list of his ships and yours so we kept an open scan for them. When the mining rigs were spotted landing at the relay station, we knew he was telling the truth."

My hope starts to fade and anger replaces it, bubbling inside my chest.

"I can't show you on your Nanosite, but watch this." She points to a monitor where a video of an installation in orbit starts to play.

The motion seems to be through the eyes of one of those drones that almost spotted me in the field. This one hurtles toward the landed mining ships and strafes them with blaster fire. Explosions fill the screen and the slaughter continues.

"No." The remaining mining ships disintegrate under the fire of multiple drones. Neman, Jali. Gone.

"Just think, this all could have been over so easily if you had just given me this when I asked." Ms. Pontane holds up a sparking and smoking piece of metal. My eyes finally adjust and recognize the shape in her hand.

Cam.

Her little fins flutter until her legs curl up under her body and she goes still.

"You could have been rich, kid." She carelessly tosses Cam's smoking remains onto the desktop. She bangs against the terminal and skids to a stop.

"You could have been the beacon of hope for everyone on this planet."

She motions to the two misshapen guards behind her and they walk to my side and yank me off the floor. My eyes settle onto Cam's unmoving form.

"Do you know why I did it?" I think the words come out right.

Ms. Pontane holds up her hand and the two goons halt. "I know you think you were doing the right thing. I know you were lied to about the so-called *Eldane*. There are no such beings with supposed *powers*."

Is she serious? I can't really tell. "Wait, you know the girl actually survived that drop, right?"

"I know you think she did. And that you faked a video of it that you thought would change the world. And so you somehow fought your way here to show it to everyone."

"But, she's here. On this moon, right?"

The look of confusion on her face is priceless. She has no idea. "There is no girl."

The two guards yank me back from the workstation toward the door. I laugh. "You are a high-ranking Scitech employee and you don't know anything. You're just as blind as everybody else on the planet."

The grip on my shoulders and arms tighten, pretty uncomfortably, and I'm dragged away from a thoroughly confused Pontane.

"Wait," she says.

The two at my side come to a hesitant stop before I exit the room. They definitely don't like it, and I'm pretty sure they're not reporting to her anymore. Or maybe they never did. My eyes settle on Cam's frame, sparking and flashing on the table.

"There's someone here?"

Poor lady. She really didn't know. What was she promised? Power? Money? Was she just living her life selling the Nanosite without questioning it?

Huh. Sounds familiar.

"Is this true?"

I'm not really sure who she's asking. The two guards seem incapable of any thought outside of seek out and kill.

There is no response, but maybe she's asking in her 'site, out loud.

"Take him to my office," she says. Her voice shakes ever so slightly.

One of the guards leaves my side and approaches Pontane. She takes a step backwards and places her hands on a desk surface to support herself. Looks like she's drunk, the way she staggers. The Sniffer raises its arm, and I see he's holding a familiar looking pistol. Mine.

"Wait, wait, no!"

Her scream is cut off as the guard shoots multiple blasts into her body until all that is left is her twitching, smoking body on the ground. Lifeless. The guard drops the gun and returns to my side. Its eyes aren't focused on anything. It's like in a dream or something. Panic clamps my mouth shut.

On the screen, there's a fuzzy video of the guard walking to Ms. Pontane and shooting her. The image repeats and loops, each time the image changes slightly, and becomes a cleaner quality. The image of the guard is slowly being replaced with someone else. In a few seconds, my own face is on the body of the killer. How is this happening? And why?

Except I do know why. I can already see the news feed going out to everyone on Magla. *Killer finally apprehended.* And this whole revolution is over.

But there's something else. Another screen lights up with an image of a single eye glancing around until it settles on me. A voice, or more like a collection of voices, speaks to me.

"You just could not stop, could you?"

"What are you?" That's all I can ask. I mean, I know I'm going to die soon. They can't just let a killer like me run around. Whoever *they* are. "Are you a Cadean?"

"No."

Well, it's not very talkative, but at least I'm not dead yet.

"Maglan?"

"No."

"You and my ship's computer should get together. You'd have a great conversation."

"You are very interesting." That stare seems to be piercing my flesh as I stand here.

"You too. You're a computer then." I yank my hand out of the guard's grip and walk to the screen. I'm shaking though. I don't want one of those goons putting a hole through my head. I mean, I know it's coming, but maybe I can talk my way out of this yet.

"That would be oversimplifying things, but for your intellect, yes."

Huh. A murderous computer and a douche. "And these Sniffers, they work for you? They're good at tracking and killing. But not much personality, huh?"

"Indeed. It's a necessary sacrifice. The nanotechnology has a difficult time interfacing with the species on your planet. I realized that early on and adapted."

Early on? How long has this thing been around? And stuck on this moon? "What, no mind controlled doctors or pilots? Or Ms. Pontane?"

"Without the ability to think, there were too many accidents. Autonomy is needed for planetary assimilation, otherwise resource production stops before Arrival."

Planetary what? And whose arrival?

It continues. "But research has led to some great new developments. Take your parents, for example."

I can't speak. I can barely breathe. My parents? Why is it mentioning them?

"Getting adequate test subjects is always a problem. We didn't want to just steal Maglans. That would have aroused too much suspicion. Instead we *recruited* them."

Recruited? But my parents were pilots, right? They were able to leave the planet and fly mining rigs. Just like every kid is told can possibly happen to them if they work hard enough, and if they're the best at what they do. Just like I was about to do. So what happened to them?

"Your parents helped. And soon you will too. And then I will be able to reach your surface and send the signal."

My parents. They weren't recruited, they were tricked into being test subjects. And were they killed, like in one of those incineration rooms back on Magla? All for what? This computer, or whatever it is, couldn't come down to Magla before? Why not? Seems like a quick trip down to the surface. But no, it's got to haul Maglans up here, and all those resources. There's something about our planet that doesn't appeal to this thing. Not yet, anyway.

And what is this signal?

This is all bullshit. I just want to destroy this monster. To unplug it. If it's a computer, or robot or whatever, then how is it powered? Some sort of fusion reaction? There's no way it could suck enough energy to run this whole facility. Unless... Something reminds me about the parasitic mines that Pran built, about what Rym always said. And it all makes sense.

Nanotech sucks the life energy out of every Maglan, cutting our lives in half, at least. And then what? Did this thing find a way to somehow move the energy through air?

Why am I even thinking of these things? It doesn't seem like I'm making it out of here alive. If I can only stall it a little longer, maybe Hira can get Stell out of here. Maybe she can finish what I started.

"You are not the first one to show a connection to the energy field around your planet. The girl lasted a long time under our tests, but she could not use the nanotechnology. You, however, have an odd blend of the two."

Stell can't be dead. No matter what this thing says. I reach out to activate the stealth tech. It's harder to feel now, and I think it's because the pill I took is wearing off, although it hasn't been a full hour. Maybe the lab computer didn't make the stuff right. It's like the effect is being pushed out of my body. Lights begin to flicker on my arms but then they stop.

Everything stops. Seriously, I can't move. I can barely breathe. It's like something else is controlling my lungs. Something is also burrowing around in my head. I can feel it in there tweaking every single nano, scouring all my memories.

I sense its thoughts, if you can call it that. It has a single purpose, but there's too much going on to comprehend what it wants.

"Thank you for showing me how *you* work. Live research is so much better than an autopsy. Although your remains will be helpful, too."

What? This is why they were grooming me? Not to be a pilot, but to be a research project?

The paralyzing grip on me lets go, and almost immediately, I feel the connection again. I sense the power from Magla, my home. I spin around to see green lights scanning up and down my body. The scans come from a hovering bot in front of the two Sniffers. With a satisfied nod, the bot flies out of the room.

"And this concludes our time together. It has been most informative."

Wait, it was stalling me? What for? What did it find out? It can't be good.

"Kill him and bring his body to me."

Oh shit, it's really not good.

The guard nearest to me points his gun at me. I step back and trip over Ms. Pontane's body just as the guard takes a shot. There's a sound of glass shattering as the bolt blasts the window.

Definitely not good.

The Sniffer shoots again, but the blasts just miss as I dive behind another desk. Okay, now that I've got my connection back, I don't want to lose it again. The stealth nanos activate with a thought, the lights flicker on my skin for a second and then I'm gone. The gun blasts again, wildly this time and it doesn't even come close. The two guards are blocking the door, though, so it doesn't look like I'm getting out that way.

"You can't hide," the computerized voices say.

The Sniffers' eyes scan the room and fall directly on me. The one with the gun stands guard while the other approaches my position. The floating robot comes back into the room, too. If it catches me, it can freeze me again. And then I'm definitely dead. The approaching guard bumps into the workstation and Cam's flickering frame knocks to the floor.

Sorry I wasn't there for you.

I duck behind the desk and reach for my pack. I can't see it, so it makes it tougher to find the thing I need inside. But I find the vial and pop it open, downing all the pills inside.

A few seconds later the hovering robot zips to my side and shines its green light on me. Then it's in my head again, probing around. My limbs seize up and I get to my feet, helpless. I want to scream, but nothing comes out. My lips don't even move. The wind coming through the broken window blows against me.

"I told you I can see everything," the computer voices say.

And then several things happen at once. My stealth field drops. The guard with the gun aims right at my head.

"Assume a prone position," a voice shouts from behind me.

"What?"

"Drop!"

I turn around and drop to the floor in one motion to see something materialize outside. Stealth tech flickers and dies, exposing a very welcome ship, the Dagger! Before I can cheer, the ship opens up its forward cannons, lacing the building with pulsing blasts of energy.

A bolt rips through the nearest Sniffer, tearing it to pieces. More firing continues, taking out the other one. While I'm watching, the floating bot reaches me and shines its green light onto me again. This time, however, I don't freeze up. The way the lights flash off and on, and the way the bot swings its single eye back and forth would normally have made me laugh. Now, though, I just grab the little bit of connection I feel from Magla, and lift the robot a little higher in the room.

P.A. fires again and the bot explodes into dust.

Alarms blare in the distance, lights flash, and a metal sheet, some sort of blast shield, begins to slowly drop over the busted window. I've got to get out of here. I lean out the window and I'm about to jump to my ship when I remember Cam. She's still smoldering, but I've got to get her out of here.

I scoop her up as gently as I can and turn back around.

"I'll get you out of here."

I hear several more guards enter the room as I'm standing on the ledge. P.A. can't fire again, I'm standing like an idiot right in front of her. These guards are carrying guns, big guns, and they don't wait to open fire. Computer screens shatter, glass flies everywhere. I step to the edge and see the Dagger's cockpit wide open, ready for me to just leap into.

Before I can jump, something explodes right behind me in a searing white flash. And then I'm shot out the window from the blast, arms wheeling and falling toward the roof way too far below me.

CHAPTER 23

Ever look up into the sky and say, *That's where I belong?*

I'm pretty sure that's going to be my last thought as I look at the flat gray surface down below. But then again, maybe not, because for some reason it's not actually getting closer at the moment. I'm just sort of hanging in the air, breathing. Calm. And focused. Not on my own, no. If I had my own head, I'd be screaming and freaking out.

But something is in there reminding me. Something familiar. Someone, I mean.

Hi Stell.

Hi yourself.

I think I'm flying.

No. It's just floating, but still, that's pretty good. Now get in the ship before you kill yourself.

The Dagger is below me now, and that's a good thing, because when I all of a sudden think about what I'm actually doing, hell, I'm fly… I mean floating, I drop. I slam into the cockpit seat and smash my arm on the control panel. Pain shoots through my body and I'm about to swear when I realize I'm no longer holding Cam.

"Cam?"

I look down over the edge of the cockpit at the roof, preparing myself to see her shattered remains. But there's nothing there. Did I land on her? I scoot around, but she's not there either. Just then I hear a slight buzzing sound beside my head.

"Cam!"

It's her, hovering right outside, but she's in bad shape. She's shaking and sparking and kind of jerking around. I quickly hold out my hand and she crawls onto it, clutching feebly with her little legs.

"Are you all right?"

She beeps weakly. Please be all right.

"Tell me you got that on video."

288

She winks her little eye. I hope that means yes, because no one is going to believe me back home.

If there's still going to be a back home.

The cockpit window seals shut and I grab the throttle controls. I crank the power and the Dagger boosts ahead with a surge of speed. It's always been fast, but for some reason, I feel like it's faster now. More responsive, too.

"Are you all right, Stell?"

Yes. Hira and my little friend found me. It says you call it Legs.

"Yeah, it's the first name that came to me."

It likes it.

"Where are you guys now?"

"Ships approaching," P.A. says.

"You're not kidding." The radar screen shows a dozen or so blips surrounding me. Stats pull up and I quickly read that they're the same drone type ships I met out in the debris field. My instinct is to quickly turn on the stealth tech and just let them pass by, but I can't access it. I shouldn't have dosed up so much, now I can't even touch them. There's no connection to the nanos, nothing on my 'site. But the thing is, I like it. I should. It's how I was able to float.

The Dagger rocks to the side as a red blast grazes my wing. "Shields?"

"I already took the liberty of—"

"All right, all right! Just go back to short response mode. I don't need the whole story." Another blast flashes past the cockpit and I jerk the controls to try to evade. "I'm sorry, I'm just a little stressed out at the moment."

"Understood."

Am I really worried about hurting this thing's feelings again? "Weapons? Please?" Yup. That's me being worried again.

"Chain pulse and mag bomb, both fully charged."

Ooh, those both sound good. I flip the chain pulse on and look around to spot the incoming ships, all the while cranking up the speed. They're surrounding me, which is unfortunate for them. The targeting link locks onto a drone right in front of me and I hold down the trigger.

A satisfying amount of energy shoots toward the ship as I zero in. The thing explodes in a shower of wreckage and I fly right through it. The metal bits pelt off the hull and one leaves a little scratch on the cockpit window. Oops. P.A. will never notice. I hope.

Several blasts streak by and my instinct is to head to the skies, but then I remember something Stell said to me.

We get up in the air and we'll be an easy target.

Just like down on Magla, there's no way I'm going to survive if I just get up into the open against all these drones. I circle lower around the broadcast station and fly as close to the buildings as I can, and then a little closer still. I crank the speed up as I sweep in and out of the buildings. At least two drones disappear off my radar and I glance up to confirm it by seeing structures topple and smoke rise into the sky.

They keep coming though, and shooting. "Keep the shield focused on the back."

"Understood."

"Any chance I have rear-facing weapons?"

"The mag bomb can be fired in the forward or backward trajectories."

Excellent. But not time for that yet. I'm still liking these chain guns. I jam the controls for a quick turn and the Dagger spins around so I'm facing 180 degrees behind, but still moving the same way I was going. Three more drones show their faces and I lace into their hopefully surprised computer brains. Two blow up in fiery explosions immediately while I wing the other one and it spirals to the ground.

Another quick spin of the controller and I flip back the other way. I don't know how I did that, how I knew this ship wouldn't just rip apart. I just felt it.

"What other things can you do?"

Another blast rocks my ship and I veer off to the side, dangerously close to some structure next to me. I can't really tell what it is; I'm going so fast, but I know it will kill me if I fly any closer.

"Whatever you got, just try to keep me alive."

At least seven more ships are still tailing me. I don't think I'm going to lose these guys, and something tells me there are more of them on their way. The engines whine as I crank them up and the buildings whip by in a blur.

"Enemies matching speed."

I risk a glance over my shoulder to see them back there. Several blasts rock my ship, but the shields take them. I wonder for how long, though.

"Shield power low."

Oh, not long then.

I steer the Dagger toward one of the bigger buildings with its hangar door wide open. Maybe I can lose them inside. I urge the engines up, noticing the energy level on the shields dip even lower. If I could just get some time to recharge those things, but these guys won't let up.

The building looms in front of me, filling up the entire viewscreen. This is the main building we saw when we got here, the one Pran said was where she used to drop materials off. Smoke billows out the chimneys at the top, reminding me it is also used for refining. I might be able to make it through. There's a door on the other side, if I remember correctly, right? The hangar door begins to close, maybe this isn't one of my better ideas after all.

A ship soars out of the closing door with its engines blasting, sounding like a huge explosion. I grip the triggers to fire but then I let go. The big ship with its familiar swept back wings soars past me into the oncoming fray of drones. The Dagger arcs around to get a better view and I smile.

The Peace Hammer!

And just likes its name, the ship magnetically grips four drones onto its belly and pummels them into the ground with a pounding motion. The ships grind into dust and fiery gases as the Hammer peels away. The remaining three attempt to scatter, but they get sucked back into the magnetic grip. Two of them disintegrate with a few more pounds, but the last one wiggles free.

"That one's yours, pilot!"

I line up the last drone and pull the triggers and the thing goes up in a quick flash of light. Its wreckage crashes into the side of a building leaving a burning trail behind.

"Nice shot, kid."

"Thanks, Rym, nice flying yourself."

"Yeah, I like this ship, but I'd rather be back in one of those."

"You flew Daggers back in the day?"

"Kid," Hira says. "He'd fly circles around you."

That I'd like to see.

"You can fly like that with your nanos?" I ask. "I'm sorry I suggested you turn them off."

Rym laughs. "Actually, I took your advice and cut myself off completely, just like you said. Thanks."

The Peace Hammer pulls up and boosts away from the base. "Link up. We're going to need your help."

I circle the Dagger into position behind them and dock with the Hammer. Instead of the way I had linked before, this time my ship spins around and faces backwards. There's a big clunk and then my display screen shows the power levels increase and the shield max out. More important, the depleted weapons charge up to full power. It's like I'm a part of the other ship now.

Four other ships are following and gaining on us. The Hammer isn't really built for speed, but I don't think that's a problem. Not for us. The cockpit lights up with all four targets. When I turn my controls now, the whole ship moves, still connected to the Hammer. I'm a cannon. A freaking cannon!

I hold down the trigger and pulses of energy shoot out. It takes me a second to get a feel for the controls, but then I zero in. The lines of light touch on the ships and each one goes up in a fiery explosion.

"Whoa."

When the smoke clears and there are no more ships coming, I press the button to bring my seat down. The Dagger has to reconfigure in the forward position first, and then the chair retracts into the bigger ship.

After it reaches the bottom, they're waiting for me. Saluting me. Not Dewey, he must still be flying the ship. But Rym, Hira, and a face I never thought I'd see again.

"Hi, Stell."

"Hi."

The voice is in my head, but she's smiling. I'm not sure how she'll take it, but I walk to her and give her a hug.

"You're safe." Although I'm pretty sure she was always safe. "Hey, that looks nice."

I point to her hair, remembering the last time I saw her pitching off the cliff wall. The fire had singed half her head and burned her face. But now her hair is pulled back off the side and the shaved looking part of her head isn't burnt at all. Or her arms. She doesn't have nanos, but she healed up somehow. And she looks bad ass.

Hira puts one arm around Stell and gently touches her face like a parent might do with their child after being parted. My hearts ache when I think of my own mom and dad, but I still smile for them.

"No time for reunions," Rym says. "What happened down there?"

"I'm not sure the message was sent. I think they knew the whole time what I was doing. I said some things, and showed Cam's feed from the jump, and after. But I don't know what actually went out."

Rym and Hira exchange glances.

"If you don't already know, we were never really at war with Cadea. There's something else going on here, something with all the nanotechnology. Hey, where is Legs anyway?"

"It found its ship and left," Stell says. "To warn its kind."

Stell already knew all this stuff. She and Legs must have bumped into each other down on the moon.

"It too was a test subject," she says. "But we communicate the same way, as Maglans used to do. When you all brought it back here, it was able to find me."

Hira and Rym smile at this, looking like a couple of proud grandparents.

"This thing, this brain or whatever, I don't think either one of our kind created it. Or if we did, it has now grown past us. It is trying to get to our planet, maybe Legs', too. Maybe it already did."

"You're babbling," Stell says.

"Right. But it got something from me. Something it was trying to get from you, Stell. I think whatever it found will help it invade. It said it was planning for an arrival. I think there's something else coming to Magla. It has an army of those drone things. They've been building them for years with our resources. Yeah, yeah, I'm babbling. Look, I think we need to destroy this thing."

"Nice idea," Rym says. "But if you haven't noticed, it's just us."

"We're Skywatch. We'll be enough."

CHAPTER 24

"If only Neman were here," Rym says. "He could help us find the core of this thing."

A pit forms in my stomach. "I saw a video of Neman and Jali's attack. They were... They didn't make it."

Rym and Hira look at each other again. So much loss.

"Why does it want to end us?" Hira says. Her fingers twitch, and I can imagine her wanting to blow something up right about now.

"I'm not sure. I only got vague images when it was in my nanos."

"It was in there?" Stell says, pointing to my head.

"Yeah. I used to wonder how Maglans could so easily let go of the powers they had, especially if they were like yours. Rym told me before that the nanotechnology appeals to our weaknesses, and once it gets in here, well, then it's got us. It's always in our heads, or it can be. It's connected to everyone on Magla. I think this moon, Naglor, is its central control station. If we can find its core, we can end it."

Stell walks up to me and places her two right hands on my head and closes her dark eyes. That's weird, but okay.

"Relax. This isn't about you. It's about what's inside you."

The feeling I get when she's in my head is kind of like when that computer brain was sifting around, too, but in a less invasive way. She doesn't seem to be checking out my thoughts, which I'm thankful for, that's kind of creepy, but she's looking for evidence of the computer brain.

"I can see it. It is here on this moon, like you said. It came to us. It taught us things. Technology. Words. But it hasn't come down to our planet. The energy that surrounds us is too much for it. It can't fully operate with the magnetic field that we have."

Stell strains under the connection she's trying to maintain. I don't know how she can read all this from what's in my head, but somehow it's hurting her to do it. She struggles to continue.

"It arrived on the moon first. It adapted to our planet by weakening the Maglans, giving them the gift of nanotechnology, all the while trying to find ways around the field. And it made an invasion fleet of drones."

"What does it want?" I ask. That's a hell of a lot of stuff she just found out. "It said it was preparing for an arrival. What does that mean?"

"First it weakens us. Then..."

She breaks the connection and slumps back. Hira catches her and helps her to her feet, but she still seems unable to stand.

Arrival. All I can picture is some alien race swooping in to take our world, or at least our resources. It's already good at doing that. How soon before they show up? And will they show up if we destroy this thing? My mind swims with every thought and my breath quickens. I'm going to have a full on freak out.

"Breathe," I say.

Stell cracks open her eyes for a moment and smiles weakly. I hope she knows I'm not joking.

I draw in several breaths, and that calms me down a bit. "Okay, so we go through all those drones, find the thing, the core, the whatever it is. And end it."

"It's not in those buildings," Stell says. "Well, it is, but it's core is in there."

Stell points down below, indicating inside the moon. That makes sense. If our planet disrupts it somehow, being inside the moon would help shield it. My mind races to what I saw on the way here, the Dust Field, a maze of wrecked moon rock, possibly all used up while mining for whatever the brain needed. What other moons did it destroy to get what it needed?

"So we get to fly inside this moon?" Rym says.

I can't tell for sure, but it sounds like he's a little excited about this. Stell nods.

Rym smacks his hands together and rubs his fingers. Yup, definitely excited. He scans the data screens in front of him.

"There has got to be a way through the blasted portion of the moon," Rym says. "The shield covers the front part of the moon, including the buildings. If we can make it through, we can get around to the other side where the wrecked part is. And find a way in."

"We're coming up on the shield now," Dewey says. "I need

everyone down here, there's a wing of those drones waiting for us. Maybe not you, Daj."

I understand and move up to my turret. It's about to get messy. Rym and Hira run down the stairs, but Stell stays behind.

"Could you watch over Cam?" I gently cradle the little Camdrone's weakly twitching frame.

Stell smiles and holds out her hands. "I've got her."

All right. I salute Stell, and jump into the chair just as it starts to rise up into my ship. The seat locks in, hisses with a quick seal, and the guns power up. "Looks like it's just you and me, P.A. You ready? And it's okay if you talk normal, I need you in top form now."

"Affirmative."

That's more like it, confident. And boring.

I twist the controls to see the extent of my firing range. The Dagger can swivel a full 360 degrees and also tilt up. Anything below the Hammer and Rym is going to only have the magnetic defensive measures.

"Rym, try and keep enemies in my view here."

"Copy," Rym says through my helmet.

The cockpit screen populates with the drone ships up ahead, appearing like a school of strange fish. There are way too many to count. Well, we just need to punch our way through some of them to get out of here.

"The shield is up," Rym says. "Hira, you were able to figure out how to shut it down, right?"

"I did, but something is wrong. I can't access the signal." She curses and then cuts out.

I turn the ship back to face behind us, better make sure no one is following.

"Uh, guys? Do you see behind us?"

Multiple ships are leaving the moon, following our path. And more seem to be leaving the buildings all the time. Great, we'll be crushed between both of these squadrons. They're not close enough to engage, but if we wait too long they'll catch up.

"Eyes up front!" Rym shouts.

That's me. I crank the sticks and face forward, sighting multiple enemies immediately. The guns light up and carve a path through the obstructing drones. Several ships explode, but others fill the space. There are just too many of them.

And they all fire back. The Hammer rocks under the blasts.

"She can take it," Rym says. "But you've got to get us through."

I hold down the trigger and spray the drones with blazing lights. The Hammer swerves and several ships jump on our tail. The others remain by the shield to keep us from escaping.

The Dagger points backwards and I lock onto the drones behind us. The seven or so back there are way faster than our ship, and far more maneuverable. No matter what swerving Rym does around giant rocks, the drones stick to us.

"Try the mag bomb," I say. P.A. acknowledges with a beep followed by a satisfying internal click whir as the weapons switch.

I aim at the center of the cluster of ships and pull the trigger. The ship recoils slightly as the blue ball of light shoots out, seeking out the drones. When it reaches them, there's a bright explosion, but instead of shooting out, the five drones right around it get sucked together in a writhing mass. I'm pretty sure they're fried, but I switch the guns to chain pulse again and finish them off.

"Re-charging mag bomb," P.A. says.

The line on the weapon gauge quickly rises from empty to a full charge. Good to know. The chain guns are down to 50 percent, but I'm not sure how long it will take to get those back. Hopefully being hooked to the Hammer will increase that rate, but that makes me worry about how long we'll both last if we can't get through.

More drones settle behind us, while the group clustered at the shield moves according to which way we go. I don't think we have the energy or the luck to get through all of them. We'll just have to see which one runs out first.

"My signal is blocked," Hira says "The shield is still up."

Trapped. And now the other ships from the moon are in range so that they start popping up onto the Dagger's radar screen.

"Keep trying," Rym says. The Hammer shifts quickly around a huge rock and one of the unlucky drones crashes into it resulting in a spray of sparks.

"Those ships behind us, what are they, P.A.?"

But I don't need to wait for a response.

"Rym, turn us around."

He doesn't respond for a second, but then I hear him laugh. The Hammer takes a wide arc and faces the approaching ships. The Maglan ships.

"Those are Maglan ships," P.A. says.

"Yeah, I got it, thanks, P.A."

The pilots and crew of the moon station must be evacuating after our attack. I can only hope that my message went through, or maybe they just saw the fighting and thought it a good idea to get the hell out of there. Hopefully we can blend in with the rest of the ships escaping once the shield drops. And then we can get into the moon.

The Peace Hammer comes around behind the first cluster of mining ships and flies into the middle of them.

"Power down the weapon systems," Rym says.

P.A. reacts quicker than I do and the energy winds down. The Dagger reconfigures into the normal docking mode and huddles closer to the hull. I glance out and see multiple craft on both sides. Sometimes I see pilots in those ships. Nervous pilots. But we'll get through this if the drones don't identify us.

Now we'll see if this old tech really works. All the other ships can be tracked, but these old things are invisible to most scans. Not all, apparently, as our previous escape attempt shows, since the visible light traces can still be followed. By shutting down the weapons, they won't be able to track those energy signatures as easily. Too bad I can't still use the stealth tech. At least not for hours now until the dosage wears off.

More and more ships begin to spill out from the moon and approach the shield. We've got some buffer around us now, so the drones can't see or get to us.

But the drones begin to open fire anyway, this time on innocent ships. Huge mining rigs, passenger ships, all start to go up in fiery explosions.

"No!" Hira says.

The radar shows the entire drone fleet surrounding the ships, penning us in. Some of the Maglan piloted rigs veer off and crash into each other in a panic.

"Maglan vessels, return to the moon or face termination," a computerized voice says on the general comms. It's the same voice as the computer that interrogated me down below.

"Are you crazy?" a female pilot says. "Negative, open the shield and let us through."

The drones don't wait even five more seconds before they fire on another transport.

Some ships with weapons return fire. It looks like there's going to be a revolution but those ships almost instantly go up in flames.

Rym doesn't wait any longer and the Hammer's systems boot up again, the engine shakes and roars. P.A. powers up the weapons and the Dagger extends back into turret formation. A cluster of drones attacks a large passenger craft and I make short work of them with another mag bomb and a spray of pulse fire. The damaged Maglan craft veers away.

Maybe all the ships will be able to get away now.

"Disperse!" Rym calls out on the general comm channel. "Maglan fleet, disperse!"

As soon as the Hammer flies out of hiding, we're surrounded by drones again. This time there are fewer rocks and it's clear we're a sitting target. Damn.

Fifty percent. Twenty. I drain my chain pulse rounds quickly, yet for every ship I take out, seemingly two more take its place. The Hammer rocks as it takes fire from all directions.

"Shields nearly depleted."

I don't need to hear that right now. The Hammer is going to be destroyed.

And that leaves only one option.

I click a red flashing button and the Dagger disengages from the Peace Hammer's top side. Engines powered up, I peel away and tear into the closest cluster of drones.

"Daj?" Rym yells. "What are you doing?"

"Drawing them away from you. Try to get into the Dust Field."

"You're crazy," Rym says. "We're not going to leave you."

"Just go! I'll distract them!"

I am one with the ship. I know I've felt connected before, but now I am an actual part of it. The Dagger twists and spins through space, lining up targets and plowing them down. I avoid incoming fire and lead drones to crash into each other. This is what I was meant to do.

But it's not enough. The radar screams at me. I'm completely surrounded, but I'll just take out as many of these things as I can before I go out.

"Weapons need to recharge," P.A. says tonelessly.

Great. Maybe this is it for me?

"The shield is down!" Rym says. "Everybody go! Back to Magla!"

Nope, not yet. Somehow, the big red shield line on my screen has disappeared. "Hira? Did you do that?"

"I think so," Hira replies. "It was as if my signal suddenly boosted and made it through."

Stell? Was that you?

But she doesn't respond.

"Everybody, go!" Rym repeats on the open channel.

But few craft are leaving. In fact, the fifty or so ships break off into groups and the ones with weapons are attacking clusters of drones. I can't believe it. I also can't believe the sight on the other side of the shield.

There's a group of starfighters waiting there that I've only read about in the history books. The distinct blocky Cadean ships. I can't believe it.

"Legs!"

And the Cadeans aren't the only ships I recognize. There are also a few squat mining rigs, and those have to be the pirates. They open fire on the drones closest to them, taking them completely off guard. Explosions fill my viewscreen. The few drone ships behind me peel off and regroup to face this new threat.

"Divert remaining power to the engines," I say.

"No shields?" P.A. asks.

"No shields. We've got to get down there fast."

It takes a second, but once the gauges show weapons and shields gone, I jam the throttles forward. The Dagger bursts away and I'm flung back into my seat. Still tuned in with the ship, I steer down to the rocky surface of the moon through the Maglan fleet. A few drones attempt to follow, but when they do, the mining rigs open up on them with their guns.

The chewed up surface of the moon opens up in front of me as I speed toward it. The power in my connection seems to grow stronger every second, or maybe it's the fact that I'm not going to die by a surrounding fleet of attack drones that pumps me up. Maybe that will shrink, though, when I'm about to die in a maze of gutted moon rocks.

Up ahead, the Cadeans have reached the fray and are openly engaging the drones. Looks like I'm clear. There's a war going on, but I have to miss it. That's understandable, though, right?

What about Rym? Should I have said I was going? Probably not, if the comms channels are being monitored, that would have been a mistake. I can just hear Stell now saying something like 'there are other ways to communicate.' But I forgot about that, and I've got a job to do.

This is a little late, but Stell, if you can hear me, I'm heading in to the core.

No reply.

I gun the engines and boost past where the shield had been, aiming toward the pitted surface. The old mining blasts have nearly cut this moon down to probably a quarter of its original size. There has got to be a way in there, right? If it leads right to the brain of this thing, it ain't going to be easy.

"No shields?" P.A. asks politely.

I shift out of the way of the first overhanging rock. "Yeah, maybe you should turn them on."

As soon as I enter the twisted maze of rocks, the darkness consumes everything. The Dagger's exterior lights flip on. Looks like P.A. is reading my mind. The rock walls are closer than I expected so I dial back the throttle and switch to repulsion mode. That ought to help buffer me from the walls and stay in the air. The gravity in this place is weird. I'm not really being pulled down or in any direction.

This place reminds me of the huge mine quarry outside of Jali's house, except there are countless pits and tunnels where mining rigs ripped this moon apart. Will the same thing happen to our own planet if this continues? Well, if I can destroy this thing now, I can end all of that.

"Hey, P.A., can you map this place? I don't want to get lost in here. Cam had a cool predictive map that—"

"Standard Skywatch subsystem. I have that, too."

I can hear the 'but mine is better' at the end of that sentence, but I don't say anything. Instead, I watch as the scanner and radar work together to build a sort of a 3D map of this place, starting with the topside portion of where we broke in and the connected part underneath where we are now.

"I will plot us possible routes based on scans."

"Good work."

Map lines slowly unravel on the complex maze in front of us, including highlighted paths colored differently based on the probability of being able to reach the center of it all. There are things other than just rocks outside the ship, like old cables and junction boxes. As I follow the most likely path suggested by P.A., the number of these increases.

It's slow going, and I have to double back on my flight path often, due to dead ends, cave-ins, whatever. With every setback, however, we seem to get further inside. My mind goes numb looking at the same thing over and over. Gray walls. Occasional wiring. I have to shake myself to wake up. How long has it been since I slept? Or ate? And no, those berries don't count.

After twenty minutes, I start bumping into the walls. I'm exhausted, and starting to panic. This whole place is surrounding me. What, am I a mile in? I can't really tell what's up or down anymore, I'm just blindly following P.A.'s directions. All radar contact with the ships fighting on the surface is gone now. I am completely on my own.

"Do you need me to resume flight controls?" The computer sounds a bit worried.

"Nah, I got this. Just a little worn out."

The Dagger drifts close to the wall, but pulls back with an auto repulsor. I silently thank P.A. for that save. Whatever's happening to me feels different than being just tired, although I don't think I've ever gone this long without sleep before, so I can't really tell. I fumble over the ship's controls a bit as I head further in.

"Is the oxygen level in the ship all right?"

"Life support is functioning properly."

Huh.

I slap myself in the face a couple of times and keep going, flying continually down and down, or up and up, I have no idea.

"Maybe you should take over."

"Affirmative. Acquiring controls."

After a beep, the controls do nothing, even if I twist the steering sticks. This gives me some time to rest, I suppose, but I only look at the unfolding radar. P.A. has mapped all the paths so far, and predicted others. It's pretty good, not as nice as Cam's, but maybe I'm biased. It also includes the wires and junction boxes, so that this whole place looks like some sort of nervous system, branching out from a single area. The brain.

We're not far now from the center of it all. When we get there, I'm going to need to unload all the ammo we have into this thing. I tap the panels. There has got to be something wrong because even though we're only cruising through on minimal energy use, the weapon systems are nearly depleted, as is the overall power. It's being drained quicker than before. We'll probably have enough juice to kill this thing, but we're not going to be able to make it out of here.

I guess that's what I signed up for when I went in alone.

It sure sucks though.

I don't have long to figure out anything else, because in less than a minute there's a light up ahead, a bigger glow than our ship is putting out. And it grows brighter and brighter as we approach. So much so that I can kill the ship lights, hopefully that will slow the draining. But there's a dead end. The light I see is coming out between the cracks of a wall of collapsed rock.

"Any way we can carve a path through that?"

P.A. beeps and the hull of the Dagger whirs and clicks right below the canopy. Sounds like some panel opened up. A green light scan flicks over the wall blocking us and then just as quickly as it came on, it's off again.

Whatever opened up on the ship is not a weapon, nothing fires out of it, but the rocks at the top of the pile begin to stir like they're being manipulated by something coming out of us. The rocks continue to quiver and shake until the pile begins to move and collapse to either side. This goes on for a couple of minutes until a path clears through it, just big enough for us to fit.

As we go through, the cavern opens up and at the far end of it all lies what looks like an excavation site with several different ships parked around it. They're old though, way old, maybe older than the Dagger. One craft looks vaguely like one of the drone ships sitting at the very center of all the digging. Like it's been buried here a long time. Wires jut out from it in all directions like weeds, or veins.

This has to be it. The core.

I'm awake now. I grab the sticks and P.A. automatically relinquishes control over to me again. My fingers rest on the triggers, ready to turn this all to dust, but I hesitate. The remains of the other ships look familiar. One appears to be a different version of something from Magla, all sleek and diamond-shaped, while the other has the box-like shape of a Cadean vessel. Seems to be that both species came together to see what had landed here.

Does anyone even know about this back home? Cadeans and Maglans working together? I'd show everyone if I could access a camera. This has to be the first contact with the nanotechnology. If we could get Maglans up here, this could change things. Figure out where it all went wrong.

I could shut down the brain, get it to work again, but under more control.

The Dagger gently lands next to the excavated vessel and a puff of dust grows in our wake. P.A. says something but I barely hear the words. My ship is so loud, I can't even focus on what's going on here. I need to concentrate. This thing knows about my parents, right? I could ask about them, and it would know everything. Even show me videos of them, or maybe tell me where they are. I flip the power to my engines off and it cycles down. P.A. repeats something to me, but I can't hear what's in this cave with it talking, so I shut the computer off with the flip of a switch.

I'm not tired anymore. I can do this. The chair lowers to the surface of the cave and I step out. It's cool in here, but comfortable. I've just got to check this thing out, make sure it's safe before I head back home to Magla. As I approach, the lights inside the old probe ship thrum and glow in sync, like a living thing.

My arms and legs are moving on their own now, like I'm being drawn to this. Wait, this is familiar. My hearts race, and I'm suddenly more aware of my senses, although I can't control them. This feels just like it did when I was in the broadcast station. When it took control over me.

How can that be happening, though? I took the pills, I made sure I couldn't use my nanos, but they're still inside of me. And now that I'm face to face with the core of it all, there's nothing to block it from using me. Back on the surface, the thing could only stop me from moving. Here it can completely control me. It lured me here. I can think these thoughts, but I can't move away. It knew I would come here to stop it, and knew I wouldn't be able to do anything.

"I've learned a lot from you," the voices say from within the ship. "And within you I can find a way to reach your planet."

I can't feel anything. This thing has got my legs moving without me. How could I be so stupid? It couldn't learn anything from Stell, she was too strong. But me? I've learned how to blend the two forces together. The power of my home, and the technology in my blood. Just what it needs.

Metallic tendrils reach from the ship toward me, ready to wrap me in a deadly embrace. I can't scream, I can't do anything. Come on, P.A., blast this thing and get it over with. Nothing happens though, and that's because I shut the computer down before I left the Dagger.

A few more steps and I'll be enveloped in the brain's waiting arms. But somehow I am able to breathe on my own. And I breathe deeply. There's something in the air, I can sense the thoughts of the brain faltering, falling back out of me. Did... I do that? I breathe again. No, it's not me, but something inside of me grows stronger because of it.

There's a pulse from the computer brain, it courses into my body with one last push. But the tendrils back away from me like they were burned. It's weakening. Something is draining its power, or preventing it from getting any.

And my senses grow sharper with every breath. There's that connection again deep in my gut. And it grows stronger, too. The brain retracts fully into its probe ship, and I feel that if it could fly, it would try to escape. But it had grown too confident in its own strength, or perhaps it was never in its original programming to try, and the ship is just a hole for it to hide in. There's no place for it to go.

A feeling like I need to vomit takes hold of me. The sense inside of me, and that's what it is, a sense like smelling or sight, begins to surface. It's that connection to some greater power, to the planet itself. It grows, and I just take it and push. There's a brilliant pain, a wash of fire that sweeps over me, but I just close my eyes and accept it.

Just as suddenly as the pain hits, it's gone. I open my eyes and see a cloud hovering in front of me. It's like a mist, but just like a spray of mist it fades away. For the first time in my life I feel free. I feel stronger and infinitely more connected. Were those my nanos?

I spare a glance at the tattoo Hira put on my arm. It's glowing with a warm white light. I smile and focus back on the thing cowering inside the ship.

It is afraid. I can sense that thought, even though it is not alive and I don't have any more nanos. I can read its thoughts. But then I also realize, this is not a single entity. No, it is a complex system, a cancer eating what's left of this moon. It has been here for so long, waiting, and calling. It is not an alien itself, but a precursor or a guide for whatever species is coming.

All the things it gave us, all the little tricks and connections, even all the words and phrases it taught, were used to connect us, but instead they only weakened everyone. Even now as it withdraws from me, it is calling out, reaching out for help. Will the others come? Are they already on their way?

P.A.?

"Yes?"

I only think my words. I don't speak aloud, and maybe that's why the ship can respond and I can pick up its frequency.

Fire up the engines.

There's a whine as the thrusters boot up and the systems cycle as I enter the ship. I don't think there's much I can do about this brain. It is more than just a single entity. It lives throughout the moon, and in every Maglan down on the planet. Maybe even amongst the Cadeans on their moon. But I can shut down this center, this thing drawing all power to itself.

And then I get what happened, why the thing was weakened. My message to the planet went through. It had to. The Maglans must have shut down their Nanosites, the thing that has been leeching their energy and delivering it up here. When they did, the flow stopped, allowing me time to get a hold of myself again. But it felt like more than just that.

No time to think about that now. I have to get out and maybe leave a parting gift for my friend here. I glance at the console in front of me.

Mag bomb, P.A. Maximum charge.

The weapon system shifts on, now at full power and all power possible is heading to the bomb.

Give it a five-minute delay.

"Affirmative."

There's a faster response time with the communication, and I sense a bit of pride in the computer's tone. It's like the ship was designed to directly communicate with the unaltered mind.

When I press the trigger, a ball of blue light shoots out of the Dagger and hovers just above the brain. Arcs of energy branch out of its ship in all directions trying to escape. With only five minutes, I've got to get out of here pretty quick. I turn the Dagger around and point it at the tunnel I came through.

P.A.'s course is still plotted into the nav system, but I'm so connected I feel like I could get out of this place blindfolded.

"Please do not."

I laugh.

A few minutes later, after twisting and turning around the passageways, we're out in open space. I turn back to the partial moon as the timer ends, and even though there's no giant explosion, with grim satisfaction I feel the rocks shift slightly underground encasing whatever entity was locked up inside.

Encased, but I can't be sure it's completely destroyed.

I turn the Dagger to go home and survey the stars. Whatever battle had taken place is over now, and most of the ships are gone. The Peace Hammer is out in front docked with the biggest of Pran's ships. Our ship looks pretty beat up, but still able to give one more smash, I'm sure.

"Rym?" There's no response.

There's something about that silence that makes me speed the ship even faster. I'm docked and lowering into the Hammer before I know it and running for the steps. It seems awfully quiet in here for having just defeated Scitech.

When I get to the cargo hold, I run into a group of Maglans and one Cadean. They're all clustered around someone lying on the floor.

"It's Neman," Dewey says, placing a hand on my shoulder.

The old technician doesn't look too good. Half of his face is scarred with burns, and he's missing an arm. They have it all bandaged up but he's not moving. Rym, Jali, Hira, and Stell circle around him, holding each other's hands and touching Neman. Just like what happened for Rym back on Magla. Bright lines glow on their tattoos, but also from under their clothes and on their faces

I push through the group of pirates to Neman's side. I'm not going to sit by this time. Jali and Hira open up their circle and welcome me in without question. I clasp their arms and touch Neman. And then I breathe.

CHAPTER 25

"Neman's going to be pissed about losing that arm," I say.

Rym just snorts. "He'll love it. This will give him an opportunity to have a robotic one. In fact, I bet he lost it on purpose."

He's probably right. I glance out of the cockpit where Neman is lying down, talking and laughing with the pirates clustering around him and Jali like they're some sort of gods. No wonder. From what I've heard so far from the whispers and conversations, it seems like they saved everybody who went with them on their mission. I'll have to check and see if anyone has a vid of it, although I'm sure anyone of them will be more than happy to share the details. I'm just happy the whole video of their "deaths" was a fake.

"The Cadeans came," Rym says. "It was strange being on the same side."

"They were just as abused by the nanotech as our planet was." Stell pats my shoulder. "In fact more so. The protective field around Magla shielded us from the full power of the tech. That is why the thing in that moon could not come to our planet. And why it was seeking a way to do so. But Cadea did not have our protection."

Legs hops over and smiles that creepy vertical smile at me. I can feel its thoughts now, but not as easily as Stell does. What I get from it is a sense of thanks, and of peace.

"They should come to our planet now. We're all friends, right?"

Stell and Legs shake their heads. "That would kill it. The energy is dangerous to them, and even being here now is hurting it. Legs took a huge risk in coming to the moon to help us."

Rym kneels down beside the Cadean. Legs shrinks back for a second, but when Rym offers his arm, it scurries over and clutches onto it with its two little ones.

"Thank you." Rym places his other hands over Legs' grip. "And thank those who came with you."

Legs takes this moment to give sort of a bow to us all and heads for its ship docked to the pirate vessel. I feel that every second here is damaging to it.

"Thank you, Legs," I say, and think.

Something very faint whispers in my head. Something like, "Until the next time." Or maybe it's, "So long, bro." Yeah, it definitely felt like that one.

Rym pulls me to the side while Hira talks to Stell.

"Did you find out anything about your parents?"

"They're gone. I know that now."

"Hey, come here." Rym, the one-time drunk kidnapper who I thought was out to steal my Cam just to make some money gives me a big hug. "We're here for you."

I may have lost my parents, but it looks like I found my family. I return the hug like he was the grandfather I never knew. In a moment, he and Hira wave and walk back to the hold leaving me and Stell.

"It's all over now, isn't it?"

Stell shakes her head again. "Hard to tell. When you were in there, you wounded it, perhaps even mortally, if such a thing is mortal."

"How do you know what happened? You weren't there."

Stell smiles.

"That was you? How?" I had felt something boost me when I thought I was alone down there.

"You will see when we return home."

I roll my eyes. No easy answers, huh? And stop reading my thoughts, it's pretty unsettling.

"I will try."

There's a whirring sound right behind my head and I jump for a second before I realize it's Cam. Hobbling along in the air, with a little structural damage, but still Cam. She blinks her little blue eye at me through a cracked lens.

"Cam! You're all right!"

I glance back into the cargo hold and Neman gives me three thumbs up.

***

The planet looks different tonight. Well, I guess I've never really looked at it from this high up. The auroras are blossoming all over like it's celebrating. And it should be.

The Maglans, though, will have different views on that. Some will accept this change easily, but most, I'm sure, will be like I was a month ago. Letting go of something that was always there will be crippling. But if what I feel inside me is from letting it go, everyone will soon feel the same.

The Peace Hammer shakes as we enter the atmosphere. I'm not sure where we're going to put down. Maybe in the middle of the ringed city? To a glorious throng of Maglans cheering for us?

Do they even know what is going on, though?

As we settle into the dark night sky, several huge shapes loom in the distance. Large pyramidal shapes. I glance over at Stell and she just smiles curiously.

"Are those what I think they are?"

But she doesn't have to answer. In a moment I see their full shapes glowing with a green light suspended in the sky. We were in one together not too long ago, talking about Skywatch. There are three of them in the viewscreen, hundreds of miles apart, and we're heading to the biggest of them.

They really can fly, or float anyway. I check to make sure no one is staring at my wide open mouth.

When we arrive, there are other ships entering the giant floating structures. Ships like ours. Rym has a smug expression on his face.

"I sent out the old Skywatch codes for everyone who could still hear it. And a few other messages as well."

The Peace Hammer approaches the structure and lights flood over us. The huge hangar bay door opens and a large group of older Maglans welcomes us in. Once we land, they swarm the ship to cheer our arrival with yells and shouts filling the air.

Hira's grandchildren, and great grandchildren run up to the ship and swarm her in hugs. The older Maglans salute us. I can see the varied tattoos on their arms, they're all Skywatch themselves.

But not all of them. I hear some familiar shouting approaching.

"I guess you were right about your two friends," Rym says to me. "They really did help us by making videos."

Two familiar Maglans run up the ramp and hug me.

"Kie? Zaylee?"

"Nice entrance," Kie says, holding some older piece of tech up to his eyes. "I think I got it all on this thing."

They both look tired, and they're gripping each other's hands tightly. A part of me still burns looking at that, but they must have been through a lot in the last couple of days. Things are different now. We all did what we had to, and apparently they're better for each other.

"We got your message," Zaylee says. "And spread the word. We figured out a way to get everyone to see it."

"It didn't take long, and then everyone was shutting down their 'sites." Kie looks at Stell with the camera. "You can fly, right? Am I going to be able to do that too?"

"Soon."

The two of them start to wander around the hangar bay, marveling at the ships around them and the view out into the darkness. Without them working together, this might not have happened.

Stell walks up a ramp amongst all the cheering, beckoning me to follow.

"You see how Scitech lost its power now, right?"

I nod. That explains why the core inside the moon weakened when I was in there. When everyone shut down their 'sites, the draining stopped and that gave me the window I needed. But that still doesn't explain how I was able to connect to Magla's power so strongly.

Stell walks past the tall Maglan statues to a door that I once couldn't unlock. Now it stands open exposing the control room inside.

"I activated these stations."

"Up there?"

She nods. Dang, I thought I was getting good at this power control stuff, but she can affect things over a thousand miles away. Well, she has been using this for a while. She's pretty old.

"Not that old."

That still messes me up, she looks like my age. I reach over to hold her hand.

She pulls back. "You know I'm as old as your great-grandmother, right?"

"I thought you said you weren't that old? Besides, I figure we're about the same age from now on, right?"

A tiny smile curls on the edge of her lips as she leads me to the room. Inside, there's a viewscreen showing holos of the planet and the multiple Skywatch platforms now in orbit around Magla. Where they should be. There's the Dust Field, and Rym's hidden Magnus base. And then the partial moon with the diseased core.

"I used these stations to focus power on you."

"What? How?"

She just shrugs, but she's smiling smugly and glancing at the room around us. Around the screens are stations with handles and controls for whatever this base does.

"This place can control the field around us. When Rym connected the uplink to the Magnus base, it made the control possible. And when all of Magla turned off their 'site, the power was there."

"Why didn't you just tell me all this stuff before when you were trying to convince me?"

"You wouldn't have believed me. You were a bit of a pain in the ass."

"True." I laugh. "You weren't a party yourself."

This time she laughs and grabs my hand.

"Thank you for saving me." I quickly add, "I mean, not just me, for saving everyone." This is what must have boosted Hira's signal to drop that shield.

She smiles and grips my hand tighter.

"So what do we do with that moon? If we leave it alone, eventually someone's going to go messing around with it. Start this whole mess up again. And if they don't, there's a beacon possibly calling out to some other alien race. They could be on their way right now."

"Come here."

Stell walks to the holographic map and touches the blue lines of the moon and instantly an energy field swells around the room.

"If that moon is sending a signal, we have to end it."

"What can we do?" I ask. "Can we blast it with some gun this place has?"

"Not quite." Stell's skin ripples with glowing lines, the marks of Skywatch. I grip her hands and feel the power of the entire planet at our fingers, and I nearly reel under it all. And then I sense everything. The planet, the Dust Field, and even the shattered moon. This temple can focus all that.

This is what we forgot. This is what it means to be Eldane.

Together we grasp the moon and push it away from us, toward the sun.

EPILOGUE

I take a deep breath and look out over my friends. "Everyone ready?"

"Got any more snacks?" Neman says and tries to get comfortable on the couch.

Jali punches him hard on the shoulder. "Come on, this is serious."

"I am serious," Neman says. "I'm worried this mutt is going to take my food."

Five-eyes growls at him from his place next to my feet.

"Again." Neman makes a snarly face at the yarel. "Why do you have this thing around?"

"He needed a home." I reach down and give Five-eyes a scratch behind his ears. He wags his tail with a few thumps and rests his head back on my foot.

Rym pats my back. "We're ready."

"Go ahead, Cam."

She beeps and her projector beam flips on, lighting up the space between us all. The video is old. I never touched it up or added anything to it. I never wanted to change how I remember. And this is how I want my friends to know them, too.

"Little Daj."

That's my mom talking.

"Hey, buddy."

And my dad.

"We're doing what we have to." My mom looks down at her lap. "You're not going to understand right now, and you probably won't for a long time. There's something wrong with this planet, something we need to figure out. Which means we have to leave you. We've taken on jobs with Scitech to get up into space."

"We just couldn't sit and not do anything anymore," Dad says. "We won't be gone long. You'll be okay, we just upgraded the house with

313

the latest tech. If you need anything, Scitech will send someone. You'll be looked after until we get back. And don't forget about Cam."

The vid bobs up and down with Cam's motion.

"We've had her forever. She's kind of like an older sister, all right? She'll look after you. It won't be very long."

Mom starts crying. "You're our special son, and we'll do everything we can to protect you. We love you."

Dad wraps his arm around her shoulder. "And remember. If you get sad or lonely, just look up into the stars and pretend to fly. We'll be up there, in the sky, watching over you."

End

ABOUT THE AUTHOR

Steve Davala is a Pacific Northwest writer and teacher. He has been creating stuff since 1977 after he saw the first Star Wars movie at a drive-in theater. His other novels include three books in *The Soulkind Series*, and he and his wife co-wrote a children's book, *Books are for Reading, Not Eating!* He is constantly wondering, "What should I do next?"

stevedavala.com
Twitter and Instagram: @sciteachah

CPSIA information can be obtained
at www.ICGtesting.com
Printed in the USA
FSHW010309050122
87337FS